GHO

Seven girls, three dressed ⸻ and four in voluminous ⸻ fitting nightcaps, sprawled on mattresses and pillows spread over nearly every inch of floor of the princess of Plötzkau's state bedroom.

Mikayla lay on her stomach eating sugared almonds from a bowl. Her attention, like that of the other girls, was focused on Johanna leaning against the heavily carved footboard of the bed as she told the legend of the Plötzkau ghost: "Eventually the count received an offer of marriage that was too good to refuse, so he sent his mistress to a convent to get her out of the way—"

"Bastard," Sherri muttered through a mouthful of kuchen, then blushed. "Sorry."

Johanna shrugged. "I don't disagree, but the girl should have expected nothing else. To continue: The mistress was locked in a cell by the nuns but escaped—and was shot by a jäger in the park as she made her way to the castle to disrupt her lover's wedding. She was buried there in unconsecrated ground, and ever since, her ghost has haunted the park at night in the form of a veiled woman in white still trying to reach the castle and her lost love."

"That doesn't sound so scary," said Mikayla, scooping up another handful of almonds.

"Supposedly she jumps on the back of any living man who crosses her path and tries to ride him to the castle, though she always vanishes when he reaches the gates," Johanna explained.

"*If* he reaches the gates," added Liesl. "In other stories she rides her victim to death round and round the walls."

"Okay, that's scary. No wonder nobody will risk meeting her," said Mikayla.

"Has anybody—" Jessie began.

There was a resounding hollow booming rolling down the halls like someone was dribbling an iron basketball. Mikayla could see the walls quiver. A long rattling noise like a chain-link snake slithering on a wooden floor followed.

"What was *that*?"

—from "The Ghosts of the Blauschloss"
by Margo Ryor

THE RING OF FIRE SERIES by ERIC FLINT

1632 by Eric Flint • *1633* with David Weber • *1634: The Baltic War* with David Weber • *1634: The Galileo Affair* with Andrew Dennis • *1634: The Bavarian Crisis* with Virginia DeMarce • *1634: The Ram Rebellion* with Virginia DeMarce et al • *1635: The Cannon Law* with Andrew Dennis • *1635: The Dreeson Incident* with Virginia DeMarce • *1635: The Eastern Front* • *1635: The Papal Stakes* with Charles E. Gannon • *1636: The Saxon Uprising* • *1636: The Kremlin Games* with Gorg Huff & Paula Goodlett • *1636: The Devil's Opera* with David Carrico • *1636: Commander Cantrell in the West Indies* with Charles E. Gannon • *1636: The Viennese Waltz* with Gorg Huff & Paula Goodlett • *1636: The Cardinal Virtues* with Walter Hunt • *1635: A Parcel of Rogues* with Andrew Dennis • *1636: The Ottoman Onslaught* • *1636: Mission to the Mughals* with Griffin Barber • *1636: The Vatican Sanction* with Charles E. Gannon • *1637: The Volga Rules* with Gorg Huff & Paula Goodlett • *1637: The Polish Maelstrom* • *1636: The China Venture* with Iver P. Cooper • *1636: The Atlantic Encounter* with Walter H. Hunt • *1637: No Peace Beyond the Line* with Charles E. Gannon • *1637: The Peacock Throne* with Griffin Barber • *1637: The Coast of Chaos* with Paula Goodlett and Gorg Huff • *1637: The Transylvanian Decision* with Robert E. Waters

1635: The Tangled Web by Virginia DeMarce • *1635: The Wars for the Rhine* by Anette Pedersen • *1636: Seas of Fortune* by Iver P. Cooper • *1636: The Chronicles of Doctor Gribbleflotz* by Kerryn Offord & Rick Boatright • *1636: Flight of the Nightingale* by David Carrico • *1636: Calabar's War* by Charles E. Gannon and Robert E. Waters • *1637: Dr. Gribbleflotz and the Soul of Stoner* by Kerryn Offord & Rick Boatright

Time Spike by Eric Flint & Marilyn Kosmatka • *The Alexander Inheritance* by Eric Flint, Gorg Huff & Paula Goodlett • *The Macedonian Hazard* by Eric Flint, Gorg Huff & Paula Goodlett • *The Crossing* by Keven Ikenberry

Grantville Gazette I–IX, ed. Eric Flint
Ring of Fire I–IV, ed. Eric Flint

Grantville Gazette IX

Created by **ERIC FLINT**
Edited by **Eric Flint,
Walt Boyes & Joy Ward**

GRANTVILLE GAZETTE IX

This is a work of fiction. All the characters and events portrayed in this book are fictional, and any resemblance to real people or incidents is purely coincidental.

A Baen Books Original

Baen Publishing Enterprises
P.O. Box 1403
Riverdale, NY 10471
www.baen.com

ISBN: 978-1-9821-9238-9

Cover art by Tom Kidd

First printing, July 2021
First mass market printing, January 2023

Distributed by Simon & Schuster
1230 Avenue of the Americas
New York, NY 10020

Library of Congress Control Number: 2021018093

Pages by Joy Freeman (www.pagesbyjoy.com)
Printed in the United States of America

10 9 8 7 6 5 4 3 2 1

To Kevin and Karen Evans

Contents

Preface by Eric Flint 1

Nasty, Brutish and Short
by Eric Flint 3

The Bad Seed
by Tim Sayeau 33

Grantville Is Crazy
by Robert Noxon 59

Hunter, My Huntress
by Griffin Barber 65

Reed and Kathy Sue
by Bjorn Hasseler 87

Nun Danket
by Clair Kiernan 133

The Ghosts of the Blauschloss
by Margo Ryor 145

The Queen's Gearhead
by Mark Huston 183

Letters from Inchon
by Robert Waters 217

A Sucker Born Every Minute
by Phillip Riviezzo 253

No, John, No!
by Jack Carroll and Terry Howard 271

Good German Axes
by Tim Roesch 317

For Want of a Nail
by Sarah Hays 335

The Marshall Comes to Suhl
by Mike Watson 349

The Tower of Babel
by Iver P. Cooper 401

Dr. Phil Rules the Waves
by Kerryn Offord and Rick Boatright 411

What Price for a Miracle?
by Terry Howard 453

The Three Stooges
by Brad Banner 479

Stolen Reputations
by Anne Keener 507

The Invisible Dogs of Grantville
by Jackie Britton Lopatin 517

A Season of Change
by Kerryn Offord 539

The Seven Dwarves and the Generals Jackson
by Bjorn Hasseler 563

Quelles Misérables
by David Carrico 567

You've Got to Be Kidding
by Tim Sayeau 575

Grantville Gazette IX

Preface

Eric Flint

This is the ninth anthology of stories from the electronic magazine *The Grantville Gazette* that Baen Books has published, and continues the "best of" format we've maintained since Volume V. The first four volumes were directly taken from the same volume of the electronic magazine, which we could do in those early days because we were only producing the magazine at infrequent intervals. But once we started coming out with the magazine on a bimonthly basis beginning in May of 2007, that became impossible.

As has been true with every Baen edition of the *Gazette*, one story in the anthology—two, in Volume VII—is a new story written by me that has never appeared before. I always write the story after the cover illustration has been done, and base the story on that illustration. As has also proven to be true with every Baen edition of the *Gazette* since we shifted to the "best of" format, the number of issues from which we select stories continues to expand:

Grantville Gazette V (from issues 5–10)

Grantville Gazette VI (from issues 11–19)

Grantville Gazette VII (from issues 20–30)

Grantville Gazette VIII (from issues 31–45)

And this volume contains stories from issues 46 to 64. The reason for the expansion was the same in each case: The magazine has been so successful that we're still scrambling to catch up.

As of the publication of this anthology in July of 2021, the magazine is up to ninety-six issues. Or, to put it another way, we're *still* more than thirty issues behind the magazine with these follow-on Baen paper editions.

I'd whine about it, but that'd be silly. A problem brought by success is still a problem, but it doesn't begin to compare with a problem produced by failure. I know—I've dealt with both in my life. One type of problem requires you to do some work. The other just plain sucks.

The Ring of Fire project is now more than twenty-one years old. The first and founding novel in the series, *1632*, was published in February of the year 2000. So far, at least, our problems have just required us to keep working. I will be delighted if that continues.

—Eric Flint
February 2021

Nasty, Brutish and Short

Eric Flint

Magdeburg
Capital of the United States of Europe
October 14, 1636

Princess Kristina burst into the room on the third floor of the Royal Palace in Magdeburg that Caroline Platzer used for a study when the sun was shining. It was a bit on the cramped side, but had a nice view of Hans Richter Square and the Dom beyond.

"There's another one, Caroline! There's another one!"

Caroline looked up from the book she was reading. She wasn't displeased by the interruption, since it was a tedious tome she was only reading because she'd promised Melissa Mailey she'd give her opinion on it—which she was now almost certain Melissa wanted simply so *she* didn't have to read the dreary thing.

Das Dilemma der Religionsfreiheit, by...

She couldn't remember the author's name. It was latinized, naturally. Opinionatus Obscuritatis, something like that. There were times she regretted having learned to read German.

"And he's here in Magdeburg!" Kristina continued excitedly. "Been here for three days already!"

Caroline heaved the book onto the side table. At least that provided her with some exercise today. "Kristina, settle down. Who is here in Magdeburg? And what's he another one of?"

"He's another famous philosopher! Like Uncle Rennie!"

Another famous philosopher . . .

There were times Caroline found her life utterly disorienting. By what bizarre transgression of all sanity and logic did she live in a world where René Descartes—yeah, him: the *cogito, ergo sum* guy—was "Uncle Rennie"?

But, so he was—at least in the view of a princess of Sweden who would someday become the empress of the United States of Europe and in the meantime had one Caroline Platzer, a Quaker born in Frederick, Maryland, in the year 1978, as her combination governess and surrogate mother.

"Okay, young lady. Start from the beginning. What is this famous philosopher's name? And do you know why he's here in Magdeburg?"

"He's *Hobbes*, Caroline! The real one! Which means I've finally figured out who to dress up as for Halloween! I'll go as Calvin, and Hobbes will be my Hobbes!"

Kristina frowned, but that was simply thought, not disapproval. "He'll have to wear a tiger costume, of course. But that should be easy enough to have one of the dressmakers put together. They do much fancier stuff than that."

Caroline was trying to catch up. "Hobbes . . ."

That name vaguely rang a bell, but only just. She'd

majored in psychology in college, not philosophy. She tried to remember the principal philosophers of the day. Descartes, of course. Spinoza—but he was just a little kid still, who'd been adopted by Rebecca and Mike. Let's see ... Did Sir Isaac Newton count? She wasn't sure where the boundary lay between philosophers and scientists. For that matter, she wasn't sure if Newton had even been born yet.

The princess lost her patience. "It's Thomas Hobbes, silly. You know, the guy who wrote about the sea monster."

Herman Melville? But ...

Oh.

Hobbes. *The Leviathan.*

Caroline had never read the book. Nor had she ever had any desire to read it.

She glanced at the tome on the side table. And it was probably not a slim little volume, either.

"Come on!" cried Kristina. She grabbed Caroline's hand, hauled her out of the chair and pulled her toward the door. "You have to explain to him what he needs to do. Halloween is only two weeks away!"

Magdeburg
Capital of the United States of Europe
October 16, 1636

"This is preposterous!" said Thomas Hobbes—for the second time in the past minute. "Deranged!"

By William Cavendish's count, that was the fourth *deranged* in as many minutes. He'd quite lost track of the number of times his tutor had used the terms *ludicrous* and *absurd*.

William was fond of Thomas Hobbes, who'd been of service to the family for many years now. Hobbes had been his father's tutor before him. William had become the third earl of Devonshire upon his father's death in 1628 and had begun employing Hobbes in that same capacity when he'd come to the continent.

But he could be tiresome, at times, especially when William—who had just turned nineteen less than a week ago—had to explain the facts of life to a man in his late forties. You'd think "practical wisdom" would be an attribute of someone who liked to think of himself as a philosopher.

It was time to get firm, he decided. "Mr. Hobbes, need I remind you of some awkward practical realities? Two, in particular. First, my father's profligate spending left me with a much-depleted purse, which has of late been still further strained by the Earl of Cork's frostiness toward the family."

Thanks in no small part to my mother's obstinacy. But he left that unsaid. "And, second, because we were for all intents and purposes forced to flee Paris due to the caprice of the new king of France. Which has so far tied up most of what funds remained to me."

Hobbes was now glaring at one of the walls. A quite inoffensive one, so far as William could determine.

"The end result," he concluded, "is that we are now largely dependent upon the good will of the Swedish princess. The one"—he waved a hand about, indicating their surroundings—"who has provided us with these very pleasant quarters in the imperial palace."

The building's official title was Royal Palace, but William saw no harm in reminding his tutor that the dynasty hosting them could legitimately lay claim to being imperial. Something which could certainly not be said of the ragamuffin dynasties now ruling Britain and France.

Hobbes shifted his glare to the vista beyond the nearest window. Which seemed to be just as innocent of wrongdoing as the wall had been.

At that very moment, Princess Kristina burst through the door leading into their chambers. "Let's go! Let's go!" she exclaimed. "The seamstress will be ready for us. And so will the boys who are designing the book!"

As it turned out, the seamstress was not ready to start working on the Hobbes costume. In any event, she was still missing an essential part of it. Kristina had insisted that the tiger suit had to be made with a real tiger pelt and it seemed there was a shortage of them in central Europe at the moment. Upon rigorous imperial questioning, the supplier assured the princess that the pelt would be arriving momentarily.

Momentarily was such a useful term, William reflected. There being, strictly speaking, no precise definition of the time span encompassed by a "moment." So far as he knew, at any rate. He'd ask his tutor later. Hobbes would know; the man was a noted mathematician, among his many other scholarly attainments.

The princess was not diverted from her course by the inconvenient news. Cavendish was by now quite certain that the future empress of the USE would be diverted by very few things once she had a project underway.

"Let's go to the book boys, then," she pronounced. "I'm sure they'll be ready to start working."

☆   ☆   ☆

That proved to be untrue as well. Or, rather, "the book boys" were willing enough to work but had no idea what they were supposed to be working on.

"'Leviathan' for Dummies?" The fellow who seemed to be the leader of "the boys" was obviously at a loss. "But . . . Your Highness, we produce the *Dummies* volumes for people seeking technical guidance. Such as—see here." He picked up a large but slender volume whose cover bore the title *Aqualators for Dummies*. "Or this one." He held up a volume bearing the title *Rotary Engines for Dummies*.

He set that one down and picked up another, which he handed to Hobbes. "And this is our latest." The title was *Electrical Relays for Dummies*.

The "boy"—who actually looked to be about Cavendish's age—gave Hobbes a dubious look. "If I understand correctly, this 'Leviathan' tome involves political theory and"—here his voice grew a tad shrill—"hasn't even been written yet."

"And never will be!" barked Hobbes. He waved the book in his hand in a grand, angry gesture of dismissal. "I am not a trained bear to be set dancing for the mob. I already wrote that book! I am not doing it again."

He flipped open the book in his hand. Cavendish thought that was done more to settle his nerves than because his tutor was interested in the contents. Hobbes was a man of theory, not experiment and physical design—much less manufacture.

He frowned at the contents. "What is the point of this?"

"Well . . ." The "boy" reached for the first book he displayed. "I am Jost Kniess, by the way." He used the book, now in hand, to point to the other young men in the small shop, which seemed to combine the function of a printer's establishment with a truly chaotic collection of devices. Cavendish only recognized a few of them.

"The fellow on the left is my cousin, Heinz Ermolt." Yes, there was a definite resemblance. "And the redheaded one is Melchior Treit. He's our mathematician."

Hobbes sniffed, but managed to restrain any further rudeness. He had a tendency to become competitive with anyone labeling himself a mathematician.

Kniess opened the book to a large diagram. "This is an aqualator, a calculating device—"

"Yes, I know what they are," said Hobbes. "But what do they have to do with these..." He glanced down at the other book. "Electrical relays?"

"They're mostly used for communications equipment but we think they can have other applications," said Ermolt. "We're trying to develop a way to circumvent the limits of aqualators. The things are just—just—"

"Too slow!" complained Treit. "And you can't push them far enough to develop really complex computations. The problem is the friction between the working fluid used—water, whatever—and the tube walls. There's a limit to the number of gates they can operate."

"The up-timers used what they called transistors, but that technology"—here Ermolt's expression grew lugubrious—"is far beyond our capabilities and will be for..."

He shrugged.

"Years," said Kniess.

"More like decades," was Treit's opinion.

As they'd been speaking, Hobbes had begun studying the diagram of the aqualator. Casually, at first, but with growing interest.

Cavendish was pleased to see that. Hobbes was invariably more cheerful when his mind was occupied. Leaving aside the young Earl of Devonshire's genuine fondness for the man, a reasonably cheerful Hobbes made for a better tutor and a less exasperating traveling companion.

But he could sense the princess becoming impatient. He turned toward her and bent down enough to allow him to speak softly. "If I may make a suggestion, Your Highness, I think it might work better—certainly more smoothly—if you used me to have your seamstress design and fit the tiger suit. My tutor and I are of approximately the same size, after all."

That was stretching the truth quite a bit. Hobbes had at least three stone by way of weight over Cavendish, and was a couple of inches taller. But William was fairly certain that no seamstress was going to be able to make a garment out of an actual tiger pelt that was going to be a very snug fit.

The princess looked up at him, and then over at Hobbes. Her expression was skeptical.

Thankfully, her governess displayed once again her skill at handling the impetuous ten-year-old scion of empire.

"I think that's an excellent idea," said Platzer. She took Kristina by the hand. "Let's go back to the seamstress."

"But she doesn't have a pelt yet," protested the princess.

"I'm quite sure there's a lot more to making a tiger

costume for a full-grown man than just covering him with a pelt," said Platzer.

As they walked out of the shop, Kristina considered that proposition. "All right," she said, once they were back onto the street, "I suppose you're right."

By now, Cavendish was better oriented. He'd found the princess's rush-about-hither-and-thither method of travel confusing at first. He and Hobbes had come to Magdeburg on a previous visit, but that had been three years earlier and the city had changed a great deal since. Now he could see that they hadn't actually gone all that far from the Royal Palace. Once you got a few blocks from Hans Richter Square, near the Big Ditch that separated the Altstadt and Neustadt from the sprawl of Greater Magdeburg to the west, you entered a zone full of small shops and narrow streets—some of them just glorified alleys. A fair number of the "shops" were really just sheds and huts set up for the day and taken down at night.

The residents' informal name for the area was the Ottomarkt, named for the city's mayor, Otto Gericke. Some of Magdeburg's upper crust had complained about the noise and general disrepute of the area, which was sandwiched between the city's municipal complex and the prestigious edifices around Hans Richter Square, but the mayor had refused to have it demolished or even suppressed.

What sort of great city doesn't have a great flea market? he'd said.

When they entered the Ottomarkt, William was surprised by the odor. More precisely, by the absence of the stench that normally emanated from urban canals—which was essentially what the Big Ditch was.

There were odors aplenty, as was inevitable in an area full of outdoor cookeries and small manufactories. But with a few exceptions—the tannery several blocks to the north being the worst—the smells weren't especially offensive and most of the ones produced by the kitchens were rather tantalizing.

That, more than anything else, drove home to the third earl of Devonshire just how vigorously—sometimes, ruthlessly—the capital's powerful Committees of Correspondence enforced the sanitation regulations. They were famous (or notorious) for it all across Europe, but Cavendish had assumed the reputation was overblown until he arrived in Magdeburg.

A man of his class probably shouldn't entertain such thoughts, but privately William was quite appreciative of the CoCs. Their sanitation patrols also doubled as informal police watches, which made Magdeburg safer than most cities of the continent and much safer than London.

Happily for the composure of the princess, the seamstress was now available to start working on the tiger costume, most of which was orange and black more or less stripy pieces of fabric sewed onto a very loose-fitting blouse and trousers. And then, about half an hour after the seamstress started her work, a shoemaker showed up to create the tiger's feet.

That created some awkwardness. Cavendish had already decided that the general tranquility of the world—his portion of it, at least—would be greatly enhanced if he continued his Hobbes impersonation all the way to the end. His tutor's rigorous sense of his own dignity being what it was, there was no chance the philosopher would acquiesce gracefully to Kristina's desire that he himself portray the tiger of the up-time fable. William, on the other hand, was perfectly willing to do it, and had intended to maintain the subterfuge as long as possible.

Sadly, "as long as possible" proved to be *now*. The royal scion was anything but stupid and unobservant. No sooner had the shoemaker sat on his stool to begin the work that she was there with the finger of accusation.

"Stop it, that's silly!" Her forefinger was aimed directly at William's right foot. "The real Hobbes' feet are much bigger than his. You'll have to wait till he's here to make the shoes."

At this point—God bless the woman—the American governess intervened again. "Kristina, what difference does it make who's actually wearing the costume on Halloween evening? You won't be able to see that much of his face, anyway. You *know* Mr. Hobbes is unhappy with the idea, whereas"—she glanced at Cavendish, who gave her a little nod—"the Earl of Devonshire is quite willing to do it. Switching them will save fuss all around and"—here she overrode the princess's gathering protest—"this way everything will go more quickly and smoothly. You always say you like things to be efficient."

From subtle undertones in her voice, William suspected that Princess Kristina's fondness for efficiency was mostly theoretical, not something she adhered to in practice. But he saw his chance in the subterfuge.

"Oh, you certainly don't want Mr. Hobbes in the costume, then," he said. "This 'Halloween' event. You're walking from place to place, as I understand it. How long will that last?"

"Might be way into the night!" Kristina said enthusiastically.

"No more than two hours, I'd think," said Caroline Platzer.

William spread his hands. "Either way, you'll be exceeding my tutor's ability to walk. He has problems with his feet, you know. He can manage most of a mile well enough." He quickly calculated how far they'd walked earlier in the day. "But once he's been on his feet much more than twenty minutes, he begins to limp."

Here, he made a face. "Half an hour...? Chancy. And within forty minutes he will absolutely need to sit down. For quite a while."

Kristina was frowning, obviously hesitant. But Platzer moved with the supple grace of a leopard. "That's it, then. Kristina, unless you want to spend half—maybe more!—of Halloween helping poor Mr. Hobbes along, we need to accept the Earl's very kind offer to take his place in the tiger costume."

"Well..."

"So, we've settled that issue." She beamed down on William. "And please accept our heartfelt thanks, Your Grace."

After they were finished for the day with the seamstress and the shoemaker, they returned to the atelier of "the book boys." Only to discover that Hobbes had left a short time earlier.

"He said he was going back to the Royal Palace."

"Not surprising," said William. "His feet must have been killing him by now."

All three of the "boys" looked puzzled by that

pronouncement, but William hustled his little party out onto the street before any of them could gainsay him.

"He'll need to soak them in hot water and salts for a good hour," he said to the princess and her governess. Kristina's expression was one of concern and sympathy. Platzer gave Cavendish the sort of look one schemer gives another. Half-admiration, half-grudge.

Back in their suite in the Royal Palace, William found Hobbes engrossed in some calculations he was doing at the dining table. He went over to look, but found the mathematics incomprehensible. It looked somewhat familiar—algebra, he thought—but he couldn't figure out the meaning of several of the symbols, some of which he'd never seen before.

On the table next to his tutor's left elbow were two diagrams. William picked up one of them and looked at it. "This came from . . ."

"From the book boys," said Hobbes. He glanced over at the one William had in his hand. "That's a diagram of the electrical relay they're talking about."

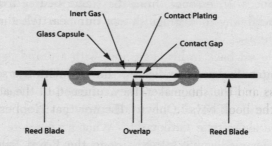

He tapped the other diagram with his finger. "This is the one that shows how the contraptions operate." William picked that one up and studied it.

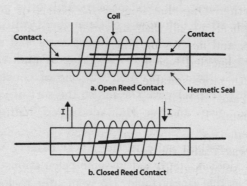

He was able to make sense of it, to a degree. A few months earlier, Hobbes had given him some basic instruction on the up-time concept of "electricity." The earl could deduce that if an electrical current was run through the coil, it would cause the two reeds to compress against each other. He couldn't remember the reason for it, though. Something to do with "positive" and "negative."

Hobbes waved his hand impatiently. "You needn't concern yourself with that. They're just practical contrivances. In essence, from the standpoint of logic, a physical way to distinguish *yes* from *no*. What really matters—"

He sat back in his chair and, with a grand gesture using both hands, indicated the calculations on the pages in front of him. "The mathematics! That's the key to it all. Those boys!" He now gestured in the direction of the Ottomarkt. "What a complete mess they've made of it all. No conception whatsoever of what's needed."

He brought his hands back together to point to his calculations. "Which is a new form of algebra altogether. One that ignores the issues of addition, multiplication—all that—in order, as I said, to focus on *yes* and *no*. Yes *or* no, rather."

He chuckled heavily. "Of course, I need to come up with more suitable terms. I'm thinking of 'affiliation' and 'detachment.' These would be the marks for them." He used a finger to point to a couple of mathematical symbols on the page in front of him. One was $\top$ and the other was $\perp$.

He scratched his jaw, frowning. "I'm thinking I need a third indicator as well. Something that refers to negation."

William was lost at sea when it came to the mathematics but quite clearheaded when it came to practical matters. Perhaps he could use the symbol Π for it. *Feet planted firmly on the ground.*

"I shall leave you to it, Mr. Hobbes." And off he went. The palace's major domo maintained a very fine selection of liquors and it was close enough to evening for an earl to partake of its splendors.

Magdeburg
Capital of the United States of Europe
October 31, 1636

"*Here?*" said Thomas Hobbes, peering out of the window of the carriage with a look on his face that was not quite one of alarm but very close. He'd come along on the Halloween expedition only because William had insisted his presence would please the princess.

Kristina didn't hear him, though, because she'd jumped out of the cab the moment it came to a stop. Caroline Platzer had followed closely.

William Cavendish swiveled in his seat, moving carefully so as not to dislodge any portion of his elaborate costume. "Where else, Mr. Hobbes?"

"Well. I thought...the vicinity of the Royal Palace, perhaps..."

William laughed. "Do you really think wealthy noble folk would agree to host a public event where unruly children would be encouraged to go from dwelling to dwelling in darkness demanding candies and such on pain of vandalism?"

Hobbes grimaced. "I suppose not. But..." His gaze fell on a small knot of men in workmen's clothing standing not far from their carriage. They had their hands in their jacket pockets to ward off the autumn chill, and were chatting with each other.

"Are those...?"

Cavendish glanced out the window Hobbes was looking through. "Yes, that's a Committee of Correspondence patrol. There will be several such guarding the event."

The philosopher's eyes widened. "And the princess does not object?"

"Ah... Actually, Mr. Hobbes, having the CoCs present was essential." He started to point his finger but left off because his finger was now encased in a clumsy tiger paw. "This residential area is a CoC stronghold. Most of the children who will be participating with Kristina in the adventure belong to CoC families, in fact."

He couldn't resist. He just couldn't. "It's a fascinating political arrangement. The nobility resents the effrontery of the CoC mobs, but the royal family gets along with them famously. The princess is especially popular."

He picked up the *Leviathan for Dummies* book—it wasn't a real book, just a facsimile—and started to climb out of the carriage. Slowly and carefully, given the tiger suit. Once on the ground, he grinned up at his tutor—who, of course, couldn't see his face. "I'm sure you must have written something about it in your famous *Leviathan*. Oh, wait, I forgot. You've never read the book yourself."

Neither had Cavendish. He'd tried once, but hadn't gotten very far into it. A dreary tome.

"I'll be back in a couple of hours or so. But have no fear, Mr. Hobbes. No one will trouble you here." Recognizing someone standing not more than thirty feet away, he turned back. "Look," he said, gesturing in the man's direction. "That's Gunther Achterhof himself. Not even the Devil will cross him lightly."

And off he went. Princess Kristina came to take his hand and pull him faster.

"Carefully, Your Highness. I'm afraid this tiger suit is awkward for a man to get about in."

"It doesn't matter. You look splendid. *Hey, everyone! Here's Hobbes!*"

Magdeburg
Capital of the United States of Europe
November 20, 1636

"So, Mr. Hobbes. Were Jost Kniess and his partners pleased with your mathematical endeavors?"

His tutor looked up from the book he was reading and gave William a semi-glare. "Yes, of course—but now I almost regret the effort I put into it. The trouble it's causing me!"

Cavendish had been reading a newspaper, which he folded and set down on his side table. "What trouble is that?"

"The princess. Such an exasperating girl! She has the notion that a philosopher can solve any problem, even one of a purely mundane nature."

"So what's her enthusiasm these days? She's always got one—usually several at once." He held up a thumb, followed immediately by a forefinger. "Riding—and I'll readily admit she's a superb horsewoman. And trying to cajole someone into teaching her how to fly an airplane. But she wouldn't be pestering you over either one of those. So what is it?"

Hobbes ran fingers over his balding pate. "It seems young Kniess and his friends approached her with a request for financial assistance. The girl has far more in the way of funds than should be allowed for any child. It's quite disgraceful the way her father lets her spend money."

Cavendish, whose father had been a champion spendthrift and come close to bankrupting the family, was strongly inclined toward frugality himself. But he didn't really agree with his tutor, on this point. It was true that Kristina had a very large allowance. But, first, her father was a genuine *emperor*, not a country aristocrat. And, second, he'd placed Caroline Platzer in command of the princess's funds, not Kristina herself. Despite the American reputation for being airheaded when it came to practical matters, William had seen no signs that the governess wasn't reasonably prudent when it came to money.

What tended to confuse down-timers on this point was that Americans were far more prone than they were to look for what they called "opportunities to invest." And while a fair number of these "investments" turned out to be what the up-timers themselves called "pipe dreams," at least as many wound up turning a profit.

"And how did the girl respond?"

Hobbes left off his skull-rubbing and waved his hand in a flipping gesture, as if batting away some sort of pest.

"Apparently, she spoke to her governess and the Platzer woman told her there was probably some benefit to be gained from the book boys' obsession with using electrical relays as calculators—they've taken to calling them computers, as if a machine were a man!—but they'd have to figure out a way to popularize the notion. 'Find an angle,' she called it. Americans can torture language like no other people on Earth. You don't 'find' an angle, you observe one. The things can be found everywhere, it's not as if they need to be searched for."

He pointed to the side table. "See? Four ninety-degree angles." His finger moved to one of the windows in the room which featured small triangular panes of glass. "And, look there! More angles. How many d'you think I can find just sitting on my posterior?"

The earl was starting to get intrigued. "Those calculations of yours? What did you call them?"

His tutor's expression became smug. "Hobbesian algebra."

"You say the book boys were pleased with them?"

"Oh, very much so. Once I explained the basic principles to them, they said it would make it much easier to design their computers. Ridiculous term." He made the batting-away motion again. "But I stopped paying attention at that point, because their discourse veered off into mechanical matters."

William decided he'd investigate on the morrow. Given his class and British attitudes—the Germans were probably not much different—he'd need to find a way to disguise his involvement in any American-style "investment." But that couldn't be too difficult, and his strained financial position could use an influx of profit. For a change.

Magdeburg
Capital of the United States of Europe
November 21, 1636

Caroline Platzer was frowning. "I don't understand what the problem is. If you're right—and I'm not questioning you on this—your electrical relay method of computing is quite a bit superior to the aqualator system. I don't see why you think you'll have trouble getting investors."

Heinz Ermolt shook his head. "The problem is we're caught in what you Americans call between a rock and a hard place."

"More like between the Devil and the deep blue sea," countered his partner, Melchior Treit.

Jost Kniess joined in the headshaking. "The problem is that German investors are wary of anything as technically—how do you say it?—'far out' as computing. And Americans"—here his expression darkened—"are like lovers who can't get over a fixation on somebody. In this case, *transistors*." He spoke the word quite venomously.

"They're okay with aqualators," said Heinz, "because

they're *charming*." He uttered that term with venom also. "But our electrical relays, they just find crude and ugly."

"Which, being honest, they are. Noisy, too, when you connect them in big batches the way you are," said William, speaking for the first time since the meeting began. He held up his hands in a placatory gesture. "I'm not quarreling with you, fellows. I agree you have a problem on your hands. But I think the solution is quite obvious."

All three of the book boys gave him beady stares. "And that is?" demanded Jost.

"Design a game using them. Something that will draw a lot of attention."

"A *game*?"

"Well, not a game, exactly. What I have in mind is something quite a bit more ambitious." He was careful not to look at the princess, lest anyone suspect him of trying to interest the only potential investor in the room who could conceivably come up with the funds for the project taking shape in his imagination.

Which, of course, he was. This would be *expensive*. On the other hand, he could see other possible benefits to the imperial family.

"Something very glamorous, as well. Exciting. Drawing lots of attention."

By now, Kristina was practically bouncing on her feet. No, now she *was* bouncing on her feet. "What is it, William, what is it?"

"Disneyland. Well, sort of. There would be quite a few differences. And we'd need to call it something else, of course. Perhaps..." His face brightened, a smile spreading. "I have it. Vasaland!"

He overshot his mark, there. Kristina immediately scowled. "You just said that because you think it'll interest my father. That's *sneaky*."

Dear God, the girl was brilliant. You couldn't ever forget that, dealing with Kristina.

"Well, yes," he admitted. "But whatever name we come up with, it will still rebound to your dynasty's credit."

The scowl didn't fade at all. "How?"

Fortunately, while Cavendish didn't have the sheer raw intelligence of the princess, he was a quick thinker. "What's the biggest drawback to living in Magdeburg?—for the working classes, I'm talking about, not the nobility and the rich." He waved his hand in the direction of the Neustadt, where the opera house was located. "They have their own entertainments. Expensive ones."

"Very expensive ones," muttered Heinz. "Whereas what we have..."

He and his partners exchanged glances.

"Not much," said Jost. "There's plenty of work and the wages are generally good. But except for that one theater that's trying to play the 'movie' things but they keep breaking down, there's not much in the way of fun. Well, leaving aside the boxing matches and saloons, but those aren't favored by most people."

"Exactly," said William. "So we give them ... for the moment, let's just call it the 'fun house.' Like the ones the up-timers had at their Disneyland."

Kristina's interest and enthusiasm came back at once. "Oh, yes! I've seen pictures of them!" She looked at her governess. "In that souvenir book you have, Caroline."

She started counting off on her fingers. "There were

so many of them! There was an adventure where you got attacked by pirates. Not real ones. What you call—robots, I think. And another one where cruel frogs attacked you! And you could ride inside a mountain with all sorts of dangers!"

"Yes, exactly."

"But what does any of this have to do with our electrical relay computers?" asked Melchior, frowning.

"That's how we'd control everything," said William. "There would be some big differences between our fun house and what the Americans had."

The next part required some delicacy. He nodded at Platzer. "Ours would be . . . ah, a lot more what I believe you Americans call 'inter-active.' In the amusements you had at Disneyland, as I understand it, the customers didn't do very much except sit and be moved about in various vehicles. Yes?"

Caroline nodded. "Pretty much."

"Well, we'd do it differently. We'd have the game players making the decisions of what to do and where to go—and the electrical relays would make it happen."

He rose, stretched out a hand, and mimed someone pushing. "If you shove this lever, this happens to you." He leaned the other way and did the same with his left hand. "Push this lever, something else."

"Like what?" asked Heinz.

William shrugged. "Could be anything. If—"

"If you push that first lever," said Kristina, "a trapdoor opens beneath you and you fall into a chute that drops you down into a pile of sawdust. But if you push the other lever, a robot monster comes at you and unless you jump really fast across a pit that opens up the monster knocks you into it"—here she squealed with glee—"and you're soaking in water because you've fallen into a canal. Then you have to decide which way to go. But if you're in the sawdust things are just as bad because . . ."

Here she broke off. "Well, something. It'll take a lot of figuring out. And the best part"—she looked at Jost—"is that I think you could change the way the relays worked so once people got too used to something you could switch it around. I'm right, aren't I?"

The leader of the book boys was tugging at his goatee. "Well . . . yes, certainly."

"This is a wonderful idea!" pronounced Kristina. "The USE's capital will have the only fun house in Europe. No, probably in the whole world!"

Magdeburg
Capital of the United States of Europe
March 3, 1637

"It's insane, Melissa!" Caroline Platzer shook her head. "When I proposed to them that they at least put guard rails on the sides of the amusement carts, they all looked at me as if I was dim-witted. 'But that makes no sense,' one of the book boys said. 'If no one has to worry about being thrown out of the cart if they let go of the handrail, what's the point of the ride?' Can you believe it?"

Melissa Mailey laid her head back and laughed. "You've been here for going on six years now, Caroline. What part of 'seventeenth century' do you still not understand?"

Caroline glared at her. Melissa brought her head upright and gave it a little shake. "For that matter, you don't even have to travel back four centuries. My mother would have understood the mindset—her mother certainly would have. Even we Americans didn't have our modern obsessions with safety and the proper care of children if you go back a generation or two. Nobody ever heard of 'helicopter parenting.' The standard so-called 'word of caution' even in my day was 'go out and play; just be back by dinner time' and nobody worried much where you went and what you did."

"I don't care. It's *insane*. On one of those rides—rides, hell; you're on foot in a narrow and dimly lit hallway—the floor consists of three boards that each slides separately and the blasted electric relays can suddenly switch directions. And you know what determines that? Which board of the walls you place your hand on to keep your balance. They have relay switches hidden behind them!"

Melissa rolled her eyes. "With my crappy sense of balance, I'd be dead meat. But I've got more sense than to plunge into an old-style 'fun house' at my age. That's for kids and youngsters."

"That's not even the worst. On part of what they call the 'voyage of doom' you're riding in a little boat and suddenly ghouls leap down on you from hidden trapdoors. They're just wooden mannequins, of course, but they're still pretty scary because like almost every corner of the fun house the lighting sucks. They give the riders wooden swords to defend themselves, which they can do by banging on the ghouls hard enough. But if you miss, the ghouls can bang into you."

Melissa grimaced.

"But that's not the worst of it! Depending on the sequence in which the ghouls get banged on by the swords—which there's no way to predict because several people are banging at once—the relay switches can either let you keep going down the canal in peace for a while, have a dragon breathe fire on you ten feet further on—it's *real fire*, Melissa; not enough to give you serious burns but it'll still hurt—or—you won't believe this!—a giant wooden sea monster rises up from the floor of the canal and overturns your boat!"

This time, Melissa's grimace was more serious. "That's cutting it pretty close. A lot of people in the here and now don't know how to swim, which is what you'd expect in a world with crappy sanitation and not a swimming pool to be found."

Caroline's lips tightened. "Well . . . being fair about it, the canal's only three feet deep and the footing's pretty good. They keep the water clean, too. They figure the little kids can get carried by their parents if they fall in—they don't let kids ride unaccompanied unless they're three and a half feet tall—and in an emergency they do have a lifeguard hidden away who can help somebody in real trouble. Still!" She took a deep breath. "You watch! Mark my words, as the saying goes. Some people are going to get hurt."

"I don't doubt it. That's part of the fun of a 'fun house' designed and built in the same year that witches are being burnt somewhere and the Inquisition is a going concern."

"It's *sick*."

"I'll tell you what else is going to happen," said Melissa. "Anybody who's been smart enough to invest in the fun house is going to make a bundle. Especially if they also invested in the relay-switch company."

Caroline sighed. "Tell me about it. Don't forget the new computer company they're planning to launch as soon as the fun house opens. Once it gets rolling, that'll probably make more money than anything."

Melissa hesitated a moment. Then: "Caroline, being completely honest here, you really have an obligation—it's a fiduciary thing—to invest Kristina's money in all this too."

"Don't teach your granddaughter how to suck eggs. We're invested up to our eyeballs." She sighed again, even more heavily. "It won't be long before the blood is on my hands."

Magdeburg
Capital of the United States of Europe
March 15, 1637

Melissa Mailey sat down in the chair facing Lennie Washaw behind his desk in his office in the Imperial College of Science, Technology, and Engineering. "Well, have you had a chance yet to read those papers I gave you?"

Washaw nodded. "Yes. I agreed to do it as a favor to a former high school colleague even though I was very busy, but once I realized what I was looking at I couldn't put it down. And I've done some research since—quite a bit, in fact—to make sure my memory wasn't off."

"I *thought* it was probably important. And?"

Washaw clasped his hands over his ample belly and shook his head in a gesture of bemusement. "In essence, what your philosopher Thomas Hobbes has done is reinvented Boolean algebra—except 'pre-invented' is probably the correct term. George Boole didn't develop his algebra until the middle of the nineteenth century, more than two hundred years from now."

Melissa saw the implications immediately. "Hoo, boy."

"'Hoo, boy' is right. So what do *we* label it in our here and now—which we're all agreed is a completely different universe? By your account, Hobbes developed this entirely on his own."

"I'm sure he did. I doubt if he's heard of Boole even now. We could question his charge William Cavendish, if you like."

Washaw shook his head. "Not now, anyway. The final decision will have to be made by the whole College in formal session. If there's any dispute, it can be settled there. But . . ." He looked down at the papers on the desk in front of him. "I doubt there will be."

The last words were spoken softly. "Dear God, it's been hard on them."

"Hard on who?"

The math professor shrugged. "Anyone—be they a scientist, an artist, a writer—anyone who was famous enough that we have a record of them in what we brought with us. What does Rembrandt do? Paint something he already painted in another world? What does"—he gestured at the pages in front of him—"this guy Thomas Hobbes do? He already wrote *Leviathan*, after all."

Melissa smiled. "The story I got is that he refuses to even read the book and flies into a temper tantrum if anyone even mentions it. He was furious when he found out they named the fun house 'Leviathan.'"

"I have got to try that fun house," said Washaw. "What the hell, I just turned forty. I figure I ought to survive it."

Melissa made a face. "Be careful, Lennie. At least two people have already broken a bone in there."

"Hasn't slowed business down any, has it?"

"Are you kidding? 1637, remember?"

She pointed at the pages. "So what are you going to recommend to the College?"

"Oh, I think we should label it 'Hobbesian algebra.' There's no indication he didn't develop it on his own, and he certainly predates Boole himself. I'm not entirely happy with that outcome, since I think the original edition was more elegant." It was Lennie's turn to make a face. "God, the ridiculous terminology Hobbes came up with! 'Affiliation' and 'detachment.' Boolean algebra uses 'conjunction' and 'disjunction.' But I figure that's a small price to pay to offset at least a little what is truly a great injustice to people who were truly great."

Magdeburg
Capital of the United States of Europe
May 12, 1637

The crowd was huge, bigger than anyone had projected.

"There must be a thousand people here!" said Melchior excitedly.

"Easily," agreed William. "I doubt we'll be able to get all of them through today."

"There's always tomorrow and the day after. And the day after that," said Jost happily.

Kristina came up, dressed again in a Calvin costume. This was the new Spaceman Spiff variant she'd had made, complete with ray gun. "Let's get going! We're the first ones in, remember?"

"How could I forget?" said William. The princess had tried to get him to agree to go into the fun house wearing his Hobbes costume, but he'd firmly refused. "That great heavy thing will get soaked right off and I'll drown."

Instead he was going in—leading the way, in fact—as the third earl of Devonshire, wearing a helmet and chainmail and wielding a sword. The helmet and sword were real, although the sword was a blunted practice weapon. The chainmail was simply a costume made of gray fabric. In a real hauberk, he'd be even surer to drown than in a Hobbes costume.

And that he would get soaked was a given. William had been intimately involved for months in the design and construction of the fun house, so he knew what to expect. But he didn't know the *sequence* in which the terrors and horrors would come at him. That was controlled by the relay switches, and their mindless "decisions" were ultimately ruled by the logic of his tutor's algebra.

Groups of twenty would go in at a time, and the starting enclosure was now full of paying customers. Each and every one of them was babbling with glee and anticipation.

A steam whistle blew. The gate rose. William Cavendish, Earl of Devonshire, led the charge toward the huge, reconverted warehouse that had flags flying everywhere decorated with the Swedish coat of arms and the name *Vasaland*.

The entrance was in the shape of a great monster's fanged maw, with red eyes glaring down.

ENTER THE LEVIATHAN IF YOU DARE
—but be warned!
Your life will surely be
nasty, brutish and short

The Bad Seed

Tim Sayeau

Paris, 22 July 1633

Master Antoine Dreux d'Aubray, Prefect of Paris in the year of our Lord 1633, stood listlessly against a door jamb, staring into the room in which his little daughter Marie Madeleine Marguerite slept. The moonlight coming in from a window illuminated her sleeping features, her blonde hair loose upon her pillow, a somewhat worn Barbie doll tucked close to her small gamine face.

There could be no cuter three-year-old in France, thought Antoine. Yes, all parents thought or should think their children were angels from God, but clearly none of those others had ever seen his Marie Madeleine as she smiled, laughed, and played.

None had ever had Marie Madeleine falling asleep in their arms, her absolute love and trust clear with every breath, her head resting upon their arms and chest.

None had ever simply stared at her, amazed that such innocence, beauty, trust, charm, intellect, and kindness could be found in one perfect little girl.

None could ever have sworn with such loving devotion as he that the cares and the cruelties of the world would be kept from her for as long as possible.

And none had ever had within their souls such despair and love as he now had.

Slowly he closed the door to his daughter's chambers, stiffening in dread that each creak might awaken his sleeping daughter. She would blink, and look around, and she would see him, and her eyes and face would brighten up, calling him "Papa!" as her arms reached out to him to be picked up and cuddled, protected from the night.

And that would let loose the tears already at his eyes, and she would look at him and ask, "Papa! What's wrong? Why are you crying?"

And he would smile, and wipe his tears away, and say, "Nothing for you to worry about, little one. Now hush, back to sleep."

And she would cuddle closer, safe in his arms, and slowly her breaths would deepen, her body relax into sleep, and he would return her to her bed, place her Barbie within her little hands, and leave.

And in the morning she would wonder why he had cried, and held her so close, and he would have to lie to her again.

The door closed, Master Antoine walked up the hall to his office.

There upon his desk lay the missive that had caused him to need to see his daughter sleeping, to know she was only three years old, still his little Marie Madeleine, his adored and adoring daughter.

He sat at the desk and stared at the document,

his hands steepled in front of him. Then he leaned forward and studied the paper again.

Like everybody who had heard of the Ring of Fire, of Grantville in the Germanies, he had of course sought to learn what the future held, to learn if the future remembered him and how it did so. To know what to avoid and what to embrace.

Why would he not? Why would anybody not?

Well, perhaps now he knew why not. Man proposes, God disposes, and God knew he, Master Antoine Dreux d'Aubray, Prefect of Paris, Civil Lieutenant of Paris, counselor of State and Master of Requests, a personal attendant to the king and member of the king's *Conseil privé*, had according to the 1911 *Encyclopedia Britannica* been disposed of in the most certain of manners.

The *Britannica*, in words he personally considered too calm and separate from emotion, stated:

BRINVILLIERS, MARIE MADELEINE
MARGUERITE D'AUBRAY, Marquise de
(c. 1630–1676), French poisoner, daughter
of Dreux d'Aubray, civil lieutenant of Paris,
was born in Paris about 1630.

No. Not about 1630. The twenty-second of July 1630. The Feast Day of St. Mary Magdalene the Penitent. Called so as, proud and beautiful, with seven devils within her, she had lived a life of sin. Then she met Christ. Who forgave her her sins, whose feet she humbly washed. St. Mary Magdalene, who three days after the Crucifixion became the first to know Christ had risen.

A fitting day for his daughter's birth, he had thought. Auspicious. And per the *Britannica*, the twenty-second of July had for years augured good fortune for the penitent's namesake.

> *In 1651 she married the Marquis de Brinvilliers, then serving in the regiment of Normandy. Contemporary evidence describes the marquise at this time as a pretty and much-courted little woman, with a fascinating air of childlike innocence.*

So. His daughter's life had been all that he or any father could want for his child. An advantageous marriage. A fascinating personality, a charmed life. An innocent life.

Then came the serpent.

> *In 1659 her husband introduced her to his friend Godin de Sainte-Croix, a handsome young cavalry officer of extravagant tastes and bad reputation, whose mistress she became.*

The irony was almost amusing, thought Master d'Aubray. Mary Magdalene meets Christ, Marie Madeleine meets Sainte-Croix. But with such different results! The first becomes a better person, the second—not.

> *Their relations soon created a public scandal, and as the Marquis de Brinvilliers, who had left France to avoid his creditors, made no effort to terminate them, . . .*

So much for the marquis, the cowardly cuckold. With bad taste in friends and finances as well.

One could not blame his other self, reflected Antoine. How was he to know? Surely when approached for Marie Madeleine's hand in marriage he had joyously consented. His daughter, a marquise!

Well, not now. Not ever. Not unless this world's marquis proved himself more worthy than that—that disgusting worm, that—*Nothing!*—who had left his marital difficulties to his father-in-law to sort.

Which he, Master Antoine Dreux d'Aubray, had sought to do.

> *M. d'Aubray secured the arrest of Sainte-*
> *Croix on a lettre de cachet.*

A *lettre de cachet.* An order of the king, or more probably his chief Minister, authorizing incarceration without trial.

Simplistic, this *Britannica* entry. Naive, even—insulting. Yes, of course he, Master Antoine Dreux d'Aubray, Prefect of Paris, Civil Lieutenant of Paris, counselor of State, Master of Requests, an attendant of the king and member of the *Conseil privé*, could obtain a *lettre de cachet.*

But not as easily as this cursed missive implied! *Lettres* were serious legal documents, not playbills and *billets doux*!

No. Clearly that other Antoine had tried all other means before this one. Appeals to his daughter, to his son-in-law, yes even to that Godin de Sainte-Croix.

None of which had been heard. The marquis—well, what of him? Useless *capon*!

Sainte-Croix? Why would that devil listen to a father's pleas?

And Marie Madeleine, his sweet child, how infatuated with this Sainte-Croix she must have been, not to have heeded her father's words!

Dear Lord, how very infatuated she must have been!

> *For after a year in prison, a year in which Sainte-Croix is popularly supposed to have acquired a knowledge of poisons from his fellow prisoner, the Italian poisoner Exili,*

and a year in which a father might reasonably hope his daughter's passions would have cooled,

> *he plotted with his willing mistress his revenge upon her father.*

Breathe, Antoine, breathe. Remember, she is only three years old!

> *She cheerfully undertook to experiment with the poisons which Sainte-Croix, possibly with the help of a chemist, Christopher Glaser, prepared, and found subjects ready to hand in the poor who sought her charity, and the sick whom she visited in the hospitals.*

Who sought her charity...whom she visited...

> *In February 1666, satisfied with the efficiency of Sainte-Croix's preparations and with the ease with which they could be*

administered without detection, the mar-
quise poisoned her father…

Thank God I made it to the window in time, reflected Master Antoine. Better I decorate the gardens with my heavings than the carpets. Dear God, there can't be anything left in my stomach, so why these pains? Why these cramps—oh God! No! Don't cry out, don't—oh Christ, stop it—oh God it *hurts*—why these convulsions—oh Marie Madeleine—Christ Almighty please stop it stop it stop *stop…*

Master Antoine Dreux d'Aubray, ashen-faced stomach-pained cold-sweating Prefect of Paris, cautiously lifted himself off the floor where for the most frightening hour of his life he had alternately convulsed in pain, unable to breathe and lying exhausted, shallowly panting.

Was that how it was for them? The poor, the sick— me? Was that how they—we—died? That pain? If so, Christ have mercy on us all.

Even Marie Madeleine?

Yes, even Marie Madeleine, you traitorous thought! Even Marie Madeleine, especially Marie Madeleine! Oh God, my sweet one, how? Why? Me, them, how? And why were we not enough? Why even not only me

but also the latter's two sons and other
daughter should be poisoned, so that the
Marquise de Brinvilliers might come into
possession of the large family fortune.

Money, Marie Madeleine? For money? Was that all I—we—were to you? Your brothers, my sons?

Your sister? Dear God, even your sister? Parricide, fratricide, sororicide, for money and—love? You and that God-damned Sainte-Croix, was it love? Was that love to you? How could you call that love? Did we—did I—not teach you love? Did we not show you love? How did we—did I—fail you, Marie Madeleine? How? Did we teach you money above all, position and privilege above all? Was that it? Did we—I—us, all, did we not—

Marie Madeleine, why?

I am lost. Worn. Weary. I am come to the end of all things. I am Antoine Dreux d'Aubray, and I am lost. All is gone, all emotion, all care, worries, joys, sorrows, all gone.

Like my sons.

In 1670, with the connivance of their valet La Chaussée, her two brothers. A postmortem examination suggested the real cause of death, but no suspicion was directed to the murderers.

My sons, thought Master Antoine, my poor sons. They didn't even have their names mentioned. As dead to history as they were to Marie Madeleine.

Before any attempt could be made on the life of Mlle Thérèse d'Aubray, Sainte-Croix suddenly died. As he left no heirs the police were called in, and discovered among his belongings documents seriously incriminating the marquise and La Chaussée.

Thérèse. Her name was—is?—will be?—Thérèse. My second daughter. My one surviving child.

I wonder, did she live well, after? Did Thérèse marry, have children, live her full life? In that other France, when Grantville was brought back, did we have family? Did they know of their many-times great-aunt and what she did? How she died?

> *The marquise escaped, taking refuge first probably in England, then in Germany, and finally in a convent at Liège, whence she was decoyed by a police emissary disguised as a priest.*

I wish—I wish they had left her in that convent in Liège. What harm could she have done there? All was in the past, all gone, all passion fled.

> *A full account of her life and crimes was found among her papers. Her attempt to commit suicide was frustrated, and she was taken to Paris, where she was beheaded and her body burned on the 16th of July 1676.*

Ha. The sixteenth of July 1676. They couldn't have waited six more days, till the Feast of St. Mary Magdalene? Life and Death, on the same day?

No. I suppose they couldn't. I wouldn't.

Did she regret it, at the end? Did she weep for what she had done? With Sainte-Croix dead, and I hope it hurt the bastard, did she awaken? Did she return to herself, to Marie Madeleine?

At the end, was she again my daughter Marie Madeleine?

I hope so. God, how I hope so, how I—hope—

Master Antoine Dreux d'Aubray placed his head in his hands and cried, suppressing the sobs lest anyone hear.

For long minutes his eyes watered his face, his hands, his clothing, falling upon the desk, the missive, the floor. Crying for Marie Madeleine, for his sons, him, the poor, the sick, Thérèsè, his sorrows a service for the dead.

I am now truly come to the end of myself, Master Antoine thought, lifting his face from his hands, eyes red, nose streaming.

Hurriedly he wiped his face clean with a sleeve. Staring at the stained document, he poured fine white sand from a small container nearby, normally used to absorb wet ink.

Finished, he carefully lifted the paper and shook the sand off. Wiping the desk clean with a sleeve, he placed the missive before him. Stared at it. Considered it.

I am a lawyer, Master Antoine asserted to himself. I am the current Prefect of Paris, its Civil Lieutenant. I am a King's Attendant, a counselor of State. As Master of Requests I am an aristocrat of the robe. I am in all humility and just recognition of self an eminent authority on the laws and the procedures of the courts of France, possibly even the authority. Within France I am an *haute placé*, second only to the cardinal and the king.

Was that why I died? Did my pride blind me? Pride in position, in family? Did I not see my daughter as

she was, not as I wished her to be? As I—forced?—
her to be?

What was it, that made her so willing to murder
myself, her sister, her brothers? The poor, the sick?
What flaw made Sainte-Croix so appealing to her that
she let seven devils or more into her?

Marie Madeleine, why?

And what do I do now? You sleep now, my little
one, safe and warm within your bed. If only I could
put time in a bottle, I would keep you there till all
the dangers were past.

Only I can't. The future comes. For you, for me. Us.

I dread it, Marie Madeleine. How will it be for
you, with the sins of your other self known? What
am I to tell you, when mothers pull their children
away, warning against you? Because they will, innocent
though you are.

You will need strength, Marie Madeleine.

Strength to know what in another world you did
and strength to not let that knowledge darken your
life in this one.

Strength to face those who will damn you for your
other self.

Strength for those times when it will seem simpler
and easier to be what the idiots and the envious
claim you are.

They will watch and whisper, see in your least
actions and slightest words proof that you are the
Marquise de Brinvilliers.

Which you are not. Which you will never be, my
child.

Yes, in another world, in another time, I died at
your hands.

As did my namesake, your little brother Antoine. Who in this world you often hold in your arms, calling him *frérot*, babbling all sorts of insights and news to him as your mother Marie and I watch on, amused and pleased.

I wonder, did you do the same with your second brother, my unborn, unnamed son? With your sister? Both of whom will never exist now.

Even should I have another son, another daughter, they will not be the same. God, even Antoine is not the same, now. Not since the Ring of Fire. We are all different now.

That is my hope, Marie Madeleine. That we are all different, now. Better, too, I hope.

So. The future has already changed. That is good. But has it changed *enough*?

Consider that fool Charles in England. Who seems to *want* to lose his head earlier in this world than in the other.

But then, consider Gustav of Sweden. Who was slated to die at Lützen this past November the sixteenth. Who lives instead.

Whose daughter Kristina still has a father. Kristina Vasa, whose life has *certainly* changed. Who is not now likely to abdicate her throne, or convert to Catholicism, or order cannons fired on unruly guests, or any of those other buffooneries—well, perhaps not the conversion—that make her up-time biographies interesting reads.

So. Don't think of what was-to-might-have-been— Lord, what a phrase!—think of what instead could be, what must and will be.

Unlike his self in that other Earth, that other thought

of God's, this Antoine Dreux d'Aubray for a certainty knew what the future held. And with God's help, or the Devil's if needs be, that future would remain like Kristina Vasa's biographies, words on a page.

Only, how?

A nunnery? His sweet Marie Madeleine, immured within a convent? Given to God in this world as penance for her sins in the other?

No. That other Marie Madeleine had enough victims to her name. Let that damned, foul, murderous creature suffer and leave his innocent child alone!

Sainte-Croix, then?

How old would he be now? Where would he be now? If Marie Madeleine's fate could be avoided, could his be as well?

Perhaps—but if need be, Godin de Sainte-Croix would one day suffer a tragic mishap in the streets of wherever, an assault late at night by footpads bent on his purse at whatever cost.

A policy of last resort, to be sure. A policy however demanding further knowledge of Sainte-Croix, his location and his conduct.

Fortunately, for one such as he, Antoine Dreux d'Aubray, Prefect and Civil Lieutenant of Paris, counselor of State, Master of Requests, an attendant of the king, member of the *Conseil privé*, such knowledge was easily to be had.

The Marquis de Brinvilliers. Who had let his wife carry on with that abomination Sainte-Croix. Whose shameful refusal to protect his marriage had left himself, Antoine Dreux d'Aubray, no choice but to take action. Most likely that contemptible cuckold is only a child himself now.

A child who depending on his age and conduct would get a sound kick to the backside and a few slaps to the head, should ever he have the misfortune to meet his once-future father-in-law!

Christopher Glaser. Who might or might not have aided Sainte-Croix in his preparations for murder. Who might be in Paris or in the provinces, or not in France at all, who might be alive or yet to be born. A ghost, really. A phantasm. Still to be searched for, of course.

Exili, now. Not directly responsible for the evils of Sainte-Croix and—and Marie Madeleine, true.

Certainly not unresponsible, however. That name, now. Clearly an alias. Probably nothing to be gained from it, though certainly inquiries would be made. Likely older than Sainte-Croix and Ma—the Marquise de B— No. *L'Empoisonneuse*. Let that be its name now. Had Exili already begun his career, then? How to know?

Grantville. That was how to know. Surely there must be more in Grantville than that almost-afterthought in the 1911 *Britannica*.

Cruel though God had been to him and his family in that other world, for whatever reasons only He knew, in this one He had let the d'Aubrays know their—erstwhile?—fate.

To reveal that much yet to conceal more, to hide why *L'Empoisonneuse* had willingly murdered her father, her brothers and others, to let no hint through the Ring of Fire as to how he, Master Antoine Dreux d'Aubray, might guide his children and children-to-be through their personal Gethsemane, that bespoke a cruelty deserving of Satan, not God. Not even the

God of the Old Testament, and certainly not that of the New, not God the Father and Christ the Son and the Holy Ghost.

Very well, concluded Antoine d'Aubray. Preparations will be made. Grantville will reveal what it knows, and Marie Madeleine shall live a better and longer life in this world than in the other.

A task which will be the easier once my wife Marie knows of this.

I wonder why the *Britannica* did not mention her. Was she already dead before *L'Empoisonneuse* began her work? Or did that creature hesitate before her mother's death?

No, Marie must have been dead before then.

Was that why *L'Empoisonneuse* was—born?

Would she have lived, would *we* have lived, had Marie lived?

Ha.

Grantville may just save more than one Marie, then.

A possibility—no, a fact I should make clear when I tell Marie of this.

He paused in thought.

The up-timers have it right. Now comes the hard part.

Marie Ollier d'Aubray, wife of Maître Antoine Dreux d'Aubray, mother of three-year-old Marie Madeleine Marguerite d'Aubray and one-year-old Antoine d'Aubray, stared at the document in front of her.

In appearance it was a most unprepossessing document. Less than half a page, water-stained, somewhat creased, flecked with white sand.

Really, a very plebian document.

She picked it up. Really, how *plain*. Look at how *easily* it tears. Look at it *rip apart*.

There it goes *again*. It just can't hold together. What a silly document, just ripping apart like so. Just a little pressure and it just falls apart. How useless a document, just falling away like that. How—how infuriating!

How dare it be so useless useless *useless* **useless** a document! I hate it, I absolutely *hate* it, I want it *gone*, it has to go *away*, I don't want to *see it*, I keep *seeing it*, I have to *put it away*, someplace I can't *see it* . . .

Why is Antoine staring at me like that? He's the one who put this useless useless *useless* document in front of me, *he's* the one who cancelled *all our plans* for today *without* telling me, he's the one who . . . *oh*.

Hurriedly Marie Ollier d'Aubray spat out from her mouth the torn, masticated remains of that useless document.

The document which described how her little daughter Marie Madeleine Marguerite had grown up to murder most of her family and hundreds of other people.

Probably hundreds, corrected Marie. Possibly hundreds. You know how people exaggerate.

Not that that makes—that—any easier to—swallow.

Poor Antoine. He must think he married a madwoman, and I think he did.

Inner monologue complete, Marie Ollier d'Aubray turned to her husband, who had remained silent throughout her fugue.

"Really, Antoine!" she said crossly. "How could you let me do that? Surely somewhere in our wedding vows you promised otherwise!"

Antoine d'Aubray did not follow his cue. "Better now?" he asked.

"Yes. Somewhat. Some wine, please. I—" She spat some flecks of paper out. "We must converse, and my throat is not at its best. The d'Angouléme, I believe."

Antoine poured out some wine from a sidebar into a glass. Placed it before her. Marie took it up and took a sip. Then another.

Swished it about her mouth. Swallowed.

"Marie!" cried Master Antoine.

"Oh hush," she said, sipping again. "With or without paper, this is still *d'Angouléme*, and besides, where would I put it? The floor? The window? Besides, what does it matter?" She looked at him.

"We have other copies, do we not?"

"Yes, Marie. I hadn't anticipated your exact reaction, but considering my own, I felt it best we have others."

"Oh good. Why?"

"Well, because—we do need to know what happened, Marie. As horrible as that up-time knowledge is, without it we are condemned, damned to—"

"No no, not that" interrupted his wife. "I meant, why tell me, why share that—atrocity—with me?" she asked, not harshly.

Antoine sat in a chair next to her. He paused, collecting his thoughts.

"I considered not telling you. It—what become of our little Marie Madeleine in the future—was horrible enough. To share seemed—cruel."

"Then?"

He shrugged his shoulders, apology on every line. "To not tell you seems even crueler. There are already several copies of the 1911 *Britannica* in Paris. The king has one, Richelieu another, Monsieur Gaston another. Not that I think any of them, even Gaston, would be so vile as to snicker, laugh and sneer, except—"

"Except some of theirs would," said Marie, finishing his sentence. "None of Richelieu's, likely. Or stay long in his service if they did. But some of the king's, even with Richelieu, assuredly. And as for Monsieur Gaston's!"

Her voice rose. "Such fine gossip to share! Madame Bovary for one would not hesitate! Such sympathy she would have for me, such expressions of care and understanding, all in that grating falsetto of hers! 'Oh my dear, how can you bear it? Such fortitude! I am in envy of you Madame d'Aubray, positively in envy!' Pfaugh! Hand me more paper, Antoine, I need to taste something clean!"

She instead took another sip of d'Angouléme.

Finished, Marie cradled the glass in her fingers as she looked over at her husband.

"What have we decided, then?" she asked.

Antoine, as used as he was to his wife, was still somewhat surprised. "You are taking this much better than I expected, my dear. Far better than I," he admitted.

"Oh Antoine, I assure you, this"—she waved a hand about—"is all an act. Inside, I am—I am—not sure what I am. Besides, I was not mentioned in that pernicious article, so presumably I was not among the dead. That is to say, not *the* dead. So I can pretend it was, it is, nothing to do with me."

She leaned forward. "Which is not what you could do. Nor what we will do. So again, what have we decided?"

Master Antoine stood up. Walked around. His wife watching him, letting him speak at his pace.

"At first I was not sure what to do. Reading this," he said, picking up the chewed remains, tossing those into a wastebasket, "affected me greatly."

"Mmmm. The rose bushes again?"

"I fear so. I sometimes wonder how those manage to do so well."

"Competent gardening, cautious pruning, and skillfully applied fertilizer. Go on."

"I decided to make inquiries into the others mentioned. Brinvilliers, Glaser, Exili. Sainte-Croix." This last was delivered with a snarl.

"Leave Brinvilliers to me," stated Marie. "No doubt if Madame Bovary and that other harpy duBarry know, there will be whispered comments. No matter. Discussing marriage plans and family *alliances* is after all my *province*. Besides, he may yet prove suitable, if he learns proper judgment and household finances."

"Not a prospect I consider favorably, Marie."

She waved a hand. "Of course not. But he is presumably still a child, so..."

"The Child is Father to the Man!"

Marie stared at Antoine. "The child is—Antoine, do explain."

"An up-time phrase, from an English poet between now and their time. The idea being that who a child is and how he behaves as a child shows how he will be as a man."

"Ah. An *English* poet. That explains everything. I admit a certain barbaric genius to it, but let us not take it too far. I doubt Brinvilliers has overspent his allowance, for one."

"I wouldn't put it past him," said Maître Antoine, sotto voce.

"I shall ignore my lord and master's last comment as a good wife should," continued Marie. "Returning to those you named—"

"Mmmm. As I said, make inquiries as to those responsible. Brinvilliers should be easy enough to learn of, and thank you."

"Marie Madeleine is *our* daughter, never forget. As Antoine is *our* son."

"Glaser and Exili—I called Glaser a ghost, and he is likely to prove one. Not so much as Exili, I fear."

"Indeed. An Italian poisoner. How redundant. How superfluous. Like saying an English thief or a Spanish braggart. Or a French conspirator, I admit."

"And Godin de Sainte-Croix, inquiries especially will be made of him."

"Quite. And should that English poet prove accurate?"

"I had considered footpads in the night. Now, in the day—" Master Antoine fell silent.

Marie stared at the wineglass in her hands. She did not take a sip. "Yes, in the day, it seems—but—he killed our daughter, Antoine. As surely as though he burned her himself, he *killed our daughter!*"

Hands trembling, she set the wineglass upon a small table. The base knocked against the table. Hurriedly Antoine removed it.

Marie clenched her hands. Stared at those as they shook.

"He killed our daughter. He. killed. Our. DAUGH-TER HE KILLED OUR SON!"

This last was a shriek, muffled into her hands.

Antoine knelt and held his wife as she screamed

her rage and her hatred into her hands, her feet stamping hard into the floor, grinding motes of paper into the wood.

He did not flinch as she gripped him, over and over screaming into his chest.

"He. Killed. Them! He. Killed. Marie Madeleine. He. Killed. Antoine. He. Killed. Them! That SALAUD killed them! Kill. Him. Kill. Him. KILL. HIM!"

Antoine carefully held his wife as her incandescent sorrow and rage peaked, then ebbed. He held her as she rocked back and forth, wordless keening coming from her lips.

Still it was long minutes before Marie returned to herself. Carefully easing her husband's cramped arms away from her, she picked up the glass of d'Angouléme. Poured some into a cupped hand. Used it to cleanse her face. Refreshed, she turned to her husband.

"Oh, Antoine. I am sorry."

"Do not be, love. This is a part of our wedding vows."

"Really?" she sniffed, an arm brushing past her nose, mouth in a rueful smile. "To hold your wife as she screams and carries on like a hysteric banshee?"

"You should have heard me last night. This morning, rather. You are still taking this better than myself, you know."

"Well, of course. I have you, you have the rose bushes. I could be quite jealous, you know. Turning to those instead of to me!"

Antoine smiled. "I thought that was what I was doing, my love, when I asked you to read that 'pernicious article.' Of course, if you had rather I speak with the rose bushes—"

"Good heavens, no. Though I may. Better those

than Madame Bovary. Who would no doubt bring up Sainte-Croix to me at every opportunity. I can hear her in my mind going on about that—that—that *monster*, that malefic thing, that—"

Antoine moved closer, to hold her again. She did not stop him.

"Thank you. I—I know he—I know he is now only a child, but—it does not matter. The rest, they do not seem—seem *real* to me, I can consider them without—hate, but *him*—I cannot see *him* as a child."

Marie moved her hands, to grasp and unclasp her husband's hands and arms.

"I am calm now. Well, calmer. Enough to hear more of our plans, at least." She retook her seat.

Antoine moved his chair to sit beside her.

"Inquiries aside, it seems to me that pernicious article is grossly incomplete. The very least of information provided. It came from Grantville, so it is my hope Grantville has more—more insight. Right now, all we know is what happened, not how. Why. Why Marie Madeleine would—did—"

"Not a word more, my heart. Marie Madeleine has done nothing save be our daughter, our laughing, playful, ofttimes exasperating, loving, daughter."

"Quite. A conclusion I myself reached. In private I refer to that other as *L'Empoisonneuse*. Would that work for you?"

"*L'Empoisonneuse. L'Empoisonneuse*," said Marie, trying it out on her tongue. "Hmm. *Non*. My apologies, Antoine, but that is too—it is entirely—almost a compliment, really. It gives her a power she should not have. Perhaps instead *La Folle* or *La Bestiole*. We need something—*La Stupide*," she said, decisively.

"*La Stupide*? Are you sure? Considering what was done—"

"*Précisément*. You dead, *petit* Antoine dead, our other son dead, all those charity cases dead, *La Stupide* dead, and all for what? Entertainment? Vanity? No, I think you are right. Marie Madeleine and Brinvilliers should never marry."

Maître Antoine stared at his wife. Blinked.

"Marie, as used as I am to your sudden turns of thought, and as oddly perceptive as those often are, this last leaves me—lost."

Marie glanced away a moment, then returned her gaze to him.

"Antoine—you wondered earlier why *La Stupide* committed her crimes, did you not?"

"Yes. I still do."

"Well" she said, taking a deep breath, "I do not know myself. But I can imagine."

She looked away.

"Antoine—do you know why I enjoy being married to you?"

"Ah—love?"

"Oh, that. Of course. But more than that, or rather in addition to that—on occasion I criticize Madame Bovary, you know."

"There is that sudden turn of thought again, Marie. And yes, you do."

"Well, she is stupid. Very. Which would be nothing, were she not also unpleasant as well. All her time on who wore what to which *soirée*, eager for the latest *on-dit*, ready to repeat and embellish whatever rumor and gossip—the more tawdry and damaging the better, alert to every error of dress and manner imaginable,

able to wrest hours of drama and attention out of the most trivial of incidents, all of it to impress and dazzle her *semblables*, and as much as I go on about her, what else does she have to do with her time?"

Marie paused, and went on.

"True, I also play the social rounds. One has to. And it can be enjoyable. At times. But often it is just—what one does. The same dance with different partners. And not that different."

"Then there is you."

She turned to him.

"Do you think Monsieur Bovary would discuss anything with Madame? Impossible. He would not think she had anything to say, not that she ever would. Even were she to try, even were she to suggest the most perfect of solutions to any quandary, he would not listen. He would listen to his horses before her. Which he should, but enough.

"You. You listen to me. You do not always do as I suggest, but you consider what I have to say. You discuss your cases with me—"

"I certainly do. You ofttimes see what I miss. And you keep my confidences to yourself. And besides, sometimes you know more of the law than I do. Comes from having been raised in a family of *avocats*, I expect."

"Quite. But could I ever be a lawyer? Be honest, Antoine. Could I?"

"Ah . . . no."

"You need not look so ashamed, *mon amour*. That is another reason I love you. You are always honest with me. Often annoyingly so, particularly when you do not agree with me. Though sometimes you are correct not to. Which is exasperating.

"As to your answer, you are correct. No, I could not be. I am a woman, of the propertied class. Expected only to make an advantageous marriage, by which is meant the richer the better."

She smiled at him. "Well, I did make an advantageous marriage. Also a *beneficial* one. Perhaps you didn't, but I did. Which I suspect Marie Madeleine—*La Stupide*, rather—did not. It may be that Sainte-Croix regarded her as more than only a decorative ornament to his arm and to his bed. Which may explain her conduct. Not that that excuses *La Stupide*, or makes *him* anything other than the rapacious *enfant de maquereau* he is!" she concluded, snapping out her last words.

"Deadlier than the male," murmured Antoine.

"Pardon, Antoine?"

"*De rien*. Another up-time English poet."

"Ah? I may alter my opinion of English poets. Or not. I must say, I do wonder at the lack of French phrases from up-time. Of course it is an English—American—village, but even so, the scarcity reflects ill of France *futur*. Speaking of up-time, what are we to do with Grantville? Send for more information, or go ourselves?"

"Oh, go ourselves, of course. Researchers, no matter how professional, can never be as concerned and as interested in the material as ourselves."

"True, but hire some even so. Ones less personally involved may see more clearly. Find connections we might miss or not understand are connections. How long until we can depart?"

"That—I am not certain. I would have us leave today, but arrangements must be made. Cases brought to a finish, others transferred. Richelieu for a certainty must be informed, and the king as well."

"So. A month, then."

"At least. Though perhaps somewhat earlier. Certainly by the end of today we can ensure sufficient funds for our stay there. The Abrabanels, after all."

"Quite so. They can also provide researchers, I am sure. Very well then. Contact them. Arrange your affairs. Myself, I will deal with the household. I believe we should expect to pass three months, and if three, likely six, in Grantville. By that I mean not only Grantville, but also elsewhere. Magdeburg, perhaps. I have heard of certain social enterprises, endeavors, I forget the exact terms—which the up-timers have begun. Many of Monsieur Gaston's circle dismiss those as peasant superstition beneath the notice of decent people, so there must be something of merit there."

Marie Ollier d'Aubray stood up, resolution in her stance. And also—care.

"But before that, I—we—Antoine, we need to see Marie Madeleine. To hug her, hold her close."

"Of course, Marie. Always."

Grantville Is Crazy

Robert Noxon

November 23, 1634
My dear father,

You said to write home with my impressions of
Grantville, and so I am penning the lines to you
before my ideas are all scrambled together by the
sheer horror of it all.

First, let me say that I arrived safely. For once
rumor has not exaggerated. The roads are as well-made
as any the Romans ever built and over 1,200 years
newer. They are as well-patrolled as rumor suggests
and few indeed are the bandits or road agents that
dare openly ply their trade near Grantville.

The inns are even more marvelous than rumor
states. Unfortunately, the prices are *also* even more
marvelous than rumor suggests, but I only plan to be
here a few nights.

Let me state, categorically, that the idea that the devil
created Grantville is wrong. *The devil could not possibly have imagined this place!* God must have done it
for reasons of his own and it stands as irrefutable proof
that mere humans will never understand His thoughts.

They claim to speak English. This is either a delusion or an outright lie. I'm not sure which. They firmly believe that if you can't understand them the first time they say something, you will understand if they just speak louder. If that doesn't work, try adding blasphemy and a few profanities. If there was a fine for the use of the words "okay" (like the French *d'accord*), "dude" (young man), and "cool" (half the words in the English language), half of Grantville would be beggared and the government could dispense with all other sources of income.

An Ami told me that we English were nice folks, but we were wrong to believe that simply because we invented the English language, that meant we were the ones who spoke it correctly. (I translate his remarks from the local patois—called "Redneck" into human speech.)

They say they are so fond of children, but they give them *milk* to drink! And yet, if you dare give that poor child a beer to kill the vile taste, they will have a hissy fit (one of the few useful up-time phrases that were poured down upon me) and swear that you are trying to kill the child. They say milk is good for children, and beer is bad for them.

They let any fool who can get his claws on a printing press take a chamber pot full of vile ideas and dump it upon an unsuspecting world. And yet, if you bid your housemaid to take a chamber pot full of vile things and dump it upon an unsuspecting gutter, they will swear you are trying to murder them by unleashing the plagues of Egypt upon them and they will have *another* hissy fit like unto the prophet Jeremiah discussing the shortcomings of the heathens. (Another thing, most of them would have no idea who the prophet Jeremiah was or what the plagues of Egypt were and they prefer it that way.)

It was at this point I began to understand how an up-timer could write a novel about a child who chased her cat into a mirror and emerged into a strange land where all logic was distorted. It is like a midget writing a novel about being short.

They believe in Universal Education and in making it so costly that no poor person could possibly afford any.

They celebrate Halloween and have many Scotch or Irish customs about it including Jackie's Lantern. (Though they do not use turnips but a much larger fruit called a pumpkin.) However, they have no idea what All Saints' Day is.

Here, the anarchists and rebels have better discipline than any king's army ever dreamed of, and better organization than most. They use the terms "democracy" and "republic" as though they were interchangeable. However, even if they can't define either term they are still the fiercest republicans to ever draw breath. "Death to all nobles!" they constantly cry. This is why they adore Princess Kristina Vasa. It is why they risked so much to help Queen Maria Hapsburg. It is why they call their most beloved singer "The King" and give to him the respect more decent folks reserve for saints. It is also why they are Gustav Adolphus' most loyal vassals and call him "Good King Gus."

They call Europe "third world." What are the first two, Heaven and Hell? Given the average Ami's level of religious knowledge, probably not. Still, in a way it is reassuring that I *don't* understand them. It proves I'm not yet insane. (At times I felt some doubt about this.)

Asking a local where I might get a cheap meal and wishing to avoid the politics of the Golden Arches, I went to a place that serves pizza. The best I can describe a pizza is to say it looks like somebody already ate it, lost it, then set fire to the remains. It looks nastier than anything even the French have ever done to God's honest victuals. However, if you can get it into your mouth, it is not bad at all and not really poisonous.

They say tomatoes are not poisonous and tobacco is. Worse, they have the effrontery to eat them and not die. They make them into a sauce which they put on everything. They will take potatoes, oats, barley, and anything else nasty they can grab and brew it into a weird, godless, horrible alchemical mess that could gag a maggot and scare a wolf. Then, they will put it between two pieces of bread, drown it in their tomato sauce, put it into their mouth, swallow it, and claim that is good for you. Yes, and the majority of them will not say grace before they commit this atrocity. They will, however, charge you a fortune for it.

But, they will not eat horse meat. (A young man at the counter said, "So many of them are a horse's ass, it would be cannibalism." If you tell them you eat horses, *then* they will be disgusted.)

What *is* poisonous is the hotel manager. He has filled most of the ground floor of the hotel with small stalls selling things you don't need at prices you can't afford. In Robin Hood's time innkeepers were often in league with bandits. In Grantville they have "cut out the middleman," as they say. He is a greedy, grasping, conniving, avaricious, swindling Shylock who would steal the pennies off a dead man's eyes then add an extra charge to your bill for "room services," or skin a flea for the hide and tallow and charge you extra for having a pet in your room. In short, the manager is a typical innkeeper, but shrewder than most. He may be the one person in Grantville who is *not* crazy.

Still, in Grantville the problem is not finding things worthy of being in a curio cabinet. A five minute stroll down any street would fill all the curio cabinets in England, and half the madhouses as well. Even at these prices I have found some curios for your curio cabinet. The ring with a chain is to keep keys. The small puzzle cube on the end is called "Rubik's Cube" after the maniac that invented it. The idea is to twist it until all the pieces on all the faces are the same color. Perhaps it is trying to solve these puzzles which has driven them insane. The book of drawings is called a "flip book" or a "thumb book" because if you use your thumb to flip the pages fast enough, the picture appears to move. This is one of the principles behind their "moving pictures," though there are many others.

I purchased one of their "fountain pens" (a marvelous substitute for quills—seldom blots and never needs dipping or sharpening) earlier, so I jot down these impressions while they are still fresh. I could easily fill a hundred more pages—this pen makes it far easier to write. Still, I have spent all evening writing this and it is meant to be a letter, not a novel. Their custom of putting lanterns on poles to light the streets means that shops do not have to close at sundown. Even though it is far past nine o'clock at night, I mean to go out and find a tavern and have a few drinks before retiring.

I will leave with this final thought. If Hell is God's prison, Grantville is clearly his insane asylum.

Your obedient son
Josiah Buckley

Hunter, My Huntress

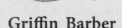

Griffin Barber

Patience growing short in the afternoon heat, Dara's favorite leopard yowled and spat at her handler, ready to hunt.

Dara grinned, ready as well, welcoming the prospect of release from the tension being around Aurangzeb always provoked in him. Now, if only they could begin. The small army of beaters had started the day before, working through the night to drive all the wild game resident in several square *kos* toward where the hunting party lay in wait. The camp was loud with the voices of men and animals, many of Father's more notable *umara* present to witness the hunt and curry favor with the *wazir*.

Seeking distraction, Dara again took up the gun he'd had as a wedding gift from Father last year, the inlaid piece monstrous heavy yet reassuring in its solidity. He sighted down the nearly two *gaz* of barrel, arms immediately trembling from the weight of iron, ivory inlay, and mahogany. Among the many refinements, the weapon sported one of the new flintlocks rather than the traditional matchlock, and even had a trigger rather than lever.

"Here," he grunted.

Body slaves overseen by his Atishbaz gunsmith, Talawat, hurriedly set up the iron tripod needed to support the hunting piece while he struggled to hold position.

"Ready, *Shehzada*," Talawat said.

Trying to keep the weight under control, Dara slowly lowered the gun onto the mount. Talawat slotted the pin that would hold the gun's weight when aimed into place, easing the awkward weight from Dara's arms. The prince knelt and placed the butt of the weapon on the cushion another slave hurriedly set in place.

Rubbing the ache from his biceps, hoofbeats drew Dara's attention. He looked down the gradual slope to the pair of watering holes that formed the two sides of the killing zone for the hunt. About one hundred *gaz* of grassy clearing lay between the slowly drying watering holes, with about half that much distance between grandfather's tent and the open space. The beaters were working toward that spot in a steadily shrinking circle.

One of Asaf Khan's men emerged from the wood line at a gallop, crossing the clearing and pounding up to the camp. In a fine display of horsemanship, the *sowar* swung down from his mount to land lightly a few paces in front of Dara's grandfather.

Asaf Khan stepped forward and listened as the young trooper made his report: "At least a hundred head of blackbuck and red antelope, a small herd of *nilgai*, *Wazir*. Tiger spoor was also found, but no one has laid eyes on it, yet. Should not be long, now, before the first of the beasts make an appearance."

Asaf Khan dismissed his man. Gray beard dancing,

the aging but still powerfully built Wazir called out: "A tiger would make a worthy prize for one of my grandsons!"

"Perhaps for Dara, Grandfather. He has yet to take one," Aurangzeb drawled from inside the tent.

Dara watched Asaf's smile dim before he turned and answered, "One tiger could never be enough for the sons of emperors."

"I did not say it was, Asaf Khan," Aurangzeb said, striding from the tent into the sun.

"I will kill it, Grandfather!" Shah Shuja crowed, raising his bow. Born between Aurangzeb and Dara, Shuja seemed always afire with desire to please his elders. At eighteen he was a man grown, however, and larger than Dara by a head. Of course, that head was rarely full of things other than those he might hunt, fight, or ride.

Asaf turned to face his eldest grandson. "And you, Dara?"

"I will take what it pleases God to place before me."

"Pious words," Asaf said, nodding approval.

Behind Grandfather's back, Aurangzeb shook his head and commanded his horse be brought up.

"Where are you going?" Asaf asked, edges of his beard curling down as he frowned.

"I will take the animals my brothers miss; that way I am sure to have a good day hunting."

Shah Shuja grunted as if punched in the belly, face darkening. He too had been shamed by the poem making the rounds of the court.

Doing his best to ignore the insult, Dara gestured at his leopards. "Brother, that is why I have brought my cats, to run down escaping game."

Aurangzeb shrugged, took up a lance. "Then I will race your cats, and beat them, to the kill."

Asaf stepped toward Aurangzeb, raising hands in a conciliatory gesture. "I would advise caution, brave one. If there is a tiger in among them, it will easily overtake a horseman. They can only be hunted safely from elephant howdah."

Aurangzeb shrugged again. "Then it will be as God wills it," he said, putting spurs to his tall horse and speeding off to the left of the firing line and the sole exit to the killing ground, a trail of attendants and guards in tow.

"Here they come!" one of Grandfather's cronies cried.

"Nur Jahan respectfully asks a visit, Begum Sahib."

Jahanara had been expecting such a request since arranging her great aunt's poisoning, if not so soon.

"She is recovered, then?" she asked the eunuch.

"Indeed, her illness has passed, thanks be to God."

"Praise Him," she answered in reflex. And because, while she had been expecting the request, Jahanara did not feel ready to grant it: "I shall consult my astrologer before visiting. He found some peril to my health in his last reading, and advised me to caution." She waved dismissal at him. "You may take my words to her."

The eunuch bowed low, yet remained before her.

She let him grow uncomfortable before asking, "There is more?"

"I pray you will forgive me, Begum Sahib, but my mistress waits without."

Jahanara tried not to display her concern—Nur Jahan's eunuch would surely report everything observed to his mistress. Still, a bit of pique was called for: "She presumes much, my grandfather's sister."

The eunuch pressed his head into the ground. "As you say, Begum Sahib. Nur Jahan commanded that I convey her assurances that the illness is not catching, and that she has words of import for your ears."

"Very well. I will trust to her greater experience in this. She may attend me. Go and fetch her."

The eunuch said nothing further, just bowed and withdrew.

Jahanara used the time to shore up her mental defenses. Tending Father's reignited grief had proved draining, leaving her tired and out of sorts. Worse yet, the result was still uncertain. Shah Jahan had risen this morning and made only one command after attending morning prayers: he ordered his daughter to summon someone literate in English to Red Fort. Knowing no other she dared call on, Jahanara sent for Salim. He had yet to answer her summons, just as Dara had yet to respond to her messenger.

And now Nur Jahan, veteran of thirty years of imperial harem politics, was coming.

She wished Dara were here. She wished Mother were here. She wished for many things, yet none of them had come to pass when Nur Jahan entered her receiving chamber.

Head high, the older woman's direct gaze immediately fixed on Jahanara. Nur Jahan approached with the supple grace of a woman much younger than her fifty-six years, a result of a life-long regimen of dance and diet. Dressed in fine silks and damasks of her own design and pattern, Nur Jahan called to mind a great cat stalking prey.

Nur Jahan came to a halt, bowed, a delicate scent teasing Jahanara's senses. "Grandniece."

Wishing to keep things formal, Jahanara used the other woman's title, "Nur Jahan," as she gestured the other to take a seat.

A brilliant, cheerful smile answered the formality and called to mind the reason for her title as "Light of the World." So great was the charm of that smile that Jahanara could not be certain it was false, despite knowing that it had to be.

"Must we be so formal, Janni?" Nur asked as she reclined on cushions across from Jahanara. "I am fresh recovered from illness, and would celebrate another day among the living with my family. And—as all the boys are hunting and your sister is with your father—I naturally thought of you."

Jahanara hid her displeasure at the other woman's use of her childhood nickname, answered in even tones: "I merely pay you the respect my grandfather bestowed upon you in recognition of your beauty, especially as you appear so well and happy."

Nur Jahan blushed, actually *blushed*, at praise she had likely heard far more times than the sun had risen over Jahanara. "Jahangir was a great man, always kinder to me than I deserved."

Marveling at the woman's control over her body, Jahanara ordered refreshments for them both.

She looked back at Nur, found the older woman regarding her with a steady gaze.

Wishing for more time, Jahanara stalled: "A new perfume, Aunt?"

A nod of the head. "Yes, I have been working on it for some time. Do you like it?"

"Very much."

"I shall see some delivered to you, then."

A silence stretched. Refreshments arrived, were served.

Jahanara let the silence linger, armoring herself in it.

"I have something I wish to tell you, Janni."

"Oh?"

"Yes."

"Must I ask?"

A throaty chuckle. "No, of course not. It is a tale. A tale from my first year with your grandfather. A tale of the hunt, in fact."

As the man's cry faded, a small herd of blackbuck, no more than eight animals, spat from the line of brush and trees. Bounding with the outrageous speed of their kind, the antelope seemed to fly across the open ground.

Dara shook his head, irritation flaring. Blackbuck were perfect game for his hunting cheetahs but he couldn't risk one of the cats attacking Aurangzeb or his horse.

Dara held out a hand. Talawat filled it with one of his lighter pieces, match cord already glowing. Shouldering it, Dara picked his target: a good-sized healthy animal just behind the leading beast.

He heard Shuja's bowstring slap bracer. A moment later Shuja muttered angrily.

Ignoring all distraction, Dara's world shrank to the chest of the beast he'd chosen. Finding it, he moved his point of aim two hands ahead along the shallow arc of its jump.

He pulled the lever and averted his eyes at the very last moment.

The gun thundered.

Dara handed it off to Talawat as the blackbuck fell, heart-shot. The gunsmith handed him another piece.

Shuja shouted, his second arrow striking the lead buck in the belly.

He ignored the cheering of his grandfather's entourage, chose another buck, aimed, fired. Another clean hit to the chest. The antelope collapsed after a few strides.

"Well done, Talawat. Your guns speak truly," he said, passing the weapon off.

Talawat bowed, presenting another piece. "The *Shehzada* is too kind."

Taking the third gun in hand, Dara waited a moment, allowing the smoke to clear. Behind him, Talawat's apprentices busied themselves reloading the discharged weapons.

"Your modesty is a sign of fine character, but—" Dara tapped a knuckle against the gun's hardwood stock—"in this instant, misplaced."

Talawat smiled and bowed again before gesturing at the field. "I merely prepare the weapons, *Shehzada*. It is not everyone that has your fine eye for shooting."

Shuja downed another of the blackbuck with an arrow that nearly passed through the animal. The first beast he'd hit finally collapsed from blood loss, blood frothing from its muzzle.

The remains of the herd cleared the firing line, only to run into Aurangzeb and his mounted party. Dara's brother took an antelope with his spear as its herd mates ran past. Leaving the weapon behind and spurring his horse into a gallop, Aurangzeb switched to the horse bow. The prey were far faster than his mount, stretching their lead even as Aurangzeb drew, aimed, and loosed twice in quick succession. Each arrow struck home in a separate neck, a fine feat of archery.

Asaf's cronies cheered, as did Shuja, who had approached Dara.

Cradling his gun, Dara smiled, despite himself.

Aurangzeb cased his bow while sending his finely trained mount circling back among his followers with just the pressure of his knees, an act of understated pride in its own right.

"I should have ridden instead of standing here with you and your guns," Shuja grumbled, loud enough for Dara to hear.

Dara did not answer, even when his younger brother ordered his horse brought up and left to join Aurangzeb.

He watched his grandfather instead, pondering the old man's place in the family history as well as his possible future: Abdul Hasan Asaf Khan had turned against his own sister to support Father when Dara's paternal grandfather, Jahangir, passed and the succession came into question once again. Dara had himself been hostage and surety against his father's loyalty after that first rebellion, and was no stranger to the price of failure for princes engaged in rebellion. Shah Jahan and his allies had emerged victorious, but it had been a close-run and uncertain thing, all the way to the end. He had been rewarded with position, titles, and power, though recent failings had reduced his favor at court. Father was considering removing him from the office of *wazir* and sending him off to govern Bengal.

As if sensing Dara's thoughts were upon him, Dara's

grandfather turned from watching the slaves collect carcasses and approached Dara.

Talawat bowed and silently withdrew a few paces, giving them some privacy.

Asaf pushed his beard out toward Shuja's retreating back. "Well, first among the sons of my daughter, it seems your brothers would hunt as our ancestors preferred."

Dara nodded. "I would as well, but for this," he said, gesturing with his free hand at the new gun on its tripod.

Smiling, Asaf bowed his head and squinted at the weapon a few moments. "Big ball?"

"Large enough to down *nilgai* in one shot...or a tiger."

"Brave man, hunts a tiger with powder and shot rather than bow and spear."

Dara shrugged. "Surely not in the company of so many men, Asaf Khan?"

Asaf Khan waved a hand. "Abdul, or...Grandfather...if it pleases."

Catching the plaintive note in his grandfather's voice, Dara smiled. "Surely, *Grandfather*, I would not be at risk among so many men."

"Jahangir once lost three favored *umara* to one, a great she-tiger. And they were all armed to the teeth and born to the saddle. The tiger does not feel pain as we do; most wounds merely madden them."

Dara was about to answer when another herd, or perhaps the larger body of the one just harvested, emerged from the wood line, dashing for the open space between the watering holes. At the rate they were fleeing, the beasts would be in range in moments.

Asaf Khan stepped clear as Dara raised his gun. He felt, rather than heard, Talawat edge closer with his remaining light pieces.

He sighted along the barrel. That part of his mind not engaged with aiming noted an anomaly: the blackbuck were running straight and true rather than bouncing back and forth along a line of travel.

Just as he was ready to squeeze the lever, a thundering of hooves caused him to lower his muzzle. Aurangzeb and Shuja were riding to meet the herd, bows in hand.

"I had only been married to Jahangir for a brief while when he invited me to join him on a tiger hunt. I leapt at the chance to join him in the howdah, and had the mahouts paint his favorite elephant for the occasion. A great party of us set out, camping of a night and slowly moving through the areas where your grandfather's armies were concentrating the game for his pleasure.

"But, as you may know, your grandfather Jahangir enjoyed smoking opium far more than was good for him, and he dozed through much of the hunt, the swaying of the howdah"—she gave a throaty chuckle—"and perhaps the swaying of my hips, lulling him to sleep a few times."

Jahanara, used to Nur's earthy storytelling, still blushed. Scandalous! To think of sexual congress in the hot confines of a howdah, of all places, *jali* or no!

Nur pretended not to notice. "It was during one of his naps that there was some consternation ahead of us. I put on my veils and opened the curtains of the howdah.

"Several slaves were running from a *wadi* some tens of *gaz* away. It was then that I saw the reason for their flight: a pair of tigers flashing through the undergrowth after them."

Jahanara noticed the older woman's gaze grown distant, breath quickening; felt her own pulse rising.

"They were magnificent. Terrible. Bloodlust made manifest. One man had his head nearly removed with one rake of claws. Others fell, were torn open. Blood was everywhere." Her nostrils flared, remembering.

A tiny smile. "The screams of his slaves at last woke Jahangir from his stupor. He moved to join me, took my hand in his.

"'Protect your servants,' I told him.

"He looked at me. Too late, I could tell my command had made him most angry.

"After a moment he pressed his great bow into my hands. 'One with this. Then one with the gun, if you succeed.'

"'What?' I asked, incredulous.

"'Protect them if you wish them protected, wife.'

"I do not think he knew then, that my brother had taught me the bow in our youth. I think he thought to test me, hoping I would fail. He sought to put me in my place as twentieth wife, however favored..." Nur Jahan let her words trail off into brief silence.

Jahanara found herself leaning forward, eager to hear more. Slowly, conscious of the other woman's skill at courtly intrigues and careful of some trap, she sat back.

Nur resumed her tale. "I resolved to show him I was no wilting flower." The older woman sat straighter even as she said the words.

"While we had spoken, another pair of slaves had

perished, and the tigers had pursued them much closer to our elephant. Hands shaking, I drew the bow, loosed. That first arrow missed. I did not miss with the second, though it was not enough to kill the beast. Enraged, it leapt into the air and spun in a circle. I loosed again. A lucky shot, it took the cat in the throat, stilling its roar."

A shake of her head. "The other tiger left off killing a man to raise its head, then coughed strangely, almost as if asking why his brother had stopped talking mid-sentence.

"Jahangir laughed, slapped me on the back as if I were one of his *sowar*, and took the bow from my hands. He handed me one of his guns, igniting the match cord himself.

"I had no experience of guns, and told him so.

"'Look along the metal, point it at his great head; when the head is covered by the barrel, tell me, and I will light it. Turn your head when I do, or you might get burned.'

"I did as he bid, aiming at a point between the great ears. I remember thinking how beautiful its fur was. 'Ready,' I whispered.

"He touched the match cord to the powder and the gun belched fire, punching me in the shoulder like nothing I felt before. I swayed back, my veil singed by the fire from the pan. I had forgotten to turn my head, you see." She shook her head. "It is amazing, what I recall of that day: I remember the feel of the elephant shivering, wanting to flee the loud noise but too well trained to move, while I tried to see where my shot had fallen."

She smiled, looking Jahanara in the eye. "I missed my mark."

Jahanara realized she had been showing her eager-
ness for the tale again, and quickly leaned back.
"Well, it is understandable: you were handling a gun
for the fir—"

Another of Nur's throaty chuckles broke Jahanara's
words. "I did not miss entirely, Janni. My ball took
the tiger in the heart, killing it almost instantly. I still
have the fur in my quarters."

Aurangzeb and Shuja had split up to either side of
the herd, and were standing in the stirrups, loosing.
Where their arrows fell, antelope staggered out of the
herd, dead or dying. Shuja ended up on the near side
of the herd, Aurangzeb disappearing into the dust
kicked up by the herd and their own mounts.

Dara shook his head. While impressive, their antics
were denying him a shot. Not that he couldn't rely on
his skills and shoot anyway; it was simply not a good
idea to go firing into a field occupied by two princes,
whether the shooter was a brother or not.

He briefly considered taking to his own horse while
summoning a drink from one of his body slaves.

"Don't want to take to your own horse?" Asaf
Khan asked.

Having already decided against it, Dara punched
his chin toward where his brothers were now racing
back toward the firing line in a cloud of dust. "When
their horses tire, there will be other game."

Asaf nodded, looked sidelong at his eldest grandson.
"Married life agrees with you, Grandson."

"Oh?" Dara asked, taking the gem-encrusted goblet
full of iced fruit juice from his servant.

"You are more patient than you were. I may presume

too much when I think it your wife's doing..." He
shrugged. "But there are worse reasons for change in
the behavior of men."

Dara hid his smile by slaking his thirst. Smack-
ing his lips appreciatively, he answered, "Yes, many
things are put in their proper places, now I have a
son on the way."

"A son? You are so sure? The astrologers tell you
it is so?"

"Yes," Dara half-lied. The up-timer history had it
that his son rode to battle with him in his war against
Aurangzeb, many years in the future.

"You must send me y—" Asaf stopped in mid-
sentence, peering into the dust beyond Shuja.

Dara followed the line of his gaze, saw it a heartbeat later: something gold orange flowing along in the
wake of Shuja's horse.

"Tiger!" Asaf bellowed in his general's voice, pointing at the great beast stalking his grandson.

Dara tossed his goblet aside, scrambled for his
newest gun.

Shuja, hearing the shout, did the wrong thing. He
reined in to look toward Asaf Khan. The tiger was
within twenty *gaz* of Shuja. When he came to a stop,
it did as well. In fact, it went forequarters down,
hunching its rear end.

Asaf was screaming, as were more and more of
his men. He started running for his own horse and
household guard.

Dara knelt and lifted the butt of his gun, surging
upright.

Shuja was looking around, trying to identify the
threat. His horse tossed its head, shied sideways, uneasy.

Dara pressed his shoulder into the stock, trying to cock the lock, find his target, and get his hand on the firing lever—and had a moment's panic when he couldn't find it: *Not a lever, a trigger, you fool!*

The tiger was rocking its hips, getting ready to charge.

Talawat was beside him, quietly urging, "*Shehzada*, please do not try to do too much at once. Slow down. Calmly."

Dara stopped. Breathed out. Found his aim point and his target. Slid his finger into the trigger guard.

Out of the corner of his eye he saw Talawat's silhouette nod. The gunsmith cocked the hammer back for Dara. "She kicks like a mule, *Shehzada*. Now kill us a tiger."

Dara squeezed the trigger. The lock snapped forward, steel and flint sparking into the pan. A half heartbeat later, the gun discharged with a thunderous roar and brutal kick to Dara's shoulder.

The tiger leapt.

Smoke obscured Dara's sight for a moment.

Shuja's horse bolted, riderless, into view.

Talawat stepped forward and turned to face Dara, hands busy as he reloaded the piece with quick, economical motions. He could hear the gunsmith praying even over the shouts of Asaf's men.

Asaf had stopped his rush to mount. It was too late.

The smoke cleared.

The tiger lay prone, part of one of Shuja's legs and a boot protruding from beneath it.

Dara's heart stopped.

It seemed years later when Shuja sat up from between its paws, face as white as bleached linen.

Hands shaking, the younger prince heaved the heavy corpse aside and stood up, apparently unscathed.

Suddenly thirsty, Dara wished for strong drink.

The line erupted in crazed shouts of joy. Asaf came charging back toward Dara, teeth bared in a smile that split his beard.

Shuja was walking, somewhat unsteadily, back toward the line.

Placing powder in the pan and stepping back, Talawat murmured, "Fine shooting, *Shehzada.*"

Dara pointed a trembling finger at his sibling. "I will give you his weight in silver, Talawat. Were it not for you, I would have surely rushed the shot." He swallowed. "And missed."

Talawat bowed his head, clearly aware of how badly things might have turned out. "God is merciful and loving-kind, to place one of my tools in the hands of one so gifted in their use: I will use the silver to make more fine guns for your use, *Shehzada.*"

Aurangzeb rode into view behind his dismounted brother, stopping over the tiger for a moment. After a moment's examination, he nudged his horse into motion. Quickly catching up to Shuja, he said something the other responded to with an angry shake of the head. Shrugging, the mounted brother rode on toward the firing line.

As he came closer, Dara noticed his quiver was empty and his face had a thin smile drawn across it. For Aurangzeb, such an expression was a broad smile of unrestrained glee.

"I see we each took a tiger this day, brother."

"What?" Dara asked.

Aurangzeb nodded his head in the direction he'd come from. "Another one, possibly this one's mate or nearly adult offspring, took the last blackbuck in the herd. He took some killing: all my remaining arrows are in him."

Asaf Khan arrived in time to hear the end of Aurangzeb's speech, sweating from his exertions. Pausing to catch his breath, he was still beaming when Dara remembered to be civil. "Congratulations, brother, I'm sure it was a fine kill."

"And to you on yours, Dara, though it appears your beast had an old wound to slow it; an arrow in its flesh, turned to poison."

"Might explain why it went for Shuja with dead game at hand," Asaf gasped.

"Anger is the poison that stirs the killer residing in the hearts of man and beast," Dara said, trying not to look at his brother as he did so.

"An entertaining tale," Jahanara mused aloud. Nur had only just departed, the air still hanging with the delicate scent of her perfume.

"*Shehzadi*?" her body slave and administrator of her personal staff, Smidha, asked.

"Nothing of import." She lowered her voice. "Has Prasad returned?"

"No, Begum Sahib," Smidha answered. She raised her voice slightly: "Begum Sahib, you asked to be informed when your ink was delivered. It arrived just this afternoon."

"Good," Jahanara said in an equally clear voice. She raised her head and ordered the remaining slave at the entrance to her receiving chamber: "Fetch my inks."

When she had departed on the errand: "What is it, Smidha?"

Smidha edged closer and bowed her head, speaking quickly and quietly. "My sister's man says a slave was found dead just outside the harem walls, Begum Sahib. Nothing special in itself, but my friend who is also your sister Raushashana's nurse, says that her mistress was heard to claim the slave betrayed Nur Jahan. Just now, while you entertained her, I confirmed with one of the eunuchs that have responsibility for guarding her quarters that Nur is seeking a new cook-slave."

Jahanara closed her eyes, said a brief prayer for Vidya. She had never personally met the young woman who, outraged by the mistreatment of her lover, had offered to spy on her mistress. Now, carrying out Jahanara's will, she would become yet another of the faceless victims of courtly machinations. Victims Jahanara would carry the guilt of in her heart to the end of her days.

She shook her head, dread encroaching on her guilt. "Which eunuch?"

"Begum Sahib?"

"Which eunuch, Smidha?"

"Chetan, Begum Sahib."

"One of the Rajputs?" she asked, running through her mental portrait gallery of the servants of her enemy.

"Yes, the great big, round-headed one with the crooked nose."

Jahanara nodded. "He is entirely Nur's. She wanted me to know she caught my spy. Do we know how Vidya died?"

Smidha bowed her head. "Poison is suspected, mistress."

The princess bit her lip. "Then Nur was never successfully poisoned at all?"

Smidha shrugged. "That is possible, though she did request the Italian doctor come and examine her."

"To complete her falsehood ... or for something else?" Jahanara shook her head. "Set someone to watch him from now on."

"Yes, Begum Sahib."

"And still no word from Salim?"

"That messenger also has yet to report success in his duties. I begin to worry he might have been waylaid."

"Where is she getting the men to do these things for her?" Jahanara asked.

"I do not know, Begum Sahib. She has not changed her habits significantly since Vidya came to us last year."

"Oh, but that's just it, Smidha. We can't know how long Nur knew about Vidya's allegiance to me. Much of our information is suspect, then."

Smidha's half smile showed Jahanara that her agile mind was working at full speed. "Yes and no, Begum Sahib. I always try to verify from multiple mouths what my ears hear from one source's lips. I do not like to look foolish, misinforming my mistress."

"So, then: what do we know?"

"That Nur Jahan is dangerous even while in your father's power."

"Who, though, is providing her with influence beyond these walls?"

Smidha shook her head, "We cannot know she is responsible for your messenger's failures just yet, Begum Sahib." Another shrug of round shoulders. "Assuming your suspicions are correct, however, I can think of a few *umara* who remember Jahangir's last years and Nur's regency in all but name as good ones for their ambitions, but none that your father and grandfather are not already aware of and keeping an eye on."

"What of Mullah Mohan?"

A delicate sniff. "That man, bend his stiff neck to treat with a woman? Hardly, Begum Sahib."

"I love you dearly, Smidha, and value your service above all others, but I think you might be letting your feelings color your assessment. She has the skill, he has the manpower."

Smidha flushed, bowed her head again. "It has been my pleasure to serve you, just as it was to serve your mother, Begum Sahib. Still"—she looked up—"I find that, of late, my heart is hard when it should be soft, and soft when it should be hard."

Jahanara patted Smidha on the arm. "You are my wisest advisor, Smidha. I just want to be sure we are not dismissing a potential truth."

The older woman bowed again, looked up sharply. "And now I think on it, the idea has merit: she did have occasion to speak with Mohan while arranging Jahangir's tomb and the mosque dedicated in his name." She shook her head again, concern drawing her brows together. "If she managed to draw that dried stick of a man into her web enough that he is willing to lend her his strength, what other dark miracles can she arrange?"

"And, having seen the steel of the trap the huntress has laid out for us, what bait is meant to bring us in, and how do we spring the trap without losing a limb?"

Reed and Kathy Sue

Bjorn Hasseler

Our House, Grantville
Tuesday, June 12, 1635

Dear Reed,

I miss you so much already. Wish you could have stayed, but they need you. I'm so proud of you.

Thank you so much for moving us back to Grantville. It was a hassle you didn't need just before you deployed, but I appreciate it so much. Lydia and Thomas do, too. We went for a walk around town—your mom and the kids and I. Grantville has changed so much just this past year! But Lydia recognized the park. She, Thomas, and Mark had a ball. Well, up until she met another little girl and told her she'd just turned six. Apparently the girl told Lydia that she's not really six yet, because "up-timers skipped whole years." She was all worried about not being allowed to go to first grade. Once we got home, and I got Mark and Mary down for a nap, we looked at the calendar. I showed her that we skipped ahead only fifty-three days. She was very excited about counting fifty-three days on the calendar.

I think Mark is developing faster than Lydia and

Thomas did, probably because Thomas is "helping" him "grow up" so much. I've reminded Thomas that Mark isn't even two yet, and he just can't do everything Thomas can, yet. These two are going to be a handful when they get older.

Mary is doing great. She woke up only once the last two nights in a row. So I'm not quite a zombie. By number four, it's practically routine. Being a stay-at-home mom in the seventeenth century is a ton of work, but every once in a while I wouldn't mind finding something I could do from home. The girls who are renting from us are all perfect dears. Anna Maria and Rosina are so happy to have the kids around again. I'm still getting to know Magdalena but Anna Maria and Rosina both said she's fitting in fine.

They were nice enough to keep an eye on the kids for half an hour last night while I went for a run. Two miles. It's great to start getting back in shape. Magdalena asked me if I was going out in public dressed like that. ☺ T-shirt and shorts.

Your mom has the victory garden all in. Your Aunt Janet and Uncle Freeman stopped by and gave us a lot of seeds. Lydia helped. Thomas and Mark mostly played in the dirt. I can't tell you how wonderful it is to have running hot and cold water in the bathtub. As soon as all four kids were in bed, I had a bath, too.

A memory—I remember when we first bought the house and moved everything over from the apartment in one day and stacked so much on the bed we ended up in sleeping bags on the carpet the first night. I was so disoriented when I woke up.

A verse, Joshua 1:9: "Have I not commanded you? Be strong and of good courage; do not be afraid, nor be dismayed, for the Lord your God is with you wherever you go."

Be careful, Reed. The whole town knows war is coming.

I love you. ♥
Kathy Sue

Camp Halle
Monday, July 2, 1635

Dear Kathy Sue,

How are you and the kids? Are you sure you're okay? Not overdoing it?

Hi, Lydia. Hi, Thomas. Hi, Mark. Hi, Mary. I'm in camp. We live in a big tent and eat outdoors. Daddy misses you. Hugs and kisses.

Your letter came Saturday. That was pretty fast. I'm afraid it's going to slow way down once we start moving. Having stamps again is great. The little things, right?

I preached yesterday. Nothing fancy—I'm not interested in lecturing on who believes what about which issue, and I don't know all that stuff, anyway. Just focusing on Jesus. I told them I've got a Lutherbibel, a NASB, and a Strong's Concordance. I'll do my best to explain a passage, and if anyone else wants a turn, they're welcome to it. Jimmy Dunn, Charlie McDow, Hans Moschel, and Alexander Ebenhöch all came. Still can't get Bruce Reynolds to come out. A few others checked us out, too.

Two Bibles and a concordance gives me a nice heavy pack to run with, so maybe by the time I get home, I'll be able to keep up with you. Sorry I missed the bath, though.

I'm doing what I do. It's pretty much the hardware

store all over again, only bigger. There are some problem areas, but mostly just because it's on a bigger scale than anything we've done before. Many of the men are veterans of last year's campaign, so they know how things work. We just have to make sure they don't requisition too many spares. But every once in a while, there's a weird one. Like that shipment of... let's call them grid squares... that just disappeared. Logged in, never signed for, just gone. It's mind-boggling how an entire shipment can go missing.

Don't worry about me. I'm surrounded by lots of people with rifles. You and the kids, be safe. I don't think the enemy could reach Grantville this time, but you know the drill if they do. Try not to dwell on it, though. Bad memories.

Please tell Mark Happy Birthday from Daddy.

A memory: You having this idea that we'd write each other. There'd be nothing for weeks, and then a whole bunch of letters would get to Wismar at once.

A verse, Proverbs 31:10: "An excellent wife, who can find? For her worth is far above jewels."

Love you, Sugar.
Reed

Our House, Grantville
Sunday, July 22, 1635

Dear Reed,

Proverbs 31? You're a sap! Seriously, though, I did read the whole chapter, and I get your point. It's okay if I find a way to work from home. It would have to be part-time and not on a deadline. I'll try to look around.

And, yes, I'm thinking about it because things are a little tight. It's not a crisis. I just have to be careful. We got the quarterly statement from OPM. Our investments made enough for the mortgage payments and the taxes with a couple hundred dollars left over. This whole idea of taking out a mortgage to make money isn't something that ever would have occurred to me, but I'm glad we heard about it. And it still wouldn't have worked if the Emergency Committee hadn't canceled our first mortgage right after the Ring of Fire, since it was through the bank in Fairmont. I know we couldn't have kept the house otherwise.

And Rosina, Anna Maria, and Dorothea couldn't have afforded it if we had to charge the going rate for rent. Magdalena was really concerned when I explained how the investments work. She thought if we were making money, then someone had to be losing it. I told her what the OPM people told us, that good investments help create wealth—and that I didn't really understand it, either, until they explained it to me.

Oh—Dorothea and Johann are doing fine. She's expecting in December. I restarted the Bible study. Dorothea came and brought her friend Elisabetha. Elisabetha is Lutheran, too, and knows the Bible pretty well. She's not entirely comfortable with a bunch of ladies having a Bible study on their own. I told her everybody's welcome, regardless of what church they go to. I don't have any formal training, but how hard is observe, interpret, apply? And the unwritten fourth step: Go ask the pastor's wife if we really get stuck.

Mark had a very happy birthday. I wish we could give the kids the sort of presents we got when we were kids up-time. But they really don't understand yet how different it is down-time. Your parents dug out your old blocks, and he's quite content to build towers and knock them down.

The kids loved the Fourth of July parade. Lydia wants to be in the marching band. This week. The adults—I think a lot of us were a little teary-eyed. It's one thing we still have from up-time. And we remember why it matters. We're set. Don't worry about us.

A memory—Our non-dates running together at cross-country practice. You know, it took me a few runs to realize that you had to be faster and were hanging back so you could flirt with me.

I'm sorry you missed the bath, too. Find any pictures yet?

A verse, Jude 24–25: "Now to Him who is able to keep you from stumbling, and to present you faultless before the presence of His glory with exceeding joy, to God our Savior, Who alone is wise, be glory and majesty, dominion and power, both now and forever. Amen."

I love you,
Kathy Sue ♥

Our House, Grantville
Monday, July 30, 1635

Dear Reed,

Are you okay? We heard there was fighting along the river. Please tell me you're okay.

The kids say, Hi, Daddy.

I love you,
Kathy Sue

Camp Halle
Wednesday, August 1, 1635

Dear Kathy Sue,

I just got your July 22 letter and package. Thank you so much! I don't know if this will make it through or not. It's completely quiet here, but there have been skirmishes elsewhere. We didn't get any supply trains from Grantville or Erfurt on Saturday, but one made it through Sunday night. It's been crazy busy.

If you're sure you're okay? Please ask my parents if you need anything. Be careful, but try not to worry. No use both of us having nightmares. I started having the one about the big open-field battle again.

Sounds like you're on top of the finances. Yeah, the original mortgage being canceled was a blessing. I'm glad we could pay it forward and give the girls a place to live. That's great news about the Bible study. Church is going pretty well here. A few more people have started coming.

I'm still looking for those...grid squares. I'd swear it was just an Army legend if I hadn't seen the paperwork myself. You know I'm supposed to watch for stuff like that. And another crazy thing—this little shipment of paper and ink shows up out of nowhere. It's not on the manifest. There's no requisition. It's just there. Addressed to an infantry regiment, no less. And then it was gone. You see the darnedest things in Supply.

Yep, I found a picture. I should have figured you'd put one there.

A memory: Since you mentioned running...I remember when you first came out for cross-country. You were putting your hair in a ponytail. Not the ditzy kind way up on top of your head or the I've-got-an-attitude kind right at the neck, but the girl-next-door kind of ponytail. I remember thinking, I need to keep an eye on this girl.

A verse, Matthew 10:29–31: "Are not two sparrows sold for a cent? And yet not one of them will fall to the ground apart from your Father. But the very hairs of your head are all numbered. So do not fear; you are more valuable than many sparrows."

Hi, kids! Happy Birthday, Thomas!

Love you, Sugar.
Reed

Our House, Grantville
Thursday, August 16, 1635

Dear Reed,

Voice of America broke into their regular program to announce that there's been a big battle at Zwenkau, and that we won. They said Mike Stearns' division was in the thick of it, and something about Polish cavalry, but that's really all we know. You're okay, right?

Don't worry about us. Some people are a little panicky about the Saxon border being so close, and now this Polish cavalry. Well, attacking Grantville seemed like a good idea to the Croats, too. We had a defense drill last week. I put Mary in the baby carrier and grabbed my deer rifle. Lydia held both her brothers' hands, and we went to our assigned building. Your parents met up with us there. Your mom took the kids while your dad and I each set up at a window.

Way smoother than in '32. Safer, too—it'd be much harder to get into Grantville now. I'm not supposed to write down what I know about that.

Being back at a window with a deer rifle sure did bring back the nightmares, though. Watching men go down and not knowing if I was the one who hit them. It's worse than knowing for sure, because sometimes I can almost convince myself I missed. Except I don't miss shots like that, not under fifty yards. Mary has settled into a routine of waking up at 1:00 just about every night to nurse. That gives me a chance to calm down. Stupid Croats.

Lydia is ready to start first grade. We bought school supplies. That's...different. She's met a couple other girls who will be in first grade, hopefully in the same class.

Thomas had a very happy birthday. I gave him a couple of my books, and your parents gave him a big old plastic baseball bat and a Wiffle ball. He's mostly hitting off a tee, but he's also very impressed that Mommy can pitch.

A memory—After I figured out you were slowing down to run with me at practice, I spent two weeks trying to decide if I had the guts to ask you to come to church. And then you said yes right away.

A verse—Since it's starting, Ephesians 6:12 and that whole passage. "For we do not wrestle against flesh and blood, but against principalities, against powers, against the rulers of the darkness of this age, against spiritual hosts of wickedness in the heavenly places."

I love you, Reed. ♥
Kathy Sue

Zwenkau
Friday, August 17, 1635

Dear Kathy Sue,

I'm fine. As far as I know, everybody else you know is fine. You probably already heard there was a battle here at Zwenkau. We won big. I wasn't actually anywhere near it, but I've been doing my thing since then. It's ... pretty bad. The field here is kind of like in my nightmare. That's probably as detailed as I should get.

If you see Jimmy Dunn, Charlie McDow, Bruce Reynolds, Hans Moschel, and Alexander Ebenhöch's families, they're all okay. We're all working together. I ran into Voss Gordon and Cody Jones, too.

I'm not sure what I'm going to preach Sunday. Things like this, I just don't know what to say. We'll be praying for the wounded and the families. Appreciate it if Grantville was, too. I think I better make sure everybody has a chance to believe in Jesus. Not much else I can do.

Anything you've written since July 22 hasn't caught up to me yet. I hope you and the kids are doing well. Daddy loves you.

A memory: Meeting you at the bookstore. Thank you for taking your break late so we could have lunch together between my last class at Fairmont State and my shift at the hardware store.

A verse, Proverbs 3:5–6: "Trust in the Lord with all your heart. And do not lean on your own understanding. In all your ways acknowledge Him, and He will make your paths straight."

Love you, Sugar.
Reed

Our House, Grantville
Saturday, August 25, 1635

Dear Reed,

Your August 1 letter arrived today. It's so good to hear from you. I've been listening to the radio news and reading the papers when I can. It sounds like there haven't been any more big battles. I 'spose the little ones are just as dangerous. Stay safe!

Lydia likes the school bus. First grade is the most exciting thing ever—so far. Thomas wants to go, too. I'm trying to set aside some time each day to read a book with him and work on the words. Mark likes exploring. It's a good thing we've got that gate to put across the stairs. Mary is getting big. She slept through the night Tuesday.

We had a dozen ladies at the Bible study this week. We had a lively discussion—by which I mean there was some hollering until the Catholics, Lutherans, Calvinists, and the rest of us all had a chance to explain what we really believe. I think it cleared the air a bit. We'd been dancing around it for too long.

The kids all say Hi. Hi, Daddy! From Lydia

A memory—Continuing from my last letter: The first time you came to church with us. All the dignified older ladies decided to give you a hard time. I almost died of a giggle fit when you told one of them, "Bless your heart."

A verse, 2 Corinthians 13:14: "The grace of the Lord Jesus Christ, and the love of God, and the communion of the Holy Spirit be with you all. Amen."

I love you, Reed. ♥
Kathy Sue

Dresden, Saxony
Monday, September 3, 1635

Dear Kathy Sue,

Your July 30 note just showed up at mail call today. To be fair, it had further to go. I'm pretty sure it came overland. Hopefully anything you've written since then will come most of the way by rail.

The fighting along the river was pretty minimal compared to Zwenkau. There hasn't been anything major since Zwenkau, either. Not sure what's coming up next. I'm running around trying to get supplies to the right places. It'd be a lot easier if people wouldn't "help" us with the supply system. It's more broken after they fiddle with it.

Tell everyone in Grantville not to worry.

Yesterday I talked about how God knows everything including what's going to happen. Or maybe I should say what He sees happening in the future. Including the Ring of Fire, however that fits in. It's the sort of thing that can give you a headache after a while.

A memory: Our dads taking us hunting. Nothing like getting used to each other's hunting styles while everyone's trying to have a non-awkward relationship discussion. Good thing our dads are both sane.

A verse, John 14:27: "Peace I leave with you; My peace I give to you; not as the world gives do I give to you. Do not let your heart be troubled, nor let it be fearful."

Love you, Sugar.
Reed

Our House, Grantville
Saturday, September 8, 1635

Dear Reed,

I'm so glad you're safe! Stay that way, please!

I'm glad your letter arrived today. The kids have just about worn me out this week. They're passing around a cold, and whoever doesn't have the cold at the moment wants to run around full speed ahead. Not really at my best.

There's nothing like being a touch under the weather and generally feeling inadequate when the doorbell rings, and it's a couple public health people on a let's-not-overpopulate-Europe kick. They may have made one or two snide remarks about having four kids before I went from feeling inadequate to getting a good mad on.

I asked them if they really thought limiting the number of descendants of up-timers was such a good idea. Seems to me that's a good way for us to die out. They gave me some nonsense about overpopulation and somebody named Malthus. So I reminded them how many times I heard my dad and his buddies complaining about how the government used to pay farmers to not grow food back up-time. And then I told them "Bless your hearts" and showed them out.

Well, that ended my pity party right quick. I can handle four kids. In fact, if you would hurry up with the war and get home, I could handle five.

The garden is keeping all of us busy. Thomas likes helping Grandma pick beans and peas. Hopefully that will last.

Bible study is going well. Elisabetha says that I ask different kinds of questions and that she would like to send them to her sisters. I really don't think I'm doing anything special. But I asked Sister Claudette about it, and she said that up-timers and down-timers have different approaches to interpreting the Bible. So I started writing out a couple extra copies of my questions and notes, and we're sending them to Elisabetha's sisters.

A memory—Aw, I miss the bookstore and lunch breaks with you, too. And going to home football games with you. It's starting to get cooler here, and I got my letter jacket out the other day. I had to explain what it was to Magdalena. She said, "Oh! It's livery, for your school." Which got me thinking. I called Calvert High, and they still do letter jackets. They're different, of course. The secretary said that some of the kids remember how their older brothers and sisters used to wear them with the hood unzipped down the middle so the two halves could lay over their shoulders. I agreed that was the style and that I didn't see any reason somebody couldn't put a zipper in. She asked me if I'd be willing to try it. I said sure, as long as somebody brings me the jacket and the zipper. So there's a Class of '36 varsity jacket next to the sewing machine right now. Wow, that got out of hand for a memory. Hopefully this year's high schoolers will have as many good memories as we do.

A verse, Psalm 46:7: "The Lord of hosts is with us; The God of Jacob is our refuge." And that whole Psalm. It's the one "A Mighty Fortress" is based on.

I love you, Reed. ♥
Kathy Sue

Saxony
Wednesday, September 26, 1635

Dear Kathy Sue,

I just got two letters from you, dated August 16 and August 25. Don't know what caused the delay, but we should have a pretty good system in place now.

I'm so sorry you're having nightmares. I wish I were there to hold you. Not sure if it will make a difference, but the Saxons are not going to be attacking Grantville. General von Arnim still has an army, but they're sitting in Leipzig. I don't think they want to tangle with us again, and they've probably heard the news: Duke John George and his wife are dead. Their carriage got blown up. It's like something from Beirut or Northern Ireland. Please pray for Saxony. A lot of people are shocked and upset. Captain-General Gustav—Captain-General Vasa—Captain-General Gars? What's the proper way to say it? Anyway, he's ordered Duke Ernst Wettin, the prime minister's brother, to Saxony to be the provincial administrator. Most of the men I've talked to from the regiments that marched down to Ingolstadt last summer say the duke is all right. But he's supposed to bring General Johan Banér with him. Banér doesn't like the Committees of Correspondence, and they're basically running Dresden right now. Good thing, too. They may be rough around the edges—no more than West Virginians, really—but Dresden's still standing. No fires, no epidemics.

We're . . . not going to be here to keep the lid on. I guess the generals have other things for us to do.

Hi, Lydia! I'm glad you like school. Hi, Thomas! Mommy says you're reading books. Hi, Mark! How high are you building the blocks? Hi, Mary! I bet you're getting big.

Thanks for sending Ephesians 6. When you've got no shortage of firepower, it's hard to remember that. We're seeing attitudes and beliefs that are different from the rest of the USE. Well, not different, but a couple years behind—like when we first got to Wismar. But truth, righteousness, faith—I can talk with Saxons about those, and after a while we understand each other.

A memory: Our parents blindsiding us with that sit-down talk about how they wanted us to join the military, go to college, or have steady jobs before we got married. Looking back on it, I see why they wanted us to wait. If I'd known the Ring of Fire was coming, I probably would've joined the Army. But then we would have gotten married three years into a four-year enlistment, and I might have stayed in, and we'd have missed the Ring of Fire. But we're here, so no use worrying about it. And having those three years to become best friends first was a pretty good idea.

A verse, John 8:36: "So if the Son makes you free, you will be free indeed."

I miss you.

Love you, Sugar.
Reed

Our House, Grantville
Tuesday, October 2, 1635

Dear Reed,

Your September 3rd letter arrived today. It's late, and both Mark and Mary are awake and fussing.

Mary's teething. So I'm holding Mary, occasionally rocking Mark, and writing.

Grantville's fine. Just about everybody has figured out that the Saxons aren't actually going to attack us. The radio makes it sound like the USE pretty much controls Saxony and Brandenburg, so I hope you can come home soon.

Things are going pretty well here. Some kid was being mean at school and asked Lydia if Burroughs were for rabbits. She doesn't actually understand he was being mean and has started signing her work "Lydia Bunny Rabbit." ☺ Mrs. Reardon was a little concerned, of course. I explained to Lydia that for worksheets she has to use her grown-up name, but when she colors or paints she can use Lydia Bunny Rabbit as her artist name if she wants to. So everybody's happy.

Letter jackets are tricky. So are down-time zippers. But I've finished two and have a third to do.

I'm having to really work hard preparing for Bible study because Elisabetha and the others ask such good questions. I went to ask Pastor Green if I could borrow a couple books. He even said he'd see if the *Bibelgesellschaft* could look up some more information for me. And that's how I met a really neat bunch of high school girls. I'm still getting to know them, but Clyde and Bettina Rice's daughter Alicia has already offered to babysit.

While I was waiting to talk to Pastor Green, I overheard some things that I don't think I was supposed to. Some folks at First Baptist are not happy with Green. It's not where we chose to go before the Ring of Fire. I miss our church in Fairmont, but I think Green's doing as well as can be expected. Some people . . .

So we could use some prayers here. You know my dad. He thinks we ought to have a house church, but he's in Erfurt. Not sure what to do but I did find this:

A verse, Acts 2:42: "And they continued steadfastly in the apostles' doctrine and fellowship, in the breaking of bread, and in prayers."

I hope everything's going well. I miss you, Reed. How are you doing? Really doing? Package on the way.

A memory—Go pull your rifle rounds out of the box. I'll wait.

Swimming at summer youth camp. ☺

The kids all want me to tell you, "We love you, Daddy." Well, Mary is mostly just blowing bubbles in your general direction. She's a cutie.

I love you, Reed. ♥
Kathy Sue

Swiebodzin, Poland
Monday, October 8, 1635

Dear Kathy Sue,

I'm so sorry people were giving you a hard time about having kids. I wish I were there with you. You handled it perfectly.

I hope you're all feeling better. Sounds like you've been pretty busy. Don't overdo it, okay?

I'm sure you noticed I'm writing from Poland. The censors were going to take it out, but word came down from Headquarters not to go overboard. We invaded Poland. It's not much of a secret. I'm sure you've already heard. And trust me, the Poles know, too. There was a battle here three days ago. Medium-sized and vicious. Kathy, HQ actually told us to put this next part in. Some of our guys from a couple units went off the deep end and started committing atrocities. Mike Stearns killed them dead. That ought to make sure there's no more of that crap. I mean there's really not going to be any more of that crap. Stearns formed a new unit to prevent it. It's called the Hangman Regiment, and he put Jeff Higgins in command of it. I've read my guys the riot act, just to be sure.

Poland is a whole different thing than Saxony. You're probably going to hear that the supply line got attacked. I'm not allowed to write details about that. I'm fine. Alex got hit. It truly is only a flesh wound. He's going to be fine, although I might have to sit on him to get him from trying to do too much. Jimmy, Charles, Hans, and Bruce are all fine. The other side, not so much. I know you'll worry. I'm sorry about that. But I figured if you were going to hear anyway, I ought to tell you what I can so you can worry less than if you just had to wonder about it.

So the church service yesterday was downright crowded. It needed to be a salvation message, so I preached from John 4 about how Jews and Samaritans didn't like each other, but Jesus talked to the woman at the well anyway. Mentioned the Good Samaritan and Philip, Peter, and John going to them in Acts. Made a couple officers mad. They don't think we should treat the Poles like Jesus died for them, too. Len Straley heard about it and told them to stuff it. They were unaware the colonel of the volley gun regiment is Pentecostal. I heard it was exciting.

I'm sorry this letter is so grim. I'll try to lighten up. Hug the kids for me, please. Daddy misses all of you.

Sounds like the Bible study is going really well. Way to go, Kathy.

A memory: You mentioned the bookstore. You working at the bookstore and me working at the hardware store. And Lydia being born. We have almost all happy memories from up-time. Down-time has been hard, but we have pretty happy memories here, too. Thomas and Mark and Mary. Coming home from all the times I've had to be away. You and the kids arriving in Wismar in that covered wagon.

A verse, John 4:24: "God is Spirit, and those who worship Him must worship in spirit and truth."

Love you, Sugar.

Reed

Our House, Grantville
Saturday, October 20, 1635

Dear Reed,

I got your September 26 letter yesterday. Voice of America announced a couple weeks ago that the USE Army had entered Poland. Some folks here don't think it's a good idea, but VOA said that Poland sent a small force to Zwenkau and took in the Brandenburg army. And took land from Brandenburg and Saxony. I'm not wild about it, but I don't see that there was much choice. If you wouldn't mind explaining what you can about it?

A couple days ago, VOA said there was a battle at a town called Zalanogora, or something like that. Then today they were talking about some place called

Warta River. I'm no expert, but they really didn't seem to have very much information. You be safe, okay?

It's getting cold here. The kids like playing in the leaves. I'm wearing sweatpants to run. I'm back down to 130.

Lydia and her friends have been playing princess at school during recess. Apparently that's a problem.

She told me they ended up playing senator this week instead. I asked her why she and her friends changed their game, and she said, "Rahel and Maria's mommies said they're not allowed to be princesses because they're not *adel*. So we play senators instead. First you have to be a 'volutiony and then you have to get 'lected." Then she leaned in close and whispered, "Then you're a senator and you can do all the same things as a princess. Shh. Don't tell."

I tucked our little revolutionary in at 7:30 tonight.

Thomas and Mark wanted to play football yesterday. I'm not sure how Thomas even knows about football, but his explanation to Mark was hilarious. "And you get four points if you take the ball away from the other team." I got to be the other team, and they wore me out.

Mary's getting so big. And sitting up.

I know exactly what you mean about how we might have done things differently if we knew the Ring of Fire was coming. I miss up-time, but if we got to go back to 2000, I'd miss everyone here.

A memory—Remember what we did after our parents asked us to wait until we were 21 to get married? The next Saturday, you took me to the mall in Morgantown. We had milkshakes and planned out the next three years. I agree—I'm so glad we were best friends first.

A verse, Psalm 3:3: "But You, O Lord, are a shield for me, My glory and the One who lifts up my head."

I love you, Reed. ♥

Kathy Sue

Bohemia
Sunday, October 28, 1635

Dear Kathy Sue,

I just got handed your October 2 letter, and supposedly this one will get to you faster. You've probably already heard what's happened. There was a hard fight here at Zielona Góra, and then the Poles attacked the Hessians at Warta River. Then they hit the Swedish Army at Lake Bledno. Kathy, the Captain-General's hurt. It was pretty bad for both sides. We got there right at the end. I don't know what people are saying, but hold on to this: The Poles left. They didn't want to take us on after facing the Swedes.

Please pray for Gustav. And Kristina, too. She must be scared. And all the wounded and the families. We're praying for First Baptist here.

Alex is back on duty and doing fine. Things are tense here, but we're doing okay. I'm doing my thing.

I apologize for the abrupt change of subject, but I need to write quickly.

I ran into some folks called the *Unitas Fratrum*. They're good people, love the Lord. You'd like them. They've been pumping me for information on up-time Christianity and comparing it to Scripture and to what they already know, like the Bereans. Um, it's pretty clear that they have people in Grantville, but I guess everybody does, and Mike and Ed are okay with it.

I trust them. Could you see if you or maybe Pastor Green can find answers to the enclosed list of questions, please? Your dad said he's sending some money. Use that to pay for researchers or paper. And why don't you start sending us copies of your Bible studies, too? I think the camp followers and the *Unitas Fratrum* would like them.

I managed to spill half a box of bullets before I found your pictures under the block. Wow! I remember you coming down to the lakefront wearing that blue swimsuit. It blew my mind that you could be so hot in what's really a very modest swimsuit.

The other one...You're breathtaking. You got Dorothea to draw you in your sparkly bikini when she came up to visit in Erfurt, didn't you? Oh! That day that Lydia wanted a swimsuit like Mommy's. I just now figured out what she was talking about. Nice scheming, honey.

A memory: The first time you wore it.

A verse, Proverbs 18:22: "He who finds a wife finds a good thing. And obtains favor from the Lord."

I'm very favored, and you're a hottie.

I've got to mail this right now.

I love you, Sexy.

Reed

Our House, Grantville
Monday, November 5, 1635

Dear Reed,

We've heard all sorts of terrible news—Gustav is hurt, his wife is dead, Landgrave Wilhelm of Hesse is dead, and Mark Ellis is missing. Nobody here seems to know much more than that. Stephanie's expecting, so I took some food over. She's far enough along that she can keep food down. She's just so worried about Mark. Mark's twin sister Mackenzie and her baby are staying with her for now.

I talked to Alex's wife, and she had already been notified that Alex was wounded. She said she was panicking afterwards, but that she'd gotten a letter from him, and he said he was okay.

That's horrifying news from Swiebodzin. I heard it on VOA. That's the same incident you wrote about in your October 8 letter, isn't it? It sounds like Jeff Higgins and the Hangman Regiment must be pretty tough.

Is there anything you can tell us? I'm worried about you. We haven't had any more defense drills in Grantville, so I assume that means we don't think the Poles could attack us. In fact, it sounds like General Torstensson is pushing them back. VOA said that before the Captain-General was injured, he appointed Prime Minister Wettin's brother Duke Ernst administrator of Saxony and ordered General Banér to move his army to Saxony. Hopefully that army can go help you. But then VOA said that Mike Stearns' Third Division has been ordered to Bohemia, and that doesn't make any sense at all. So maybe all of this is just speculation. (Look at me second-guessing your commanders, like I know what I'm doing or something.)

I hope the church is doing well. I sent Brenda Straley a note and thanked her for what Len did.

The women's study is going well here. A couple girls from the *Bibelgesellschaft* came and explained some stuff to us. A Marta Engelsbergin did a church history of where all the denominations came from and a Katharina Meisnerin did the history of the Bible. And Alicia Rice is a great babysitter. All the ladies are concerned about the war, but it's starting to feel like we're all in this together.

Things aren't so good at First Baptist. People are really divided over the down-time Anabaptist service. Alicia told me about her friend Nona Dobbs, who is one of the people caught in the middle. Please pray for us here. Reed, I think my dad's right—that we should be reaching out to the down-timers, and that a house church is the best way to do that. I asked Marta, and she promised to get back to me with some more information.

I had to explain to Lydia that it's fine to be revolutionaries, but she has to let everyone else play. Apparently the girls have discovered telling on each other. So I had a talk with her about what happens when revolutionaries start using the government against each other. I don't need college to explain why police states are evil. But I might need college to stay ahead of Lydia in a few years. I couldn't remember that much about Martha Washington and Abigail Adams, so mostly we talked about Becky Stearns.

The boys are doing well. All the kids send hugs & kisses. Mary sends a big smile.

A memory—That was quite a list of memories! Wismar was really cold. Had to cuddle to stay warm. ☺ Erfurt was fun. I hope you get to come back to Grantville soon. It's . . . different. I'll always remember what it was like when we were growing up. And the town meeting in the gym right after the Ring of Fire. And you guys rolling back into town after the battles in '32.

A verse, Isaiah 40:31: "But those who wait on the Lord Shall renew their strength; They shall mount up with wings like eagles; They shall run and not be weary, They shall walk and not faint."

I love you, Reed. ♥
Kathy Sue

Prague, Bohemia
Saturday, November 17, 1635

Dear Kathy Sue,

Thanks. I needed that letter, your October 20 one, with how the kids are doing. Good for them. It's great that the boys want to play "football." I think Lydia and her friends playing senator is a wonderful idea. Please tell Lydia that Daddy thinks she is very grown-up for playing games about people who do things rather than about people who think they're better than everyone else because of who their family is. We do have a few members of the *adel* with us—General Knyphausen and General Brunswick-Lüneburg, to start with—who are stand-up guys. But a lot more of the *adel* could get off their butts and help out.

Generals Torstensson, Knyphausen, and Brunswick are still in Poland, and they've driven the Poles back to Poznan. I knew I can say that because I've already seen it in the papers. But we're in Bohemia, and I'm not sure why. The Poles sure aren't here. But General Banér is still coming north. Please be praying. Something's off.

A memory: Going hunting the first winter after the Ring of Fire, putting our skills to use, and realizing it actually mattered, and we were going to make it.

A verse, Philippians 4:6–7: "Be anxious for nothing, but in everything by prayer and supplication with thanksgiving let your requests be made known to God. And the peace of God, which surpasses all comprehension, will guard your hearts and your minds in Christ Jesus."

Love you, Sugar.

Reed

Our House, Grantville
Monday, November 19, 1635

Dear Reed,

Your October 28 letter got here in three weeks flat.

We're all praying for Gustav and Kristina and Landgravine Amalie and everybody else. VOA and the papers covered the battles. Now we're hearing that General Torstensson has Poznan under siege. It sounds to me like the war is going better—except that now we're hearing that Third Division really is going to Bohemia, and that doesn't make any sense to me.

Not much has changed at First Baptist. Our women's study has had a couple really good weeks. We talked about faith and works. As long as we were sending copies to Elisabetha's sisters, I figured we probably ought to send them to Mom in Erfurt as well. It's kind of weird. We're almost a church. Really the only reason we aren't is that we don't agree on baptism and communion. And there are no guys. So I invited all the ladies to bring their husbands and boyfriends to Thanksgiving dinner.

Anna Maria, Rosina, Magdalena, and Elisabetha are concerned we're close to being a church, but Marta told us about the Moravians. They developed from the *Unitas Fratrum* that you met. I'm including her summary. Marta said her brother actually met some of them here in Grantville—they belonged to some sort of military unit called Battlegroup Procopius.

I hope you found all the bullets. ☺ Glad you like the pictures. Do you want another? Any requests on what I'm wearing?

A memory—Date nights. I really miss date nights with you, especially the ones since the Ring of Fire where we'd try to cook something elegant and laugh because we were making it up as we went.

A verse—You're being sappy again. But let's go with that. Proverbs 5:18b: "And rejoice in the wife of your youth."

I love you, Reed. ♥
Kathy Sue

Our House, Grantville
Thursday, November 29, 1635

Dear Reed,

There's been an outbreak of measles in Grantville. Dr. Abrabanel announced travel restrictions. The schools are going to be closed. I don't know much else yet. Please pray for us.

I love you, Reed. ♥
Kathy Sue

České Budějovice, Bohemia
Sunday, December 2, 1635

Dear Kathy Sue,

We just got word that Grantville is under quarantine for the measles. Our guys picked up a radio message.

We prayed for all of you in Grantville at church today. I know you guys are probably scared. We sure are. Can you call the guys' families, please? Alexander Ebenhöch, Jimmy Dunn, Charlie McDow, Hans Moschel, Mike Marcantonio, Friedrich Patzscheldt, Caspar Treiber, Bruce Reynolds, Len Straley, Voss Gordon. Just let them know we're all thinking of them. Other guys in the division, not from the Ring of Fire area, have been stopping in to offer their sympathy, too.

Yeah, Mark Ellis is missing. I'm sorry. I knew about it, but I couldn't say anything. Please tell Stephanie and Mackenzie there were people out looking for him. The Army's on it. I know, we're cooling our heels here in Bohemia for no good reason when we could be looking for Mark. I'm not happy about it, either.

I got your November 5 and November 19 letters yesterday. The second one was really fast. You're absolutely right about the military stuff. It doesn't make a lot of sense.

I'm really excited the women's study is going so well. And I hope you guys had a great Thanksgiving. We had a pretty good one here. A few of the *Unitas Fratrum* came, and I've met the guys who were in Battlegroup Procopius.

I always want more pictures. Next letter maybe I can tease you about it. Right now...

Take care. I want to give you all kinds of advice, but you're the one who's there. Stay well, honey.

A memory: Remember the cold spell the first winter down-time? How we just stayed in the house and rode it out? I guess you're doing that now. Please hug the kids for me and tell them Daddy loves them and misses them.

A verse, Psalm 18:2: "The Lord is my rock and my fortress and my deliverer; My God, my strength, in whom I will trust; My shield and the horn of my salvation, my stronghold."

Love you, Sugar.
Reed

Our House, Grantville
Saturday, December 8, 1635

Dear Reed,

A lot of kids have died of measles. Or measles and influenza. Reed, the Crafts' little girl Nora died. They were up in Jena. I feel so bad for Norris and Alysa. I don't know what I'm going to tell Lydia and Thomas. How do I tell them Nora died?

We're okay. The TV says they're getting the outbreak under control. We had St. Nicholas Day by ourselves. Magdalena, Rosina, and Anna Maria are wonderful. They're able to go back to work Monday. We've got a washing station set up so they'll scrub back in when they come home. We got a message that Dorothea, Johann, and little Friedrich are doing fine.

I got your letter of November 17. I'm glad the USE Army has good officers. General Banér's army marched through Thuringia on their way to Saxony. It sounds like he's going to put Dresden under siege, and that makes absolutely no sense. You already captured Dresden.

Everything seems to be spiraling out of control.

A memory—How many times since the Ring of Fire have we told each other, "God has this under control?" Been right every time, too.

A verse—Luke 1:1–2:20. Merry Christmas! Merry Christmas from Lydia, Thomas, Mark, and Mary.

I love you, Reed. ♥
Kathy Sue

České Budějovice, Bohemia
Wednesday, December 19, 1635

Dear Kathy Sue,

We're praying for you and the kids and the Crafts and everyone else in Grantville. And for Gustav and Kristina and for the government. The radio guys told us the measles are winding down, that the doctors have it under control. I hope you're all still okay. Stay safe.

You and the kids must be tired of being cooped up. I hope it's going okay, and I'm sorry I'm not there with you.

We're trying to do our thing here. Quite a few people are coming to church, including some *Unitas Fratrum*.

I know it's not a happy time right now, but it's almost Christmas. It will be by the time this gets to you. Merry Christmas! Please tell the kids Merry Christmas from Daddy.

A memory: Our first down-time Christmas. And then the second one when all of Grantville tried to get together. And last year in Erfurt.

A verse, Ephesians 3:20–21: "Now to Him who is able to do far more abundantly beyond all that we ask or think, according to the power that works within us, to Him be the glory in the church and in Christ Jesus to all generations forever and ever. Amen."

Love you, Sugar.
Reed

Our House, Grantville
Wednesday, December 26, 1635

Dear Reed,

The Sanitary Commission lifted the quarantine before Christmas. VOA and the newspapers say there haven't been any new cases of measles in over a week. There's still influenza going around, so we'll keep being careful. But your parents were able to come over on Christmas. It was nice. I told the kids we'll do presents on Three Kings, the same day that the wise men brought presents to baby Jesus. They're rolling with it.

I wasn't quite ready to take the kids out in public yet. I'm probably just being overcautious. We have gone out and played in the snow a couple times. So we didn't go to church on the 23rd. Deacon Underwood announced that the deacons had voted no confidence in Pastor Green on the 17th and that there will be a congregational vote on January 6. Word spread pretty quickly. I don't know how it's going to go, Reed. It wasn't our church, so in some ways we're just as much outsiders as any down-timer. But in other ways, it shouldn't matter.

I think Lydia is going to be ready to go back to school. Thomas and Mark need to spend some time around other kids—once we're sure the measles outbreak is over. Mary is crawling around and cautiously standing up.

A memory—The two of us wanting summer vacation to be over once we figured out we saw each other a lot more during the school year.

A verse, Numbers 6:24–26: "The Lord bless you and keep you; The Lord make His face shine upon you, And be gracious to you; The Lord lift up His countenance upon you, And give you peace."

I love you, Reed. ♥
Kathy Sue

České Budějovice, Bohemia
Thursday, December 27, 1635

Dear Kathy Sue,

I'm so sorry Nora Craft died. If you see Norris and Alysa, please tell them how sorry I am. Nobody should have to deal with that but so many parents have had to.

The radiomen have been keeping us up to date. I know the doctors are getting the measles under control. And I know you're being careful. And I know it's been a sad Christmas. I hope you're all well.

We're doing ok here. Mostly we're bored. We had a nice Christmas, but I'd rather be home with you and the kids. There's no real reason for us to be here.

Thank you for sending Luke 1–2. It'll help keep me focused.

A verse, Rev 21:4: "and He will wipe away every tear from their eyes; and there will no longer be any death; there will no longer be any mourning, or crying, or pain; the first things have passed away."

A memory: Coming home from work and seeing you and the kids.

Love you, Sugar.
Reed

Our House, Grantville
Thursday, January 10, 1636

Dear Reed,

Banér opened fire on Dresden. The Crown Loyalists really are going to try to suppress us, aren't they? Or so they think. Did you see this Charter of Rights and Duties they issued? They really think they can go back to how things were before the Ring of Fire? They say they're moving the capital to Berlin. I don't think they understand that we're not going to have that kind of Germany this time.

And then Bavaria attacked Ingolstadt. VOA said that Tom Simpson sent a radio message, but they haven't heard anything since. The National Guard already marched out. It's been on the radio, so it's safe to write.

Our block captain came by and told us to make sure we had winter clothing ready. So I had a winter go-bag ready for the kids when they called a defense drill on Tuesday. The girls and I grabbed the kids and got to our positions. Grantville's ready. Reed, I didn't have any nightmares that night or last night. Maybe later. Right now, I think I'm too mad. Your mom says she needs some grandma time with the kids. I was going to work on the next Bible study, but I'd better get in some range time instead.

On the 6th, First Baptist voted out Pastor Green. Great example on Three Kings, huh? The Greens are going to move up to Old Joe Jenkins' place on the mountain and open a Bible school. Joe left town a while ago. I don't know where he went. We hear stories sometimes. I'm pretty sure some other folks are leaving with the Greens.

I can't see going back to First Baptist. You're in Bohemia, Dad's in Erfurt. I guess I'll tell the ladies they can come by on Sunday morning if they want to, and we'll have church. Or they can go to church somewhere else and come here for Bible study. Whatever works for them. I'll have to see if we can get a pastor to preach sometimes.

The measles outbreak is definitely over. The schools are open again. Lydia was so glad to see her friends again. Mary took her first steps. Now that she's got it figured out, it looks like she's stuck on full speed ahead. Mark's pretty happy she's walking. I think in his mind it promoted her from "baby" to "playmate." Thomas is really energetic, as in wearing Mommy out. I think it'd be good for him to play with somebody his own age so I'll try to figure something out. We had a good time on Three Kings.

A memory—Our dads and grandpas talking about being in the military. And our moms and grandmas telling us what it was like at home.

A verse, 1 Corinthians 7:23: "You were bought with a price; do not become slaves of men." The song that Marla Linder sang reminded me of this verse. I had to hunt around in a concordance to find it while the kids were at story hour.

I love you, Reed. ♥
Kathy Sue

Česke Budějovice, Bohemia
Saturday, January 12, 1636

Dear Kathy Sue,

I can't tell you how relieved I am to hear that the outbreak is over. I hope all of you had a fun Three Kings.

One crisis down, three to go. What is First Baptist thinking? How did the vote go? Kathy, you've got a lot on your plate, but can your women's study take in anybody who doesn't have a church anymore?

The other two are Oxenstierna and Maximilian. We got word that Oxenstierna has arrested Prime Minister Wettin. I have no idea what's going on. But this could get very bad, Kathy. And Maximilian attacking Ingolstadt? It's insane. I mean that. The guys call him Mad Max. Please talk to my dad. Have a plan ready, just in case. We're doing our thing.

I can't wait to see you and the kids again. I'm so glad they're doing well.

A memory: Mike's speech right after the Ring of Fire. We might be back there.

A verse, Psalm 23, especially verse 4: "Even though I walk through the valley of the shadow of death, I fear no evil, for You are with me; Your rod and Your staff, they comfort me."

> Love you, Sugar.
> Reed

Our House, Grantville
Friday, January 18, 1636

Dear Reed,

Thank you.

I went over to see the Crafts. Alysa and I had a good cry. They're hurting.

I told Lydia and Thomas. Sometimes I don't think they really understand but then Thomas asked if Nora would grow up in heaven or if she'd always be four.

I told him I didn't know but that Jesus would have a really long time to teach everyone lots of things so maybe we'll all seem more grown-up than we look. He seemed okay with that. I hope I'm at least somewhat close to correct.

You probably hear all this before I do. The Bavarians are in the Oberpfalz, Banér is still besieging Dresden, and a bunch of nobles who got thrown out of Mecklenburg during Krystalnacht tried to take it back. They lost.

VOA is saying it's no accident that the USE Army just happened to be out of the country when this all happened. It's also saying that some Crown Loyalists are honorable and trying to stay out of it—like Landgravine Amalie of Hesse and your General Brunswick.

Alicia Rice has agreed to teach Sunday school if we have church. Plus, Marta Engelsbergin said that there are a whole bunch of Anabaptist pastors and elders who don't get to preach as often as they'd like. So we're going to start Sunday services this week. Of course having an Anabaptist preacher is a problem. So I told the ladies that we'd go in alphabetical order: Anabaptist, Arminian, Calvinist, Lutheran, Roman Catholic for the next five weeks. They've all got assistant pastors who think they don't get to preach often enough, too. Half of them objected to our arrangements, but that just narrowed down who to pick.

Alicia says A&A Day Care is really good, and she wants to work there. What do you think of having Thomas there one day a week to get him used to playing with other four-year-olds before kindergarten next year?

Mary is walking and sort of talking—mostly "mama-mama." We'll work on "dadadada." Mark is getting into everything. Lydia has settled back into a routine at school.

I don't suppose they'll let you guys come home soon? I miss you.

A memory—The Fourth of July, 1631. I think that's when a lot of us realized that not only we were still going to be us, but it was going to work, too.

A verse, Joshua 1:9: "Have I not commanded you? Be strong and courageous! Do not tremble or be dismayed, for the Lord your God is with you wherever you go." I know I sent you this verse in my first letter in June. It's still appropriate.

I love you, Reed. ♥
Kathy Sue

Our House, Grantville
Monday, February 4, 1636

Dear Reed,

Yeah, we had a good time on Three Kings. Thomas wanted to put out gold, frankincense, and myrrh for Jesus. We've still got some work to do. ☺

I got your letter on Saturday but waited to write back so I could tell you how this Sunday went. It was our third service, so it was Calvinist Sunday. We had nine ladies and twenty or so kids. That's about average, although it's different people each week. Next is Lutheran week, and then Roman Catholic week. And at that point we'll have to decide if we've got one mini-church or if people might as well go to five different churches.

The vote at First Baptist was actually pretty close, but they voted Pastor Green out. Some people left with the Greens, some more since then. I just heard that the Chengs have had a house church for a few months, so I sent them a letter telling them a little about us, asking for advice, and trying to make sure we don't accidentally step on their toes.

I think you and I should coordinate, too. I know it could be dangerous to send lists of who is attending, especially since people think Oxenstierna will try to take away freedom of religion. But I also know that a couple of the ladies have husbands in Third Division who've come to your services at least once. I even thought about coded messages but I don't know anything about super-secret spy stuff. I'm trying to remember missionary stories from up-time, how they dealt with this.

Yes, the papers call them the Ox and Mad Max. I don't know how much you can say, but I can't figure out why Third Division isn't attacking the Bavarians. I mean, nobody thinks the Austrians can take Wallenstein, do they? I talked to your dad. We're set. Can't write anything down, but you know your dad.

It is really cold out today. I hope you guys are staying warm. As soon as it warms up a bit—like gets back to zero—I'm going to take the kids over to the middle school so we can run around in the gym. They need to run off some sap, and I need to do something, even if it is just running in circles inside.

A memory—Going to the movies up-time. You know that kind of movie where the bad guys finally just push the hero too far? I think the Grantville television station has been playing all of them. There's no way that's a coincidence.

A verse, Acts 11:20–21: "But there were some of them, men of Cyprus and Cyrene, who came to Antioch and began speaking to the Greeks also, preaching the Lord Jesus. And the hand of the Lord was with them, and a large number who believed turned to the Lord." I heard that's what Okey Rush preached on yesterday at First Baptist.

> I love you, Reed. ♥
> Kathy Sue

Bohemia
Friday, February 8, 1636

Dear Kathy Sue,

I'm glad things are better in Grantville. Be safe. We just got word of two things. Yesterday, Banér tried to storm Dresden and got his butt kicked. And then earlier today, Princess Kristina and Prince Ulrik flew into Magdeburg. Which means Oxenstierna isn't as in charge as he thinks he is. We need to keep praying about this.

The church is doing well here. Well, some of Wallenstein's men think we're pretty sketchy, but we're getting along great with the *Unitas Fratrum*. We're learning a lot from each other, but I wish I could answer their questions. Half the time all I can say is, "I don't know."

A memory: I've been telling them about up-time missionaries. They're fascinated. And sometimes they already know up-time stuff. It's weird how that

knowledge gets around. I told them about the time
that pastor spoke at your church, way back when we
were in high school, and had a translator. Remember
how he had to be so careful?

A verse, Matthew 28:18–20: "And Jesus came up
and spoke to them, saying, 'All authority has been
given to Me in heaven and on earth. Go therefore
and make disciples of all the nations, baptizing them
in the name of the Father and the Son and the Holy
Spirit, teaching them to observe all that I commanded
you; and lo, I am with you always, even to the end
of the age.'"

Love you, Sugar.
Reed

Our House, Grantville
Thursday, February 28, 1636

Dear Reed,

I was wondering what was going on with our letters. Now I know. Please tell me you're okay. VOA
reported the Battle of Ostra yesterday. Mike really
attacked in a snowstorm? I'm sure you'll hear it before
you get this, but Captain-General Gars is awake—
alert—I'm not sure of the right word, but he's back,
and Oxenstierna's dead. You guys did it! Thank you!
Grantville's going crazy.

I just got your February 8 letter. I get what you
were saying. And now why. I've got some questions
for you that I don't think I'll be writing down.

It's over, right? Thomas is very proud of Daddy.
Lydia's worried so we prayed for you tonight. Me, too.

Hoping to hear from you soon. But I know—you're doing your thing. Get 'em organized and supplied.

> I love you, Reed. ♥
> Kathy Sue

Dresden, Saxony, USE
Sunday, March 2, 1636

Dear Kathy Sue,

I'm positive you've heard. Third Division defeated Banér at Ostra, just outside Dresden. Mike left our unit at Děčín, and we had to move up fast. This is the first time I've sat down since we got here.

Another huge answer to prayer: The Captain-General's better. I'm sure Princess Kristina is overjoyed to have him back. So are we.

Banér's army is gone. Casualties are heavy on both sides. A lot of the survivors are joining us. We're trying to get them straightened out. It's pretty bad.

I got your January 18 letter, but couldn't answer. Your analysis was right on.

Uh-oh. They're calling us back in to resupply somebody.

A memory: You know how it feels coming home from camp? Can't wait to see you and the kids.

A verse, Acts 22:28: "The commander answered, 'With a large sum I obtained this citizenship.' And Paul said, 'But I was born a citizen.'" Preached on that this morning. To Banér's men. Well, used to be Banér's men.

> Love you, Sugar.
> Reed

Grantville
Tuesday, March 18, 1636

"Lydia, please help Rosina clear the table," Kathy called as she plunged another glass underwater.

"But Mom, I want to play, too." A crash told Kathy that Thomas and Mark were already knocking down towers of building blocks.

"Right after you bring me those plates, honey." Kathy rinsed the glass and placed it in the drying rack. Magdalena attacked it with a dish towel.

The doorbell rang.

"Is Anna Maria back already?"

"She has a key," Kathy reminded her. "I'll get it." She shook dishwater from her hands and hurried to the front door. She unlocked the door, swung it open, and screamed.

"Reed!" Kathy threw herself into his arms.

"Daddy! Daddy! Daddy!" Lydia, Thomas, and Mark charged into their parents, arms outstretched.

Kathy took the opportunity to kiss her husband properly, whether the kids were jumping up and down and pulling on them or not.

"Wow," Reed said when they came up for air. "I should come home more often."

"Yes, you should."

Reed picked up each of the kids for a hug. Mary studied him intently.

"This is Daddy," Kathy told her. "Daddy."

Mary ducked her head but allowed Reed to hold her.

"How did you get here?"

"Sleigh from Dresden to Altenburg and railroad

from there. Kathy, I'm not home for good. We've got orders to take care of Bavaria, and you can probably figure out the rest."

"Mike sent your Supply Company on ahead to have things ready and waiting. You'll make sure the supply depot in Grantville is all set, and then you'll move on. Bamberg, probably."

"Not bad. Not bad at all."

Kathy's smile vanished quickly. "How long?"

"A few days."

"Darn." It came out more mildly than she felt.

Reed shifted Mary to one arm. "I know. I was hoping that once we got settled in Bohemia, they'd let us rotate home. But, well, Oxenstierna had other plans. And now we need to deal with Mad Max."

"Daddy! Daddy! Daddy!" Lydia and Thomas tugged in opposite directions.

"Let's go sit on the sofa," Reed suggested.

"I'm sitting on Daddy's lap," Kathy declared before any of the kids could. She did.

"That's silly," Lydia pronounced. But she joined her siblings in piling around and on top of their parents.

Kathy exchanged glances and a quick smile with her husband. He gave her a squeeze. They'd let the kids talk to Daddy first, and she and Reed would have time alone later.

She raised her voice. "Magdalena! Rosina! Come meet Reed!"

Kathy cuddled up next to Reed and pulled the blankets up to her chin. "I missed you so much."

Reed kissed her. "I missed you."

"Do you know where your pajamas are? Because

in the morning, the kids are going to pound on the door and want to jump in bed with us."

Reed stretched, trying to reach toward the floor.

"Not yet, silly," Kathy teased. "We might wake up before the kids do."

"Oooh, I like that plan," Reed told her. "I do have to go to work tomorrow. Camp Saale handed us a full inventory of the USE supplies that have been pre-positioned there, so I need to place orders in the Grantville area to fill in the gaps. I should be able to be home for dinner, but don't wait on me if I'm not."

"Okay."

Kathy snuggled closer and started to drift off to sleep. Then she remembered something.

"Reed, will you still be here Sunday?"

"I think so."

"Good. Can you preach? We were supposed to have a pastor, but he canceled. I was going to start making calls tomorrow to line somebody up..."

"Huh. Funny how that works out," Reed observed. "Almost like it was planned. Sure. I'll bring my guys. Oh—a couple letters ago you asked about comparing who was attending. Remind me in the morning. I have a list in my pack. Can you check them against yours:..?"

"And see if I need to make sure to invite anyone's family for this Sunday? Or if you need to invite any of your guys in particular?" she finished for him.

"Exactly. And there's this monk we need to pray for. I didn't dare write down anything about him."

Kathy sat up. "There's a girl who comes to the Bible study and church. She's *Unitas Fratrum*. Remember how you said they had people in Grantville? I couldn't tell you..."

"...because she's technically a spy, even if we not only don't care but are actively encouraging it," Reed murmured. He sounded distracted.

"Reed?" Then Kathy realized she'd lost her blankets when she sat up.

"Definitely a picture I want to remember," her husband told her. "C'mere." He pulled her down close.

"How's the PTSD?" he whispered.

"I'm good, Reed. I could really do without any more defense drills, but I can handle a raid if I have to." She waited a moment. "You?"

"I'm good, too, Kathy. The battles are different than the dreams. It makes the dreams less real."

"Do you want to talk about it?"

"Maybe tomorrow. Right now I just want to hold you."

Kathy really couldn't object to that.

A few minutes later, Reed murmured, "Thank you, Jesus, for protecting us."

"Please keep Reed safe," Kathy chimed in.

"And Kathy and the kids."

"Amen."

Author's note:
Kathy is using a New King James Version.

Reed is using a New American Standard Bible.

Nun Danket

Clair Kiernan

*Grantville
Summer, 1637*

The train from Jena was crowded, but Martin hardly
noticed the people around him as they flowed out of
the station and into the amazing wonderland from the
future. Martin had thought he was used to the rush of
changes that had come with the up-timers. After all,
it had been more than six years! But his little town
of Eilenburg was in Saxony, and until spring of last
year he had never even seen an up-timer. The fall
of Dresden and overthrow of the Elector had shown
him what change really was—change that was like a
dam bursting, a dam he hadn't realized was there.
But the flood had brought prosperity and plenty, not
destruction.

Martin chided himself for woolgathering, and tried
to orient himself in this strange city without walls. He
walked toward what he hoped was the center of town.

In a place where everything was strange it was
hard to determine which thing shouted loudest of its

strangeness. The houses were too far apart. There were too many windows, and they were far too big. The houses were too short—how could people stay warm in a sprawling low house with only one chimney in the center? What were the streets made of, and how did they make them?

The wires strung from poles would have been a greater mystery, but a kindly person on the train had explained them. "Radio" remained an enigma, however, even though he had seen and even listened to a crystal set. Then, of course, there were the things he had been told that were probably *not* true, and Martin only hoped he wouldn't make a fool of himself believing some of the things he had been told.

In the meantime, he realized, he was near the famous Thuringen Gardens, and it was close enough to lunchtime that he could justify stopping long enough for a meal. Perhaps when his errand was done he could take time to be a mere tourist, but what harm would it do to stop for a meal at one of the most popular tourist attractions in Grantville?

The Thuringen Gardens at noon on a weekday was nowhere nearly as rowdy or lively as it was on a Friday night, but it was loud and busy enough for a humble pastor with a turn for poetry. He was shown to a table in a large and crowded room, and ordered a small beer while he studied the "menu card" printed in English and German. Martin was bemused at the idea of a tavern offering its customers a choice of food items, instead of whatever was cooked that day.

He was reading the German description of that day's "special" when a voice came from nearby. "Mind if I join you? If I wait for a table I'll be late getting back."

Martin gestured a welcome to the stranger standing before him. He was disappointed not to be sharing a table with an up-timer, but at least the form of German the stranger spoke was close enough to his own to be easily intelligible.

"I'm Hans. Are you new in town?"

"Yes; just visiting, though. I hope to come back sometime and show my wife around."

The waitress returned with Martin's beer.

"Small beer for me, too, *bitte*, and I'll have the special," Hans said quickly. He smiled at Martin. "If you're in a hurry, the special is not only cheaper, it's faster than choosing something else."

A *"hamburger"?* Martin hesitated for only a moment. The description in the menu had been vague but not completely discouraging. "Very well, I will have that too."

"They're very popular," Hans assured him. "The Americans mostly eat them with this red sauce here, and the yellow sauce." He pointed out the bottles on the table. "Don't use the red sauce in this smaller bottle unless you like eating fire."

Martin nodded his thanks. Hans went on, "Best to get your bearings before you bring the family into Grantville. It's no more dangerous than any other town, of course—in some ways much safer, except to your wallet. You'll want to know how to steer the wife to things you can afford." He grinned wryly.

Martin thought about bringing Christine to see Grantville and perhaps buy something pretty. It was a charming idea, and she certainly deserved the treat. "So you're an old Grantville hand, then?"

"I guess so. We've been here a little over a year,

since Saxony opened up. Father wanted some business contacts here amongst the up-timers."

"Saxony! I am also from Saxony, in Eilenburg."

"Well, then, I've no need to explain to you that we need to catch up with the folk in Thuringia-Franconia! The old Elector held the entire region back."

Martin nodded soberly, thinking of the wasted opportunities and needless deaths of the past few years. His own church had finally gotten the last of its refugee families resettled into new homes and lives. The up-timers had come none too soon. John George was not widely mourned.

". . . and Father hopes to bring some new methods and materials into the business. Fortunately, my older brother is more bookish than I am and willing to study the science and math. He's taking a correspondence course in mathematics! Voice of America is broadcasting the lectures once a week."

The waitress returned with their food and fresh drinks. Martin was surprised at how quickly it was ready, but Hans answered his raised eyebrow before Martin could ask.

"The items for each day's special are cooked in advance. They have to be efficient, you see? Everyone in Grantville is rich compared to back home, but there's a price for it. The Americans call it 'hustle.' Or their other phrase, 'you snooze, you lose.' You can't sit back and keep doing things the old way; someone else will come up with a better idea and before you can blink, you're eating their dust!"

While he spoke Hans briskly dressed his hamburger with yellow sauce and the red sauce from the large bottle, making a puddle of the latter in the center of his "Freedom Fries." Martin copied him, taking a cautious taste of the hamburger. It wasn't quite what he had imagined, but it tasted good. He was pleased to see that the Americans also took their largest meal at lunchtime; it made them feel less alien. The two men applied themselves to their food, and even Hans was mostly silent during the rest of their meal.

When they had finished, Hans claimed the receipt and left a paper bill weighted down with his beer mug. When Martin demurred, Hans insisted. "After you let me sit at your table and yammer at you during your lunch, it would be rude of me not to pay. Besides, it was nice to hear speech from home. This Amideutsch is easier than learning English, but I still have to think too hard before I talk."

Martin chuckled. "Very well, but I insist on paying the . . ." He struggled to remember the advice he had been given about service in taverns or taxis. "The tip," he said firmly. He found a coin in his pocket that was the right proportion to the banknote, and set it carefully on the table. He followed Hans out, weaving a path between tables filled with businessmen, shoppers, families and tourists. "Thank you again for lunch, and making me feel more welcome here. Before you go, could you point me toward the Leahy Medical Center?"

Hans gestured down the street. "I would walk you there, but my office is in the other direction." He gave Martin directions, shook hands with him, and strode quickly away. Martin went his own way, not quite so fast.

There was a soft knock at the door. "Enter," Gary Lambert called, without looking up from his paperwork. Like many up-timers, he had far more to do than he could finish in a day, and saved time whenever he could.

Instead of one of the hospital's department heads, a stranger entered, a down-timer older than himself and soberly dressed. "Herr Lambert? My name is Martin Rinkart, of Eilenburg, and I have come on an errand from the burghers and guild masters of the town."

Gary rose and reached across his desk to shake hands with his visitor, and gestured to a chair. "How may I help you?"

Martin refused the chair. "I know you are a busy man, Herr Lambert, and do not wish to take up much of your time. I am only here to express the gratitude of our town for the help that has come to us this past year. Ever since the Elector fell, we have found out what good neighbors Grantville is made of! For the first time since the war began my wife and I do not have our home filled with refugees, nor must I beg for assistance for them. Instead the countryside has farms and villages filled again and plenty of work for the asking.

"Because somewhere in your books it was written that there was plague in Saxony in 1637, teams of volunteers came in last year with DDT and chloramphenicol," he pronounced the unfamiliar words carefully, "and then the ratcatchers came in, and the sanitary inspectors. The town has never been so clean and healthy! Not a single case of plague was in the town this year. And so when the burghers and guild masters looked for someone who would be available to take our thanks to the good people of Grantville, why, I am the only one of them who has less work to do than last year, so they asked me." Gary smiled bemusedly. "But why thank me? I didn't go to Saxony.

I should think the ratcatchers and sanitary inspectors would deserve your thanks more than me."

"Oh, but we did, Herr Lambert! We thanked everyone who came to Eilenburg. But then last month it occurred to me that there would be no DDT for killing the rat fleas, no chloramphenicol for healing the sick, without the people of Grantville. We would thank every up-timer personally if we could, but we chose you, Herr Lambert, because you are the administrator of this medical center, and thus had to find the materials to send us without running short for your patients here."

Martin reached into his satchel and pulled out a wooden plaque, carved to show two hands clasping in friendship, with "With thanks and friendship, to the people of Grantville, from your brothers in Eilenburg, for you have been brothers to us" engraved on a metal rectangle inset below. He held out the plaque to Lambert, who took it as gently as if it were a baby. "Without you and others like you, our town would have been overwhelmed with plague. Who knows how many would have died, how many would have been left to grieve, how many children would have been orphaned and impoverished? A plaque is nothing, Herr Lambert, compared to the gift you have given us."

Gary cleared his throat. "You were more than welcome, Herr Rinkart. After all, stopping plague in Eilenburg was in our interests as well . . ." He froze suddenly, then set the plaque down on his desk. "Eilenburg?" he murmured, searching through his bookcase. Was it here? Yes, it was! He practically snatched the book off the shelf and began flipping through it. "Yes, here you are. It says you are the only pastor who was left during the height of the plague . . ." Gary faltered. "You said . . . your wife . . . ?"

"She is at home, Herr Lambert. I hope to persuade her to visit Grantville in the future. What is wrong?"

"Nothing, now," Gary replied. He took a deep breath, trying to dismiss the sudden swooping sick feeling that reminded him so poignantly of his first realization that he would never see his wife Sheila again. It felt strange to think of it, but he had been married to Anna Catherina longer than to Sheila. "Nothing now, Herr Rinkart, but in the other world we came from, the plague was very bad. Apparently you were officiating at forty or more funerals every day." He looked directly into Martin's face. "Including that of your wife."

Martin sat down, but held up his hand to stop Gary from coming over to assist him. "I am all right, Herr Lambert. I have had many years to realize that your people are from another world. It is just the first time that I have contemplated that there was another me in that world. How he must have suffered! I was grateful when I came here, but more grateful now, to be delivered from that ordeal."

"And you have thanked me, Herr Rinkart. But truly, none of this would have happened without the Ring of Fire. It is God who deserves your thanks more than us."

"Oh, I have, Herr Lambert! We have given prayers of thanksgiving every Sunday, along with prayers for the well-being of all the up-timers." He reached into his pocket and pulled out a small leather notebook, and opened it to the place marked with a tattered ribbon. "And among my other scribblings, I have written this."

Gary took the notebook. On the open page was a poem, written in Fraktur, which Gary still found hard to decipher. The top line said "Nun Danket Alle Gott." There were several verses, complete with scribbled corrections and edits.

"I have to write it out more cleanly, of course, but I hope to have it published. If you know of any place I should send it, I would appreciate the suggestion."

Gary looked at Martin, then back at his bookshelf; his eyes rested on the Lutheran Hymnal, and smiled widely. "But you already have, Herr Rinkart." He went to the shelf and held the book in his hands, slowly turning the pages until he found the page he was seeking.

> *Now thank we all our God,*
> *with heart and hands and voices,*
> *Who wondrous things has done,*
> *in Whom this world rejoices;*
> *Who from our mothers' arms*
> *has blessed us on our way*
> *With countless gifts of love,*
> *and still is ours today.*

Gary wondered how close the up-time English translation was to the lyrics Rinkart still held in his hand. The German pastor was looking over his shoulder, moving his lips silently as he worked through the English. Gary wondered if Rinkart's ability to read English was better than his own ability to read Fraktur. The pastor looked up ruefully. "It would be too much to ask for your book to have the same words that I have written in this world."

"If the butterfly effect is right, they aren't the same." Gary gave Martin a searching look. "Does it really matter?"

"Maybe. The words written by that other me were a better expression of faith than mine. He wrote of light in the midst of darkness. I wrote of light when dawn was breaking. He was a stronger man than I am, perhaps stronger than I will ever be."

"Strong because he had to be." Gary frowned down at the floor, then looked up. "When we came here, I lost everything—my home, my job, my family, the whole world. All I had was my faith. I had to be strong because I didn't have a choice—and the words that your other self wrote were a great comfort. But I didn't have to see my loved ones die to get that strength." He gave his guest a wry smile. "You may have to accept being thankful in place of being stronger."

Martin smiled back. "That will have to be enough." He turned to leave, then stopped. "Perhaps you can suggest a gift I can bring back to Christine? Something pretty, but not too expensive."

Gary looked at the pile of papers on his desk. They would, alas, still be there in the morning. "I think I should come with you. Have you ever heard the expression 'tourist trap'? A native guide is definitely a good idea."

"You are the second person today to give me such a warning. I will abide by your wisdom in the matter of shopping. And perhaps we shall stop by a publisher; there are many more verses in my notebook."

Gary followed Martin out the door.

☆   ☆   ☆

*O may this bounteous God through all our
    life be near us,*

*With ever joyful hearts and blessèd peace
    to cheer us;*

*And keep us in His grace, and guide us
    when perplexed;*

*And free us from all ills, in this world and
    the next!*

*All praise and thanks to God the Father
    now be given;*

*The Son and Him Who reigns with Them
    in highest Heaven;*

*The one eternal God, whom earth and
    Heaven adore;*

*For thus it was, is now, and shall be ever-
    more.*

The Ghosts of the Blauschloss

Margo Ryor

August 1635

Mikayla Barnes squinted against the late morning sun bringing the town of Plötzkau into focus. Set well back from the lazy loops of the Saale, it looked exactly like an illustration out of Grimm's Fairy Tales—just like all the other German towns Mikayla had seen since she and the rest of Grantville accidently landed in the seventeenth century. Then she spotted something not at all fairytale but distinctly twentieth century; a crowd of protesters on the docks waving signs.

"Johanna," Mikayla said, "come look at this."

Her pen pal, Princess Johanna of Anhalt, turned from giving some instructions to one of the barge crew. She looked first at Mikayla, then toward the docks, frowned, and came to the railing for a better look.

"Do you know what's going on?" Mikayla asked, looking up at the tall princess. She was still getting used to the real Johanna, as opposed to the imaginary one she'd been writing to for over a year. Even though she'd known better she'd still somehow imagined her

145

pen pal as thirteen like herself, and shorter and, well, more American because they seemed to have so much in common.

Johanna shook her head. "No idea. Can you make out those signs?"

Mikayla squinted harder trying to force the distant lettering into focus. "UMWA. What's the Mine Workers Union doing in Plötzkau?"

"There's a potash mine on the other side of the river," Johanna answered absently, gesturing vaguely behind herself.

"A what mine?" Mikayla asked blankly.

"It's a kind of mineral salt," Johanna explained. "It's good for fertilizer and the chemical company in Stassfurt buys it, too. Papa says we're doing very well from the profits."

Mikayla was a coal miner's granddaughter and great-granddaughter. She instinctively sided with the protesters and frowned darkly at her friend. "Why is the UMWA upset with you?"

"I didn't know they were," Johanna answered, eyes still on the shore.

As the barge got closer it became clear there were two different and entirely separate groups waiting to greet it. A cluster of portly men in formal seventeenth-century dress constituted one and a number of much younger men and women dressed in homemade knockoffs of up-time clothes the other. Guess which one was waving the signs. A fairly large crowd stood well back in the fields between the docks and the town proper watching avidly but at a safe distance from ground zero.

By now the rest of the girls making up the Anke Treuer Mysteries writers' circle had gathered round, all of them eyeing the reception committee with some unease. Mikayla joined her Grantville friends, Sherri Hinson and Jessica Samuels, at the back of the group. They weren't exactly cowering behind their older downtimer friends but they definitely intended to let the princesses deal with the problem—whatever it was.

"Maybe they've got nothing to do with us," Sherri said, clearly dreaming.

"I bet it's got to do with Johanna and Lies," Jessica answered.

"I fear Jessie is right," Lies, aka Princess Elisabeth of Anhalt-Zerbst, agreed a little grimly. She was the eldest of the four down-timer girls, a full eighteen years old like their heroine Anke Treuer. She was also Johanna's cousin.

The other two down-timers were just seventeen, like Johanna. Julia Felicitas was yet another of Johanna's many cousins and Anna Sophia wasn't. Like the Americans they seemed more than willing to hold back and let the Anhaltiners face the music. Both halves of the welcome committee surged forward as the barge docked, leaving the girls with barely enough room to disembark.

"Your Grace," the senior of the official detachment, marked as such by his heavy gold chain, began, "welcome back to your loyal town of—"

There was probably more to the speech but the girls didn't get to hear it as it was drowned out by the sign wavers howling union mottos. The local dignitaries turned on them and both sides forgot all about the girls yelling insults at each other. Mikayla saw a punch land on chain guy's nose followed by a gush of blood and a howl of fury as he dove into the protesters, fists swinging.

She tugged nervously at the back of Johanna's jacket. "Maybe we should get back on the boat."

"That's a good idea," Anna Sophia agreed with considerable feeling.

The whole clump of girls edged back toward the gangway which luckily was still down but then the free-for-all in front of them heaved and split right down the middle the combatants shoved apart by men wielding long poles topped with wickedly pointy axe-heads.

Lies heaved a sigh of relief. The other princesses relaxed too. "What?" Mikayla asked, still nervous. "Who are those guys?"

"Guards from the castle," Johanna replied.

"So, on our side. Good."

The guards got the girls through the crowd and into a capacious carriage painted with the Anhalt arms.

"What was that all about?" Mikayla asked her pen pal breathlessly as they rattled off.

"I don't know and I can't say I care," Johanna snapped, looking thoroughly put out.

"We're here to write, not to settle local quarrels," Julia added, staring pointedly at Lies.

The eldest princess nodded agreement. "Johanna and I weren't sent as envoys from Uncle Augustus. We should definitely not get involved."

"Yeah, politics. Not our problem," Sherri chimed in on behalf of the up-timers.

Mikayla didn't disagree. She just wondered if they could ignore riots practically on their doorstep. Of course having a wall and a mile or so of park around them should help.

☆　　☆　　☆

Schloss Plötzkau looked more like a mansion on steroids than Cinderella's castle but at least it had a wall, if not a very high one, lined with two-story buildings and enclosing a courtyard that was mostly dirt with scattered patches of grass and weeds. Directly ahead was the castle proper, three or four stories high, with rows of rounded gables and a tall, thin tower topped with yet more gables rising over all.

The carriage rattled through a sort of tunnel into a cobbled inner yard and came to a jerking halt in front of an open door flanked by rows of men in the yellow-and-black Anhalt livery standing at attention. Mikayla nudged Jessie who nudged Sherri. The princesses were clearly unimpressed, taking it totally for granted.

The coach door opened. Johanna went first, then Lies, then Julia indicated it was Mikayla's turn. One footman held the heavy door open, and a second offered his hand to steady her as she gingerly descended a pair of rickety wooden steps to the cobbled ground.

The two princesses were accepting the bows of an important-looking fellow in furred gown and gold chain. Johanna answered him in a friendly tone, meaning he was somebody important. The princesses were kind of abrupt when talking to servants, not mean exactly but not nice, either. Mikayla reminded herself that it wasn't their fault they'd grown up in the seventeenth century.

The man with the furs and chain was introduced to Mikayla and the other guests as Burgmann Schenk, the castellan in charge of the castle now that the prince had moved away. He bowed a good deal as he escorted the girls into a hall made darker by lots of carved paneling. But they left him behind as Johanna and Lies led the way up a massive staircase to an upper hall where they were greeted by a row of capped and aproned maids dropping deep curtsies.

Jessie nudged Sherri who nudged Mikayla who nudged sharply back. "Don't gape!"

A lady in formal dress wearing an order's decoration turned out to be Frau Schenk who would act as their chaperon or, in twentieth-century terms, their babysitter. "We have prepared the princess's apartments for Your Grace and your guests," she said to Johanna, curtsying but not as deeply as the maids.

"Not the guest quarters?" Johanna asked, surprised, then shrugged like it didn't really matter. "Very well."

The first room of the apartment had deep-set windows overlooking the park and gilt on the elaborately carved paneling. Mikayla saw it was furnished as a dining room, dominated by a big table surrounded by brocade-covered chairs and wasn't at all surprised when Johanna said, "We'll take our meals here."

"Nice," said Sherri, fingering the heavy silk covering the chair nearest to her.

Frau Schenk opened another door. This room was brightened by a thickly gilt wallpaper. Mikayla joined Sherri and Jessie in oohing and aahing over the heavily carved sofas and chairs upholstered in blue and red silk. A mechanical typewriter stood on a long table under the windows, clashing with the rest of the decor. Seven gilt inkwells and fountain pens stood in a row ending in a carved box. Mikayla opened it and found it full of neatly cut eight by eleven sheets of paper.

"I see this is where we are expected to work," Johanna remarked behind them.

"That seems pretty obvious," Julia agreed dryly.

"Looks like Burgmann Schenk has seen to it we

have everything we need." Lies smiled at Frau Schenk who smiled back and opened the next door.

The girls, led by Johanna, filed through into another large room. This one was dominated by a tall four-poster bed all hung with multicolored tapestry.

"Who's going to sleep in here?" Sherri asked brightly. The princesses all looked at her like she was crazy.

"Nobody," Johanna answered. "This is just for show. The real bedrooms are on the third floor."

A twisty staircase tucked behind the bed took them up to a much more reasonably sized room hung with red curtains on bed and windows. Green tapestries covered the walls and open doors on either side showed a row of similar rooms all connected. "You see?" asked Johanna. "Which room would you like? Take your pick."

Rooms were picked, and Johanna led her guests back downstairs to the first room of the suite for the midday meal, leaving the unpacking to the maids.

The long table was now spread with white linen and set with majolica ware and silver plate. Johanna seated herself at the head of the table and gave Mikayla the place of honor at her right hand. She had spent the last year or more pouring out her every thought and opinion to her Americaness pen pal, so why was she finding it so very hard to talk to Mikayla to her face? She'd always known how old her correspondent was, but somehow she'd never imagined her so young.

"Mikayla, what is a 'slumber party'?" Johanna asked abruptly, breaking the awkward silence between them.

Mikayla seemed considerably taken aback by the question. "What?"

"Frau Nelson wished me pleasure of my 'slumber party' when we left Quedlinburg," Johanna explained. "I have been wondering what she meant ever since."

"Well, it's a girl thing, a twentieth-century girl thing I mean," Mikayla began a little uncertainly. "You invite some friends over to your house to spend the night—"

"If it's just one or two it's a 'sleepover,'" Sherri interrupted. "It's only a slumber party if there a lot of you."

Mikayla nodded. "Yeah, that's true. A real slumber party won't fit into your bedroom. You have to spread sleeping bags in the living room or somewhere."

"But what pleasure is there in sleeping on the floor?" Anna Sophia asked, puzzled. All three up-time girls laughed.

"Oh you don't sleep at a slumber party," Mikayla said. "You sit up and eat snacks and watch movies—"

"And talk about school and boys and stuff," Jessie added. "I guess you don't do any of that."

It was the down-time girls' turn to laugh. "Oh yes we do," said Johanna. "We are always sneaking into each other's rooms to share good things to eat and talk about our teachers, classes, and boys."

"But there are no boys at your school," Jessie pointed out.

"All the more reason to talk about them!" said Lies with a grin.

They all laughed, and the atmosphere became more relaxed and friendly.

"What else do you do at 'slumber parties'?" Anna Sophia asked Sherri across the table.

"Well, since the main idea is to keep awake, we tell each other scary ghost stories," she answered.

"I thought up-timers didn't believe in ghosts?" Julia said in surprise.

"Depends on the up-timer," Mikayla said and looked at Jessie.

"I don't believe in ghosts. I am interested in parapsychology," she answered primly. Mikayla and Sherri both rolled their eyes, and Jessie went on defensively, "Hey, we're sitting in a castle in the seventeenth century having lunch with girls who died three hundred years before we were born!"

Johanna joined the rest of the older girls in a disapproving frown. "The Ring of Fire was a miracle of God," Lies pointed out stiffly.

"I know it's on a whole different level," Jessie backtracked hastily. "What I mean is we're not in a position to make absolute statements on what's possible and what's not anymore."

The older girls looked at each other. "That's true," Lies conceded.

"I know what psychology means," Julia said, "but what is 'para' psychology?"

"It's the scientific study of things like ghosts, premonitions, and other stuff that doesn't fit in with the standard scientific view of the world," Jessie answered. "According to parapsychology all those things are really perfectly natural—just rare and governed by rules we don't understand yet."

Julia looked dubious.

"Does your castle have ghosts?" Mikayla asked Johanna.

"Not that I've ever seen or heard," she replied, "but the park is supposed to be haunted by a ghostly nun."

"Who hasn't been seen in living memory because

nobody dares to go into the park at night." Lies added dryly.

"Must be some ghost," said Mikayla.

After the meal Johanna took her friends on a tour of Schloss Plötzkau. The three little up-timers were rather flatteringly impressed by everything, starting with the stiff two-dimensional paintings of Johanna's medieval ancestors hanging above the wainscoting of the corridor.

"Oh, gosh, look at these," Sherri gushed.

Johanna did and they still looked flat and old-fashioned to her. The American girls were even more impressed with the dark-paneled council chamber and all but overwhelmed by the chamber of estate.

"Oh, Go—gosh! An honest to goodness throne room!" Mikayla was practically jumping up and down, and the other two looked just as excited.

Johanna exchanged a bemused look with Lies. The room in fact wasn't particularly impressive as such chambers went; it had a rather nice parquet floor and a geometrically coffered ceiling painted with armorial motifs. The walls were covered with red and yellow damask, and the chair of state on the dais had no canopy as these days it was the seat of a deputy, not the prince himself.

Mikayla saw and correctly interpreted their looks. "Royalty and thrones are things from books back in our time," she explained. "That's why it's so exciting to see it real."

Johanna smiled at her pen pal. "Come and see the Fürstensaal."

"Oh, wow, just—wow," Sherri breathed as they came

through the door. The other two Americanesses seemed incapable of saying anything at all. Even Julia and Anna Sophia were impressed, and the looks Johanna and Lies traded were smug.

Prince Bernhard had imported craftsmen from Italy to paint the white plaster walls with the grotesque designs and classical medallions fashionable in those days, and unlike the medieval painted panels these decorations had aged well. The coffered ceiling was also decorated with classical scenes and the whole room dominated by a massive, heavily carved stone fireplace.

"Is it the ballroom?" Sherri asked in awe.

"Well, if we'd ever had a ball, this is where we'd have held it," Johanna answered. Looking at the little Americanesses' respectful faces she gave way to a sudden impish impulse. "Let me show you what we did do in here!" She pulled off her shoes and in her stockings skated smoothly forward on the well-waxed parquet floor.

"Seriously?" Mikayla gaped as Johanna made a creditable figure eight in front of her.

"Seriously!" she called over her shoulder, skimming toward the far end of the hall and the fireplace.

Lies laughed, kicked off her own shoes and joined her cousin.

"We did the exact same thing in our Knight's Hall," Anna Sophia said as she shed her shoes.

"We used the marble floor of the old Romish chapel," Julia added, catching Anna Sophia by the hand and spiraling round and round with her.

"You guys are nuts!" Mikayla kicked off her sneakers and made a spectacular running slide. "Wheee!"

"You're all going to break your heads," Jessie told them. "Wait for me!"

"And me!" cried Sherri.

Some considerable time later the seven girls were exploring a low-ceilinged and dark-paneled corridor running between the state apartments and the kitchen quarters inch by inch.

"I can see why they weren't all that careful about matching the paneling in this light," Mikayla remarked, nose inches from the walls as she searched for the hidden door.

"The light is bad," Johanna conceded. "Give up?"

"Yes," said Mikayla.

"Yeah," said Sherri.

"Yes" and "Yes," said Julia and Anna Sophia.

"No!" said Jessie.

"Shut up, Jessie," said Mikayla and Sherri in rough unison.

Johanna laughed. "I'm sorry, Jessie, you are outvoted." She opened the shutter of the dark lantern she'd been holding, flashing the light onto a section of the paneling near the door to the kitchen lobby. "See?" The outline of the door was very obvious—even the paneling was a different color and grain.

"Wow, talk about obvious!" said Jessie.

"When you can see it," finished Julia.

Lies pressed an invisible spring and the door clicked open. "See—it's double thickness just like the one in *The Hidden Staircase*."

The downward-slanting tunnel was very low and disappeared into darkness. "So what's this oubliette thing you got down there?" Sherri asked.

"An oubliette is a sort of dungeon—" Jessie began.

Sherri glared at her. "I was asking the princesses, thank you."

"It's the sort of dungeon where you throw people and leave them to die," Lies said.

"My nurse told me they took hundreds of bones out of it when Prince Bernhard remodeled the castle," Johanna added.

"Ewwww!" Mikayla made a face. "And you say this place isn't haunted?"

"Nope," said Johanna.

The next stop was the subcellar of the keep and the rather better-concealed entrance to the castle's escape tunnel.

"Where does it go?" Jessie asked as the girls peered into the stone-vaulted darkness of the narrow tunnel.

"We're not quite sure," Johanna admitted. "There's a roof-fall about fifty feet down blocking the way but it seems to be heading toward the river."

"That would make sense," Anna Sophia said. "There were probably boats hidden at the other end for a quick escape downriver."

Jessie looked at her with interest. "Does your castle have a tunnel too?"

"All properly constructed castles have escape tunnels," Julia answered for Anna Sophia. The three up-timers looked very impressed.

Johanna led her friends back toward their quarters detouring into the council chamber to show them the secret room. She didn't make them hunt for the door this time because the intricately carved paneling made it literally impossible to see. But it also made it very easy to remember exactly where the spring to open the door was located. She pressed the knob concealed in a spiral of gilt scrollwork and the door popped. Lies hauled it all the way open, and all peered inside.

"Wow, this is big." Sherri sounded impressed.

It was in fact a fair-sized room, wedge-shaped with stained plaster walls and lit by a long slit window. It was large enough to hold all seven of them and a pair of iron-bound chests that stood on the floor under a set of shelves against the short outer wall.

"The oubliette was to get rid of people you didn't like. The tunnel in the keep was for escape. So what was this for?" Mikayla asked.

"Papa used it as an archive for important papers and a treasury," Johanna answered, "but it had another use too." She ran her fingers along the rough plaster wall on the council chamber side until she found a raised edge. She pried open a hinged oval of wall revealing a pair of peep holes at eye level for a man of average height.

"Ooh, do they look out the eyes of a portrait?" Sherri asked eagerly.

Johanna laughed. "No, they're in the shadow of the chimneypiece. You'd never see them if you didn't know just where to look."

"So the prince could spy on his council?" Jessie asked. "Isn't that kind of paranoid?"

"A paranoid prince stays a prince," Julia answered dryly.

"How very Machiavellian," Jessie said.

A second door led from the secret chamber to a withdrawing room adjoining the prince's private apartments. From there they got back to the hall lined with medieval paintings leading to the princess's apartments.

"Mikayla," Johanna asked, "do you think Mama's state bedroom is big enough for a slumber party?"

Seven girls, three dressed in colorful twentieth-century pajamas and four in voluminous white linen nightgowns and close-fitting nightcaps sprawled on mattresses and pillows spread over nearly every inch of floor of the princess of Plötzkau's state bedroom.

Mikayla lay on her stomach eating sugared almonds from a bowl. Her attention, like that of the other girls, was focused on Johanna leaning against the heavily carved footboard of the bed as she told the legend of the Plötzkau ghost: "Eventually the count received an offer of marriage that was too good to refuse so he sent his mistress to a convent to get her out of the way—"

"Bastard," Sherri muttered through a mouthful of kuchen, then blushed. "Sorry."

Johanna shrugged. "I don't disagree, but the girl should have expected nothing else. Counts don't marry peasant girls outside of fairy tales. To continue: The mistress was locked in a cell by the nuns but escaped—how, the legend does not say—and was shot by a jäger in the park as she made her way to the castle to disrupt her lover's wedding. She was buried there in unconsecrated ground, and ever since, her ghost has haunted the park at night in the form of a veiled woman in white still trying to reach the castle and her lost love."

"The poor sap," muttered Jessie.

"That doesn't sound so scary," said Mikayla, scooping up another handful of almonds.

"Supposedly she jumps on the back of any living

man who crosses her path and tries to ride him to the castle, though she always vanishes when he reaches the gates," Johanna explained.

"*If* he reaches the gates," added Lies "In other stories she rides her victim to death round and round the walls."

"Okay, that's scary. No wonder nobody will risk meeting her," said Mikayla.

"Has anybody—" Jessie began. "What was *that?*"

There was a resounding hollow booming rolling down the halls like someone was dribbling an iron basketball. Mikayla could see the walls quiver. A long rattling noise like a chain-link snake slithering on a wooden floor followed.

Without a word Lies rolled over and grabbed a shawl from the pile of dressing gowns and bathrobes in the corner, snatched a candle from the stand, and hurtled out the door. Johanna was right behind her, followed by the rest of the girls.

Mikayla stumbled along in Lies' wake. The princess's rapidly moving candle sent shadows soaring and swooping over the medieval paintings rattling on the wall as knocks and raps boomed behind them.

Light flooded out of an abruptly opened door ahead, and Mikayla almost collided with Anna Sophia as the girl gang slid to a sudden stop. Burgmann Schenk stood outlined in the light which also showed his dismayed, going on horrified, expression as he caught sight of them.

"Burgmann Schenk," Johanna asked regally, "*what* is going on here?"

His face crumpled and for an awful moment Mikayla thought she was about to see a grown man cry. "Your Grace," he all but wailed, "I *don't know!*"

The whole story poured out of poor Burgmann Schenk

with great force and speed, making it a little difficult for Mikayla, Jessie, and Sherri to follow his German as they all sat around the table in the council chamber. His account was punctuated by the continual racket inside the walls and overhead, which didn't contribute to its clarity. Eventually Johanna succeeded in stemming the flow and tersely summed up the few facts:

"In short this chaos has descended every night for the past two months and repeated searches of the entire castle have failed to reveal the cause?"

Schenk heaved a huge, relieved sigh. "Yes, Your Grace. The disturbances seem to center around the state apartments, I had hoped that the princess's quarters would be distant enough to allow you and your guests to be undisturbed—" He was interrupted by explosive noises overhead. All winced.

"Poltergeist," said Jessie.

"It certainly is," Johanna agreed.

"When did the trouble begin in town?" Lies asked.

"About two months ago—" Burgmann Schenk answered automatically then blinked in surprise. "Surely Your Grace doesn't think there is any connection?"

"How could this"—Julia waved vaguely at the noisy walls—"benefit either the burghers or UMWA?"

"If this was a Nancy Drew mystery, one of them would turn out to be behind it," said Sherri.

"Hello," said Mikayla, "Real World to Sherri: this isn't a book!"

"The correlation in timing strikes me as suspicious," said Lies. Everybody looked at her. She looked at Johanna. "It seems we are going to have to get involved in Plötzkau's troubles after all."

☆   ☆   ☆

When the girls entered the chamber of estate the next morning, Mikayla saw right off that a canopy had been erected over the throne. Johanna seated herself in the big chair looking exactly like a princess should. Burgmann Schenk took up position just below the dais on her left hand and Lies went to stand next to the throne on her right. The rest of the girls settled themselves on a velvet-covered bench farther to the right and below the dais.

Jessie nudged Mikayla. "I feel like one of Queen Amidala's handmaidens."

It was kind of like that. There were even five of them. "All we need are the hoods," Mikayla whispered back.

Burgmann Schenk stamped the long white staff in his hand on the parquet floor, making a satisfying booming sound. One of the guards flanking the anteroom doors reached over and opened the left-hand side door. Schenk's staff boomed again:

"Mayor Friedland and Union Master Weintraub, Your Grace!"

Mayor Friedland turned out to be Chain Guy from the riot on the wharf. Mikayla didn't recognize the younger man in down-time jeans and a UMWA T-shirt but assumed he'd been there, too. Both men were looking defensive—like they were expecting a dressing-down. Johanna had a surprise for them.

"I have no mandate to deal with your dispute," she began. "That is a matter for the prince and the estates. I would however remind you, Friedland, that unions have the prince's favor, and you, Weintraub, that there are laws against slander and libel."

The two men exchanged an unfriendly look but said nothing.

"I have called you here today for quite another purpose," Johanna continued. "Burgmann Schenk, please describe the disturbances in the castle."

Schenk did so at some length and with considerable emotion. Friedland and Weintraub listened with widening eyes and sagging jaws. If this wasn't news to them they were both in the running for the seventeenth-century equivalent of the Oscars.

Once again Johanna found it necessary to cut Schenk short. "Thank you, Burgmann Schenk. Friedland, Weintraub, have either of you any light to cast upon these happenings?"

"No, Your Grace!" Friedland said emphatically. "Why should we do such a thing? What purpose would it serve?"

"That was not an accusation, Friedland, just a request for information," Johanna assured him. "Weintraub?"

"I know nothing, Your Grace," the union man said, but very, very unconvincingly.

Johanna had to have noticed but she didn't press the issue. "Thank you. You may go."

They went.

"Wow," Sherri breathed from the end of the bench. "Now that's what I call Girl Power!"

All seven girls—and Burgmann Schenk, too, for that matter—agreed Weintraub had been lying.

"He knows something, or thinks he may know something," Lies said, expressing their unanimous thought. "Something he is not willing to admit in a public hall."

"But might be willing to tell privately," Johanna finished and stood up. "I'll talk to him. Schenk, Miss Barnes and I will need an escort."

Mikayla brightened. "Me, too?"

"Yes," said Johanna. "You're an up-timer and you know all about unions. If he won't trust me, his princess, he might trust you." She stood up, shaking out her wide satin skirt. "But first I must change. You probably want to, too, Mikayla."

Mikayla looked down at her 'best' dress and agreed.

A short time later, the two girls were on the road into Plötzkau with two castle guards, minus their big halberds, at their heels. Johanna asked the first person they met where they could find Union Master Weintraub and was given complicated directions that she seemed to understand perfectly, though Mikayla couldn't follow them at all.

She noticed that nobody seemed surprised—and certainly not awed—by the sight of their princess calmly walking the streets. A good number of them greeted her with a polite "Good morning, Your Grace," and got an equally polite "Good morning" in return. Johanna seemed to know an astonishing number of the citizenry by name. Or maybe it wasn't all that astonishing. Plötzkau was a small town, smaller even than Grantville, and Johanna and her family had lived up at the castle for years and years.

Weintraub's usual home was the workers' village across the river but when in Plötzkau he stayed with cousins at a small, well-kept house on a winding back lane. Only he wasn't there now.

"He didn't come back here, Your Grace," Josepha Meltzer said. She acted like she had princesses sitting in her parlor every day of the week. In fact, she seemed a lot more interested and impressed by Mikayla—a genuine up-timer.

So it was Mikayla who asked, "Do you have any idea where he went? This isn't about the union troubles. It's about something up at the castle that he might be able to help us with."

Frau Meltzer seemed to believe her. "He has probably gone down to the Old Stork Inn—that's where the union holds its meetings."

Of course Johanna knew where the Old Stork Inn was. So did the guards, and they were less than happy about going there. "It's a disreputable place," Sergeant Schieffer reminded Johanna.

"That's what you are here for, Sergeant," she answered calmly.

The main room at the Old Stork didn't just look seventeenth century; it looked medieval. The rafters of the roof were so low Mikayla found herself ducking though they cleared her head by half a foot at least. There was a strong smell of beer, smoke, and less salubrious things. The customers, barely visible in the gloom, did look like a rough crowd, but they also looked kind of shocked and pretty dismayed at the sight of Johanna—or maybe it was the bristling, protective guards.

Johanna marched right up to the long, sagging bar and asked for Union Master Weintraub in her crisp, unfriendly talking-to-servants voice. Mikayla couldn't understand the host's mumble but his pointing finger stabbing the air in the direction of a low door needed no translation.

Sergeant Schieffer opened the door warily, one hand on his sidearm, while Johanna and Mikayla stood well back protected by Corporal Heine. Schieffer's eyes went wide, and he gasped.

The girls pushed forward to see what the problem was. Mikayla found herself looking into a long room whose only furniture was an equally long table and assorted benches. Union Master Weintraub was lying bent uncomfortably back over one of those benches, eyes and mouth wide open with a small black hole between those eyes and blood dripping from the large exit wound in the back of his head into the red puddle spreading slowly over the floor.

Mikayla backed away from the sight and kept backing up until her legs intersected with a bench. She collapsed onto it. But she didn't scream; she was proud of herself for that.

Johanna looked about the way Mikayla felt—paper-white and green around the gills—but that didn't keep her from spitting out orders like a machine gun. "Don't touch the body, Schieffer, but see if there are any other doors or a weapon. If you find one don't touch that either. Heine, go for the watch."

"Yes, Your Grace," said Heine, "but first I think you should sit down, Your Grace." He steered the princess respectfully to Mikayla's bench, and she collapsed next to her friend. "Shall I get you something to drink, Your Grace?"

Johanna swallowed hard. "Yes, please, and bring the owner over here. I have some questions for him."

The inn's owner claimed to know nothing, nothing at all, and said so repeatedly and emphatically. Johanna shot a look at Mikayla over her mug of small beer and got a nod of agreement. Either the man was telling the truth or he was another Anhaltiner in line for a down-time Oscar.

Mikayla took a sip from her own mug. The beer

tasted awful but it settled her stomach. Too bad the alcohol content was too low to do anything else.

Sergeant Schieffer emerged from the murder room, closing the door carefully behind him. "There's a door leading to the cellars, Your Grace," he reported. "I bolted it. No sign of a weapon."

Mikayla had been subliminally aware of the bar emptying like it was on fire and was more than a little surprised when a patron approached them rather than making for the exit. He was young and dressed in the T-shirt and jeans that seemed regulation for the UMWA demonstrators, and he looked pale and distraught. "Your Grace, I'm Heinrich Farber of UMWA." He swallowed hard. "I—I know some things that might help."

"Excellent," said Johanna. "Please continue, Farber."

He swallowed again. "We had a meeting scheduled. Stefan sent word for us to start without him, and we did. Then he came storming in, very upset, and threw the rest of us out so he could talk to Berners alone."

"And this Berners is?" Johanna prompted.

Farber clearly didn't want to answer that but: "An undercover man from the CoC."

"What?" Mikayla and Johanna said in unison.

"He came down from Bernburg to help us organize the workers here in Plötzkau," Farber explained, "undercover so the capitalists wouldn't stop him—"

"No," Mikayla interrupted firmly. "Just no. That is not how the CoC operates, not in the USE, anyway. They march into town with banners flying and a brass band if they've got one, set up a Freedom Arches, and start pumping out pamphlets. They don't *hide*, and let me tell you they would have cleaned up this place first off!"

Johanna was nodding agreement. "That is certainly how they operate in Dessau and our other cities."

"I don't know who this Berners guy is," Mikayla told Farber earnestly, "but I'll bet money he isn't CoC."

"But . . . but then who is he?" Farber faltered in dismay.

"A suspect," said Johanna with visible satisfaction.

Returning to the castle, Johanna and Mikayla were welcomed by a girl avalanche from the hall door. Sherri and Anna Sophia both excitedly shouted, "We found clues! We found clues!"

Anna Sophia grabbed Mikayla's hand and Sherri Johanna's, and they practically hauled them inside, through the hall and into an adjoining room where Lies, Julia, Jessie, and Burgmann Schenk were sitting around a table spread with assorted exhibits.

"We didn't feel like writing," said Anna Sophia.

"Why should you have all the fun?" Sherri added. "So we decided to split up and look for clues!"

Mikayla gave a snort of laughter. Johanna looked questioningly at her cousin. Lies shrugged and mouthed, "I'll explain later."

"Anna Sophia, Sherri, and Lies decided to be Fred and Daphne and check out the ground floor—" Jessie said, taking over the story.

"Taking a couple of guards with us just in case," put in Lies with a smile.

"First we found marks on the floor like somebody had been dragging something heavy—" Sherri chimed in.

"Then we found a barred door that wasn't—" added Anna Sophia.

"The bar had been cut through," Lies explained,

"so it looked like it was still sealed but it opened easily enough—"

"Too easily—the hinges were oiled!" said Sherri.

"Somebody was using it regularly—" added Anna Sophia.

"So we started prying around under the furniture covers and found crates that didn't belong and look what was in them!" Sherri finished with a dramatic gesture.

Johanna looked, and suddenly felt much more serious. A new-style military rifle lay on the table still in its packing. "You found that in my castle?"

"Crates and crates of them," said Lies.

Johanna exchanged glances with Mikayla. "Something worth killing over." Her friend nodded.

Jessie took up the story. "Meanwhile Julia and I were making like Velma in the archives and we found the plans for Prince Bernhard's remodeling."

A large paper was unrolled on the table next to the gun, its corners held down by pieces of silver plate from the sideboard. The ink had faded but the plan could still be made out. "Look at those spaces between the old walls and the new ones," Jessie said, using a pencil as a pointer. "Just enough room for a man or men to move around and make noise."

Burgmann Schenk spoke for the first time. "We still haven't found how they're getting into the between spaces, Your Grace, but I had the wall of the corridor flanking the Prince's Hall broken open and found this." A length of heavy rusty chain lay coiled beside the parchment completing the exhibits. "What did Weintraub have to say, Your Grace?"

"Not much," Johanna said. "We found him dead, murdered." She saw the excitement drain out of the other girls. Their mystery had just stopped being fun.

"He knew about this," Mikayla said slowly, thinking it out. "He knew who was doing it and why, and they killed him before he could tell."

"Let me tell you what Weintraub's UMWA friend had to say." Johanna repeated Farber's story about the fake CoC man.

"Sounds like this Berner is the murderer," Lies said when her cousin had finished.

"If this were a book it would be more complicated than that," Sherri observed, "but being reality you're probably right."

"And Berner is smuggling up-time style guns to somebody, and we are right on the border with Brandenburg and Saxony," Lies continued thoughtfully.

"Five gets you ten the UMWA guys think they're for the Saxon rebels," said Mikayla.

"What do you want to bet that they are dead wrong?" Johanna asked her grimly.

"Nothing," Mikayla answered.

"The real question is what does this Berners do now?" said Julia. "If he's smart he'll cut and run—"

"But that would mean leaving all these guns behind," said Jessie, "so maybe he won't do the smart thing."

"So we set a Scooby trap," said Sherri. "Just in case."

"A what?" asked a bewildered Burgmann Schenk.

All three up-time girls started talking at once, stepping on each other's sentences and creating more confusion than clarity, but finally Schenk nodded.

"Yes, I see, an ambush." His fingers drummed the table as he thought. "Yes," he said again, "they might come again and we should be ready." He turned to Johanna. "Your Grace, this castle is no longer secure.

You and your guests should remove to Bernburg at once. How soon can you be ready?"

For an instant all seven girls just gaped at him, then Johanna recovered enough to answer, "Don't you think you're overreacting a little, Herr Schenk?"

He set his jaw. "Armed men are running through this castle at will, Your Grace. Security breach doesn't even begin to describe our current status. I cannot guarantee the safety of Your Grace and your guests."

"Be reasonable, Herr Schenk," Johanna argued. "Either they won't come back at all or you'll catch them tonight. Either way the situation is resolved, and we'll have made the trip for nothing."

His expression showed he was wavering.

"You are right to be concerned," Lies said persuasively, "but surely we'll be safe enough in our quarters." She pointed to the plan. "See, there are no false walls in the private wing."

Schenk turned the paper around and studied it carefully. The girls held their breath. "Very well," he said at long last. "I take Your Grace's point. If you ladies will be so good as to retire to your quarters, I will make the necessary dispositions to secure your safety."

"There are guards on the downstairs door, too," Sherri reported.

"Schenk is nothing if not thorough," Johanna said ruefully.

Sherri dropped into an empty chair. The girls had gathered in their writing room but nobody was in the mood to work. Anke's mystery held no appeal compared to the real one they'd found. The girls lay draped over assorted pieces of furniture; Johanna and

Mikayla sharing one couch, Jessie and Julia another, Lies and Anna Sophia curled up in two of the armchairs.

"We should try to get some work done," Lies said after a long moment. Nobody moved.

Jessie got up and went to the window. "I don't see any guards outside," she reported.

"Of course not," Julia said reasonably, "Schenk doesn't want to risk scaring Berners off if he does come."

Mikayla sat up in sudden excitement. "That means we can get outside through the garden door!"

Lies sat up, too. "No! Absolutely not. It would be much too dangerous!"

Mikayla opened her mouth to argue but a knock at the door made her close it, words unsaid.

"You may come in," Johanna called, and Schenk entered rubbing his hands and looking quite pleased for a change.

"Your Grace and Miss Barnes were quite right about where the guns are going," he said. "I've just heard from the ABI office in Zerbst. They've stopped one or two shipments of SRGs on the Brandenburg border and have been trying to find out where they came from ever since."

"The *what* office?" Mikayla said blankly.

"The Anhalt Bureau of Investigation," Johanna answered. "It's a county level police agency using up-time methods. Papa got the idea from—"

"We know what he got the idea from," Mikayla assured her.

"The Bernburg office is sending a team of agents to investigate this Berners' operation," Schenk continued quite happily. "If we are fortunate tonight we will have prisoners for them to question."

"I certainly hope so," Johanna said politely.

Schenk left the room in an excellent mood, which would have ended abruptly if he'd heard the first words out Anna Sophia's mouth:

"That settles it—we can't miss this."

"This is wrong. It is dangerous. What if something happens? Poor Schenk will be blamed!" Lies pleaded, practically wringing her hands.

The other six girls turned almost identical impatient expressions on her. They were gathered in the princess's state bedroom all ready to go, the up-timers in their jeans and the down-timers in short, dark-colored petticoats.

"Nothing is going to happen, Lies. Don't be hysterical." Johanna sounded annoyed.

"All the danger will be inside the castle," Julia explained yet again. "We'll be as safe outside as in our rooms. And we'll see Berners arrive."

"*If* he arrives," Jessie added, also repeating herself. "There's a very good chance nothing will happen at all."

"Don't say that," Mikayla pleaded.

"Don't be such a killjoy, Lies," Sherri said.

Johanna handed her cousin one of the two dark lanterns. "Here, you bring up the rear." Dark lanterns were the seventeenth-century's version of a flashlight—sort of. They consisted a candle in a tin box with a handle and a shutter that allowed the light to be cast or shut off at will without blowing out the candle.

Lies threw up her hands in despair, but she took the lantern.

The girls passed through connecting doors from the bedroom through a maid's room to the sitting room adjacent to the walled garden terrace built against the castle under the princess's windows.

They moved as quietly as possible so as not to alert the men patrolling the passage. Fortunately, Schenk's precautions were aimed at keeping Berners' people out rather than the girls in. Apparently it had never occurred to him that they might try to get out, which showed a certain lack of imagination on his part.

"This is a really, really bad idea," Lies said from her place at the end of the line as Johanna slid back the bolts on the garden door.

"We know, we know, now be quiet," her cousin answered. "All right, everybody follow me, watch your step, and no talking."

Johanna slipped through the barely-opened door followed by Mikayla and the other girls, one by one. Lies brought up the rear, carefully closing the door behind them. They flitted single file, hugging the castle wall. Suddenly Johanna came to a full stop and Mikayla almost walked into her. Anna Sophia did bump into her and she could hear muffled ouches as the reaction moved down the line.

Johanna opened the shutter of her lantern a little more, sending the square of yellow light rippling down a flight of moss-covered steps descending into a hole. "Be very careful here," she breathed, "the stairs are slippery and quite steep."

"Gotcha," Mikayla whispered back, then turned to pass the word over her shoulder.

They descended, still single file, into the damp tunnel, Johanna and Lies opening the shutters of their lanterns all the way so they could at least see where they were putting their feet. The tunnel was short and they soon emerged from the foundations of the garden terrace. Johanna and Lies promptly closed their lanterns all the way, plunging the girls into pitch-blackness.

The shadow of the castle cut off what moonlight there was and the girls had to feel their way along the rough stone of the castle's base to their goal, a clump of trees growing up against an angle of the wall. Once there Johanna and Lies opened their lanterns just a crack, enough to make out the tree trunks and the statue of some old Roman goddess. Seven pale faces blinked at each other.

"See," Johanna whispered to her cousin. "We're under cover; nobody will even know we're here."

Lies said nothing but looked unconvinced.

Johanna rolled her eyes impatiently. "Everybody find a hiding place."

The girls arranged themselves as comfortably as possible under the trees overlooking the open slope running to the edge of the wooded park. As soon as everybody was settled Lies and Johanna closed the shutters of their lanterns.

Then nothing happened for what seemed like a very long time.

Mikayla shifted her weight off a particularly knobby root and wondered if this had been such a good idea after all.

Apparently she wasn't the only one. "Maybe Berners isn't going to come at all," somebody whined off to her right.

"Be quiet, Anna Sophia," Julia hissed.

"Look, do you see that?" Anna Sophia said, ignoring her.

"I said be quiet—"

A white light flickered among the trees and was gone. "I see it!" Mikayla burst out, then bit her tongue.

"Shhhh!"

"You shhhh!"

"Mikayla!"

"Julie!"

"Everybody be quiet!" Johanna snapped, and just in time, too.

Dark shapes detached themselves from the mass of blackness brooding under the park's trees and moved at a brisk pace up the only slightly lighter slope toward the castle, the unbarred door, and the waiting Scooby trap.

Holding her breath in excitement, Mikayla watched with eye-tearing intensity as the dim figures passed the girls' hiding place and entered the castle. The last disappeared and she let out her breath in a long sigh. She heard the other girls shifting position around her.

"I guess that's that—" Jessie began uncertainly when she was interrupted by the sound of gunfire, muffled by the castle's heavy stone walls. "Oh, God." It wasn't taking the Lord's name in vain but a genuine prayer.

The door burst wide open sending a fan of light over the lawn. Three or four men tumbled out followed by further bullets and hoarse shouting. Clearly something had gone wrong. Come to think of it, Scooby traps almost always did go wrong.

Naturally the fleeing men turned toward the nearest cover which—of course—was the girls' grove. Mikayla watched them coming, mouth hanging slightly open, unable to think of a thing to do about it.

Fortunately Lies had more presence of mind. She

sprang to her feet, opening the shutter of her lantern wide. Johanna instantly followed suit. The gun runners shied away from the lights, heading down the slope to lose themselves in the woods.

Burgmann Schenk showed no signs of pursuing them. Instead he stared at the girls, mercilessly revealed by the light, his face slowly purpling. "Your Grace!"

"Not now, Schenk, they're getting away!" Johanna cried.

"No, they are not," he answered grimly. "What is Your Grace doing out here? And you other ladies?"

Before anybody could come up with an answer to that entirely reasonable question, the woods erupted in screams. Horrible, hoarse, grown-men screams. The girls clumped closer together as Schenk and the guards turned their guns toward the sound.

The screams came nearer. Bodies crashed through the brush and into the open. The light from the castle and assorted lanterns was bright enough to show more men emerging than had gone in. They were also empty-handed, so the guards held their fire. The men scrambled up the slope to throw themselves on the guards' mercy. A few surrendered themselves to the stunned girls, groveling and sobbing in complete hysteria.

Mikayla looked blankly at the man at her feet then past him down the hill. A light flickered white deep inside the trees and disappeared.

"We're grounded?" Mikayla said in disbelief.

"Can Schenk do that?" Sherri wanted to know.

"Oh, yes," Lies answered grimly.

"Believe me, we're lucky he hasn't decided to report us to Papa," Johanna added.

"What *happened* out there, anyway?" Julia wondered.

Johanna had to admit that was a very good question. Pity she didn't have an answer. "I have no idea."

They were back in the state bedroom and in deep disgrace. Schenk hadn't had much to say to them but his look had said volumes. The girls sprawled on the mattresses covering the floor and for a little while nobody said anything—but a great deal was thought by all.

"Typical Scooby trap," Mikayla commented at last.

Sherri nodded agreement. "Everything goes totally wrong but somehow it works out in the end."

"If you call this working out," Mikayla said dubiously.

"We caught them, didn't we?" Sherri said.

"If you call them throwing themselves at our feet wailing and crying 'catching,'" Lies said dryly.

"What the heck was all that about?" Mikayla wondered.

"You know," Anna Sophia said. "You saw her, too."

"I saw a light," Mikayla said a little nervously.

"A bright white light like one of your electric bulbs in the middle of the haunted wood," Anna Sophia shot right back. "Why don't you just admit it? It was the ghost."

"That's jumping to conclusions," Jessie said.

"I thought you believed in ghosts," Anna Sophia snapped.

"I believe in evidence," she replied. "That light could have been anything."

"Sure it could," Anna Sophia snorted.

There was a knock at the door. "You may enter," Johanna called, sitting up and trying to look dignified.

The man who came in was dressed in an up-time-like

camouflage uniform with a pistol strapped to one hip and a helmet with a light like a miner's under his arm. "Your Grace," he said with a slight bow to Johanna, "I'm Agent Bauer, ABI, at your service."

"Yes, Agent Bauer, what can we do for you?" Johanna said politely.

"You were in the forest, weren't you?" Jessie asked not at all politely before he could answer, her eyes on the helmet.

"That's right, miss," Bauer answered. He turned back to Johanna. "My team had located the gun runners' barge downriver and backtracked them into your park."

"So you're what scared those men so badly," Johanna said with some relief. Jessie sighed, and Mikayla shot a triumphant look at Anna Sophia.

But Agent Bauer said, "Not exactly, Your Grace. Which of you young ladies were playing ghost there in the woods?" he shook his head. "That was very dangerous. You shouldn't have taken the risk."

"Playing ghost?" Johanna echoed weakly.

Agent Bauer looked from one wide-eyed girl to the other, puzzled. "That's right. All I saw was a flicker of white light but you certainly convinced the gun runners. They're still terrified."

Johanna swallowed. So did Mikayla. Anna Sophia looked scared rather than triumphant.

"None of us were playing ghost in the park, Agent Bauer," Johanna said as steadily as possible. "Whatever those men saw, it wasn't one of us."

Schenk came to their workroom the next morning, and the girls could see immediately that he was much calmer than he had been the night before. He even wished them a good morning before getting down to business. "I am told that none of you young ladies were playing ghost last night?" he said, inflecting it like a question.

"Absolutely not!" Johanna answered emphatically, and the others nodded like bobbleheaded dolls. "We were irresponsible—we realize that now. But not to that extent!"

"It was a real ghost," said Anna Sophia.

Schenk cleared his throat. "Most unlikely, Your Grace. It seems our park was full of people last night: the gun runners, the ABI team, and Union Master Weintraub's friends. We're still not quite clear whether they were there to help Berners or to avenge their leader, but I am quite sure they were responsible for those mysterious lights."

Anna Sophia looked dubious. So did Jessie, but neither girl seemed inclined to argue.

"You were right, Herr Schenk," Johanna admitted, "and we were wrong. It wasn't safe, and we shouldn't have been out of our rooms."

The much-tried Burgmann actually cracked a smile. "I will remember to be more thorough in my precautions another time."

He withdrew, and the girls slumped back into various boneless postures, draped over the armchairs and sofas of their writing room, every one of them feeling let down, discouraged, and thoroughly disinclined to work.

Mikayla finally broke the silence, putting the thought all of them were nursing into words: "Well one thing's for sure. Our book is no good at all." Groans of agreement showed her friends agreed entirely.

Then she sat bolt upright and shouted one word: "REWRITE!"

The other girls also jerked up, staring at her in shock. Mikayla grinned manically and one by one the rest of the writing circle grinned back. Energy cracked through the room.

"Rewrite!" Johanna shouted like a battle cry and led a charge on the pens and paper.

The Queen's Gearhead

Mark Huston

The buggy was running good. The open exhaust behind Trent's head roared into the night with just the right tone, a low rumble with a harsh rasp at the end of the note. It sounded right. The breeze in his face over the windscreen felt great. Trent Haygood was motoring toward home after visiting what he considered a rather pretty Polish down-time girl. He was driving briskly, relaxed, and thinking about the pretty blonde with green eyes, cute accent, very nice figure, and even a fair brain. Not that he was overthinking the brain thing.

The headlights illuminated his path as he worked his way up Route 250. He barely slowed the last few hundred yards before the turn onto his street on the outskirts of town. He geared down, and began to make the turn. He was going to move in a nice simple arc, and zip down the street to his driveway.

As he turned the buggy into the corner, he saw movement in his path, and a flash of clothing.

"Shit!"

Trent tossed the buggy sideways with a quick flip

of the wheel and managed to miss the man. He still hadn't touched the brakes. If he had, he would have ploughed straight into the pedestrian. The tires were squealing as the buggy slid sideways.

He corrected, and now the buggy was slewing back in the other direction. Anticipating the spin, Trent flipped the wheel quickly back, jammed on the brakes while putting the clutch in, and let his buggy slide in a controlled spin, harmlessly down the center of his street. His three-quarter rotation put him facing the side of the road. He smelled the rubber from the tires. Expensive and irreplaceable tires. The buggy came to a stop. He was pissed. Unbuckling his seat belts, he leapt out of the vehicle and headed toward where he had last seen the pedestrian.

As he strode back to the corner, he saw the man standing on the gravel shoulder, slack-jawed. In the diffuse light of the headlights, which were pointing in the wrong direction to see clearly, Trent saw a short man, who from the look of him was a down-timer, wearing the uniform of an officer. He appeared to be in shock.

Great, Trent thought, *just what I need. Some big-shot down-timer gettin' all pissy. Wonderful.*

He towered over the man. Trent finally stopped in front of him, took a breath, and clenched his teeth into something resembling a smile. He needed no more problems with the police, after what was being called the "Horsepoop Pursuit" concluded with the pursuing squad car half-full of horse manure.

"Hasn't anyone ever told you to not stand in the street after dark?" He asked as civilly as he could manage. Which was not very.

"How did you do that?"

"Do what?"

"How did you control that—that vehicle?"

"It's a damn good thing I did, else y'all would be a bug in my grille." He inhaled slowly, and then let his breath out. Slowly. "What the hell were you doing standing in the middle of my street?"

"You are still in the army, is that correct?"

"Yeah." Trent decided the shortest answer is the best when dealing with "Army" questions.

The officer, a colonel Trent could see now, stood up straight and looked Trent in the eye. "I was not certain at first, but I am now. I think you would be perfect. Report to your commanding officer first thing tomorrow morning, at zero seven hundred hours." The colonel smiled. "And that is an order, Corporal Haygood. Good night."

"You *will* stand up straight when I am talking to you, Haygood. Dammit, you are still in the army and I am giving you orders. So pay attention!"

Trent Haygood chewed on his lower lip and nodded.

"Can't hear you, Haygood!"

"Sorry, sir. I mean, yes, sir."

His CO at the Grantville radio school looked at him with frustration. Karl Orht was a down-timer. Trent knew he transferred from Magdeburg, where he learned up-time soldiering, as well as up-time-style ass-chewing, from Admiral Simpson. And Orth looked grumpy this morning. "You were never much of a soldier even when we were in a first-class shooting war. Since you've been here in school, you've spent more time building that damn buggy of yours than you have learning CW. You are not a good radio operator, Haygood. Do you know that?"

Trent began to feel perspiration bead on his forehead. "I have made passing grades, I believe, sir."

"Barely, Haygood. Barely. And you will graduate in a couple of weeks, assuming that you don't screw up again."

"I hope so, sir."

Orth's tone softened. "Why did you pick this assignment, Trent? Why radio?"

"Well, sir, it is the wave of the future. Radio techs are going to be in incredible demand when we finally stop the wars. It would be a good way to earn lots of money, sir. And when I broke my ankle during the battle, it was about the only duty I could do."

"Do you like it, Haygood?"

"Sir?" Haygood swallowed and began to sweat again. Things were going so well here in town. He had his garage, the car/dune buggy he built and was racing around the streets when he could. He had started to build a couple more cars for customers, and he had made a fair number of dollars when he taught Herr Gribbleflotz to drive. When that word got around, he was certain that he was going to have a lot of customers who wanted to learn how to drive. And now, in this office, it sounded a lot like he was about to get transferred to some other duty. Obviously the CO was setting him up for something. But what?

"I said, do you *like* it Haygood? Are you paying attention to me, son?"

Trent brought himself back to the present. The crappy, unpleasant, seventeenth-century present. With little to keep him interested, and even less to be excited about. Especially when he thought about the future he could have had—

"Haygood!"

"Sir!"

The man's expression softened again. "I asked you if you liked it."

"It's okay, I suppose. I mean, well, radio is important. And with my ankle. Well, there is not a lot I could do running around in the army hauling a rifle, sir."

"Honestly, Haygood. I know your old man is one stubborn SOB. It's obvious *that* apple didn't fall far from the tree, by God. Just give me the answer that's true, don't try to guess what I want to hear."

Trent shifted uncomfortably from foot to foot. "Well, sir, I . . . I suppose the answer is no. I don't much care for it." He stood up a little straighter and added, "Sir."

The CO looked at him square in the face, and smiled. "Finally. We're making some progress. You don't like radio." The bulky man waited for an answer with a raised eyebrow.

"Well, no, sir. Not very much."

"Very well." There was a smile on the man's face that Trent found a little too gleeful. "Have some new orders for you. You will need to be fully certified in CW before you leave here, but these orders are going to be a little more to your liking, I think."

"Am I being discharged, sir?"

The CO laughed a long time over that one. Trent slumped.

As the CO finally got his laughter under control, he moved around his desk and put a hand on Trent's shoulder. "Son, you are being reassigned, and your name came right to the top for this special assignment."

"Sir? That sounds like a load of—well, it doesn't sound likely, sir." Trent quickly faced forward again.

"Seems your little buggy is getting famous. As are you."

"Me, sir?"

"Yes, Trent. You." The man returned to his desk, rummaged for some papers, and sat down. "It seems that while you were running that buggy of yours around, you happened to buzz past a few highly placed down-timers. Course, you can't take a shit in this town anymore without running into a handful of highly placed down-timers. But you, umm, let's say, attracted someone's attention. At the time it was brushed off as a crazy up-timer, but when the emperor's son in Vienna hired a couple of up-timers and bought a sports car, well, it seems that lots of royal courts want their own automobile or two to race around in, and an up-time crew to run it for them. So you are volunteering for special duty. As a member of the USE Army, of course."

"Special duty? Sir?"

"How do you feel about the Spanish Netherlands, Haygood?"

The Netherlands, as it turned out, were not all that bad. At least, once he got there. Which he finally did when the war was over. Trent had trouble keeping track of which war was which. But one or more of them ended enough for him to get there. For Trent, the wars in this century all kind' of ran together after a while. One after another. After another. After another. But he didn't care all that much. He had cars to play with.

There was the delay with plagues, of course. After almost two and a half years of building and buying cars and parts, scrounging tires, tools, and equipment, crating it, shipping it all across Europe, setting up in The Hague, fixing all of the shipping damage, training assistants, and finally getting the little dirt track built where the driving could take place in a reasonably safe manner, he could kick back a little, and relax. Hard work never bothered Trent, but it was nice to have the end in sight, a goal that he could sit back and admire a bit while he had a beer or three. Finally.

It was a late afternoon in the fall, warm for the lowlands, in the infield of the racetrack not far from the center of Brussels. It was a sandy area, and Trent was sitting on the front porch of his garage, drinking the third or fourth of his hard-earned beers, and feeling rather satisfied. He purposefully built the garage area with a porch. Sipping his beer, Trent reflected this wasn't exactly what he had planned for himself before the Ring of Fire, but in this universe of kings, queens, plagues, nonstop wars, way too much religion, and a whole lot of folks who thought they were way better than anyone else, he was doing okay. Nobody was actively trying to kill him in some war; plenty of girls—but no girlfriend; enough business going on the side to create a good income; a couple of guys who were starting to understand the buggies and the cars—things were honest-to-God damn good.

And then he met her.

She got out of her carriage, ignored the footmen and the carriage driver—in fact she seemed to ignore everything around her. She looked down her nose at the entire world, and expected it to get out of her way.

Her slightly pursed lips, combined with her look-down-the-nose, would plough a furrow through any crowd. It was working so well that Trent figured it would work on animals and insects to boot. She stepped up onto the porch, expertly tossing skirts to the side to take the stairs, and stopped directly in front of Trent. The haughty look on her faced changed only a little with the addition of a slightly raised eyebrow.

"I am the Countess Kristina von Bulow, Trent Haygood. I am sure you have heard of me."

Trent paused. Allowed one of his eyebrows to elevate slightly. He had been around the court of the king in the Netherlands for over a year now. He was learning to not stick his foot in his mouth too badly. There had been a challenging learning curve, to be sure. For instance, he now understood he couldn't just call any dandified, limp-wristed, piss-ass, lisping courtier with a sword an insulting name without consequences. He discovered that during his first month. As a result, he now took lessons every other day from the court fencing master, just in case his sarcastic hillbilly humor was misunderstood. Again. Trent pushed back his baseball hat ("Chevy, Heartbeat of America"), lowered his beer mug, and studied the woman who was addressing him. He made a decision not to stand up. He usually hated this type.

"Nope. Can't say that I have." He paused a moment to make sure the woman understood the pause, and then added, "Ma'am." He was disappointed when she didn't even harrumph a little.

"Then that is your mistake, Mr. Haygood. I am well known at court, and have the king and queen's favor, above many. You should keep yourself informed and updated on the goings-on at court, who is in favor, who isn't. There is much I can do to help you, Trent. Improve your dismal standing at court for one thing."

She certainly seemed sure of herself, Trent had to admit. And she didn't come right out and demand a ride in one of the royal cars or one of his buggies, as was the usual approach for one of the court hangers-on. And Trent wasn't easily given over to handing out rides in vehicles that technically didn't belong to him. There was a lot of money tied up in these things, and if he granted a ride to everyone who wanted one, there wouldn't be any gas, tires, oil, or anything else left when someone from the royal family truly wanted to go driving. Not that he was against giving a pretty young lady—well, the woman in front of him was not that young, but still pretty, in a well-shored-up sort of way—a gentle ride in the Ford Crown Victoria he brought along from Grantville. The king really liked the name of that car, and it wasn't one of the old police cars. This one had belonged to some old man in town, and the thing was still in great shape. Plush seats, AC, nice stereo, wire wheel covers...

"Mr. Haygood, are you listening to me?"

Trent blinked. "Umm. Not really, no." He sipped his beer again.

"You really should listen to her, you know. She is trying to help you. And Lord knows you need the help." That new voice came from the guy who had appeared at her side on the porch. He was bulky, looked like he was strong at one time, but was now going soft, mid-thirties, and no hair on his head. Eyebrows with a Vandyke beard and mustache, and that was it. The rest was a cue ball. He had piercing blue eyes and such a level of earnest sincerity in his voice that it was arresting to Trent.

"Why do I need help?" He was beginning to wonder why they hadn't asked to see the cars yet. Usually they did that first.

"The queen likes you, Trent. Do you know that?"

"Well, she has told me that. She is a natural, picked up driving the buggies like she's been doing it all her life. I rather like her too." *For a royal*, he added, into his beer mug.

Kristina paused. "Do you mind if we sit down?"

"Uh, no. Go ahead."

"Thank you. Trent, this is my associate, Bryan DePayne."

"Hello, Trent," DePayne said sincerely. DePayne didn't have that courtier swishiness about him like some of the other ones Trent had met. Some of the Spaniards in the court carried swishiness about them like a badge of honor. DePayne gave the impression of a regular sort of guy, not a puffed-up hanger-on. "Solid" was the word that came to mind with this guy. Trent nodded to him.

Von Bulow continued. "We understand up-timers are rather direct people, and I have been told that you prefer people to be direct, Trent, so I am going to lay this out plainly and simply. We have been sent by the queen, who, as I said, likes you and what you have done to improve your standing in the court."

"I really don't care about my standing in court all that much, Miss von Bulow."

"Countess."

"Countess?"

"You need to address me as *Countess* von Bulow."

"Uh, okay."

"Okay, what?" DePayne asked with sincerity. He had a way of peering out from behind her that was a bit disconcerting.

"Okay . . . Countess?"

She leaned back in her chair and put her hands together. "Very good, Trent. Thank you. We are going to improve your life here in Brussels, at court. Make it much better than it ever was. You will be more engaged, more involved, and have a much higher level of prestige within the court than you could have ever imagined."

"The queen sent you?"

"She asked us to help you." DePayne nodded vigorously in support, and Trent had an image of him as a dog wagging a tail, if he had one. Which Trent decided he might. The image of a bald, Vandyke-bearded dog wagging its tail made Trent smile.

"Well, if the queen says so, then I guess I need to pay attention."

The rest of the afternoon was wasted with what Trent felt was a whole lot of bullshit. It was sophisticated bullshit, full of gilt, fine languages, hand-waving, and perfume, but bullshit all the same. Trent admired a certain amount of bullshit, if it was done well. And these two were absolute professionals. Trent smiled, nodded in the affirmative, listened, allowed them to schedule a tailor for some fittings. It seemed his Torbert overalls and T-shirts were not appropriate for wearing when seen in public. He had better clothes for his court appearances, but for just hanging around the garage he dressed much as he always did, with work boots, T-shirts and the down-time copy of overalls that were called Torberts. His remaining blue jeans he saved for special occasions. Down-time girls had a hard time resisting a man in a good pair of Levi's. But, a new wardrobe was called for—nay, not called for—a new wardrobe was decreed! And etiquette lessons were scheduled. Trent had taken such lessons when he was first posted here, but he patiently allowed the pair to lecture him some more.

But never once did they ask to take a ride in a car, or a buggy, or even to see the garage area. Trent wondered about that. He looked at his watch. It was getting late. He noticed, very briefly, as DePayne's eyes flicked to his watch—a quick, hungry flick of the eyes. A working wristwatch was a very valuable thing, and it was the first tiny indication Trent had that there might be more to these two than met the eye. But then again, that pretty much defined life at court. Which is why he hated it.

Trent drove his buggy into Brussels the next day, to his favorite machine shop/hardware store/blacksmith/ fabricator to meet with Nulens Ruff. Ruff's shop provided the royal garage with all of the bits and pieces that maintaining a fleet of ageing and hand-built vehicles required. It was a win-win, as the information flowed from Trent as he required parts, then into the knowledge base of the team at Ruff's shop, and then on into the local and national economy.

It was also handy, in that Nulens was Trent's handler. Handler, as in spy. Trent was, after all, still technically in the army. The time Trent spent in the shop office, one-on-one with Nulens, wasn't all about discussing suspension design or shock absorber rates. But it was a perfect cover. Nulens was connected to the Nasi clan, somehow. Trent didn't ask how. And he had been here in Brussels for years. And he wasn't Jewish, as far as Trent knew. And he ran one hell of a good shop. He had taken to the new technology coming out of Grantville almost immediately, and Trent noticed he didn't just ape whatever tech he came across. The man was smart enough to adapt it to his own level of fabrication and production.

"May as well play along, for a while. I will see what I can find out for you." Nulens Ruff was the antithesis of a burly blacksmith. Slight and soft-spoken, he wore wire-rimmed spectacles. He was fastidious in his manner and his shop showed it. It was one of the reasons that Trent liked his shop. Nulens nodded at Trent. "Yes, play along. But be careful, court is full of want-to-be courtiers, and those who may have some sort of agenda. I will let you know if I find out anything about them. You know, Trent, we have always wanted you more involved in court activity. This may be your opportunity to become more involved, or more influential. The voice of an up-timer carries weight, more than you realize."

"Yeah, right. I'm sure it does," Trent replied with more than a hint of sarcasm in his voice, "but I'm not really sure if my opinions on tire wear, or the fact that I can't get the wheel bearings I need out of Grantville, influence a damn thing. And I'm not going to talk about foreign policy, or domestic policy, or any kind of policy when there are folks around who know a whole lot more than me. Hell, Nulens, I'm just a wrench-turning guy from the backwoods of

West Virginia. Not some royal advisor. I never even bothered to vote back home."

"They listen to you more than you realize, Trent." Nulens pushed his wire-rimmed glasses back onto his nose. "And even if they don't, who knows? Maybe something you say will have an influence, a positive one, on what they do."

"Okay. I will take another set of etiquette lessons from this Kristina von Bulow—excuse frickin'me, *Countess* von Bulow—maybe this hardheaded hillbilly will learn something."

The lessons went on fairly routinely for a couple of weeks, with Countess von Bulow and Bryan DePayne. When the queen eventually sent a messenger to him that she wanted to go for a driving lesson in one of Trent's motorized buggies, Trent thought he would try out some of his new lessons on the queen. Trent actually rather liked the queen. Maria Anna was a looker, and physically athletic, unlike some of the more rounded girls in town. He tended to go for the twentieth-century look with his girls, while the down-timers were more favoring to what Trent would have called "chubby." To each their own, he figured.

So for the first time, he tried his new courtier bow to the queen, and the proper greeting, "I am so grateful to see you again, Your Majesty."

"Trent, it is time to go driving. I have had a very stressful week, and I want to go fast. Very fast. Let's go."

Trent stood up straight from his bow. She had that look in her eye, that look that Trent had seen before. It must have been a very bad day. He smiled. "Buggies?"

She smiled a crooked smile. "Buggies."

Moments later they were both strapped into the little modified two-seater ATVs, and went tearing around the track, spewing sand and dirt out behind like a pair of giant roosters. The Buggies, as everyone called them, had started out life as ATVs. Trent had modified one into a cross between a dune buggy and an ATV for his own use, and the design caught on. There were a lot of ATVs in Grantville, and he ended up building a handful of them for customers and for himself.

The queen was a little rusty, and it took her a couple of laps to really start to tear it up. Trent drove his buggy beside her, pacing her, showing her the fast way around the tiny track, ducking under her in some corners, passing her on the outside on some corners, allowing her to pass him, then retaking the lead as she followed. He pushed hard, and she was able to keep up with him. They tore around the track for nearly an hour, until Maria Anna finally pulled off into the pit lane. Trent took another lap at top speed, tail hanging out as he drifted the car around the final set of turns, until he grabbed the brakes and hauled the small car behind Maria Anna, who was just climbing out of her buggy. Her safety straps dangled to the side as she pulled her helmet off. Her grin was ear to ear.

Trent hopped out and pulled his own helmet off. "Damn, Your Majesty! You were hauling ass today!" They were both standing by the cars, the retainers and Trent's mechanics hanging back. Trent would many times offer critiques to the queen, and others had learned to keep their distance until the conversation ended.

"That was very good, Trent. I needed that after this week. It is so exhilarating. I try to explain the feeling to my court, but the closest I can come is horseback riding. But you have so much more control and so much more power. It is only you and the machine."

Trent could only match her grin. "I understand, Your Majesty. Nothin' better. You know, you are still a little heavy on the throttle mid-corner in the south turn."

"I keep forgetting that the tail out is the fastest way around, not just mashing down on the throttle. I want to go faster, all the time."

"Sometimes you need to go a little bit slow, to go faster."

"I know, Trent. I know. You have told me many times." She grinned while shaking her head, a mix of fun and frustration.

"Your Majesty, you've done this driving thing for what, eight months now? And in that time, you have done more performance driving than a lot of folks who have been driving their whole lives have done. You are a natural at this."

The queen nodded. "You know, Trent, people compliment me endlessly, tell me how good I am. But you have also told me, at least when we first started, how terrible I was, and how worried you were that I was going to damage the equipment or myself. You have always been quite forthright with me, Trent. It is one of the things I like about you." She glanced at the group of hangers-on, courtiers, and townsfolk who gathered for the session. "When they compliment me, there is an agenda. With you, not so much."

Trent felt himself blush. "Thank you, Your Majesty. I just like this stuff, and I like it when someone else likes it too. Especially in this time and place."

"Thank you, Trent Haygood."

"You're welcome, Your Majesty!" Trent actually didn't mind bowing his head, just a little bit.

Another month went by, and Trent got used to having the Countess von Bulow and DePayne hanging around the garage. He eventually gave them a ride around town in the Crown Victoria, and they fell in love with the car, asking about how fast it would go, how far it could go without stopping, and DePayne just about wore out the electric window mechanism on the side where he was sitting. He let DePayne try to drive it a few feet, and the man was such a clod with the controls that Trent forbade him from attempting to do it again. DePayne agreed as Trent's quick action saved them from what would have been a minor accident. Von Bulow was simply not interested.

"So, on a full tank of fuel this remarkable vehicle can travel something like three hundred and fifty miles, at least?" DePayne was shaking his head in amazement. "On just nineteen gallons of fuel?"

Trent shrugged. "On the old interstates, it could be a good four hundred miles, and cover that in less than six hours. But here? With these roads, and the lower-grade fuels? We are lucky to get ten miles per gallon. But this car can haul ass when it needs to. Plenty of room, and most of the roads in the country around here are pretty good. I can get cross-country a lot faster in my buggies, but this will still do better than any horse. And it's a hell of a lot more comfortable." DePayne continued to play with the power window. Up. Down. Up. Down. Trent sighed. "Bryan. Please. You will break it."

"This car is so cool!"

"Great, Bryan. Maybe sometime I will take you for a ride and you can hang your head out the window."

"That would be wonderful!" Trent could almost see his tail wagging.

A couple of weeks later, Trent had his head buried under the hood of a Chevy pickup truck that he had dubbed "Frankenstein." The truck made the trip from Grantville to Brussels as part of the king's fleet. It was in a fire before the Ring of Fire, and was abandoned when he bought it with royal dollars. Somehow it hadn't gone to the scrap yards for steel production like so many others. All of the wiring, the ignition system, the battery, the interior, seats—just about any soft part or electrical part—was of down-time manufacture. The engine, transmission and body were all up-time. The metal parts had survived the rather severe fire. Everything else was re-created from scratch. He was looking for a short somewhere in the down-time wiring. Fuses were not in great supply, and the short circuit was one that only happened sometimes, not all the time. So he was deep in thought when someone quietly whispered into his ear.

"May I speak with you, Trent? Alone?"

Trent twitched, and promptly bashed his head on the hood. "Dammit!" He turned and was face to face with von Bulow. She smiled at him. Then she placed her hand on his upper arm, and stood a little close. Certainly closer than she had ever been. Trent glanced around the garage, and there was nobody else there. The countess made him uncomfortable. He rubbed his head where he bashed it on the hood.

Von Bulow looked at him with a pout. "Did that hurt? I am sorry, Trent."

"Not too much, no. I was just—"

"Working hard, as usual."

"Yeah. Well." He pointed back under the hood. "I'm kinda busy here, Countess. Tracking down an electrical problem; takes some concentration."

"Trent, I would really like to speak with you." She stood even closer, and began to gently stroke the growing goose egg on his skull. He turned to face her, his back to the fender of the truck. She leaned into him, brushing her hips against his as she stroked his head. "Does that hurt?"

"Uhh. No." He paused a moment and thought. "Well, yeah. A little."

She pouted again, and continued to gently stroke his head. "Does this feel better?"

"Uhh. Y-Yeah."

She smiled at him, and looked down demurely. Her hand left his head, brushed across his face, and then rested lightly on his chest. She then looked up at him. "I have been watching you, Trent. You are special."

"And I have been watching you too, Countess." Her eyes flashed up to him. There was a darkness in them, Trent decided. Pretty, intelligent, hopeful, but at the core deceitful. He knew she was up to something. Nulens Ruff had told him that the only von Bulows he could find were in Schleswig-Holstein, which even *he* knew was nowhere near Bavaria, and there was nothing on a Kristina. That didn't mean she wasn't who she said she was, but it didn't confirm it either. He knew it was more than sex, whatever it was she was after. And he knew, with all certainty, that it wouldn't turn out good. It never did with this sort. He smiled back at her after a moment. "You are special, too."

Her smile widened, and she pressed against him fully. "I knew you would say so."

Trent smiled back. "Forget it, Countess. I'm not your type."

She stepped back, and her eyes flashed. "What do you mean? You prefer those tavern girls in town to me? I have watched where you go, Trent. Those girls in the taverns, trollops for the most part, whores otherwise. I am far more worthy of you."

Okay, he thought. *She's been following me. Crap. What the hell is she up to? God, I hate court life, hate it, hate it, hate it. All I want to do is work on cars and drive fast. And for that, I have to deal with crazy women . . .*

"Trent, are you listening to me? I am far better for you than them. More to your station, more to your kind."

Trent had had enough. "Countess. I didn't ask you to come here. You just came." He stopped and put down the screwdriver he was using, and stepped away from her. He was angry, and he didn't want to start waving around a screwdriver and give the wrong impression. He began to pace, and he raised his voice in frustration. "*You* are up to something." He pointed at her. "*You all* are up to something. Everyone in that whole damned court. You are *all* full of shit. Some sort of agenda. Some sort of angle. Wanting favor. Wanting a leg up for your family. Wanting something for nothing. And I'm tired of it, lady. Countess. Duchess, princess. Whatever the fuck you are. Because I don't care. You know why I don't care? Why?" He turned to face her. Her face was a mask. A porcelain mask. No expression, just blue eyes staring at him, dead. It spooked him momentarily, until she allowed a little anger to show through the mask. "Those tavern girls." He pointed toward the center of town. "Local girls. Sure they have an agenda, some of them. Sure they would love to snag some rich up-timer. I'm not stupid, lady. Don't make that mistake. But they are who they are. What they are. No bullshit. Simple agendas. So as far as I am concerned, they are one hell of a lot better than you, Countess. If that is what you really are."

Her face went back to the mask, the anger shoveled behind it. "I don't think you are stupid, Trent. Naive, yes; spectacularly so. Stupid, no." She sighed, then looked at him with what might have been sadness. "And I *am* a countess."

It was a week later that he finally figured out what they were up to. But like most lessons in the here and now, it didn't come easy. He came back from a night on the town in his buggy, and pulled it into the shop like he always did. Cars were much easier than horses that way. You could come home at two in the morning, feeling little pain from the evening, and just park the damn thing. No taking off the saddle, no putting the damn thing into the stall, no brushing it down, no removing the tack and putting it away. Just park it. He really hated horses. Slow and stupid, and a shit ton of work. Crappy brakes. Plus, he rode like a sack of potatoes.

As he was climbing out, he saw von Bulow standing in the lamplight by the big Crown Victoria. "Hello, Trent."

He stood next to the buggy, listening to the engine make quiet *tink-tink* sounds as it cooled. "Countess..."

"Well, at least you learned that from our lessons. My proper address."

"So, why are you here?"

She motioned him over. "Let me show you." He walked over to the big Ford, and she opened the passenger side door. The interior lights came on, and Maria Anna sat in the back. The queen's hands were tied behind her, and she was gagged, seat belts snugged down, but conscious. Her eyes flashed as Trent looked at her first, and then back to von Bulow. He sensed someone come up behind him, and felt a blade go to his throat.

"DePayne."

"Trent."

Trent slowly turned to von Bulow. "So, what is it? What's the game?"

"We are going to take the Crown Victoria. You are going to drive us to Ostend, by the sea. It is about fifty miles. You will do it before word of the missing queen reaches there."

"I don't even know if the roads will take this car. It's big. Much bigger than a buggy—" He felt the knife tighten on his throat.

"Get in and drive." He felt DePayne grab him by the back of the neck and steer him toward the driver's seat. His grip was like a vise. "I have the route."

They piled in while Trent started the car. "It needs some gas. The gauge is only at a quarter tank."

Von Bulow was sitting behind him. "We have already taken that into account, Trent. I have two of the spare cans in the trunk, an extra ten gallons. We have plenty of fuel. Let's go."

He started the car, DePayne got out and opened

the doors to the garage, and Trent pulled out. He glanced in the mirror as DePayne closed the doors behind them, and then adjusted the mirror to look at von Bulow. She smiled at him, and leaned forward. She held a six-inch dagger in her hand, and playfully touched his earlobe with it. "Trent, I am quite good with this. I can kill you and the queen in a moment, if I wish to. So do as you are told, and you may survive."

DePayne piled into the car, sitting heavily and fumbling with his sword. Trent noticed it was impossible for the man to fasten his seat belt with the sword and belt. There was a pile of papers on the dashboard. "Take the north road out of the track, and head for the village. We will go through the center of the village. It will be deserted this time of night. Everyone knows this is the king's car and will get out of the way. Your buggy drives in the night have shown the local populous that much, Trent." He laughed for a moment. "I have the rest of the route plotted out here. I have been working on it for weeks. They'll never catch us, and Maria Anna will be on a ship before they know she is gone."

The big car eased out of the now unmanned gate, and toward the small village nearby. This was a route Trent knew well. The headlights illuminated the absolute darkness of the seventeenth-century night. It was not only quiet, but deeply dark. Trent glanced at the clock on the dash, and it showed 3:00 A.M.

"This is why you came on to me, finally. You wanted me to be here, with you, tonight. Keep me in bed, keep track of me, and keep me ready to do your bidding." Trent glanced in the mirror to try and catch a glimpse of von Bulow's face in the darkness. He heard

DePayne snort derisively next to him. "You wanted to make sure I came home in time."

"Drive, lover boy." DePayne was no longer a puppy dog. He was turning into a nasty bear-baiting dog, the kind that snarled and bit, when the bear wasn't looking.

They drove on through the village, and he took the main road to the west. The car had a small compass display stuck to the windshield, and it was reasonably accurate. Trent knew the nearby roads, and some of the other more distant roads. He also knew that many were impassable to the big Ford. The big sedan didn't have the ground clearance of the buggies, didn't have the turning radius, and was just too damn wide for some of the bridges. Shipping the vehicles here had been a nightmare, and he knew that a cross-country run, at night, at speed, was going to be challenging. "Slow down, you are coming to a turn." DePayne growled at him. "We had to make a bridge here, in the field. Follow that chalk line." Powdered chalk had been dusted down in a line for the car to follow across a pasture. The pasture ran alongside a creek, and the headlights showed a new set of planks, placed across the creek. "The bridge for the road isn't wide enough. This is. Drive across it slowly." Trent squared the car up with the temporary bridge and eased the car across. He felt the planks dip and clatter, but they more than held the load. Trent figured they were slightly more than two tons of weight. He eased the car off of the bridge and then up a small, sloped embankment. The rear tires slipped a little, but he had enough forward momentum to pull them up to the crest. He followed the chalk lines back to the main road.

"You have been planning this for a while, Countess.

That much is clear." Trent glanced in the mirror, looking at the countess and the queen. The queen was watching carefully. Her eyes met with Trent's for a moment. He nodded imperceptibly. An instant later he felt the cold edge of the dagger under his earlobe.

"Trent. Don't be a hero. It isn't in you. You don't join, you don't participate. You don't become part of something. It's because you are a loner. And loners aren't heroes, Trent. Loners are not part of something greater than themselves. No reason to be heroic, except when it comes to themselves. And if you behave, you will live." She played with his earlobe again with the tip of the dagger.

"And Maria Anna? What of her?"

"You can go faster here, for three miles the road runs straight and clear." DePayne shuffled his route notes and shifted in his seat sideways, facing von Bulow. "We are right on schedule. We will be in Ostend in less than an hour, we should be able to get up to fifty miles per hour on this road, Trent. So step on it."

Trent looked in the mirror at von Bulow. "And Maria Anna?"

"She is going to end up back in Bavaria, to answer for her crimes." Trent shifted his gaze to the queen, who was staring straight ahead. "We will meet a vessel in Ostend, and from there we will be out to sea. We will eventually make our way back to Bavaria, where I will claim what is rightfully mine, once again."

Trent eased the speed of the car up to near fifty, and focused on the road ahead. The car danced in the ruts, but the soft suspension and wider tires made it controllable. It was a broad lane, by down-time standards, with mature oak trees on either side. It looked like an alley, the faster he went. It was wide for wagons drawn by horses at walking speed, but for the big Ford, at speed, it was deceptively narrow. He let his vision go as far down the road as he could. "Any turns coming up? I don't want to fall off the road."

DePayne looked at him, grinning. "You stop, you die. Very simple."

"So, why? Why are you doing this, Countess? What's to gain?" He glanced in the mirror quickly, searching for her eyes. He found them. Her porcelain mask was back, but the eyes were calculating. His eyes flicked to the road ahead, and then back to her, feeling the road as much as seeing it.

"My father." Trent put his eyes back to the road, and then noticed DePayne stir next to him, turning to look at von Bulow. DePayne was turned nearly two thirds around in his seat to look at the countess. Trent brought the speed up slightly. The oak trees whizzed by. The car danced.

"Kristina..." DePayne cautioned.

She held up her hand. "It doesn't matter now, DePayne." She shifted in her seat and leaned up to speak to Trent. "My father was a great man. But what she did to him was criminal."

"What did she do?"

"She killed him. Oh, not with her own hands, but by her negligent, selfish actions. When she ran away from her responsibilities, her commitments, there were many that were thought to have helped her. And my father was one of those who were caught up in Maximilian's nets of vengeance and suspicion. We lost everything. Everything that should have been mine. You asked me if I was a countess once, Trent. And

I *was* a countess. We had lands, respect, position. All destroyed by her." She pointed casually with her dagger. "And I intend to bring her back to pay for her crimes, and to set right that which was taken from me. So you see, Trent, I have every reason, every right, to do whatever I need to do, to return this woman back to justice. You have no idea how many died because of her selfishness. Her inability to do her duty, her weakness." She spat the word, and then looked directly at the queen. "Maria Anna isn't fit to be queen of a pigpen, much less the Spanish Netherlands. My father was a great man."

Trent looked at the trees going by. With his right hand, he reached down and snugged his seat belt as tight as he could. He then placed both hands against the bottom of the steering wheel. In one rapid motion, he tapped the brakes to settle the front of the car to give the front end additional grip on the rough surface, and snapped the wheel to the right. He hit the massive oak tree at about forty miles an hour, and he centered the tree immediately in front of DePayne. The impact was massive.

One of the lessons that Trent always tried to teach down-timers was about the damage that was created by high-speed impacts. As speed went up, so did force. An impact while walking hurt. An impact while running hurt a lot more. At five times running speeds, the impacts became fatal. Since down-timers had little experience at these sorts of speeds, the concept of the impacts, and the damage they could do, it was something they just couldn't grasp. Trent tried to get down-timers to wear seat belts all the time. They almost never did.

The nose of the big Ford hit the tree in the center of the headlight on the passenger side. The car began to crumple as it folded around the tree, the sheet metal deforming first. The rest of the car slowed slightly, and the airbags went off. They did DePayne no good, as Trent had a fleeting image of him flying out of the car to impact against the oak tree with a wet *thwock*, and the body pinwheeling into the darkness.

Trent felt pain in his foot as the engine and transmission hit the tree, and the heavy components displaced backwards into the passenger compartment, folding under to absorb the crash. He was dazed by the airbags. He was vaguely aware of the car rotating off of the tree to his left, still continuing after the immediate impact. He felt another thump and then it was very quiet.

He smelled gas and engine coolant. He unfastened his seat belt and looked around him. Taking inventory. His foot hurt, and looking down he could see why. It was turned at a right angle to what it should be. The foot well where the pedals were was about half the size it should be. Somewhere in the accident the brake pedal had impacted his foot. The headlight on his side of the car still worked, and it illuminated up into the tree, casting a harsh yellow light over everything. The left blinker was on, flashing steadily. His vision was clouded and his ears were ringing from the airbags going off. His wrists burned. He looked around for Maria Anna. She was still belted into her seat and was clearly unconscious. Von Bulow was nowhere to be seen.

Trent tried to open his door, but it was stuck. He could see the start of a small fire under the hood, probably a result of the fuel injection system leaking onto something hot. It wasn't large, and he wasn't particularly worried about it. He had seen several cars burn to the ground, and he knew he had time. It wasn't going to explode like in the movies.

He also knew he had time before his foot really started to hurt badly. He had broken it once while marching when he stepped into some sort of European gopher hole, and ended up missing some battle that everyone always talked about. So he crawled over the back seat to get Maria Anna. He could see she was breathing. He unfastened her seat belt and began to drag her out of the driver's side. That door was already open. He looked around for von Bulow again.

Half crawling and half limping, he pulled Maria Anna away from the car onto the far side of the road. He grabbed his pocketknife and sliced through her bonds. He kept a spare blanket and a first aid kit in the trunk of the big car. Limping badly, as his foot started to hurt by now, he opened the trunk. The rear of the car was elevated, and the front was pointing down so that he had to reach up to get into the trunk. He was met by the smell of gasoline. One or both of the cans had ruptured in the trunk. He grabbed the blanket and the first aid kit and began to attend to the queen. He elevated her feet with the blanket and opened the first aid kit. He heard a moan from the queen, and her eyelids fluttered open.

"Can you hear me? Maria Anna? Can you hear me?" He used some of the gas from the blanket, and waved it under her nose like smelling salts.

There was another small moan. "Yes, T-Trent. What happened? It was so fast."

"I wrecked the car. On purpose. DePayne is dead, and I don't know where the bitch is."

"She's dangerous. Watch for her." The queen struggled to sit up.

"Take it easy. It was a big hit. But I knew you were belted, and they weren't. It had to be fast enough to take them out, but still not hurt us. Looks like I was a little faster than I wanted to be." The queen fell back, and Trent cradled her head. "You might have a concussion, Your Majesty. Don't try and sit up." She moaned and made a confused gesture with her hands, then put her head back down.

The car had started to burn a little more by now, as the plastics under the hood caught fire. It was a very up-time smell, burning plastics. Trent heard a cry for help. It was faint. He winced as he made his way back to the car and peered inside. "Hello? Countess? Are you in there?"

"Down here, in front, I think. I-I'm trapped." Trent peered into the front seat. Somehow in the accident von Bulow ended up on the floor of the front passenger seat. She was now wedged between the floor and the distorted front seat, her head facing up and out as she tried to wriggle her way free. One arm, the left one, appeared to be still stuck. Trent crawled into the back seat, and leaned forward, with both arms extended to pull her out. The fire was growing and the smell of gasoline was strong. Stronger than it should be. That's when Trent remembered the two cans of gas in the trunk.

"I need to get you out of there! Grab my arm." She reached, but couldn't get a good grip. The interior started to fill up with smoke as the plastics and the wiring under the hood began to aggressively burn. Trent knew he was running out of time. He leaned further over the seat, crying out in pain as he put pressure on his damaged foot. "Grab my arms, I'll pull you out!"

He could barely see, but suddenly von Bulow's left hand was free. And it held the dagger, which was streaking toward his throat. He jinked back, and he felt it tick into the side of his jaw, and saw his blood spray before his eyes. "Fuck!" Trent realized that by shouting, he knew his throat hadn't been cut. He put his hand to the side of his face, blood oozing between his fingers. "What the hell's the matter with you?! I'm trying to save your life!"

She laughed at him. He couldn't believe it. Laughing. "You are so, so naive, Trent Haygood. You think you are so smart. But you don't understand us at all. You up-timers are all the same. You don't get it. You don't get how we think. You are trying to save me. I have no life left to save, you fool. I am nothing. The only thing I have left, is for *you* to die." He could feel the blood continuing to ooze between his fingers, and he felt woozy. The smoke thickened, and he began to cough.

"You have got to get out"—*cough! cough!*—"now!" He reached across one more time, taking care to keep out of range of the dagger. He could see she was truly pinned under the dash. "Give me your hand." The dagger whipped through the smoke toward his fingers. He tried again, and the dagger swept by again. His foot slipped to the floor and it went squish as gas from the cans began to run down into the passenger compartment from the trunk. He tried one more time, and was met by the swish of a dagger once again. He crawled out the door to the ground, moving away from the car, one hand still on his neck. He felt the *whump*, the movement of air, and the flash of heat as the gasoline ignited. The car became a fireball.

Trent remembered the scream of the burning von Bulow for a very long time.

"I was a fool to trust her, but she was very, very good. We began by taking walks in the evening, in the gardens. She had a good mind, good ideas—or at least was well coached. How is your foot coming along, Trent?"

"Better, Your Majesty. I'll be on crutches for another couple months at least. The last time I did this it took a while to heal. Is that when they grabbed you? During an evening walk?" Maria Anna and Trent Haygood were sitting on the porch to the garage. He drinking a cold beer, Maria Anna sipping wine. He rubbed the scar on his neck.

"You know you cannot talk about this, Trent. This is, as you Americans say, 'classified.' Word cannot get out about a kidnapping attempt on me. I ask you this as a personal favor to me."

"I think they know about it, at least now. My people in the USE, anyway. The guards for the garage were killed. Car wrecked the same night. My intelligence people will figure it out. And if they don't get some kind of report from me, then they will get all wigged out. So I gotta. But I will tell them to keep it need-to-know only. Sorry."

Maria Anna nodded. "I appreciate your discretion and honesty, as always, Trent." There was a pause and they looked at the sun, setting across the porch, and casting long shadows through the wood trim. "This is nice here."

"Thanks. You paid for it, Your Majesty." Trent smiled at her.

"You seem different, Trent. Something has changed."

"Never killed anyone before, for one thing. I know it was necessary, but, still, first time. And something tells me it won't be the last." He took another sip, this one much longer.

"There is something else. What is it?"

He sighed. "I think I am beginning to understand something. Something about this time. People are different. I mean I have always *known* they were different, you know. I'm not totally stupid. But I thought they were the same. Different clothes, different hairstyles, technology, but still the same people. People are people. And in a lot of ways, they are. But on the other hand, there are some things that are so damn different. The way folks think, the value of life, rights of common men. I mean, you ask somebody where they are from, and they answer with who they belong to. I mean they don't say, I'm from Brussels, they say, I am Baron Fredric's man, or some such thing. On one level, I knew that. But until I met Countess Kristina von Bulow, I didn't realize the difference. She *was* her position, a countess. She wasn't *separate* from it. Deep-down understanding, you know?" He shrugged. "Does that make any sense to you?"

The queen nodded. "You are very wise, Trent Haygood."

"Now, Your Majesty, I like you and all, but don't go blowing smoke up my butt. I'm just a wrench-turning hillbilly from West Virginia."

They raised their glasses, and continued to watch the sunset.

Letters from Inchon

Robert Waters

Grantville
July 1636

Arnulf Langenberg found the dusty, crumpled shoebox beneath a pile of rags smelling of mildew and up-time 2-cycle oil. Tucked between dirt-encrusted aluminum badminton stakes and an olive drab duffel bag, the box called to him, as if saying, "Save me, Arnie, from all this junk." For junk was pretty much all that one could find in Herr Grooms' garage: useless debris from a future that Arnie could imagine, but would never know in truth. Yet, he always enjoyed coming in here, always made a point to make up some excuse to rummage through the piles of old boots fallen to dry rot, or rusty carburetors, or broken chain links from a Poulan chainsaw, or oddly shaped gardening tools with soft green handles, or spark plugs lying about like errant nails on wooden shelves. To Arnie, it was a testament to what life could be in the future, a life filled with all kinds of neat gadgets and "gizmos," and oh how he wanted to live in that world. To him, the old man's garage was like a treasure chest. But he had never noticed the shoebox before. Now, it was the only thing that he could see.

He pulled it from its hiding place. Nothing much to look at: a nondescript light tan box with a brown top, damp fungus near the back that made it smell old and rustic. He held it delicately like a jewel, careful to keep his hand flat on its bottom lest it fall apart and crumble to the grease-stained concrete floor. He removed the top carefully and looked inside.

Letters. Scores of them. Some in blue-and-white envelopes; some without envelopes at all, but folded at the center in neat, tiny squares. All of them dog-eared and yellowing with age. They smelled too, and Arnie wiggled his nose at the combined fragrance of aged mold and some kind of stale cologne or perfume. He couldn't tell which. He plucked one carefully from the box and turned it around. It had been opened long, long ago, the tatters of paper at its top sticking out like gnarled, rotten teeth. The address on the front held Herr Grooms' name and street in West Virginia. The postage was strange, and nothing like Arnie had ever seen before. Certainly not like the old American stamps that he had seen in books at the high school library. He pried the envelope apart and began pulling out the letter.

"Did you find the hammer?"

The sudden voice made him jump, and he nearly dropped the box. He turned quickly to find his employer, Jim Grooms, standing at the entrance of the garage, a cane supporting his old, weakened body. Herr Grooms had had a mild stroke in February, but by the grace of God, he had recovered and could walk reasonably well under support. His speech had never been impaired, though the left side of his mouth drooped a bit still, and it made his smile look a little clownish. But there he stood, the thick glass of his spectacles making his eyes seem larger than they really were . . . and more concerned and menacing as well.

"I . . ." Arnie began, then realized the error of what he was about to say. No need to speak a fib; as an up-timer preacher he knew often said, "The truth shall set you free." He lifted up the box as if offering it to sky. "No, Herr Grooms. I found this box."

The old man seemed to deflate from the offering, his shoulders slumping as if laden with weight. He stared a moment at the box, then moved forward carefully. "Where . . . where did you find that?"

Arnie pointed to the box's hiding place. "Right there, behind all that stuff. What are they?"

Herr Grooms set his cane aside and took the box in his shaking hands. He pulled the top letter out, put it to his nose, sniffed. A tiny smile crept across his mouth like the scribbling of a red pencil, thin and barely recognizable between the darker, leathery skin above and below. But it was a smile, no doubt about it. Arnie hadn't seen Herr Grooms smile often, but the man could smile under the right conditions. It was indeed a smile, and a small spot of tear lined the bottom of his left eye. "They're letters," he said, smelling again, then setting it gently back into the box. "Letters I thought lost long, long ago."

"Where did they come from?"

Herr Grooms didn't seem to want to answer at first,

grabbing his cane to give his legs rest. He handed the box back to Arnie, then said with a sigh, "Korea."

Arnie ruffled his brow. "Where's that?"

Herr Grooms moved as if to point toward the east, but then put his hand down and chuckled. "Far away, my boy. Far, far away."

"Is that where you got your wound?"

It was not a subject Herr Grooms liked talking about; in fact, whenever it was raised by anyone, the old man changed the subject quickly. And his wife, Vellie Rae, gave anyone the evil eye who even mentioned the Korean War in the presence of her husband. Arnie didn't know why it was such a touchy subject, and he didn't know if he was violating that unspoken rule now, but he couldn't help it. Something about this box of letters, and the reaction that Herr Grooms had when he saw it, made him want to know more.

Herr Grooms looked at Arnie with eyes wide, and smiled. "Yes, it is. Now . . ." He guided Arnie over to the shelf and directed him to put the box away. He moved aside a piece of warped pressboard and pointed to a hammer. "Grab that hammer and let's get cracking. Those boards ain't gonna nail themselves, you know."

"Yes, sir." Arnie tucked the box away, and made a half-hearted gesture to conceal it with the oily rags. He reached for the hammer and followed Herr Grooms out of the garage. "Perhaps you can tell me about the war someday."

The old man didn't stop, nor did it seem as if he even heard what Arnie had said. Then quickly, as if to keep from being overheard, he cleared his throat and whispered, "Someday, my boy. Someday."

Near Seoul, South Korea
September 19, 1950

Corporal Jim Grooms watched Sergeant John Nearing die in his arms. John was shot through the neck with a Kar98k. Jim tried staunching the blood, but the Eternal Footman would not be denied. By the time the medic arrived, the sergeant was dead. His eyes in death were so peaceful that Jim didn't want to let him go, wanted to fall into those peaceful eyes and forget about the chaos surrounding him. But one of his men grabbed his arm and shook him awake.

"What are your orders, Corporal?"

My orders? He knew this day would come eventually, but he never planned for it to arrive in the midst of a firefight while holding his dead sergeant. Luckily, they were now in a good defensive position, so he had a little time to consider their options.

They weren't good. They never were. His unit was working alongside the 1st Marines, in an attempt to retake the city after the North Koreans had come across the dividing line in the summer, smashing through nearly all of South Korea. The KPA were doing surprisingly well, though General Douglas MacArthur's amphibious Operation Chromite, which had landed in Inchon, had finally broken the back of the North Korean Army. Now Seoul lay before them, and by order, they were supposed to help retake it. That was the order given to the 2nd Battalion, 32nd Infantry Regiment, 7th Infantry Division. The private who was asking the question knew that. What he wanted to know was what *they* were going to do in this bigger scheme, now that their sergeant was dead. And the private was right: at this moment, the lives of the six men remaining in their squad were more important to Corporal Grooms than any general's overall strategic plan.

He looked around quickly. Other elements of 32nd IR were engaged, fighting all along a line that overlooked the very edge of the city. The KPA were entrenched and determined to stay. Funny, but at that moment, Corporal Grooms couldn't think of anything else but West Virginia, and how much it resembled Korea. Well, the mountainous parts of it anyway. Similar topography, similar foliage. Cold as hell in the winter. All this talk of exotic Asian jungles back home had been quickly dashed when he had arrived in-country. It almost felt like fighting in his own backyard. He shook his head. What a silly notion!

He peeked around the rubble protecting him and his soldiers, making sure his helmet was on tight. Kar98 rounds struck nearby. He pointed to the guts of a building. "There. That's where we'll go. Right in the center of the line; good defensive position. We get there, that might give the rest of the battalion a chance to anchor and then push forward."

"They've got a light machine gun, Corporal," said PFC Monk.

Corporal Grooms nodded. "I know, but it's the best choice. Either that, or stay here and look like pussies. Sergeant Nearing wouldn't want that. Now, get ready!"

He was mad. He didn't know why. Of course he did. His sergeant and friend had just been killed, and there was nothing he could do about that. What he could do, however, was honor the memory and press forward, to kill the son of a bitch who had just killed his friend. It didn't matter what dog he killed, in truth, as long as he was North Korean. One was just as good as the other.

"Get me a Garand with a grenade launcher!"

Someone found one among the bodies and handed it over. Corporal Grooms checked it. Still functional. Good. He'd prefer a rocket launcher or a Corsair dropping a bat bomb, but this would have to do. He'd discovered in training that he was a pretty good shot with one, so long as he could keep the snipers off of him while he set.

He waited until his men assembled beside him. He looked at them. Damn! Some were so young, hardly eighteen. He wasn't much older than they were. Young men killing other young men. Didn't someone say once that all wars were started by men, but fought by children? That certainly was the case here. Even the sergeant had been in his mid-twenties. But what did all that matter now? Now, they had to get across the small, deadly open space, take those ruins, and press on. They had to do it now!

He gave his order through hand signals. They nodded, readied their rifles. "Now!"

Together they rose up and fired on the building. Their rounds peppered the concrete and pinned the enemy gun. Corporal Grooms steadied the grenade rifle on the rough surface of the rubble in front of him, aimed carefully, and pulled the trigger.

The grenade flew inside the window where the machine gun resided and exploded. He felt a sudden rush of elation, then stowed it. "Go!"

They climbed over the rubble and pressed the attack, pulling grenades from their belts and launching them to cause even more suppression. KPA units farther away tried responding with grazing fire, but the machine gun in the building had been taken out. Good! That made Corporal Grooms very happy.

PFC Hadley fell with multiple shots in the chest and abdomen. His live grenade rolled away. Corporal Grooms crawled after it, caught it before it fell into a ditch, and tossed it wildly to the left, just in time to see it explode harmlessly in a patch of weeds.

The other men had reached the building and were taking up defensive positions among its ruins. He noticed someone stabbing the machine gunner with a bayonet. He smiled, climbed into a crouch, and pressed toward the building.

That's when the bullet struck his right side.

It felt like a bee sting. Then a warm, comforting sensation spread through his stomach, down his legs, and up into his chest. He dropped to his knees. He looked down, expecting to see blood. What he saw and felt was piss.

Grantville
July 1636

"You peed yourself?"

Arnie regretted the question as soon as it came out, but the expression on Herr Grooms' face settled his concern quickly. The old man smiled, even chuckled.

"Well, yes, I'm embarrassed to say. I took the bullet right through the kidney." Herr Grooms set the glass of tea down and leaned back in his rocking chair on his porch. The creak of the old gray-painted pine slats below the chair was eerily comforting to Arnie, and in direct conflict with the seriousness of the story. "Right through my kidney and right out the back. A pretty clean wound, all things considered, but I guess the shock of that made my bladder pop. I remember lying there thinking, 'Damn! I hope no one saw that!' More concerned about my honor than if I was going to die or not."

"But you didn't die."

Herr Grooms shook his head. "No. I passed out shortly after that and woke up several days later in a MASH unit."

"What's that?"

"You don't know what a—" Grooms paused. "Sorry, I forget sometimes where I'm at. Of course you wouldn't know. A MASH unit is a Mobile Army Surgical Hospital. They were used a lot in Korea, popularized through the sitcom *MASH* in the seventies. Vellie Rae might have some old episodes on a VCR tape somewhere if you want to see what they looked like. But I can assure you, young man, that there was nothing funny about the real thing, about being in one."

"Did it hurt?"

"Not at first, as I say. It was kind of a warm feeling. But when I woke up, it started to...bad. I got an infection, and that didn't help. But I pulled through, in the end."

Arnie set down his empty tea glass, cleared his throat, dreaded asking the next question, but couldn't resist. He thought of his mother, who always slammed him for his intellectual curiosity. "It'll get you in trouble one of these days," she'd say.

"May I see it?" he asked. "The wound?"

Herr Grooms stopped rocking, clearly debating

whether or not to let this impetuous down-timer see his up-time battle scar. Finally, he shrugged and pulled his shirt free from his waist. He leaned forward and motioned Arnie to come around. "Go ahead. Take a gander."

Arnie walked behind the rocking chair. In his lower back, Herr Grooms had a large mass of red tissue, like a little mountain of flesh that had smoothed over the hole that had obviously been there. Surgical scars ran from it, but they had faded to near invisibility over the years. To Arnie, the wound almost looked like a spider, or some kind of nasty starfish. How could anyone survive such a wound?

"My word," he said, "you're lucky to have survived."

Herr Grooms put his shirt back down. "No. I'm lucky *she* was there."

"Who?"

"Mee-Yon Cho."

Arnie cleared the lump in his throat. *You'll get in trouble one of these days* . . . "Was she the girl who wrote those letters?"

Herr Grooms did not speak. He nodded.

"Can you tell me about her?"

Suddenly, the old man's expression and demeanor changed as he saw his wife Vellie Rae returning up the path toward the house. She cradled a basket of ripening tomatoes in her arms.

"Shh! Enough talk for today. Some other time. Now," Herr Grooms said, rising slowly from the chair and grabbing his cane with Arnie's help, "get those weeds out of the rose bushes, and then get home. Your mama's probably worried about you."

"Yes, sir," Arnie said, taken aback by Herr Grooms'

sudden change in spirit. The old man didn't even bother waiting for his wife to reach the porch. He turned and entered the house as quickly as his old bones could take him, letting the screen door slam behind him.

"What was that all about?" Mrs. Grooms asked, stopping at the bottom of the porch steps and setting her basket down.

Arnie shrugged and walked by her. What could he say? He didn't know what that was all about either. He didn't know why Herr Grooms had suddenly gone cold and curt at the sight of his wife.

It's those letters, he said to himself as he grabbed the hoe and began work. *Those letters and that girl with the exotic name.*

The girl he liked was named Jessica Yvette Tyler. *Yvette... how exotic!* Named after her mother; French in origin. He had looked it up in the Grantville library, its meaning being yew or archer. Well, she had definitely pierced his heart with her arrow.... *Get a grip, Arnie! Stop swooning like a fool.* A girl like her would want a man, one like Herr Grooms who had led his men into a hail of enemy gunfire. A man who would take a bullet for someone.

In his various waking dreams of her, Arnie had decided long ago that he would do anything for Yvette, even take a bullet. He'd decided on that first day he had seen her at school; the first time their eyes met innocently over the lunch table; the first time she smiled and waved at him across the crowded hall. Or was she waving at another boy? Of course she was, for why would Jessica Yvette Tyler wave at such a "nerd," as the up-timers often called boys like him; the booky-boys, the brains. Arnie was so studious, with a book constantly glued to his hand, with tiny wired glasses and such a thin frame that his mother had had to get him a summer job just so that he would know what it was like to make an honest day's wage. "Get out there, and get dirty," she had told him, pushing him out the door with a kiss toward the Grooms' house. "Get out there like your father used to."

Father was the kind of man who had been willing to take a bullet for someone. He had taken one for the Protestants, but he didn't survive it.

He felt kind of creepy watching her this way, as she and her friends communed outside Johnson's Grocery, having pedaled over from her home to get an ice cream on a warm afternoon. If she knew he was watching her, she'd probably flee, and rightfully so. No real man stalks a woman, as the up-timers might say. But he wasn't stalking her; not technically. He was just trying to get up the nerve to go and talk to her.

But what do you say to a vision like her? he wondered as he looked down at the dog-eared paperback in his hand. A Mickey Spillane special. Mike Hammer at his best. Borrowed from Herr Grooms' extensive collection of up-time *crime-noire* paperbacks. There was no wisdom in those pages, at least not on how a sixteen-year-old down-timer should approach a fifteen-year-old up-timer to ask her for a date. *A date?* Arnie found himself blushing at his own forwardness. *Is that what I really want?* Her parents might be strict, might not let her be seen with such a worthless creature as Arnie Langenberg, with no father and few good prospects. No. He didn't want a date. He just wanted to say "hello."

He breathed deeply and wiped sweat from his brow. The sun was setting, and Yvette wouldn't sit around the grocery store all day. He peeked out from hiding again and imagined the store as the ruined building that Herr Grooms and his men had worked to secure. He imagined Yvette and her friends as the enemy—*no, you fool!*—not the enemy. The target. And all Arnie needed to do was come out from hiding and walk over to her.

He stood up, tucked his paperback into his back pocket, and began walking across the street. At first, Yvette and her friends didn't see him. That was good, Arnie thought, because that meant they didn't see him climb out from hiding. *Play it cool, Arnie. Saunter...*

Finally, she noticed him, as he made it across the street and into the parking lot. He buried his hands into his pockets, and made at first as if he weren't paying attention. Then he turned to her, smiled, and was about to speak, when three other bikes rolled up in a whoosh of rubber tires, creaky frames, and boisterous smack talk.

Arnie had been so fixed on Yvette's face, so focused on the first word he was going to say, that he nearly ran right into them.

"Watch yourself, brainy!" Erich Becker said as he swerved to keep from ramming Arnie. The bigger, brawnier, and shirtless boy clapped on his brakes and skidded to a halt in glorious fashion in front of the girls. They scampered out of the way as if they were going to be hit, acknowledging the new arrivals with playful banter and fake outrage. The girls seemed pleased with Erich's dazzling two-wheeled showmanship. Even Yvette seemed impressed, and Arnie stopped dead in his tracks and looked round as if he were casually measuring the parking lot for drapes. He pulled the Spillane novel out and pretended to read the back.

He inched closer to their conversation without seeming as if he were doing so. They were talking fast, and their words were often interrupted with laughter and jibing. Something about horses and riding; something about a farmer up where Erich lived letting them shoot skeet. The girls didn't seem all that keen on that activity, but the horses were another matter. Decisions were made, promises tendered.

Arnie turned to leave, that leery, bashful spot in the hollow of his heart aching fully. Foiled again, like the great devious masterminds in those up-time novels, like the one in his hand. Close, but no cigar. He sighed deeply, looked both ways, then stepped out into the street.

A hand caught his shoulder and turned him around.

There she was, right *there*, mere inches from him, her body so close he could smell her light perfume. Arnie fell back, suddenly realizing that he was in the street. She smiled. "Hi, Arnie. Would you like to come with us? We're going to try to ride some horses at old man Foerster's farm."

The world was right again. Arnie breathed deeply and was about to say yes, when he looked up and saw the three boys on their bikes staring at him across the pavement. Their stern eyes and furrowed brows made it clear what his answer should be. Erich straddled his bike as if he were Atlas himself, his arms crossed, his expression pure ice.

"No . . . no," he said, waving her off. "That's okay. You guys go on."

"Are you sure?"

He nodded, too afraid to speak again lest his cowardice show.

Yvette seemed genuinely disappointed. She shrugged. "Okay, well, talk to you later then?"

He nodded and backed away across the street.

Yvette returned to her friends, and Arnie watched them ride away.

He stood there along the side of the road for a long while, letting the fragrance of her perfume ride his thoughts. He smiled. The scent reminded him of Herr Grooms' box of letters.

1st MASH Unit, Near Inchon
September 25, 1950

He awoke in a bed, his muscles stiff, his arm attached to an IV. He tried to move, but the pain in his right side, covered by thick white bandages with blood stains, kept him glued to the mattress. He managed to lift his head and look left then right. He was in a room, but it looked more like a long hallway, a half dome with row after row of beds, soldiers in every one, some wounded far more badly than he. *I guess I should be thankful*, he thought at first, then let that notion drift away from his groggy mind. The morphine coursing through his veins would not allow him to think clearly. Maybe it would have been best to die there on that desperate charge. Maybe if he had pushed himself just a little harder, he might have dodged that bullet and finished it off with his men. His men! Where were they? Had they survived? Had they—

He tried getting up again. A delicate hand held him down.

"Now, now, be still. *You* are going nowhere," a voice said, soft yet firm.

Jim pinched his eyes shut, shook his head, and refocused on the shape that stood over him on his right side. He blinked, and she came into focus. It was a woman—no doubt about that—dressed in white, the insignia of the nurses corps emblazoned on her soft blouse. She was not American.

He let her push him down, her smile guiding his head gently back to the pillow. "You must rest," she said, her English decent, but heavy with accent. "You were wounded badly."

"You're Korean," he said, not realizing the word had come out.

She smiled, and dimples on her pale face accentuated a bun of thick dark hair. Her eyes thinned to slits. Her teeth were nearly perfect, though one of her canines stuck out a little, giving her mouth an almost fang-like appearance. Jim smiled back, not caring for that one tiny imperfection. To his dreary eyes, she was perfection.

"Yes, I am. And you are an American soldier, wounded in action. And you must rest."

She leaned over and fluffed his pillow. She checked his vitals, scratched some numbers on a piece of paper attached to a clipboard. Jim refused to take his eyes off of her.

"How badly am I wounded, miss...?"

She put the clipboard back on its peg and sat down next to him, careful not to jostle the bed. The curve of her body as she sat mesmerized him; the petite nature of her frame surprised him. Standing over him, she seemed almost giantlike. Beside him, she was thin and small. He marveled. She couldn't be more than nineteen, eighteen maybe.

"My name is Mee-Yon Cho," she said, laying her hand on his chest. A warm, sleepy feeling spread through this body. "I'm glad to meet you, Corporal Jim Grooms."

Grantville
July 1636

"Then what happened?"

Arnie was literally on the edge of his seat in Herr Grooms' kitchen, listening intently, as if the old man was reading from one of his yellowing ten-cent Doubleday paperbacks. Arnie had already read a number of them; one was in his pocket now, replacing the Mike Hammer tale just that morning. He hung on every word as if they were parables. Herr Grooms looked surprised, clearly not realizing why the young boy was so enthralled with the story. Arnie hadn't told him about Yvette. He hadn't told anyone.

"Well," Herr Grooms said, sniffing and leaning back in his chair. "She was my nurse for the time I was there. Soon after that first meeting, the doctor came along and explained to me my condition. I wouldn't be going back in the field; that was certain. Losing a kidney like that, it's a life-changing experience. Going back to war would be a death sentence, and they were afraid of infection. A person can live a pretty normal life with only one kidney, but I was done. That pissed me off, I'm not ashamed to say—forgive the pun. I had gone to Korea to fight for my country, to fight for the Army, to fight the Communists, and I hadn't been in-country for long. And here I was being told that I was no longer fit to fight." He hung his head as if ashamed. "It was a tough time."

"But she helped you through, right? Mee-Yon?"

Herr Grooms perked up, sniffed again, angled his cane so that it lay against his chair in a more secure manner. "Oh, yes. Definitely. She smiled all the time, even when men, far worse off than me, were hauled in with wounds so bad that there was nothing they could do. One time, she walked by my bed alongside a stretcher. The man on it was leaking blood from his jugular, and she held a cloth over the wound as best she could, talking to him all the way, rubbing his forehead, while his life poured out of him. She was crying, and that was the first and last time I saw her cry, break down, when finally the poor boy gave up the ghost. And yet, even through something like that, she kept her spirits high. She cleaned herself up and was back making her rounds within an hour, smiling like always. She was amazing, and a damn fine nurse."

Arnie cleared his throat, measuring his words carefully. "Did you... when did you know you loved her?"

Herr Grooms smiled and rubbed his reddening face. He looked around the kitchen as if he were afraid that his wife would pop in unannounced, obviously forgetting that she and a neighbor had gone to the market. "Well, at first, I thought it was the morphine. That would wear off, however, but the feeling wouldn't subside. I looked at her the same way no matter what kind of drug I was on, had the same feeling each time. So, I guess from the very beginning, from that first time she sat down beside me and we talked. Love at first sight. Silly, eh?"

Not at all. "So, what happened next?"

"Well, I was in her care for about two weeks, and I got better as the days wore on. And she would visit me every day, several times each day. And sometimes she'd linger too long, and the head nurse would get on her case. We'd laugh about it later, after she'd come back with a little food from the mess. And when I got strong enough to try walking, she was the one who helped me with that. Whenever she'd bend down to check my temperature with a hand across the brow, I'd hope she'd come in close enough so I could steal a kiss." Herr Grooms chuckled about that. "And sometimes she'd be close enough for it, but I never tried."

"Why not?"

Herr Grooms shrugged. "Too afraid, I guess. Too worried that she might recoil from it. I wasn't sure how she felt about me, you understand. I knew how I felt about her, but behind that grand smile, those smooth cheeks, those pleasant, hopeful eyes, she was difficult to read. I didn't know how she felt, and I thought moving too fast would be a mistake. It's a decision I've regretted all my life.

"Through our letters, I did finally tell her how I felt. But I never said it to her face. I wish I had. She deserved to hear it once."

Arnie sat back, breathed deeply, taking in all that he had heard. Herr Grooms had not told the woman of his dreams how he felt, and he had spent over fifty years regretting it. How long would Arnie regret it if he didn't, at least once, approach Yvette and...

"When did you start writing letters to her?"

Herr Grooms heard the question, but he didn't give it any mind. He looked past Arnie, through the kitchen window to the setting sun. He pushed his iced tea aside and got up as quickly as his cane would allow. "Look at us ... sitting here like fools. You got me talking again, boy, and we ain't finished painting the fence we promised Mrs. Grooms we'd get finished before she got back. Come on, get up, and let's go. Grab your brush."

They walked outside, and Arnie grabbed his brush. He sighed. Painting was not on his mind right now. He wanted to tell Herr Grooms that right away, to tell him that his thoughts were on more important things, but he couldn't speak. The kinds of words he wanted to speak were not for an old man's ears.

They were for a girl named Yvette.

Arnie sat alone on a bench outside Johnson's Grocery, a small pad of paper and a pencil in his hands. He scribbled a line, marked it out, scribbled another, marked it out too. Over and over, until the page was so full of failed words that he tore it off and tossed it in the wastebasket nearby. His frustration grew.

Why can't I write like Spillane, he wondered, *or Hammett, or Chandler? Sure, they didn't write love poetry, but their words had bite, pizzazz, and punch. Why can't I write like them? Why can't I write a letter like Herr Grooms did?*

He hastily wrote a few new lines, then read them aloud, so he could hear the words. "My dearest Yvette, I want to tell you so much, but I'm afraid that if I say the wrong words at the wrong time, I'll ..."

"Hi, there."

He froze, the paper clutched tight in his hand. She was behind him. Quickly, he crumpled the paper and turned, seeing her there silhouetted against the backdrop of a setting sun. "H—Hi," he said back.

"What are you doing here?"

Her question was valid. What the hell *was* he doing here? She couldn't know the truth. "I . . . I was just jotting down a few things Frau Grooms asked me to pick up for her."

"Oh, well, I'm getting some things for my mother too. Shall we go in together?"

Yvette stepped out of the way and allowed him to take the lead. He took it, though he would have been much happier to walk behind her. He enjoyed the way she walked and the light fragrance of her hair. "Okay."

He had lied, of course, about needing to get groceries for Frau Grooms, but he played along, picking a couple potatoes and a little bit of dried bacon. Luckily, he had some money in his pocket, though he had been saving it for a newspaper. He acted like he was referring to the "list" crumpled in his hand. Yvette picked some potatoes too, and some beets, and a small container of milk. "I don't know why Mom gets beets. I hate them." She laughed, and Arnie laughed with her.

"Yeah," he said, another lie. "I hate them too."

"Are you looking forward to school starting again?"

"Yes, I am. Especially science. I'm anxious to do some dissecting."

"Gross!"

Oops! Maybe he'd made a mistake confessing that. "I—I don't really like it, but you know, it's kind of interesting to learn about things like that. Anatomy and all."

"Oh, are you thinking about being a doctor?"

The idea had crossed his mind a few times. With the arrival of the up-timers, medicine had taken a major leap forward. If he got into the profession now, by the time he was in his late twenties, he could very well be one of the premier doctors in the USE, maybe even in Europe.

He shrugged. "I don't know. I'm thinking about it. But I like to write also. Maybe I'll be a writer."

"For one of the newspapers?"

"Maybe . . . to start. But I like fiction, stories."

Yvette nodded. "I see that you're always carrying around a book. Where do you get them?"

"Herr Grooms mostly, sometimes from others. The library has some."

The small talk continued until they reached the counter, paid for their items, and left.

Ask her . . . ask her now before she turns away!

"Yvette? I mean . . . Jessica." His heart was beating so fast he could barely stand. "Would you . . . I mean, would you like to meet up here on Saturday for some ice cream? I don't have anything to do that day."

He waited for her reply, leaning against the post outside the entrance. She gave him a quizzical look, but the smile that spread across her face was all the answer he needed. "Sure. How about three?"

He nodded, taking a deep breath. "*Ja*, that's fine. See you then."

They said their goodbyes and Arnie, a smile on his face and a spring in his step, crossed the road and headed to Herr Grooms' house.

1st MASH Unit, Near Inchon
October 8, 1950

The infection had subsided. The fever was gone. It was a near-run thing, however, and Corporal Grooms felt lousy. The initial days after the wound had been hopeful, and then he had taken a turn for the worse. There were nights that he felt he wouldn't make it; Mee-Yon was there to see that he did.

He cried for morphine; she refused. He threatened. She ignored him. He clamored for a doctor, but there were too many wounded, too many more immediate concerns for them. Mee-Yon was all he had, and she ran the show. "I have seen too many men become addicted to it," she said, her beautiful mouth having difficulty sounding out the name of the drug. "I don't want that to happen to you. You will live without it; I have prayed for you."

And she was right. He survived again, and one morning he awoke pain-free with a small bit of the sun peeking through the rough green canvas of the tent he had lain in. It was cold outside, but the errant breeze that found its way through the canvas folds felt good to his sweaty skin. Mee-Yon bathed him with a sponge.

She averted her eyes when she worked his thighs. He worked hard to keep from concentrating on where her hands were rubbing, thinking of fat old Mr. Barnes from high school, or the shot that destroyed his kidney. Images that evoked disdain, disgust, anything to keep from focusing on the most beautiful woman in the world touching him in places his mother would have considered scandalous. But even with those terrible thoughts in his mind, he could not avoid the fresh fragrance of her skin, the mild curve of her lip as she hummed one of her soothing lullabies. And there was no concealing the fact that she kept looking at him, more intently than any nurse should, and he didn't keep her from doing so. Their eyes lingered on each other's faces, and he so wanted to reach out and touch her skin. But she turned away, any expression of joy erased from her face.

For the rest of the day, she avoided him, working quietly with other patients. He tried getting her attention, but she would scoot past his bed with nary a glance his way. Then she erred and drifted into his reach. He grabbed the hem of her dress and tugged. "Tell me, what's the matter? Did I do something wrong?"

She paused, turned to him, and he could see that she was fighting back tears. "No. You did nothing wrong, Jim Grooms. But . . . we are leaving. We are packing up tomorrow and heading to Seoul. And you are not coming with me. You are being sent to Japan, and then back home."

She did not wait to hear his response.

The rest of the day, he tossed and turned, ate sparingly. The idea of going home was exciting, sure, seeing family again, being safe and at peace in the West Virginia wood. But at what cost? To leave his men, his unit behind, and more importantly, to leave her behind. A million thoughts raced through his mind, none of them soothing.

The night before he left Korea forever, she came to him, quietly and without a light. She was a shadow to him, a shape in the darkness that made it even more difficult to say goodbye. She did not let him speak. She cupped his face in her hands. She kissed his forehead. She kissed his cheek. She nuzzled his neck, whispered something in her language he could not understand. She pressed a letter into his hand. She left.

He never saw her again, but the letter told him everything he needed to know.

Grantville
July 1636

"We corresponded for twenty years," Herr Grooms said, putting one of the letters back in the box.

"Even after you were married?"

That question seemed to hurt the old man as he hesitated, leaned against his cane, then pushed the box across the workbench so that he could rest his arm.

"Yes. She gave me an address in that first letter, and after I was shipped back home, I finally got up the courage to write her. Honestly, I was surprised that she wrote me back. The war was still going on, you understand, and a combat nurse's job is dangerous. It took a while for her to respond; she just wasn't in a place where she could stop and mail a letter. But she did, and I was glad about it."

"Herr Grooms," Arnie said, nervously sweeping the cold garage floor with his shoe, "I—I like this girl. Yvette Tyler. I've asked her to get some ice cream with me but—"

"You sly dog!" Herr Grooms winked and snickered.

Dog? What does a dog have to do with this? "—but I want to tell her more. I'm afraid, though, that I'll creep her out? I want to write her a letter, tell her how I feel, but—"

"Patience, my young Lothario," Herr Grooms said, walking forward. He placed his hand on Arnie's shoulder. "Take your time. Don't go from cream and sugar to marriage in one date. Hold her hand before you neck in the backseat. You understand what I'm saying? I didn't tell Mee-Yon how I felt in my first letter. I took a few years to confess it, and I still—"

"You still what?"

Arnie turned and saw Frau Grooms standing there, in the entrance to the garage, her dirty-gloved hands on her hips. Arnie looked in her face, saw anger and pain there. She looked as if she were about to cry. The look reminded him of how his mother looked when she thought of Papa.

"Vellie!" Herr Grooms said, backing away from Arnie as if he'd seen a ghost. He turned toward the workbench, toward the letters. He moved as if he were going to reach for them. Frau Grooms blocked his way.

"You still what, Jim? Still love her? You still love your Korean girl? You promised me you had gotten rid of them. You promised."

Then Herr Grooms got angry, defensive, though he could barely express it physically. "Well, I didn't, did I? And what do you care, anyway? They don't mean nothing. They're just letters."

"Just letters . . ." She trailed off, no longer able to contain her anger, her hurt. Arnie turned from them, looking for a way to slip out of the garage unseen, but before he could make a move, she said, "Well, then, there it is. You have your letters, Jim Grooms. And you can keep them. They've always meant more to you than me."

She stalked away, leaving her husband standing there,

dejected, speechless, grasping for a response to her abrupt departure. The old man mouthed something at his wife Arnie could not understand, then he turned to the letters again and fumbled through them under the faint light of the overheard lamp, as if searching for a place to hide.

Arnie left the garage and found her in their small garden, leaning over a hoe that she slammed into the dirt like a cleaver. At first, he was afraid to approach, worried that she might turn on him and sink the hoe's business end into his face, but he paused, breathed deeply, and stepped forward. "Frau, Grooms. I'm sorry. It's my fault. I found the box. I asked him what they contained. I—"

"It ain't your fault, boy!" She said, chopping away at the weeds. "You didn't write those letters, did you? You didn't make a promise to me to destroy them and then break that promise, did you? Don't cover for him, Arnie. Jimmy's had a thing for that girl for fifty years, and there ain't no down-timer gonna take the blame for it."

She let the dirt fly, but her anger finally subsided. She dropped the hoe, stepped back, rubbed a glove across her brow, and said, "I guess it's partly my fault. I've always held this notion that I could compete with a memory, that I could, in the physical, wipe away what she meant to him in the ethereal. Know what I mean?"

"No, ma'am."

She pulled off her gloves. She tossed them to the ground and moved a little closer. Arnie thought about backing off. "But . . . surely, Frau Grooms, you have meant something. You have been married for a long time, no? Over fifty years?"

She chuckled, looked up at him. "You're a good boy, Arnie. Your mother must be proud."

No, he thought. His mother had never said so directly, and she was always trying to dirty him up, get him out the door, working, toiling in sweat and muscle. She didn't seem to care much about his more intellectual pursuits, about his reading. *I don't think she is*.

"Did I hear you say that you had a girlfriend?"

Arnie shook his head. "No, ma'am. Not really. I've asked a girl to get some ice cream with me, but she's not my girlfriend."

"Well, don't pay any mind to what Mr. Grooms says. Patience is fine when it comes to gardening, hunting, or dealing with a stubborn old coot like the one I married. But it don't hold water when it comes to love. It sounds crazy coming from me, I know, but Jimmy should have gone to her a long, long time ago. He should have confessed his feelings in person. But he didn't. And he regrets it. That's why he clings to those letters. That's why they mean so much to him, because as long as they exist, there's hope, even now after we've gone through the Ring and are living in a time way before she was even born. It's silly, but that's my husband for you. An impetuous dreamer."

She placed her hand against Arnie's face, then leaned in and gave him a light kiss on the cheek. "When the time comes, young man, don't waste your time with letters. Face your girl . . . and *tell* her how you feel."

She walked away, and Arnie stood there watching her go, Yvette's smile drifting again across his confused thoughts.

☆   ☆   ☆

The ice cream was tasty. A vanilla cone with a preserved maraschino cherry on top to give it "zip," as the grocer described it. Arnie got what Yvette got, so he tried it. Too sweet for his tastes, but he smiled through it. What mattered was that he was trying it with her.

He had dressed in his best shirt, vest, and cap. He had even scrubbed his shoes and had put on clean socks. She arrived pretty much as she always did, in a light-colored dress. Sometimes she wore a hat, but not today. Her hair flowed down her back in brilliant fashion. He liked it that way. The only negative was that her mother had brought her to the store, and then proceeded to spend her time shopping while they sat on the bench outside. Arnie's enthusiasm dropped like a sail in the doldrums. Frau Tyler was a nice lady, but what boy wants a girl's mother hovering around? Arnie didn't need a chaperone. He wasn't going to try anything. *Am I?*

"Have you worked for Herr Grooms all summer?" she asked, finishing off her cherry.

Arnie nodded. "Most of it. Since his stroke, he can't do much himself. Frau Grooms does some work still, but only little things, like weeding. They have me do the big stuff." He arched his chest as if he were stretching, hoping she'd notice. "I'll be doing some reconstruction work on the concrete block support wall along his driveway. The blocks are starting to crack and break away from their mortar."

Yvette seemed impressed. "Sounds like hard work."

"Yes, but I can handle it. Herr Grooms showed me how to mix the cement, and I read up on it in the library."

She smiled. She worked on some ice cream that was running down the cone. Arnie watched her, a question on the tip of his tongue, but he shelved it and asked another. "Do you read?"

Yvette shrugged. "Some, but for school mostly. My mom has old Nancy Drews. I've tried a couple of them."

Arnie nodded. "I've read some Hardy Boys." He reached into his back pocket and pulled out a paperback. "But I've been reading a lot of this kind of book lately." He held it up to her.

Yvette squinted in the sunlight to read the title. "*The Big Sleep*. Interesting. What's it about?"

"Not what you might think," Arnie said, smiling and flipping through a few pages. "It's a crime novel, like the Nancy Drews, only better. I can read you some if you like. Or, better yet. Herr Grooms has an old VCR. It doesn't work too well anymore, but he says he can usually get it to go. He said he's got the 1978 version of the movie, with some up-timer named Robert Mitchum. I haven't seen it, but I was going to ask next week if I could." He beamed at an idea, sat up straight. "Hey, would you like to come by and watch it with me? I'm sure the Grooms wouldn't mind."

Yvette thought for a moment, then nodded. "Okay, I'll ask my mom and see what she says."

"Great! I know you'll love it. It's a little adult—well, that's what Herr Grooms calls it—but it's really good, and—"

He was interrupted by the rumble of bicycle tires on loose gravel. He looked up, and here they came, Erich Becker and his posse. Arnie's stomach clenched.

They rolled up, ground to a halt, spreading gravel and dust everywhere.

"Watch it, Erich!" Yvette said, holding her cone up high to escape the dust.

Arnie put up his hand to help protect her cone. "Back off, Erich. You're getting dirt everywhere."

Erich made a face. "Oh, is that so? Herr Brain has decided to speak. What are you trying to do here, Arnie, protect your girlfriend?"

"She's not my—" Arnie paused, refusing to finish that line. She wasn't his girlfriend, not really, but he couldn't admit that truth, not even to himself. "Just go away, will you? Leave us alone."

"Why don't you make me?"

"Erich, shut up!"

Arnie's heart raced, his stomach churned. He risked a glance toward Yvette. She was upset, angry perhaps, or more likely afraid. Her expression made Arnie mad, and he turned back to face Erich. *I have to do something. But what? What would Marlow do?*

"You want me to make you, eh?" He said, standing and tossing aside his half-eaten cone. "Okay. I'll make you, tough guy."

With his fist balled up and ready, he took a step toward Erich, but something on the bench caught one of his socks. He tried pulling away, but the impetus of his move caused him to trip, and he fell forward. Erich moved aside and let Arnie fall face-first into the gravel.

Laughter erupted. "Nice move, Herr Brain! You learn that one in a book? Come on, guys," Erich said, climbing back on his bike. "Let's go before Arnie here breaks a nail and starts to cry."

They rode away, and Arnie lay there, not wanting to move, wishing that the world would just go away, wishing that the Ring had never come and changed all their lives. Yes, life was hard before the Americans, but at least it was simpler, easier to understand.

He felt her hand on his shoulder. "Are you okay, Arnie?"

He pushed her away. "Please, leave me alone." He got up, rubbing grime and dirt out of the scrape on his left elbow. It stung. He didn't try to hide it. What was the point now? She had already seen him humiliated. "I'm sorry. I have to go."

"Wait, Arnie. Don't—"

He didn't stop. He crossed the road, not looking back, not wanting her to see his face, the fear and pain there, the embarrassment. He walked away, leaving her there holding melting ice cream.

Arnie smelled the smoke before he saw the fire. He rounded the corner of the house and found Herr Grooms standing beside the old bonfire pit in his backyard, picking letters from the box and tossing them into the flame.

"What are you doing?" He yelled to the old man. "Stop!"

Herr Grooms tossed another letter into the fire and watched it crackle and burn. "Doing what I promised her, years ago. I should have done it then. Now, why keep them? Mee-Yon doesn't even exist in this world, and probably never will."

"But they're your memories. You loved her."

Herr Grooms nodded. "Still do, but I don't need letters to remind me of that. And Vellie Rae has been patient long enough. She deserves better from me. It's time."

Arnie wanted to lash out, to knock the box from Herr Grooms' hands, but that would be stupid, disrespectful. And what would it accomplish anyway? They weren't his letters; Herr Grooms could do whatever he wanted with them. But to burn them, to throw away all that sentiment, to walk away from a relationship so fully defined by words and paper, a relationship more real than Arnie had ever experienced himself, more real than the one he was trying to have with Yvette. How could that be thrown away? He wanted to cry.

Herr Grooms upended the last letters into the fire, then tossed in the box as well. They stood there together, watching as the heat and smoke spread slowly through the old, yellowing paper. "Mrs. Grooms said you went on a date with that girl you mentioned?"

Arnie shrugged. "Yeah, we got some ice cream."

"How'd it go?"

Arnie's heart sank. "Not very well."

Herr Grooms huffed and turned on his cane. "Well, what the hell you standing around here for? There ain't no work for you to do today. Go find her, and make it right. You got one big advantage over me and Mee-Yon. Your girl ain't thousands of miles away, in another timeline. Go!"

The old man walked away, and Arnie watched him go. When Herr Grooms disappeared through his porch screen door, Arnie knelt beside the pit, stuck out his hand, and plunged it into the fire.

Her mother greeted him at the door. Arnie removed his cap quickly. "Good evening, Frau Tyler. I'm sorry to disturb you, but may I speak to Yvette—I mean—Jessica?"

She noticed the white bandage on his hand. "My word, what happened to you? Are you okay?"

He smiled. "Yes, ma'am. It's just a little burn."

She nodded. "Wait here."

She went back inside, and another silhouette joined her behind the door. They spoke a few indiscernible words, then Yvette emerged with a smile. He stepped back and let her come out on the porch. She noticed his hand as well.

"Are you okay?"

He nodded. "Yes, nothing to worry about. Just a small burn. It's healing already."

She grabbed his injured hand and stroked the fibers with tender fingers. "Poor thing."

"I—I wanted to come by and apologize for running off on you today. I didn't mean to do that. But—well—"

"That's okay. I know it wasn't your fault. Erich's a jerk! I'm not hanging around him or his friends anymore."

Arnie nodded, sniffled. He put his cap back on, fumbled around with the bandage, trying desperately to delay. But she stood there, her eyes staring deeply into his face, not blinking, waiting. "Yvette...there's a lot I want to say to you, but I don't know where to start."

"Wait," she said, taking his hand again and leading him onto the porch, away from the door. She whispered, "My mother is listening, so don't say anything."

She grew sullen and sad. "Arnie, I wanted to tell you at Johnson's. I—I'm not allowed to date until I'm seventeen. I asked my parents if I could go watch that movie with you, and they said no. The subject matter is too adult, whatever that means." She shook her head, rolled her eyes. "Anyway, what I wanted to tell you was that, I like you. A lot, and if you will be patient with me, seventeen isn't that far off."

In a matter of seconds, his emotions went from utter defeat at the fact that she couldn't date, to the faint sliver of hope that within a couple years, she could. Sweat began to build on his brow. He wanted to wipe it away, but he didn't. He couldn't move his arms, so fixed he was on her soft expression, her kind, searching eyes. "Okay...I can wait."

She jumped a little, then reached into the pocket of her dress and fished out a note. A letter, folded twice and tucked neatly in a beige envelope. "Here, I wrote you this," she said, still whispering. "It tells you how I feel about you. And maybe some of my words are yours as well."

She leaned in and kissed him on the cheek. "Bye, Arnulf Langenberg. I'll see you around."

He opened the letter as he walked away. The faint light of the moon made it difficult to read, but he figured it out. Most of it. And he was happy, for Yvette was right.

Her words *were* his words.

Grantville
August 1636

Herr Grooms was in an anxious mood. "No, do it like I showed you, boy," he said, waving his cane at Arnie as the boy worked his trowel through the thick mortar in the wheelbarrow. "Mix it up right, and slather it on thick. Let the brick settle, then scrape it clean. Understand?"

"Yes, Herr Grooms."

"I'll come back and check on you soon."

Arnie did as he was told, set three concrete blocks in place as directed, until he was certain Herr Grooms was inside the house and well into his nap. Arnie smiled, reached into his pocket, and pulled out Mee-Yon's letter. The one he had saved from the fire.

He opened it carefully and read the passage that had not been burned. The lines were precise and straight, as if she had used a ruler. Her English was spotty, articles missing here and there, but it hardly mattered. The sentiment was there, the love, and whether Herr Grooms would admit it or not, he needed her words, like Arnie had needed Yvette's. Her letter was tucked into his latest Chandler novel and would be in every novel from here to 1638 until he could cash in on her promise.

"Well, Herr Grooms, you may have thought you burned them all, but you didn't. Your Korean girl will be with you always." He rolled the letter up and tucked it into one of the cement blocks. "Take care of him, Frau Mee-Yon. He needs you now more than ever."

And with a smile, Arnie scooped up a trowel of mortar and buried the letter.

A Sucker Born Every Minute

Phillip Riviezzo

March 1635
Naumburg

Lamplight flickered over the table as Jan partitioned out what profits they had made the past few days. After subtracting costs of buying more food, care for the horses, repairs to the wagons, and the requisite contribution to their threadbare emergency fund, not much was left to share around.

Kurt took his handful of coins glumly—but then, the ruddy-faced dwarf did most things glumly, except when he was drunk. And he was drunk quite a bit of the time, having the alcohol capacity for a man twice his size and the thirst of two men that size. The money went into his pouch, as it always did, but Jan knew a good portion of it would disappear into tankards of ale before they left town, and the rest into more tankards when they arrived at the next one. Kurt was his friend as much as his client, and had been ever since the two of them met in a coastal tavern. Both roaring drunk, they'd sworn a partnership to tour

Europe's countrysides, showing off an authentic dwarf to villagers who had never seen the inside of a royal court where dwarves were still in fashion.

Marie counted her share of the pot carefully, dropping each coin one at a time into the small pouch she kept in a pocket of her dress or beneath her bed at night. They would stay there, gradually hoarded, until she had saved up enough to buy a tiny bottle of expensive perfume, or a handful of colorful ribbons— trinkets and scents to enjoy in privacy, letting her feel like the lady she wanted so desperately to be for a short while. Her table-length beard was neatly groomed, but as soon as they had left town, Jan knew the woman would be hard at work with a razor in her wagon. Shaving off the rest of her tangled body hair would give her a day or two of itch-free relief, and still leave enough time to grow enough arm and facial hair for a proper display at the next fair.

Between now and then, she'd also tell Jan just how close to destitution they were this time. At nineteen, she had as good a head for numbers as any man he'd known, far better than Jan himself, and handled the troupe's account book. Buying her custody from those who had presumably been her parents—Jan preferring to think of it as paying ransom for a hostage—had been one of the best investments he had made in his life. From the perspective of the French peasant girl, life as a traveling oddity was undoubtedly heaven compared to years of imprisonment in the basement of a tiny peasant cottage, and who knew what sort of mistreatment by superstitious village priests attempting to purify whatever demonic curse left her with body hair rivaling the hairiest of mountain men.

Furthermore, Jan had never tried to impose himself on her as a less scrupulous manager might have. She was a woman, and minus the hair a quite attractive young woman at that... but there was the hair. He'd truly never so much as been tempted, and instead their relationship had become a sort of odd fusion between friend, father-surrogate, and manager.

With his typical taciturn lack of expression, Albrecht swept the meager share of profit in front of him into his own coin pouch, where they bounced and rattled alongside the rest already there. As with Marie, Jan knew those coins would be hoarded until the troupe reached a sufficiently well-populated city, but Albrecht wouldn't spend his earnings. Instead, he always packed what money he'd collected securely and brought it to a courier office, for delivery to parts unknown. For that matter, Jan didn't really know much about where Albrecht had come from before the day he'd approached Jan in the wake of a show with inquiries as to a possible job. A few demonstrations of his incredible-approaching-inhuman flexibility had served as an audition, yet aside from a rare habit of emitting bouts of profanity in what Jan was fairly certain was Italian when drunk, none of them had so much of an inkling regarding the soft-spoken contortionist's past.

Regarding his own equally lackluster personal earnings—as opposed to the money used communally to keep all of them in business—Jan pondered, as he all too frequently did, how the third son of a prosperous Dutch merchant ended up managing a trio of malformed and outcast human beings as they displayed their aberrant appearances for the amusement or horror of townsfolk and villagers. With two elder brothers between him and ownership of the family firm, he had never considered, nor wanted, a prominent role in the business. At best, his education and natural talent for oratory could have given him a position recruiting new customers or bargaining with suppliers.

Unfortunately for him, he'd been on one of the family ships when a freak North Sea storm sent it to the bottom of the waters. He and a handful of other survivors had clung to assorted wreckage for two days before luckily being rescued by another merchant ship heading the opposite direction. The ship was easily replaceable. Jan, on the other hand, walked away from his near-death experience with an overpowering terror of open waters larger than a river. There was no place in a Dutch shipping firm, son or not, for a man who feared the ocean and could not set foot on a ship with his senses intact. It was live on family charity or find a job on land, and Jan's pride demanded the latter. He'd come close to signing up as a mercenary soldier, but encountered Kurt in that tavern before taking the martial plunge.

The four of them, touring through France and Austria and the Germanies, had been able to eke out a passable living for a time. They migrated from town market to village seasonal fair, and where neither could be found, gave some small inn a night's entertainment for food and a place to park the wagons overnight. They would have never been rich, but there was enough cash in the hands of curious and bored commoners, or very rarely an idle local nobleman demanding a command display, to keep them fed, clothed, and comfortable.

But war had not been kind to Europe in recent years, and even in the lands not ravaged by armies the belts got tighter and the purses smaller. Jan had heard stories of a genuinely bizarre man—an Italian by the name of Lazarus, whose half-born twin brother hung grotesquely out of his stomach—traveling the cities and courts of Europe to market himself much as Jan marketed their troupe, and to much greater success. If only he'd been born Italian, and in a place to forge a partnership with the Italian Lazarus instead of the German Kurt. The thought faded quickly, though, beneath the ingrained habits of a life's Calvinist upbringing, and disappeared entirely as Kurt broke the morose silence.

"Where to next, Jan?"

Marie and Albrecht looked over at him as well, and Jan felt the weight of authority bearing on his shoulders once more. He took out the schedule of fairs and festivals they'd accumulated, folding it down to the relevant section of Germany, and spread a map over the tabletop. "It looks like our best odds are heading south, through Rudolstadt, and planning for the big summer fair in Saalfeld, then continuing on toward Nuremburg."

Albrecht spoke up, laying one long finger on Saalfeld and moving it a hairsbreadth westward. "What about here?"

Jan and the others stared down at the dot labeled "Grantville." They'd all heard about the amazing town full of people from the distant future. By this point it'd be difficult to find a man in Europe who had not heard the news. Jan had even seen a few of them when the troupe passed through Magdeburg some weeks past. Even in a crowd, the up-timers stood out unless making an effort to blend in. But he'd never considered actually going there.

"Why d'ya want to go to Grantville, Albrecht? They're all mechanical wizards from the future there. I'll bet where they come from a dwarf sits on every street corner, a bearded lady stands in every shop window, and all of them down to the babes can tie their own limbs into knots. We'd be nothing special. There's no money to be made there."

Kurt was as surly as ever, but Marie looked at the map with a wistful expression. "Do you really think so, Kurt? It might be nice, to see a place where no one looks twice at us. I'd like to spend a few days being normal."

"And if not, there might be something there we can use, or someone who can use us. It's not as if our options are increasing, Jan, and there's more than enough time for us to detour there and still make Saalfeld's fair."

He couldn't argue with Albrecht's logic, either part. Nor was Albrecht often wrong when he chose to comment. Truthfully, Jan wasn't the only one who wanted to see something wondrous for a change, rather than being (or selling) the wonder. Grantville it was.

Grantville
April 1635

It was incredibly difficult not to stop and gawk as the small caravan made its way down the main street of Grantville, but the trio of horse-drawn wagons was just large enough to make a significant obstruction in the thoroughfare. Seeing as how one of the primary aims of their visit to the town was not drawing close attention to themselves, Jan felt causing a roadblock on their first day there was contraindicated. Albrecht, driving the second vehicle, was undoubtedly of a similar mind. However Kurt felt about the matter, he would be too busy keeping the horse pulling the third wagon on a steady course to rubberneck at his surroundings. What he lacked in muscle power was made up for in volume, and the poor beasts were by this point thoroughly intimidated by the bellowing dwarf, but it was still a task for full-time attention. Marie, inside the wagon Albrecht was driving, could see nothing at all.

The first step was to find a hostelry with enough space to accommodate them. That took a fair bit of time to accomplish, but eventually an inn was located at the perfect confluence of yard space (plenty) and room price (cheap) for the troupe to afford. The somewhat dilapidated condition of said inn, and its distance from the bustle of downtown, were undoubtedly contributors to these facts, but Grantville remained enough of a vibrant economy that the business stayed afloat.

A long-sleeved dress and hooded shawl were Marie's usual attire on the infrequent occasions she went out in public. Keeping her head down to hide her face meant next to no attention from the innkeeper or any of the other guests, particularly with Kurt to look at instead as Jan rented two middling-quality rooms for a weeklong stay. From there, the three men drifted out separately.

Kurt interrogated the innkeeper with regards to the source of Grantville's best beer, and left for someplace called the Thuringen Gardens, mildly befuddled by the other man's fascination with his short stature and how quickly it became mundane. With any luck, he wouldn't get into trouble this time; too much beer broke Kurt's usual sullen immunity to taunts about his size from strangers, and where a regular-sized drunkard would resort to fists, Kurt had a tendency to go straight for his knives. He'd yet to kill anyone, or be killed, but it was always a constant worry for Jan. Americans were said to be quite fair as civil authorities went, but that simply meant they'd collect evidence before hanging a murderer, dwarf or otherwise.

Albrecht asked for and received directions to the couriers, or "post office," and set off on his own errands. Where all that money was sent, Jan had no idea. He'd asked once out of curiosity, and been rebuffed in such a vehement and atypical display of emotion that the subject was never broached again.

After checking that Marie was settled in her room, Jan set out trailing the other two, with no specific destination in mind other than sightseeing. At a gentle stroll, he looked here and there at buildings of obvious up-time design and construction, outstanding amidst the sprawl of down-time construction produced by four years of enthusiastic expansion. Polite nods came from up-timers he passed on the street, who seemed to be in a similar proportion to down-time immigrants as their buildings were.

Pausing at one corner to rest his legs, his eye settled on an up-time building across the street, the sign outside proclaiming it to be the Grantville Public Lending Library. Grantville was famous for its weapons, machines, and attitudes, but it had been the printed books brought back from the future that changed the fortunes of kings and princes. Idly, Jan wondered if those same books could change his fortunes as easily.

Inside, the building was brightly lit despite the relative lack of windows, thanks to a series of heatless lamps attached to the ceiling—an up-time mechanical marvel, evidently. Long rows of books on shelves filled the entry room and at least two adjoining chambers, comparable to a bare handful of private collections Jan had seen in his youth, but far beyond anything usually accessible to commoners. Behind a large desk to one side, a woman not much older than Jan himself looked up from her work with a smile.

"Can I help you?"

"Perhaps. Do you have any books about traveling shows? Entertainers and performers, going from one town to the next?"

"Do you mean, like, a circus?"

It took a few moments for Jan to retrieve the word from distantly remembered Latin lessons—great arenas of the ancient Romans, spectacles of bloody "entertainment." "Something like that, I think."

"I went to see the circus as a little girl, once. I wanted to go down and climb on the elephants, and almost got sick on cotton candy. What about them were you interested in?"

"Their masters. I'm curious to learn about your up-time showmen, the men who ran these 'circuses.' Who was the greatest show master of the world you came from, and how he managed it. That sort of thing."

The woman pursed her lips in thought. "I couldn't say for certain who was the greatest circus manager up-time, but I can certainly point you toward someone who thought he was."

After a short burst of activity at the device on her desk, she rose and headed toward one of the side rooms, gesturing for him to follow. As they walked, he spoke up again. "What were these circuses you had up-time? I know the origin of the word, but you may have used it differently."

Her reply was a cheerful, somewhat rambling narrative of performers and acrobats, buffoons and trained animals, and strange foods, all together under a structure called the "big top," recited while the helpful woman found her destination shelf and began running a finger along its contents. A small book proved her goal, triumphantly retrieved and handed across to him—*The Life of P.T. Barnum, Written by Himself.*

"Back up-time, they called Barnum and Bailey's Circus 'The Greatest Show on Earth.' If anyone qualifies to be up-time's greatest showman, P.T. Barnum is probably it. I'm afraid it's in English, though. No one has expressed interest in translating it. Can you read English?"

Jan matched her smile with one of his own, replying in English. "Enough to get by, I think I can manage. My thanks, *Frau* . . . ?"

"Calafano. Cecilia Calafano."

She offered a hand, and Jan shook it in the up-time fashion after spying the ring adorning one finger and quashing his initial impulse to kiss it instead. "Jan Barentsen. A pleasure, Frau Calafano."

"Likewise. Checking books out requires Grantville residency, if you plan on staying. Otherwise, you're welcome to stay and read until closing hours, and I can set it aside for you to continue tomorrow."

Accepting of the terms, Jan took his prize and

settled down at the nearest table, opening the slightly battered tome.

"Few men in civil life have had a career more crowded..."

When the librarian returned to close up for the night, it took three tries to break him free of the book. She took it away gently, adding it to the top of a small pile dominated by a book depicting a man wrapped in chains.

On the third day of their visit, Jan convinced the rest of the troupe to come with him. The library failed to impress anyone else to the same degree, thanks to assorted individual degrees of shyness, impassivity, or hangover. It was not the volume of books Jan had brought them to see, but one in particular, sitting somewhat forlornly on its shelf where he had left it after reading and from which he retrieved. Later, he would discuss the tricks of the illusionist Houdini with Albrecht, but this was for all of them to share.

"Albrecht suggested we come to Grantville in hope it would have something we could use, and he was right. This is the history of an up-time pioneer of entertainers, a master showman. He took what was ordinary, and made his fortune by convincing people it was extraordinary. He sold stories as much as he did shows, and succeeded so well that his business bore his name a hundred years after he died."

Finding a table with enough chairs for everyone, Jan opened to the story of General Tom Thumb and began to read, doing his best to translate.

Saalfeld
May 6, 1635

Jan wiped his palms on his trousers, looking over the small crowd of townsfolk gathered in the darkened tent. There were more of them than a first showing usually drew when he set up shop at a new fair, but not a great deal more. If this didn't pan out like he was counting on, the extra money the troupe had spent preparing for their "new look" could leave them all in somewhat dire straits. There was, however, only one way to find out for sure.

Showtime.

Standing on the elevated lectern, he lit the lamps next to him, illuminating him with light and drawing the eyes of the crowd to where he stood at the front of the tent with hanging curtains on either side. "Good sirs, gentle ladies, welcome to the first showing of Barentsen's Fantastic Display of Living Wonders! I am Jan Barentsen, and today you shall feast your eyes upon sights you have never dreamed of, amazing human oddities of unusual appearances and origins! When you tell stories to your grandchildren, many years from now, the tale they will clamor for most will be the day that you paid to see what you are about to witness."

So far, not bad. No one was leaving, and no one looked incredibly bored.

"Thus, without further hesitation, the first of the three fantastic spectacles I bring today to your town. There was once a mine, from which men worked long to dig coal from the earth. Their foreman was tall and strong, and led his crew with skill. Yet one day, disaster struck! A support gave way, and the tunnel began to collapse. As the miners fled to safety, their brave foreman stepped forth and took the weight of the tunnel upon his own back, bearing the world on his shoulder as did the Titan of mythic Greece. Only when the last of his crew had fled did he allow them to pull him free as well, and by then that immense weight had left its mark, crushing him down to half his size. So thus a mighty giant did fall, and thus to you I bring today...Atlas, the Shrunken Titan!"

With a tug, he hauled back on a rope, pulling the leftmost curtain aside. On his now-revealed platform, Kurt posed with dramatic exaggeration, flexing his biceps at the audience. His tight, colorful shirt and breeches were well stuffed to resemble bulging muscles, and when he knelt to lift the cloth-over-wood "boulder" above his head, several sets of breath drew in from the audience. Jan gave Kurt a few more seconds to show off, then raised his hand again for attention.

"Before this next tale, the faint of heart amongst those gathered here should be warned to steel themselves. Many miles from here, in distant France, a young bride with impending child and her husband did go for a comforting walk in the forest near their home. To their misfortune, it was the husband who fell and injured himself, senseless and helpless. His wife called for help, but drew at first not men, only the attention of ravenous beasts, a pack of savage wolves! About the couple they prowled, drawing ever closer, and it was surely the fate of both to be devoured where they lay. Salvation came as huntsmen appeared, hearing the lady's cries of distress to drive the fell beasts away. Yet, the terror she had known never left her, and the experience forever marked her. Months later, the couple's child was born . . . but woe! for what came forth was half man, and half beast, covered in fur and bearing sharp fangs no human child could possess. See now, as she has grown, the one and only Wolf-Lady!"

The curtain slid aside at his pull, behind which Marie sat demurely in her usual chair on the small stage. They had paid a carpenter to build the wooden cage surrounding her, including the false rear wall— the other three sides as solid as any true cage would be. For the new show, they had trimmed and shaped her facial hair and beard into a close approximation of a lupine visage, shorted the sleeves of her dress to reveal the tangled hair of her forearms, and glued small, pointed bits to the ends of her fingernails.

"Do not fear, for despite her terrible appearance, she is as meek and proper as any could be. Yet be wary, for when the moon hangs full and high in the night, it is the bestial portion of her soul that rises strong within."

On cue, Marie reached forward to grip the bars of her cage with fake claws, baring her teeth in a sort of grimace and giving the crowd what Jan thought was a rather lackluster growl. Evidently they disagreed, though. Quite a few closest to the front went slightly pale and pulled back into the safety of the group, even after she settled back calmly into her seat.

This time, the assembled townsfolk turned back to him with some reluctance, occasionally sneaking sidelong or outright glances at Kurt and Marie on their platforms. "And finally, to you from the far distant lands of the exotic Mughal Empire, a tale of heathen magic and the infinite mercies of God. In faraway temples, sorcerers toy with power no man should carry, transgressing in heresy as their dark spells warp exotic beasts and animals into semblances of Man's blessed form. Yet by being given Man's body, they now share in both Man's sin and his grace, and the luckiest of them find solace. Here, today, is one such would-be man, an animal freed of its evil creators and taught as a child ignorant yet innocent. Here, today, is The Human Serpent!"

For his new look, Albrecht had found a skin dye that darkened his flesh to the brown of a Mughal. Lying on his belly as the curtain revealed him, he slid forward to the edge before rising up on his knees. From there, he bent backwards, curling into a chest stand and staring at the hushed audience from between his now-spread legs. His eyes narrowed, he waved his outstretched tongue at the watchers with a hiss, flipped his legs over his head, and slowly rose to his feet without using his arms for balance.

This was the riskiest of the troupe's new looks. For some reactionaries, the story they'd concocted might be enough to justify charges of peddling witchcraft, and Jan eyed his onlookers with no small amount of anxiety. No one seemed angry, though, at best shocked and mostly fascinated by Albrecht's sinuous movements back and forth.

One by one, Jan pulled on his second set of ropes, sliding the curtains between each "wonder" and the audience closed, then clapped a final time to draw eyes. "Wonders I promised, and wonders you have seen! Let them stick forever in your memory, and should there be charity in your hearts to aid the care and comfort of these benighted souls, you may leave coins in the bowl by the exit. We will remain until the end of the fair. Tell your friends, your families, of what you have seen today and let them experience such sights for themselves. Good day, and thank you!"

The generous heap of money going into his cash-box was an excellent promise for the future, Jan decided. Overall, they had taken in nearly twice as many visitors—and twice as much profit—as a fair this size usually produced. Even after the expenses for the new displays and costumes, there had still been a great deal more than usual for the four of them to split. The tensest moment had been late in the second day, when the pastor of the town church and his assistant came to view the show and linger afterwards. But when Jan and Albrecht explained the truth of Albrecht's flexibility, the latter reading a few lines of Scripture to prove his humanity, the church-men went away satisfied.

A beggar caught his eye as he neared the edge of the market square, and Jan paused to toss a coin into the legless man's bowl. Almost too fast to follow, the beggar flipped his bowl into the opposite hand and snatched the flying coin out of midair for deposit, all without spilling a single pfennig. Amused and impressed, Jan tossed another coin toward the bowl, and the crippled man repeated his trick in reverse. Jan started to turn away, but stopped as an idea struck him, and he looked back at the beggar with closer scrutiny. Both stumps ended just above the knee, yet those brawny arms, shriveled by slow malnutrition as they were, could only have belonged to a sailor even if the tattoos had not given it away. Flashbacks of the shipwreck fluttered in the back of Jan's mind, but he quashed them brutally. Stepping closer, he met the man's suspicious glower with his friendliest smile. "What is your name, friend?"

Balancing on his hips and pulling the bowl of coins protectively close, he replied somewhat grudgingly, "Jacob."

"A pleasure to make your acquaintance, Jacob. My name is Jan, and I might have a job offer to make you. Have you ever considered learning how to juggle?"

No, John, No!

Jack Carroll and Terry Howard

The Mountain Top Baptist Bible Institute
West Virginia County
Early summer, 1636

Martha Button woke up alone in a strange bed.

A strange bed, in itself, was no novelty by now. There had been one strange bed after another since the family's desperate flight from Cambridge, and some nights no bed at all. But being alone at any time was altogether out of the ordinary.

As the mists of a troubled dream dissipated, she came to herself, opened her eyes, and looked around at the unfamiliar room. The very cozy, welcoming room, with its varnished pine walls, braided rug, and gently blowing curtains. And remembered.

With a start, she realized that the sun was already pouring full into the room. There were sounds of people moving about their tasks on the floor below. And yet, she had slept on into the morning and done nothing this day of whatever her yet-to-be-explained obligations might be. She swung to her feet, pulled up the coverlet, dressed in haste, and hurried from the "new barn" where she and her family had been quartered on the second floor, across to the kitchen in the house, expecting a scolding.

"Sister Friedeberger, I . . ."

Katerina Friedeberger turned from the cupboard where she was just putting away a stack of plates, and smiled at her. "Good morning, Sister Button. Are you feeling more like yourself today? You looked like you were about to drop where you stood, by the time you let us lead you off to bed yesterday afternoon."

"But I did so little! I didn't mean to shirk, but . . ."

"After traveling all the last day coming here, then praying all night at the hospital for your stepmother and your new sister, and giving blood besides? Really, we didn't expect any of you to do anything but sleep around the clock recovering from it all. I tell you, you all surprised us.

"But you haven't eaten yet, yes?" She reached for a bowl, ladled in something from a pot on the back of the stove, and handed it to Martha. She fluttered one hand toward the dining room table. "You can sit there. You like sausages? There are a couple left in the pan, I'll just warm them up again." She did something to the front of the stove, and there was a soft *whump*.

Martha found herself floundering. She took the bowl, and a spoon the older woman handed her, and stood uncertainly in the doorway to the dining room. "But shouldn't I be doing something?"

"Well. After you eat, girl. We'll talk then. I'll show you where things are and how they work." She hefted a pot with a spout, and set it down again. "The chamomile tea is all gone, I'm sorry to say. I'll pour you a glass of cold water. The water here is safe, did anybody tell you?"

Tears threatened to come as Martha sank onto a wooden chair and set down the bowl in front of her. "Sister Friedeberger, I'm overwhelmed by your kindness. Yours, and everyone's. Father said we would be among friends when we finally reached this place. It seems it is so."

The first thing Katerina put in front of Martha was a book. This was yet another new thing; she had heard of books of cookery, but never seen a book in a kitchen. But this was not a printed book, nor was it bound. The handwritten pages were encased in some soft material as clear as glass, yet as thin as paper, and they were held by metal rings passing through holes in the pages and fixed to the covers.

It was lying open to a page headed "Potato Chowder." As she looked at it, Katerina was explaining, "The recipe calls for peeling them, but we don't do it that way here. I just cut them up small so they cook down in the soup. Like this." She took up a knife lying on the worktable and cut off a slice, then cut it crosswise to make some pieces about the width of her little finger. "Sister Green told us there are important things in the skins that we need in our diet, and she should know. I could name some oh-so-proper people who will happily tell you that's no way to make a soup, but we have better things to do with our time than unnecessary work, don't we?" She grinned. "You're well enough rested to use a knife today, yes?"

Martha barely had time to nod "Yes."

"Good, good. I'll get the water started heating while you're getting the potatoes ready to go in, so we can have it done in time for lunch. Once the soup's going, we can finish off the breakfast pots."

Katerina took down a large pot from a hook and carried it to a sort of basin fixed to the wall. She turned a handle on a metal fitting projecting above it, and water poured out of a spout.

Pipe-borne water here in the kitchen as well? Oh, yes, I should have foreseen it.

"Oh, and after lunch Brother Green wants to meet with you. There are your studies to plan."

My studies?

Clearing away after lunch was yet another surprise. Instead of leaving the dishes where they were for a couple of the women to take away and attend to, the whole company around the two dining tables rose and formed a line to the worktable in the kitchen, and started passing plates and serving bowls from hand to hand. In a remarkably short time, it was done, and one of the men set to wiping up the spills.

Before Martha could figure out her place in what was clearly a well-practiced routine, Brother Albert Green looked her way and smiled. "Ready to sit down and talk?"

"Oh! Oh, yes! Where shall we ... ?"

"In my study." He turned and led her through the parlor and around the corner, into a large, sunny side chamber.

Her jaw dropped. Two whole walls were lined with bookshelves from floor to ceiling, and stuffed so full of books and manuscripts that there wasn't room to stand them all upright. Some were lying on their sides atop the filled rows.

As a printer's daughter, Martha had dealt with books often enough, usually proofs or uncut sheets, now and then a whole book. On a few occasions she had accompanied Father on business to the university library and seen the great collection there. But that was the accumulation of centuries, in a rich university with many endowments and land holdings. There were not so many books as that here, but this college of their small and scattered faith was said to be only a year old and not at all wealthy. How was such a thing possible?

But surely this library was for the learning of those destined to preach the faith, the men. The lot of women in this world— Suddenly she felt as if she were starving, in the midst of a bakery. Before she could carry the thought further, her host waved her toward one of the chairs in the room, and sat down himself. His eyes crinkled for a moment. "I'm sorry we had to rush all of you around the other night, without time to explain much of anything."

Sorry? For serving all her family with his own hands the moment they arrived at the end of the long journey, and then without an instant's hesitation carrying Stepmother to the only doctors in the world capable of saving both her and the baby? Before she could open her mouth to express her gratitude, he went on.

"Your father and your brother John have enrolled as divinity students. Right now the rest of you are here as family members, but that's not the only choice you have. What you should do now, and what you should study, depend on what you want in life. So let's start with that. What are your thoughts?"

Nobody had ever asked her that. Indeed, she had never thought of asking herself that. "Do? Well, I'm a printer's daughter. It was thought that I would marry a printer and be a printer's wife, knowing the trade well enough to put my hand to it, and perhaps to the apprentices at need. I can set type and correct proof in English, French, and Latin, and Stepmother has been instructing me in keeping accounts. There was a suitor in England, but he wasn't really of our own faith, and I'm not sure he was even sincerely of the Church of England. And he wanted the press and fonts Stepmother inherited from her first husband as a portion of my dowry, which Father would not agree to. Father had thought to bring us all to Massachusetts and find me a husband there so we could all be together, and have the press with us to carry on our trade, but it was not to be. And we had to flee without the press. So, now? How is the printing trade here? Would I have prospects?"

He sat silently for a few moments, turning from side to side in his chair, before he spoke. "Probably. There's a whole lot of printing being done around here. We'll know better when your father and brother get back from the errand I sent them on—they're visiting all the print shops, finding out what we'd have to do to get some of these reprinted." His hand swung vaguely around at the books surrounding them. "But this is West Virginia County. It's not like the guild towns, where all the trades are tied up with rules and practically nobody can get in. Even the traditional trades are pretty free around here, and the new trades and professions are pretty much wide open to anybody who can learn them. Want to be a doctor or a machinist?

You could if you're smart enough, and I think you are. For that matter, there's nobody to say you couldn't set up in the printing business yourself. Not in this town." He stopped again for a few heartbeats, and put one hand to his chin. Then he turned and took a thick pamphlet from a stack of papers on the desk behind him, and handed it to her. "I think maybe a good way to start is to make this your first piece of study material and talk again tomorrow, after you've had a chance to absorb it and think about it."

She saw at first glance that it was cheaply printed, on a thin, somewhat grayish paper, in an Italian typeface. Then she took in the cover page.

> *Getting Acquainted with Grantville Laws,*
> *Customs, Society, and the Working World*
> *by Sarah Cochran Reardon*
> *and William Oughtred*

She stared for a short moment. It was not unheard of that a woman would be one of the authors of a published work, but the first one handed to her in Grantville?

The Bible Institute was no monastery, but it had at least one Rule. Father had said it: All share in the bounty, and all share in the work. It could hardly be otherwise. The seminary was a place of learning, but it was also a home to the students and those accompanying them, and a farm that fed them all. Schools, homes, and farms all mean work.

That afternoon Martha wielded a hoe in the grain field. A student named John Stewart, perhaps a few

years older than her nineteen by the look of him,
showed her the manner of it. He was dressed for
work the way the up-timers did, and spoke much
like them, yet there was a flavor of Scotland in his
speech. A long, straight scar on one forearm where
his sleeve was rolled up spoke of battle sometime in
his past. Well, this was the Germanies, and there had
been battle enough everywhere. He pointed with the
handle of his tool.

"It's easy enough telling crops from weeds. You see
these rows? The seeds weren't broadcast; they were
driven into the ground with a seed drill. It's a mechanical thing on wheels, a great help. So everything that
belongs here is in a row. Anything that isn't, is a weed.
If you see something in a row you're not sure about,
leave it, because there are three different grains all
mixed together. Something's bound to thrive."

They fell into conversation as the sun crossed the
heavens, working along with a few rows between them
for elbow room. Some of it was mundane enough,
what the weather was like hereabouts, what crafts
were practiced on the farm, what plants grew in odd
patches that could be steeped for a tea. After a time
they spoke of what they had done in life, and what
they hoped to do. Martha supposed they were more
or less chaperoned, being within clear sight from the
house. Anyway, he was polite, and good enough to
look upon. And so the afternoon drew on.

When the college sat again at table, it was left to
Sister Claudette Green to bring the glad news that
Stepmother was gaining in her recovery, and that tiny
Providence still lived, though she required constant
care in that incubator, and likely would for weeks to

come. "I got to spend a few minutes with Melisa just before I left for the day. She's doing all right. The doctor thinks she might be able to leave the hospital in a few more days, and finish recovering up here. They're already cutting down on her pain medication. She's awake some of the time and reading a Bible to pass the time."

Father and John heard that news from Sister Green, the same as everyone else. Though they'd ranged from one end of Grantville to the other in the course of the day, their commission on behalf of the college left them no more chance to visit the hospital than Martha and her younger brothers had. After a brief prayer of thanksgiving, their contribution to the dinner conversation was a meticulous recounting of what they'd seen and heard in the print shops they'd visited so far. The printing arts here, it seemed, differed even more from what they'd known in England than Master Triebel's shop in Hamburg had. That was something to think upon.

Martha could have gone to their quarters across the yard to begin reading the pamphlet, but at that moment she wanted to be with company, even if some of the other women were carrying on a spirited study time in the dining room. Her younger brothers Andrew and Harry were seated at one end of the smaller table, puzzling out answers to questions on a "placement test." They were to be sent to school in town; that was already decided.

She settled into a soft chair in the parlor. This time of year, there was still daylight enough to read by. Soft music was coming from a cloth-fronted box atop a cabinet in a corner; the heavy paper sleeve leaning against the contrivance proclaimed it to be the work of an English composer of the eighteenth century, performed by a Swiss chamber ensemble of the twentieth.

She began to read. There were a few short words of welcome from some of the notables, and then the chapter on laws began. It would be *most* important to know the country's laws and not fall foul of them. Much was familiar. Murder, theft, robbery, rape, arson, fraud, contracts, leases, lawsuits. There were entirely novel strictures against polluting air, water, or public places. But not a word about sedition? But, then, "Treason shall consist only of levying war against the nation, or adhering to the enemies thereof." *Nothing concerning opposing the authorities, or speaking out against their acts?* And then, "Congress shall make no law abridging freedom of speech, or of the press, or concerning an establishment of religion, nor prohibit the free practice thereof." She stopped. That, in one sentence, was why they were where they were, able to do what they were doing.

She started turning pages and running her eyes down the topics, faster and faster. She would have to go back again and read through with deliberation, but she wanted to grasp the shape of it all first.

Citizenship! After three months she would be eligible to take the oath of citizenship, and it mattered not that she was a woman. So was the Mayor of Grantville!

Martha's thoughts were still spinning in a dozen directions when she took her seat to meet with Brother Green again—in truth, *Doctor* Green, a title seldom spoken aloud outside of an occasional visit to a university. John Stewart had explained it to her. As Baptists, they took the priesthood of all believers seriously, no one more so than Albert Green himself, and so there was no precedence among them before the Lord.

She was still marveling. "Do I understand from what I have been told that I am not only permitted to study here, but while I stay I am almost obligated to do so? That this learning all around us is for all and not reserved to the men destined to preach?"

A broad grin lit up his face. "Well, that might be overstating it a little, but this is a college, and learning is what we're here for."

She let out a long breath. "So. I was prepared to plead, and beg, to be allowed to delve deeply into these works, and know and embrace the word of the Lord—with little thought that my desire might be granted. And now you tell me that here it is hardly less than a duty laid on us all? What delicious irony!"

He was still smiling, but it was a more thoughtful smile. "Well, our faith can't be *all* that you study. Or it shouldn't be. Remember, the Bible isn't a shovel. By that, I mean that as long as we truly practice the priesthood of all believers, we can't make our living from religion alone. We each need a way to support ourselves, a trade or a profession. And if you're planning to make your home in this state and become a citizen, there's a lot to learn about civic affairs, so you can take part and make sure your interests are respected. It might look like an awful lot at first, and I suppose it is, but let's talk about what you want to do. Then we can set some priorities."

"Oh. Yes. Well, then, the first pamphlet, the one

you gave me yesterday, speaks of an 'equal opportunity law.'" She raised her eyebrows. Green nodded, an encouraging nod. "And you said that I would be free to practice the trade I already know, I would be looked upon as a printer, and not as merely the daughter of one?"

"I'm pretty sure you would be. Your father says you know the trade as well as most journeymen."

"But Father said at dinner that printing here is different and still changing, so I would need to learn some of it again, and then again." She paused for a breath, then went on. "But perhaps I could be taken on as a journeywoman, for all that. But what of civic affairs, then?"

"The classes at the high school are probably the best place for that. And it's important. We can't just leave it to the government to run everything."

What an extraordinary thing to say!

Brother Green was taking out another pamphlet. The cover identified it as an "Adult Education Course Catalog."

A couple of weeks later

As Al Green was pulling up his pajamas, he became aware of his wife giving him a funny look. Claudette was sitting up in bed, with her face turned down toward the paperback book in her hands, but her eyes were turned up beneath her brows looking diagonally across the room at him. She had a quirky half smile on her face. He stopped buttoning and looked back at her, trying to figure out what that was all about.

Finally after about five seconds or so, he gave up and shrugged his shoulders. "What?"

"What, sweetie? I think you've lit a great big firecracker. I hope it's got a long fuse."

"Now, what's that supposed to mean, honeybunch?"

She sniffed. "A little bird says you told Martha Button she could enroll here as a full student. The whole divinity program."

"Well, not in so many words, but I did say everything we have is open to her. She's college material, for sure. You saw her placement exams from the high school, didn't you? She needs to learn Greek before she can get past the translated Bibles to the original words, and she can get that down there while she's taking civics and filling in the rest of the gaps in her education, and of course she needs to get up to speed in German to function in this country. So sure, why not?"

She tucked an expired grocery coupon into the book and put it down on the bedside table. "Why not? Because you'll get a revolt from the rest of the women here if she gets treated the way the men are, and gets a full student's hours for study and lectures. But right now she's in the same position as the younger kids, going to school in town, so it won't come to a head for at least a year. And maybe in that time she'll find something else she wants to do. There are opportunities enough. But if she doesn't, you're going to have to figure out how to play Solomon and keep everybody happy. Or at least not terminally upset."

"Upset? Why?"

She sighed. "Why, is because we're trying to run this place on the cheap without a staff, so we can admit anyone who's qualified. And that means we, and the students, and the families, have to do everything. Look, the hours the men spend on the heavy work and whatever other chores they do is nowhere near what it takes to keep this place going. Half a day of work, and then the rest of the time on lectures and study. The wives and daughters put in close to twice that on chores, and they believe in our faith just as much as the men do. They want their share of learning. But they put up with it, because the men are where the preachers are going to come from. It's called 'putting hubby through.' Ever heard of it?"

That threw him for a moment. "Well, why can't a woman study for the pulpit?"

She sat up straight and gave him a half-cross look. "Albert Green, you're a true idealist, and I love you for it. But where is a woman going to find a pulpit in seventeenth-century Germany? Even right here in Grantville, the only one we have is Mary Ellen Jones, and she's a Methodist in an up-time congregation. None of those old reactionaries in the Baptist church in town are ready for one, let alone the down-timer churches all around us. They still think Paul had the last word on what a woman can and can't do."

He tapped his fingers on the bedpost a couple of times. "I Timothy 2:12? 'Do not let women teach men or have authority over them?' That the one you're thinking of?"

"Yeah. Can you imagine Albert Underwood and his crowd seeing it the way you do, as Paul's personal opinion conditioned by the times he was brought up in? No, to them it's the literal word of the Lord. And the down-time cultures, outside of the Dutch—

"Look, there isn't a woman here who wouldn't rather study an extra four hours a day. But they know they can't, because the work has got to get done and that takes time. If you let Martha knock off at lunch to spend the afternoon studying, you are going to get a rebellion. Right now, the ladies are happy. They're eating well, and sleeping warm; the clothing is good, and they get to study some; there is hot water on tap for the showers, and the washing machine is a treat. As long as nothing breaks that Stewart can't make a replacement for on that old milling machine in the barn. Doing laundry is a preferred job, even before cooking—and cooking in that kitchen is a treat for them, playing with the gadgets and only using the wood stove for big meals when they can't fit it all on the gas range. Plus, it's communal work so they get to chat while they're working, more often than not. And what they get to chat about is last night's lecture or the discussion or their own study course work. In short, the work here is easier, and gets done quicker than it ever did before in their lives.

"But if you give one woman the afternoon off to study, the others will rightly ask, 'Why not me?' They'll look at what has to get done, and they'll do it because it has to get done, but they won't like it. And your collection of happy slaves will suddenly start asking questions like 'Why do the men only have to work a half day?' And you really don't want to explain that to them, because this is Grantville, and they just might say no. The best you can hope for is that a female full-time divinity student might be accepted if she's rich and can pay for her room, board, and tuition in money, or maybe bring along a husband, but I wouldn't bet on it even then. We've got a social philosophy going here. As William put it, 'All share the work, all share the bounty.' Best not start rocking the boat."

Al finished buttoning his pajamas, and paced back and forth between the door and the clothes closet a couple of times. "That stinks."

"Yeah, it does, and thank you for admitting it. And we're changing things. But we've got four hundred years' worth of changing things to slog through. So think harder about what you promise Martha."

Martha wondered if she should perhaps feel a little guilty at indulging in this course of study, for which she could hardly defend the necessity if it came to a challenge. Clearly, it was impossible for her to be anywhere but at the high school during this hour, if she were to attend lectures in Social Studies with Mr. Dwight Thomas in the period before (the celebrated Mrs. Sarah Reardon being at home with a new baby), and Introductory Greek with Mr. Augustine Ashmead immediately afterward, and Print Shop to follow at the technical college across the way for a rapid introduction to the new methods. But the course catalog offered nothing at this hour that directly applied to preparing for the responsibilities of SoTF citizenship, nor to the study of scripture in its original, uncorrupted languages, nor to the new skills of her chosen trade. And so her counselor, Mrs. Tito, had suggested, "How about Algebra 1?"

It was that, or let the hour go to waste. To her surprise, on the first day when the lecturer had risen to address the class, he had done so in her own familiar Cambridge turn of speech. John Rant, M.A., 1635.

Today he was going on, "And why is it useful to know how to solve a second-order polynomial for x, my friends? Let us examine a problem in accelerated motion, shall we?" He raised a wooden pointer to an equation high up on the chalkboard. "Here is Newton's second law of motion..."

Martha found Master Rant altogether pleasing to look upon with his elusive hint of a smile and his grace of movement, and his most impressive intellect. Had his gaze lingered a moment too long when he called on her to explain the next step in a chain of reasoning? Perhaps it was her imagination.

"Follow me, please. Mrs. Elias's office is this way." The young man led Martha and her younger brother Andrew to a small chamber upstairs in the Grantville University Press building. It had a door with a window of that very clear, smooth Grantville glass in it. The bespectacled woman who rose from behind a cluttered desk to greet them was perhaps in her fifties, though it could be hard to tell with some of these folk.

"Hi, I'm Ellen Elias. What can I help you with?"

By now, Martha knew that according to Grantville's customs, it would be proper for her to shake the proffered hand. "Thank you for receiving us, Mrs. Elias. I am Martha Button, and this is my brother Andrew. Our family was formerly in the printing trade in Cambridge. My father was master of printers at the university." She paused, and took a breath. "We are new to Grantville. I would like to inquire whether you might have work."

"Possibly. For both of you?"

"For me, while I carry on my studies at the high school, so that I can help pay our debt to the hospital for saving my stepmother and new sister. Andrew is fully occupied with his schooling, but I hesitate to go about the town unaccompanied."

Mrs. Elias nodded. "Oh, I see. But is your experience all with letterpress? Setting type by hand and running it on a flatbed press?"

"Yes, but Father has told me of the changes hereabouts. One of my courses of instruction is Print Shop at the technical college, to learn the new ways."

"Uh-huh, that's the smart thing for any printer to do. With so much of our work going to photo reprints these days, we do a lot less letterpress work. On some jobs we bang out the columns of copy on typewriters now, paste up the page layouts, and shoot foil plates. You'd probably cringe at the quality, but it's cheap and fast for short-run jobs. We do use new ribbons. Anyway, let me take you around the shop and show you what we're doing." She added over her shoulder, "But you might try Van Loon's shop, down the street. They do a lot of advertising and translated book work, and that's still mostly letterpress. Oh, and be sure to take typing at school. On a German keyboard."

She led them down the hall to a large open room, where someone was smoothing down a two-page spread from an unbound book onto a white board, beneath a pair of intense lights.

The man glancing up as Martha and Andrew came though the street door was of an age to be the proprietor—Adrianus van Loon, according to the gilded sign. His eyes crinkled as he came toward the front counter and acknowledged their presence with a small wave of his hand. It seemed a kindly face, rather broad, with a dark goatee. "A good day to you. Shall we speak English? *Oder Deutsch*?"

She gave a quick, shallow curtsey. "English, if you please, sir. My German is still poor." She'd already glanced around the room. It was filled with the familiar thump and clatter of a busy print shop. Andrew was staring at some freshly printed sheets lying on a nearby bench, waiting to be folded. Probably presuming to judge the work, though he had the sense to hold his tongue. The master printer was resting one hand lightly on the counter, evidently waiting for her to say on. Well, hesitation would accomplish nothing; she'd learned that much.

"Herr van Loon, I am Martha Button, and this is my brother Andrew. We are of the family of William Button, formerly master of printers at the University of Cambridge. We have all helped in the work, and Father says I have skills like unto a journeyman. Mrs. Elias at the Grantville University Press has suggested that you may have work."

Van Loon pursed his lips for a moment, and nodded a couple of times. "Perhaps, perhaps. So you are the daughter Master Button spoke of some time ago. Yes, he and another of your brothers were here, and we talked at length. Hmm . . ." He turned to face back into the shop, and called to a young man working one of the presses, "John! Lay that aside for now, and come here."

"A moment, Papa. Nearly done."

"That's all right, you can let it wait an hour. There is someone here you should meet."

"All right, then." He laid down the sheet he was about to load, and wiped his hands on a rag.

The fellow had some of the appearance of his father,

and at first sight, some of his temperament too. He seemed little older than herself, and while his father's English had only a small tinge of a Dutch accent, his had even less. Not the English speech of Cambridge, though, nor of the Americans.

The elder Van Loon performed a quick introduction, then pulled a ten-dollar bill from a cash drawer and handed it to his son. "John, it's nearly noon, and it's noisy in here. Why don't you take our guests to the cook shop next door, and discover what they have to say?"

In a remarkably short time they found themselves seated around one of a warren of small tables, with savory-smelling bowls of stew in front of them. Generous bowls, at that. Evidently meant to satisfy the appetites of apprentices and journeymen, who rarely had the chance to satisfy their appetites, in Martha's experience. Not that Grantville truly had apprentices and journeymen, if the pamphlet was to be believed.

"So, your father has given you the task of questioning me? To see if I'm fitted for the position of a printer?"

The younger Van Loon gave her a small smile. A rather friendly smile. "I think he means for each of us to take the other's measure. I do believe the position he has in mind is daughter-in-law. He has been speaking to me of beginning to seek someone suitable for a courtship."

Martha was taken aback for a moment. Laughter danced in Andrew's eyes. For lack of any other thought of how to answer that, she blurted, "I wondered, your name is really John? Not Jan?"

The sudden retreat from the delicate subject seemed to relieve him as much as it did her. "Oh. Yes. We have family connections on both sides of the Channel. I'm named for my grandfather. My mother was from Salisbury."

"Was?"

"Yes. She took a chill during the flight from Amsterdam nigh on three years ago, and fell into a decline. There was nothing to be done."

"Oh, I'm terribly sorry. Would you rather talk of printing? Do you use stereotypes, as the printer we worked for in Hamburg did?"

It wasn't often that Al Green got a chance to meet his wife for lunch on a weekday. But there'd been a meeting of most of the Protestant clergy in town—just ordinary pastoral matters. Father Kircher had been invited too, and would have come, but he had a conflict. So here he was in the middle of the day, headed back to the farm. It was easy enough to swing by Leahy Medical Center and its coffee shop.

Hot dogs and beans were on special. Well, the mild sausages weren't really hot dogs, but they were close enough, and the bakery had no trouble turning out the right shaped buns. A darn sight better buns than any supermarket would have had up-time, to tell the truth. Mustard and ground pickle relish were no trick at all. A taste of home, it was.

Claudette patted his hand across the table. "How'd it go?"

"About the way you'd expect. Kastenmayer gets uptight pretty easily, but he agreed with the rest of us that if someone needs to go out of town or gets sick, we'll cover for each other with any parishioner who needs comfort or counsel. And we won't preach sectarian doctrines outside our own congregations. We've been doing it all along as personal favors, but now there are some ground rules and we can count on each other. It was a good meeting."

She took a sip of her coffee. "That's a relief. And I bet I know who wasn't there, or there wouldn't have been any agreement on anything."

"Heh. You'd be right about that. May I be forgiven for un-Christian thoughts." He paused while he took a bite of hot dog, and chewed. "But I had the oddest conversation with John Stewart when I crossed paths with him. He asked me whether it would be all right to approach William Button for permission to court Martha. And he had a logically airtight line of reasoning on why they ought to marry each other, if you accept his premises. It came down to he's available and she's available."

"Oh, he did, did he? I wondered when that would happen. Did he say whether Katerina put him up to it, or he came up with the idea all on his own?"

"No, why, does it matter?"

She looked up at the misshapen, overly orangish light bulb in one branch of the chandelier overhead. It was kind of hard not to notice the thing. More and more these days, they were running on new-build light bulbs. Fortunately, they were starting to last longer. She brought her gaze back down. "It probably does. I think her sense of what's proper at the seminary is that an unattached full student throws an extra share of work on everybody else. He's been making moony eyes Martha's way, though. You probably haven't noticed. And what did you say?"

"That I only lead the college, in what it does as

a college. I've got no right to tell anyone what to do with their lives, for pity's sake. And that Martha would be smart to listen to her father and stepmother, who love her, and consider what they say, but in the end it's her life to live and her choice to make. This isn't medieval England."

"Mmm-hmm. I've been keeping my ears open. I think she's starting to really understand that. And I think she's taking notice of him, some. And what will you say if she comes to you for advice?"

"Same as with anyone. I'll try to help her understand what her desires really are."

She squeezed again, and raised a hot dog in salute with her free hand.

Mechanical drafting at Marcantonio's was a decent enough job, but Henri Faveau had seen what the mechanical designers were paid. He would need geometry and algebra to even begin to advance toward that position, and so—

Class ended, and he was almost laughing as he stepped into the corridor. His daughter Clothilde looked at him sidewise. "What has so amused you, Papa?"

"Heh. Our instructor, the handsome Monsieur Rant. A great dancer, I am sure. Have you seen those so-brief glances he throws toward the always-proper Miss Button, who affects not to see them? I think a fire burns in him. In class he speaks only of mathematics, but I wonder what he says to her when there is nobody else to hear, eh?"

Martha stopped just inside the door, and looked back at the chalkboard. She began to talk, slowly. "Master

Rant, I've been looking at that shape you drew. It's all complicated curves and irregular angles. Calculating the area of such a figure is no simple matter of dividing it into a few rectangles and bisected rectangles we could easily calculate, and then adding them up. But what if we were to divide it into as many small squares of a size as would fit within? Then the sum of their areas would be close to the area of the whole. And if we made those squares smaller and more numerous, the area not accounted for would become smaller. And thus we could come as close as we wish to the true area, and though we would never have it exactly, it would be good enough for any purpose of commerce."

He turned to face her, and rolled the pointer between his fingers for a heartbeat or two. "That is most brilliant, Miss Button. That thought, if pursued to its logical conclusions, leads on to a most useful mathematical theory which can produce exact answers in a great many cases."

"It does?"

"Indeed. But there is no need to perform that great labor, for a countryman of ours in a world we shall never see, Sir Isaac Newton, has done it for us. Do you know that Newton once said in a rare moment of humility, 'If I have climbed higher and seen further than other men, it is only because I have stood on the shoulders of giants?' If you were to stand on the shoulders of *that* giant, Martha Button, I wonder how high you might climb and how far you might see."

Martha wondered what to make of that, as she made her way to her next class. Newton, she knew by now, was a name to conjure with.

☆　　　☆　　　☆

John Rant found William Oughtred in the teachers' lounge. "I've been meaning to speak to you. I have a student in Algebra 1 who I think would make better use of her time in your accelerated class. Let me tell you what she said yesterday..."

John Stewart hesitated once again to speak his mind. He looked briefly across the parlor. Martha was so pretty, so neat in her person as she sat in evening study time—and a good Christian, true enough. Far from waiting to master Greek to begin serious study of the faith, she was using her few hours at home to dive deep into what copies of Latin works they felt safe in keeping at the farm after so much had been put in the care of the Academy of Conservators. For that matter, she was one of the few women even willing to spend time on Greek.

What if he should say the wrong thing, to her or to her father? But there was time enough. They both had a great deal to learn and to do, both for matters of the Word and matters of the world, before it would be time to leave the college and move on to a new life.

Thuringia-Franconia State Technical College
The print shop

This paste-up method of composition was truly intriguing, even with nothing better than cloth-ribbon typewriters to set the columns of text. First, Herr Hennel had demonstrated how to use the drafting board to lay out the space where columns and headings would go, ruling pale blue lines that would be invisible to the camera onto a heavy sheet of coated stock—this was to be the foundation for the work to follow. Then Martha and her classmates had practiced the technique. Next he had given them already-typewritten columns and shown how to wax the backs and secure them in place on the base sheet. Within an hour they were all assembling accurately composed pages. No apprenticeship Martha had ever heard of had advanced at such a pace. But Herr Hennel had said on the first day, "This is no guild shop, though we do real printing here. That's how you learn. We are here to turn out printers, so let's get on with it."

It went at a dizzying pace. The rub-down transfer type used up-time to create headings and titles was mostly used up by now, so they learned to slice single letters and common words from preprinted, pre-waxed font samples with little knives, and paste them in. They learned to cut in single-word text corrections and not have them show on the photo plate. Pen-and-ink drawings replaced woodcuts. They learned to use the strong lights and the large-format camera, sensitize the metal foil plates and process them through the chemical baths, and then run them successfully on the temperamental new-made rotary press.

Today Herr Hennel drew a complicated-looking mathematical expression on the chalkboard, and turned to face the class. "Suppose you were asked to set this into a column of type. How would you proceed?" He looked around for a moment. "Artur?"

"Not possible on a typewriter. I suppose we could do it the way we do headlines. Or we might set it in type, then print it on a slip of paper to be pasted in."

Hennel nodded. "We could, if we had a symbol font with all the parts we'd need. There would be a lot of fiddly wedging, to hold all the subscripts and super-scripts and ratio terms in place. What if speed were more important than elegance? Any other choices?"

Martha raised her hand.

"Yes?"

"We could calligraph it by hand on the drafting board, with pen and ink. We would rule the paper with blue layout lines first, of course."

He smiled in approval.

When Martha arrived for the next class session, Hennel told her, "I think you're ready to do a complete project. A small one, but a paid job. Would you like to try?"

"If you think so, Herr Hennel. What is it?"

"You will see. I have someone for you to meet." He beckoned to a striking blonde woman standing near the door, well dressed in one of the styles Martha had come to recognize as a woman's business suit. There was only one piece of jewelry visible on her, but it was a watch chain in some silvery metal. She crossed the room with a brisk, confident stride. "Frau Anneke Decker, meet Miss Martha Button. Please show her your treatise."

"Sure. Call me Annie." She favored Martha with a friendly grin and stuck out her hand to be shaken, then took a folder from under her other arm. "I'm an engineer at American Electric Works. The company is licensing my designs for induction motors to a new shop in Eisenach, and I need to send them the complete theory and technical data so I don't have to get involved with every different model they want to make. This"—flicking the folder—"is the design manual. It will free me to put some serious work into several types of synchronous motors that we need. The boss wants it published so we can train some more help, since I had to write it anyway. Here's a carbon copy of the English manuscript for you to look at while they finish typing up the text in columns. I'm told that should be finished by tomorrow. I expect to have the German manuscript written by next week."

Martha paused with the folder in her hand for a few moments, taking in the newcomer. She looked to be in her middle twenties. By her stance, her manner, and the style of English she spoke, she might almost have been an up-timer, if it weren't for the German rhythm of her speech. She was a *presence.* Martha opened the folder and leafed through a few pages to see how the document was organized, then looked up again and delivered a wry smile. "This being Grantville, you may as well call me Martha. Hereabouts, I hear it said, 'When in Rome, shoot Roman candles.' Yes, the methods we have been learning are well-suited to this. What page size and format would you have?"

Anneke cocked her head. "Well, your teacher tells me you were an experienced printer before you ever came here. What would you recommend? It's for working designers to refer to as they make calculations and develop their ideas."

"To be surrounded by other papers on a desktop, then?"

"For sure."

"Octavo might be best." She went to a bookcase at the side of the room and selected a small handbook. "About like this."

Anneke smiled. "Looks good to me." She pointed to some numbers written on the inside of the folder.

"That's my office phone, if you need to go over anything with me."

A few days later

Martha stared at the half column of text she was about to paste into place, and hesitated. Something was inconsistent. She went to Herr Hennel's desk, picked up the shop telephone, and dialed.

"Hello, Anneke Decker."

"Annie, this is Martha Button. I hope this isn't a foolish question, but under your fifth equation, where you give a list of the variables and their units, it says phi-prime is given in webers per square meter. Should phi-prime not be expressed in webers per square meter per second?"

There was silence on the line for two or three heartbeats. Martha began to wonder if she had transgressed some rule or custom.

When Anneke spoke again, her voice was subdued. "You're absolutely right. It *is* per second. And how did you reach that conclusion?"

"Well, you said elsewhere in the text that the force turning the rotor is proportional to the current flowing in it, which is in turn proportional to the voltage induced in it, but you also said the voltage is proportional to the rate of the magnetic field's increase, not the instantaneous magnetic field. Why that should be so eludes me, but..."

"And you took the trouble to read all that, and understood it right away? How far have you gone in math? Did you study calculus when you were in Cambridge?"

"Well, no, I've only just been transferred to Master Oughtred's algebra class. It was suggested I would make swifter progress there."

Silence again. "Apparently so. Somebody believes in you. Well, I'll get that line corrected. Would you believe two of us took our time proofreading, and that mistake still slipped past us? Tell me if anything else raises your suspicions, all right?"

"Thank you, I will." Martha paused for just a moment, with the phone still held up to her ear. "I wonder, if I might be permitted to see one of these machines, the motors, that you write about here?"

"Well, sure. Any time. Just call an hour ahead, to make sure I'm here. Take the tram out to the power plant, we're right next door. Look for the sign on our building. I'll give you the whole shop tour. And I think my boss would like to meet you."

"He would?"

"Oh, yeah. You have more talents than just printing other people's words, Martha. It would be good to find out how much more, don't you think?"

Nobody could say Martha shirked, in what few waking hours she was not at school or at Bleiler's print shop in Deborah, earning the wages to repay the college's generosity in the hour of her family's arrival. Father had learned that the hospital care that had saved Stepmother and Baby Providence was an outlay the college could not easily afford. But perhaps, with her earnings added to what Father and John's diligent reprinting of the college's books might bring in, the family's obligation of honor would soon be met, and she could in good conscience begin to save for her own future. It was a relief that Rudolf Bleiler, having hired her on the strength of her work on the Dead Sea Scrolls, had no thought of Martha as anything but a part-time printer.

This morning, she gathered the eggs, promptly fried a platter full for the college's breakfast, and had barely time to wolf down her portion before it was time to hurry down to the tram stop by the foot of the hill.

She skimmed ahead in the social studies book as she rode toward the high school. It seemed to put great importance on the federal principle of national government. Why was that, and what did it imply for this time and place? Perhaps Mr. Thomas could shed some light on that. She made a mental note to ask.

American Electric Works occupied a long brick building, two stories high. It had a good many windows, but they were of the ordinary kind, not the large, near-perfect panes of the buildings at the town center. A railroad siding extended into a large closed door at a rear corner.

When Martha arrived with an unbound copy under her arm, Anneke came out to meet her wearing work clothes of good quality, with the sleeves rolled halfway up her forearms. Her face lit up with a smile. "Hi, good to see you! You found some time to come over?"

"Yes, I've finished your printing. We have two days before the other students finish their projects and Herr Hennel takes us on to intaglio and photogravure. Do you know what bookbinder you want the copies sent to? Here, I've brought you one set to approve."

"Oh, thanks. I'd better leave it in your hands until I wash up. There's a batch of motors going through production right now. Want to go watch somebody put one together?"

"Oh, yes, please."

"The factory floor's this way." Anneke opened a door at the back of the lobby and held it for Martha to pass through. When they emerged from the far end of the offices, the production hall was cavernous and noisy, a hive of activity. Anneke led Martha down an aisle to a worktable flanked by racks of shelving and boxes of small parts.

"*Wie geht's, Johann*? How's it going?"

Johann flashed a corner-of-the-mouth smile. "*Gut, gut. Und* who's your pretty friend?"

Anneke responded with a firm voice and a twinkle in her eye, "Behave, Johann, this is business. Our visitor needs to see how a motor goes together."

He waved a hand in acknowledgment. "Okay, okay, at least when you talk in English, you don't call me John like some up-timer." He reached to a shelf, and took a dish-shaped metal part from a pile and set it flat in a wooden cradle.

Martha searched her memory of the manual she'd just printed, and recognized it as an end bell. He took four threaded rods from a bin at the back of the bench and screwed them in upright. Next he picked up a cylindrical stack of thin metal plates with cloth-wrapped wire coils set into slots running the length of the interior. So that was what a stator assembly looked like in real life. He slid it down over the rods. From another shelf he took a cylinder of smaller plates girdled by a spiraling cage of copper bars, with a shaft running through the middle. That was the rotor, then. He oiled the shaft ends, and slid that inside the stator. He slid down a second end bell on top, with the stator wires sticking out through an opening, added four nuts, and tightened them with a crank-handled wrench. Anneke swung one hand toward it, palm-up in a theatrical gesture. "*Et voilà!* A four-hundred-watt three-phase induction motor. The simplest of all possible motors." As Johann lifted the motor off the work cradle and laid it on a four-wheeled cart half-full of completed motors, Anneke turned to Martha. "And if you look up there"—pointing toward the roof—"that's one of them, running a ventilation fan."

Martha put her fingers to the shaft of the just-finished motor, musing. It turned with the lightest of touches. "And everything fits together perfectly, just like that? I've watched smiths at work. How is that possible?"

Anneke glanced at a clock on the far wall. "Let's go visit the machine shop. There's time for that, before Lan gets out of the budget meeting."

The president's office was on the second floor, close to a stairway but out of the way of the comings and goings just below. The man who turned from an open filing cabinet when Anneke led Martha in wasn't the venerable figure she had imagined would oversee such a large enterprise. He looked to be no more than thirty, and was dressed more for comfort than to project authority. "Hi! You must be Martha Button."

"Yes. And you are Mr. Landon Reardon?" She wasn't altogether sure what the custom might be, and dipped a slight curtsey.

"That's me, all right. Like to have a seat?" He came around to one end of the small conference table in the middle of the room.

The furniture was plain wood, but looked well crafted, and when she settled into one of the solid-looking chairs, she found it surprisingly comfortable. Anneke took the next chair.

He went on, "It's good to meet you. Annie has been telling me about you."

That was a little puzzling. He hadn't seen the finished work yet. She laid it on the table and opened the folder so he could look. "She has? Do you have other manuscripts to be printed?"

"Well, we will from time to time, but that's not what got Annie and me so interested. I'll get straight to it. The reason I asked to see you is so you and I could find out together whether we could offer you a job, and whether you'd like to work here."

"I— I know nothing of what you do here. Everything is strange to me. What would be my tasks? Would I do your publishing? I understand that all the books you have from up-time are in English. Would I translate them into Latin? Or French? I know no other languages, not really."

A smile danced in his eyes. "There's *nobody* we could hire who knows anything about what we do here, Miss Button, and we're short of people in every job. So what we look for is people who can learn fast. And that seems to be you. I hear you got recommended for Will Oughtred's accelerated algebra class. Are you keeping up all right?"

"Yes, though sometimes I must ask to have something explained again."

"I can imagine. He's good that way, though, a teacher I admire. Keep doing that, and he'll make sure you don't get left behind. And Annie says you didn't just

check her design manual for spelling and grammar,
you caught a math mistake. A simple one, but you
caught it. So you must have read the booklet as you
went along preparing it for printing. Why don't you
tell me what you learned about induction motors?"

The next half hour passed in a whirlwind of revela-
tions, filled with drawings on the chalkboard beside
the door, and meanderings along chains of reasoning.
At the end...one simple sketch, and a few short equa-
tions... "That's the key to it all? The transformer
and alternating current, and with those you can send
power great distances?"

"You've got it. Plain algebra isn't the best way to
explain it, but the rest can wait."

She stood, turning it over in her mind. "What
would I have to learn?"

"Once you finish algebra, and take plane geometry
too, you'd have enough math to understand manuals
like the one you just worked on. Mechanical drawing
would be good too. They're basically great big cheat
sheets, to let someone carry out the detail work of
a product design and help transfer it to production,
without needing to understand all the deeper complexi-
ties. That's what an electrical designer does at AEW.
Most students need about a year of high school study
to get that far. I don't think it would take you that
long. And if you take the job, you'd be taking some
of the load off my half-educated engineers Annie and
Gottfried, and maybe they'd have a little more time
to finish their bachelor's degrees. And then they could
take a little more load off me."

Anneke chuckled. "Three-quarters educated, Lan."

Landon laughed. "Okay, I won't argue with you."

Martha looked at them both. "And this is a respectable job?"

"Respected, and decently paid, too. And plenty important." The hourly rate he named was three times what she could expect as a printer. "And by the way, the company helps with tuition if you decide to go on to engineering courses at State Tech. I've got no doubt at all you'd make good use of them."

Some days later

William Button was at a desk downstairs in the new barn, preparing to copy the text of one of Brother Green's books onto mimeograph stencils, when Adrianus van Loon came calling. He laid aside the work—not one with any great potential to sell outside the seminary, but it would be one step closer to restoring the college's working library from the up-time originals kept safe at Schwarza Castle.

"Good morrow, Master van Loon. What brings you to us today? Are you offering your shop's services to the college?"

"No, Master Button. This is not business. Not exactly.

"You may know that some time past, your daughter Martha visited my shop, seeking work. My son John and I formed a favorable impression of her, and I hope she did the same of us. You may remember him. He is to inherit the business when the time comes, and he is already of an age to marry. Yesterday, one of my hired men mentioned seeing her at a meeting of the United Printers, Compositors, and Editors. He said that she is well regarded among the union members. It reminded me. I would like to inquire whether you and your family might find a courtship acceptable. Yes, I know that by the laws here, the decision is hers, but it seems only respectful to speak with you and her mother first."

William was silent for a few moments. "It's most encouraging that you and your son should find her so. I'm sure you will understand that I would like to know more of your son and your business prospects before I say yea or nay, but I shall be diligent in making some inquiries. By the by, my present wife Melisa is not her mother, but loves her as if she were. She is away at the moment, but perhaps we may all call on each other and become better acquainted?"

"That would be fine, Master Button. I shall not take up your time further today, then."

John Stewart came in to get a buck saw, just in time to hear most of it. It was suddenly clear that the time for hesitating to speak to William Button about any matters more personal than the studies of the day had just come to an abrupt end. Words said in another place to another man sprang to mind. *You must speak for yourself, John.* As the visitor left the barn he gathered the resolve to approach Brother Button and speak his mind and his heart.

". . . so, we'd have a good life together. Will you allow me to ask Martha what she thinks about marriage?"

Button's expression was unreadable. Mixed feelings? He spoke. "John—" He paused, and sighed. "You are a decent man, and a true servant of the Lord. I have the greatest regard for you. We all do. But you speak of returning to Scotland, and taking up the trade of building steam engines for the mines, and bringing the other blessings of the industrial age there. And I have seen enough here to understand what you hope to do. It could make life better for many poor souls. But going there would bring Martha once again within the reach of the king's men and a ravening swarm of lawyers.

"I have not told you all the circumstances of our departure from Cambridge. It's best that you know now, so that you can understand why none of us can return. And then I must ask, are you willing to change your plans and do your work in a place where Martha can remain safe?"

It was late when Martha came home, well past the supper hour and into evening study time. That was unavoidable, between school and the hours she worked at Bleiler's print shop. Tonight there had been a rush to complete an order, and she'd finished her typesetting at the overtime rate. Still, it had been a good day. The proofreader had passed her work without a correction, and she had the week's paycheck in her purse. One step closer to making good the family's obligation. Father and John were doing their part toward that goal; the latest of the photo-reprints they had done for Brother Green was selling well and bringing income to the college.

There was leftover stew in the refrigerator. Step-mother came into the kitchen with Providence in her arms as Martha finished warming a bowlful. "Martha, will you join your father and me in Brother Green's study? We need to speak privately."

When they came in, Father was already seated. He motioned Stepmother to Brother Green's comfortable

chair. She settled in and arranged the coverlet over
the baby and her bared breast. The chair awaiting
Martha was conveniently by the worktable. He even
made a quick gesture toward the bowl as she set it
down. *Eat it while it's hot.* The expression on his
face—she was unsure what it meant.

"Martha, where have you been? You're late. We've
been waiting for you."

"I'm sorry. The work at Bleiler's ran over. I was
offered overtime, and I took it. We need the money."
She reached into her purse and pulled out the check.

"Yes. We do. I praise your diligence in this, though
your brothers had to cover your evening chores. But
you should have let us know. There are telephones
in Deborah."

She noticed through her tiredness that Father was
using more of the turns of phrase of the up-timers.
Well, they all were. "Again, I'm sorry. But all's well."

He looked from one to the other of the three
women of his family, with that same solemn expression. "Is it? Daughter, I have had some misgivings of
your attending these union meetings with question-
able chaperonage, and these 'study dates' at school
without teachers present, but I have kept silent. Other
countries, other customs, and they seemed perhaps
necessary. But of that, later."

He paused and took a breath. "The most remarkable
thing has happened today, Martha. John van Loon's
father came to see me, to ask if a formal courtship
might be welcome. And immediately afterward John
Stewart asked the same thing. We know Stewart well.
He is a fine man. I made him understand that you
cannot go to Scotland or anyplace else where the king's

writ runs. Van Loon we would need to find out more about, but I'm willing to make the inquiries. On the face of it, either would make you a good husband and secure you a place in life. And I must tell at least one of them 'No.' Your stepmother is quite right that we must consult with you now. We would like to ask, what is in your mind and heart?"

Stepmother leaned forward a little, and looked down at the tiny head nestled against her breast. "I am overjoyed at the thought that such choices as you have now, in this wonderful place, will surely come to your little sister in good time."

Martha swallowed the spoonful she had just taken, and laid the spoon back in the bowl, taking a few seconds to gather her thoughts.

"Father, as you say, the choice is mine. But it's much more than which man to accept as my suitor. The choice is what sort of a life to have. Before we came here, I had no thought that I could be anything but a printer's wife and a mother, and do the same thing every day. But now? My eyes are opened. Things here are different. Much different.

"I look at the achievements of Helene Gundelfinger. Gretchen Richter. My friend Annie Decker at American Electric Works—twenty-three years old, and already doing work vital to all our futures, honored in her own right, and well-enough paid to employ a servant so that she can have the time to study further and advance in her profession. And I was told by those in a position to know that I am capable of the same.

"If I were to marry now, how could I do anything but keep a household? I do want to be a wife and a mother someday, but not now. Not until I finish what

I need to learn, and establish myself securely in a respected profession. I've found my shovel. I wish to become an electrical engineer. There are far too few of those for the good of this world. And unless I'm much mistaken, it's one of the many parts of God's work, and one of many reasons why we and Grantville are here. Perhaps, now and again, I might find time for a date in the style of Grantville's customs, with no promises asked or given, but I shall not seek a betrothal or even a courtship.

"So please tell Herr van Loon that I shall not even think of getting married until I have finished my education and am well established in my career. But of John Stewart, we have been much together. It could not be otherwise, here at the seminary. Surely, he deserves the courtesy of hearing it from my own lips."

Father slapped his palms flat on the chair arms, and bent forward, looking like a bulldog. "What? As your father, young woman, I have something to say about that!"

Stepmother raised a hand from her lap, palm slightly raised, a cautionary gesture she used now and again. "Yes, husband, that is precisely correct. You do indeed have *something* to say about it. And I am sure that when you have taken the time to think, and spoken with the Lord, and consulted with our pastor, or better, Sister Green, that then, when you are ready to tell your daughter what it is that you have to say, you will say the right thing."

It did no good. He flew into a red-faced rage. "No! You"—facing Martha—"defy me and you"—facing Stepmother—"resort to bare-faced manipulation. That I must tell two worthy, good men 'No' for no reason

that I can give save that it is the will of a slip of
a girl, is more than an embarrassment—it throws
doubt on the good judgment of our whole family. The
shame that I did not raise an obedient daughter will
follow me for the rest of my days. I shall go down
to my grave disgraced. And you speak of seeing men
socially alone, without a chaperone? That 'tis done in
Grantville is not nearly reason enough, many a foolish
girl will surely rue it. No! It is most unseemly. Were
we Catholic, I would send you now to a nunnery to
forestall sin. That you will not join with John Stewart
and his steam engines, nor with John van Loon and
the print shop one day to be his— No. I will not have
it. Not while you abide under my roof!"

"Father, father." She shook her head in dismay. "It
is not your roof."

He rose from his seat and struck the table with
the flat of his hand so hard the bowl jumped. "You
have your place here as the dependent of an enrolled
student. If you are dependent on me you will be
obedient to me!"

"Has it come to that? Must it? If it is truly so, than
I shall gather my belongings and be gone tomorrow."

"*What?* Would you wander the streets, then?"

"No. I could share a room with one of the women
on the production line. I saw notices on the bulletin
board at the factory, seeking roommates to share the
rent."

"The rent? How would you pay rent?"

"You need ask?" She pointed to the paycheck lying
on the table. "As the Lord decreed shall be the lot of
Adam and all his line, I shall 'eat my bread by the
sweat of my brow.' And within a year, when I pass

the school examinations in algebra and geometry, I can leave the print shop to be the assistant to an engineer, and earn much more."

Stepmother broke in again, "Martha? When did this come about? How long has it been in your mind, and when did you intend to tell us?"

"It began a few weeks ago, when my school project in the new printing methods was a small manual Annie wrote. My work so pleased them that they told me of a fine position I could take there, if I would take the courses of instruction at the high school necessary to do the work. I have seen what they do there, and how they are treated. I forbore to speak of it until I should be ready to pass the examinations and there could no longer be any doubt the position is mine. But this forces my hand."

Father loomed over her. "But you do *not* have it in your grasp, do you? No, 'tis moonshine, and you discard two good suitors to pursue it! The Lord's will is that women marry, and obey their husbands. And young women obey their fathers."

"Not here, Father, not here. Not when they are grown and able to take responsibility for themselves. If I devote myself to learning until I am an engineer, then I shall earn enough to hire a cook and a nanny when I finally marry and have children. Why should I not then do something that makes use of my mind, and not just my hips and breasts?"

Father strode to the door and flung it open with a bang. "Brother Stewart!"

John Stewart was sitting at the far side of the parlor, looking wide-eyed straight at the door.

Father's voice fell to half a gale. "Brother Stewart,

I ask your services, and the services of the station's wagon." He still got the name of the thing wrong, but then he was in a roaring passion. "I need to see what goes on at this American Electric Works, this den of . . . I know not what!"

He turned back to the room behind him. "Wife, would you please see to it that my daughter is still here when I return?" It was in no way a question.

Stepmother said, "Finish your dinner." Then she sat silently for a minute or more, rocking softly and burping the baby. And finally, "What will he find there, at this time of night?"

"He will find the factory running full speed, filling orders for Eisenach. He might find Annie burning the midnight oil, or Gottfried Bley, the mechanical engineer. Either one could show him everything."

Stepmother's eyebrows rose. "Midnight oil?"

Martha fluttered a hand. "A turn of phrase Annie uses. They seem to burn a lot of it there."

"Ah. Do you suppose they sweeten it with sandalwood and myrrh?"

"Heh-heh. Would that anyone ever had for us, when we proofread by candlelight. But if ever anyone would, I think it might be them."

"A pretty thought. And would they show me everything, too?"

"Yes, they certainly would. I think you'd like them."

"Hmm." She fell into silence again for a time.

"He really does want what's best for you, you know."

"Yes. The difficulty is understanding what that is. The world is changing. I don't want to be left behind—I want to be part of the change. No, I want to set my hand to making this a better world."

"Then be patient. He will look, and listen, and consider. He will surely master his passions before he reaches the far side of the Ring. He will treat with these people courteously. And do not force his hand with intemperate speech. But when you are ready to marry, late like these Germans? Stewart, then? I think he might wait for you."

"Perhaps, Stepmother, perhaps. And perhaps not. But that is for another day."

Stepmother smiled softly, and rocked Providence to sleep.

Good German Axes

Tim Roesch

Wittenförden
November 1635

Kunigunde stood in the quiet dim coolness of her mother's house near the very center of Wittenförden, a small, secluded village where she knew she was not welcome.

The house, before, during, and after her mother, had been slowly expanded so that the loft was now more of a shelf, and the central hearth was large enough to heat the interior without the addition of farm animals.

Good, strong German trees had been felled by good German axes, some of which her papa had made from good German ore, to hold up the well-made roof. What had been an exterior meeting area with an awning rather than a roof was now an interior room with a long, heavy table that had seen much, carried much, and been scarred, burned, and gouged by much.

Those who experienced it called it a section of castle wall laid upon its side.

The door was a good, strong German door held

together by strong German hinges with a lock that held the door tight to the frame. For all its inherent value and strength and thickness it could not prevent the silence from coming inside.

"Papa?" she asked quietly. She did not expect her father to hear her. Not yet.

If there was anything in the house that was her mother it was the hearth Kunigunde had her back firmly turned to; more of an oven and a stove than a mere fireplace. In the winter it could heat a house three times the size of this one and make meals for ten times the number of people who commonly ate at the table that was also behind her.

The hearth was a clever combination of brick and cast iron with a clever collection of tools; each one made to the sort of exacting specifications her papa was well known for from Schwerin to as close to Berlin as anything from her papa dare come.

Even Danzig knew of her papa's specifications.

Once a year, sometimes twice, a wagon came and took away tools and pieces of carefully crafted metal to places in Poland that might not know her papa's name but knew her papa's work well.

Wittenförden might not be well known or easily locatable but it was well thought of.

Like her mother . . .

"Papa?"

In the end it was the silence that made her open the door, forced her out into the very late morning, almost midday. There should be loud, raucous noise, and there was not.

"Papa?" She was louder this time.

From sunrise to sunset her papa's forge, his smithy, was never silent, and he was the loudest thing or person there. Wittenförden rang with his blows upon red-hot metal. Not now.

A wagon had come and there had been voices and the rumble of unloading. There had been horse sounds and wood sounds and the sounds of footsteps but no sound of the forge. No sound of her papa.

When her papa awoke and found the apprentices gone for the holiday in Schwerin he had not bellowed, so she had hunkered down in her mother's kitchen awaiting the inevitable, which never came. She struggled through the baking of bread and simmering of broth and the cutting of vegetables but, all morning, there had been silence.

"Papa?"

The wagon had gone with the normal sounds such things make, diminishing in the slow distance along a road, a path really, back to Schwerin.

Kunigunde had finally taken off her mother's apron, the one she wore while working inside the house, and put on the leather apron, the one the women of Wittenförden looked at with disapproval. She left the house and strode across the yard and stopped at the boundary between house and smithy.

She would have dared the women of Wittenförden and even those of Schwerin to say any single thing about her leather apron, the one she wore in the smithy when she worked beside her papa, whether he or the women of Wittenförden approved or not.

In the distance she could just hear the wagon, its sound diminishing, respectful of the silence of the smithy.

"Papa?" she inquired of the silence that haunted the smithy, a silence so unnatural in a usually loud and busy place. The crackle of flames or the sizzle of the quenching trough would have been loud in this silence.

The heat was there and the smoke and the smells of metal, hot and cold. There was nothing obviously amiss. Everything from brooms and baskets, hammers and wood and coal and charcoal were all where they belonged. Work waited to be finished and finished work waited to be paid for and taken to market.

Such were the tides of the smithy of Wittenförden.

"Papa?"

Her papa was a big man. Normally he dominated the smithy and the vast sound of him filled the countryside. He was called "the Smith," rarely by his more common name, Ernst.

Few from Wittenförden, fewer from Schwerin called him Ernst. No one in her memory used his family name, his surname. Formally, which was rare, he was called Herr Ernst.

To her, he was simply Papa. The surname didn't matter to her, not here, certainly not now.

"Papa?"

Wittenförden produced two things: axes of all sorts and the trees those axes felled.

Her papa made the finest axes in the north of Germany, possibly Poland and the south of Germany as well, and his skills at fixing wagons and harness, at least as far as the metal that bound the wood and shackled the leather, were well thought of.

Any farmer or shepherd who needed a knife fixed or a pot mended could depend on her papa's strong arm and firm, well-placed hammer blows. With those same hands and same hammers he made needles and pins far too fine to come from a place so obviously a smithy created to make axes and horseshoes and loud, large things of metal.

When he made needles and pins Kunigunde thought, for a moment, he was remembering her mother, his wife.

"Papa?"

"Stay away!" His voice finally burst out of the smithy like a flock of geese thrown up and off the nearby lake. "Go back in the house where you belong! Go!"

Kunigunde did not stay away. She did not go. It was not in her nature to do so. Besides, the memory of her mother was in that house. Better she should be here, being bellowed at by her papa, than inside remembering the mother she never knew.

Kunigunde strode forward into papa's command as if it were a stiff wind, cold and forbidding, full of ice and snow, but between her and where she needed to be.

In the end, it was not her papa's command that stopped her, but his silence.

"Papa?" Kunigunde began. "What is wrong? You are not working? The forge is almost cold. Look..."

"You are like your damned brother. He doesn't listen either. Off being chased about...swinging that damned sword like he knew what he was doing! Instead of coming to show himself, show that he was well, he sends me this damned...trash. Both of you don't listen."

"I am not like my brother! I am here. He is not. You should thrash those lazy apprentices!"

The silence was oppressive, stifling. She expected a response, a noise, a shout. Anything?

She had to walk around the large, brutish hulk that was her papa to see what had silenced him.

It was a pile of metal on the smashed and pounded dirt floor of the smithy.

Armor.

"Is that blood, Papa?"

"This is no place for a woman. I told you to stay away! Why can't you follow directions? Why?"

She stood beside her papa and looked at the pile of metal on the ground, before her.

"I should marry you off..." he muttered. "But who would have you?"

His hands clenched. She could hear muscles creak.

"What will you do with it all, Papa?"

The silence was hot and lasted a lifetime, or so it seemed.

"It is good metal...the best..." her papa whispered. "Some fine man had it made to protect his precious son, and see what good it did? What a waste..."

That frightened her. The whisper frightened her. In her fifteen years she had never heard her papa whisper. He was too big to whisper. Even his soft good night could wake the dead then frighten those very same dead back into their graves!

There was no fear in that whisper, no reverence or the quiet of men waiting for just the right moment to set loose an arrow at a rabbit tempted close and careless. His was a whisper of remembrance, when louder words might scare a memory away.

He was remembering her mother, and events even more tragic, and because he did she must.

In that silence her sigh was loud.

Kunigunde took a deep breath, adjusted her leather apron and began.

She let her loudness speak for both of them. Her actions were obvious, designed to confront her papa's silence, to challenge his whisper. She clattered and banged and stomped. She slammed and clashed and grunted. Smithies were excellent places for noise and clamor!

This was the part she liked: early in the morning, scaring the night away with the awaking of the forge; the eager clanging of the smithy ready to do work.

But this was midday. Kunigunde sighed and forged forward, anyway.

She made up for the time of day with loud rattling and shaking of the metal armor as if to wake the dead; even if that dead was the one who had worn this armor.

She cut off the leather straps, carefully, putting the knife down as loudly as she dared when finished. You did not live in a small town like Wittenförden and not understand the concept of "waste naught, want naught." Everything, even silences and memories and forgetfulness, had a use.

Even the distaste and frowns the women of Wittenförden made when she appeared had a use.

Once the cloth and leather was taken away, the metal need only be heated and pounded and used to make other things, useful things. There was a myriad of things to do; bring the forge to the right temperature, collect the appropriate tools, check the metal for anything that might interfere with the work.

She could see where a few "garnishments" had been gouged out of the metal. The enameling had been light and she left it alone. The blood was more like a thin, powdery mud now; easy to ignore.

The silence from her papa was almost unbearable. She wanted to shriek at him! But shrieking was something women did.

Papa told her once that her mother never shrieked until that day, that horrid and not easily remembered day, when Kunigunde had been born.

She let the clanking of the metal shriek for her. She slammed the bellows into action until the coals glowed and the leather shrieked.

The idea was to heat the metal and pound it back into an ingot which could then be reforged, cut, shaped into useful things.

Usually her papa was loud with comments and instructions, loud proclamations and deep, bellowing reprimands. Even his compliments came as loud as his recriminations, but not now.

Silence.

Once heated, once the stench of scorched blood was removed, she pulled the red-hot metal from the furnace and placed it on an anvil.

Her papa had many anvils and woe betide the apprentice or daughter who chose the wrong tool for the work at hand.

She chose a hammer.

Her papa had many hammers and woe betide the apprentice or daughter who chose the wrong one for the work at hand.

This was a critical part of the process and usually there was a loud, brutal chorus from her papa on which hammer and which anvil to pick and which not to even consider, let alone touch.

She had learned early to never touch a single tool in the smithy without permission. That she did so now, using his silence as permission, hammering her papa with his own silence, frightened her, scalded her.

Her papa often fought with her. Until now, she had never fought with her papa.

Even that time when she had stolen one of her papa's hammers for a purpose it was not meant for,

applying to a boy's forehead, she had not fought, not
dared to fight, with her papa.

The memory came and she smiled as she slammed
and clattered and made noise in the once-silent smithy.

She had been nine in that memory; a shorter version of her present self. She had been angry, fuming
like a red-hot forge, even at nine.

The memory of that nine-year-old girl came silently
to her mind.

Kunigunde knew she was not pretty, then and now.
Forges, though, do not make such unnecessary judg-
ments. Anvils did not care about beauty. Hammers
merely hammered.

A group of boys from Wittenförden had once made
her lack of beauty well known, even as far away as
Schwerin, and the nickname "horse face," *pferdegesicht*,
had been used once too often, and when a nine-year-
old daughter of a well-respected and busy blacksmith
is annoyed she reaches for a hammer.

Her papa had many. Would he even notice? When
you are nine you do not think of many things that
you consider long and quietly when you are fifteen.

Papa did notice, of course, but that was for later
in the memory.

She chose the largest boy in the smirking, mocking
pack and applied the hammer to the front of his skull
in as unwomanlike a manner as could be imagined
by any woman of Wittenförden.

Sons had worth, value, preciousness and wore armor.
Daughters had a place, a kitchen perhaps or shrieking
in childbirth, little more.

The boy, now older, still bore the mark. The women
of Wittenförden and even Schwerin remembered the

girl who gave it and marked her, therefore, as a woman outside her place.

If anyone used the nickname *pferdegesicht*, it was done out of her hearing, though. Sometimes "horse" was replaced with "ox"; sometimes unconscious fingers rubbed uninjured foreheads when she was seen in public.

What was one to do with a girl who did not have a mother and did not know her place?

Her papa had used a strap on her for taking one of his hammers without permission but only smiled whenever he thought of the village boy who now became very quiet around his daughter and rubbed the spot on his forehead and found other things to do and other places to be.

His approval of her was silent, but a smiling, approving silence.

Not like this present silence.

Finally, a hand pushed her roughly aside and she staggered and, suddenly, the smithy erupted into noise—good, hardworking, hammering, clanging noise.

Together, papa and daughter beat the hot metal until only memory remained of its former use.

But that memory was more than enough, possibly too much.

Later that night at the supper table, between the hearth and a good German door

Kunigunde had an aunt, her father's aunt, who often came to the house to help with womanly chores in an effort to show her, force her to see, how a real woman behaved and where her place was.

This aunt cleaned like a man beat a disobedient dog. She cooked like a wagon driver whipped a lazy horse.

Tonight she had not come, and Kunigunde did the cooking.

Reluctantly.

Supper preparations began just after breaking of the fast, with an interruption for a quick, hasty lunch. Her arms were tired, and her mind did not need the memories cooking brought.

This had been her mother's house, her kitchen, her place, not her daughter's.

The kitchen was well ordered and scrubbed and clean and the house as tidy as one could imagine when so few used it so very infrequently and cleaned it often.

It was almost as if someone had tried to erase the memory of her mother; except for the letters shaped into the metal of a little, cast-iron door—To H.

She closed her eyes and trembled with the memory of those molded words.

Kunigunde, Gundie to her brother, brought the large metal pot to the heavy oak table and set it down like a hammer blow. Her papa made many pots and pans and other cooking utensils but, in this house, there was one pot used to cook almost anything from chickens to carrots or both at the same time. As pots went it was very utilitarian, no embellishment, nothing fancy.

She stabbed the ladle, the only ladle available while the smithy burst with tools of every sort, inward, smashing aside the vegetables, splashing the liquids like blood, forcing aside the chunks of good, German meat, then sat down with all the grace of a sack of coal dropped beside the forge.

Her papa knew not to comment and her brother didn't even look. That was how she liked it.

To H—these were the letters on the little, cast-iron door on the stove.

It had been her large head that had done the deed.

Cooking reminded her of that fact, which was one reason why she hated it.

Papa clapped his hands together in what should be, but never was, quiet prayer.

Kunigunde had taught herself, much to the disdain of the women of Wittenförden, to cook quickly and efficiently. This, of course, gave her more time to be in the forge despite whatever her papa said to the contrary. The forge wasn't work to her as the house was. Her memories of the forge were pleasant. Memories of the house and hearth were not.

Papa began the prayer. Her brother was silent throughout the prayer.

It had been her large head that had done the deed.

Kunigunde pretended the smell from the stew wasn't a smell she had anything to do with.

"God bless the memory of my mother, amen," she added to the very end of the prayer her papa almost bellowed and her brother barely acknowledged.

Eating began slowly, quietly, like the heating of a forge.

Kunigunde did "stew" well. Throw it all into a pot and heat. Pretend not to see To H.

It was her great, big...

"I had them send you some of the metal, father!" Reichart stated as proud as a spring sun rising over the mountains it thought it had conquered. Kunigunde almost smiled.

His name, like hers, was far older than he was. Reichart wore it like he wore his clothing; like it was in style or would be or had been.

Her papa, ignoring his son, ate as one who was deaf or deafened.

"The apprentices will be back tomorrow at sunrise, father," Reichart stated. "They are celebrating the victory over those who thought they still ruled here. The fools were coming from Berlin to set things straight. We set them straight, instead! We sent them straight back to Berlin...those that survived. We sent a message that we are not serfs waiting for our masters to come back and tell us what we must do!"

Her papa, ignoring his son, ate as one who was deaf or deafened.

She prodded the stew with her spoon. Her father had made an entire set of spoons and even forks as a gift to her mother whom she killed with her...

"Father..." Reichart began.

"I am eating!" Papa bellowed like a mishandled forge.

The silence was punctuated with the sounds of slow, methodical eating.

Her brother made one more attempt, though oblique.

"I brought this for you, Gundie." He smiled, purposefully not even looking at his father. He reached out his fist and opened it just above the good, German table, beside her almost empty bowl.

They were metal; that much was obvious. They were shining bolts with nuts screwed on them. They were too small to be bolts with nuts screwed on them. There were no tools in her papa's smithy to make bolts this small, let alone tighten them.

Her papa made needles and pins with his biggest

hammer on his largest anvil, like he was challenging the challenge.

What could possibly require bolts that small?

How were they so shiny? They were not silver or silvered.

Kunigunde looked up quickly at her papa who was cleaning the bottom of his bowl with a chunk of bread torn like a limb from a tree, not cut from it with a good, German axe.

"Now these . . ." He produced two . . . things that she could almost explain. They were bolts with some sort of sleeve on them. The sleeve was metal, and the bolt screwed into it. ". . . I don't know what they are. There is so much I do not know."

Her brother paused as if listening to his father's grunt, as close to a laugh as she had ever heard him make.

"I traded for them. Tell father I am going to find out. I am going with my friends from the Committees of . . ."

The hand came down on the time-scarred table that many compared to something like a wall. The sound was like thunder and the table actually shook. It required at least three strong men to move this table, but it moved under her papa's single hand.

"Not in my house!" her papa bellowed.

". . . next spring, when all this mess goes away . . ." her brother continued as if his papa's hand had not come down and the heavy, oak table, with bolts large enough to kill a man with a blow delivered to the forehead perhaps, had not moved.

". . . and how will you know this mess, the mess you and the fools you call friends created, will 'go

away'? How do you know that you and your foolish...friends have not brought it here? Those who
are born to rule do not give up easily what they are
taught they deserve. They are not iron that can be
made into gold or gold that can be made into iron.
They are men! Men!"

"...I will go to Magdeburg or Hamburg at least and
find out what these are and how to make them..."

"...we do not need them! We do not need to know
how to make these things!"

The silence was loud. Kunigunde knew to wait
through the silence.

"I might even go to this...Grantville, Father."

Kunigunde waited for her papa to explode. When
he did not she looked at him.

"Your grandfather..." her papa began as he so often
did in situations like this. He turned to his papa like
a priest turned to the Holy Cross. Her brother turned
away, at such times, like a heretic.

"...first you call my friends fools then you want to
remind us all of this revolt of the peasants and your
father. His revolt failed, Father! This one will not!"

She waited for her father to explode. He did not
and his short silence frightened her.

"And what will you do when your friends take
control and become the monsters you killed out there
somewhere? Will you kill them, too? Iron does not
change. Men do."

"Iron rusts, Father!"

"And with a simple procedure it can be made into
iron again. Men age and piss all over what they once
revered and cherished! Men pray to God on a Sunday
then do evil to make the devil weep on Monday. Men

smile and rub their hands before a meal then squat and shit and fart. Men rust then change into something else and then forget how to be men again! Iron does not forget it is iron! Even when it is rust it remembers!"

"Father..."

"All this... this Grantville did was remind men they can be what God never meant them to be. Boys need to be trained to be men and men need to be reminded where they came from and to where they will all go!"

"Father..."

"Papa!"

"Go. You are almost nineteen. I will not stop you. Wait for spring. Wait for all hell to freeze over! When you go, take your friends with you. When you go... don't come back. Don't bring your human rust to my forge!"

With that papa stood and receded into the darkness that huddled like memory around the table.

"I don't understand him," Reichart said softly, almost whispering. "So much is changing. Why will he not change with it, Gundie? How do I make him understand?"

"The armor you sent to us... it was made for a very young man and resized to fit a man... a few years older, maybe one about your size. You don't understand. His tears sizzled on the metal, on gashes and gouges. You did not see those tears, Reichart. He is afraid for you. He sees you in the stories he remembers from his grandfather and his papa. He sees you on those battlefields, hung from trees, heads cut off with good German axes. He is afraid and papa does not... fear well."

"This is different! Things are different now! Things will be better...I swear..."

Kunigunde heard the whirring and felt, through the table, the crisp *thunk* of the good German axe into the large, wooden pole, once a good, German tree, that helped to hold up this part of the roof.

There was more than enough space, overhead, for a whirling axe; a good, German axe. Papa wanted his wife to feel she cooked in a large kitchen, not a hovel somewhere in a secluded place in Germany. He was proud of that tall roof and the open space.

The silence was stunned, brittle; like the silence after a tree falls hard onto good German soil.

"You might need your grandfather's axe for this... new, better, different world, this bright shining whore you will be running to this spring," came the pronouncement from the darkness that surrounded the table like the past. "Take it when you go. When you hold it...maybe you will remember who held it before you and...remember that someone might hold it after you are gone."

"I wish you luck, brother," Kunigunde told her brother, speaking as soft and still as the dust that was rattled out of the rafters, as the memory of her mother. "Will you help me clear away the meal?"

For Want of a Nail

Sarah Hays

Early March 1636

The fourth ring hadn't finished yet when Alyse Glazer caught the phone in a corner of her apron. "Howdy, this is Alyse..."

Claudette Green's voice over the line sounded vaguely scratchy. "Alyse, we've got a bit of a situation..."

"What's happening at church"—Alyse glanced at her tall-case clock and shifted to a hipshot lean against the counter where she'd been wrapping slender, corn-shuck bundles of tamales for the morning Farmer's Market—"at *nueve y media* Friday night?"

"I need transportation quick as I can find some," answered the pastor's wife. "Moving a family; there's a kerfuffle. Al says if you can't help you'll know who can."

"Kerfuffle? *¿Sobre qué?*"

Claudette answered, "Broken axle on the movers' wagon. Might have been overloaded with four adults, nine kids and all their stuff."

"Stuff like bedrolls and spare clothes, or stuff like house furniture?"

Claudette's sigh gusted down the telephone line. "Yes."

"Well, I can find you a draft team easy enough," Alyse said. "Maybe a driver, too, but I haven't got a wagon the size you need."

"Do you know who would?" Claudette's voice sounded weary. "The movers and the family are both threatening lawsuits, right now. I doubt they'll agree to try again."

"Talk to Huddy Colborn."

"The housing secretary?"

"Approves all the moving vendors, doesn't he?"

"Hadn't heard about that."

Alyse's snort had no feminine delicacy about it. "We do for one another, so Dr. Green's not burnin' daylight at the housing office. Huddy's had his hands full over spats like those Spitzenbergers claimin' the Hilltop Moving men deliberately wrecked all their portraits of saints. *Nadie quiere* believe accidents happen."

Contemplating the hullabaloo that must have landed Huddy Colborn with, Mrs. Green replied, "We have enough troubles without making them for each other, don't we?"

"Now," Alyse murmured, "*si sólo* people would believe that."

"People believe what they want, oftener than they ought," Mrs. Green commiserated. "Have you talked to Powell?"

"He sent me a letter full of orders. Sell all my trinkets and whatever's left of the livestock. He'll manage the money." Alyse gritted her teeth. "Make us a better life in the here and now, leave all that Texas and Mexico malarkey behind. Like I can just get shut of everything at a yard sale."

"That," replied Claudette, "won't do. You two need to talk, face to face."

"Sí," Alyse said wearily. "But I can't take home with me, so he sees *mi trabajo* to get us here... That's another thing. I'm not sure he's willing to keep our foster kids."

"Surely," Claudette said sharply, "Powell wouldn't renege on that commitment?"

"I don't know," Alyse answered. "He did want to help Marty when his wife died."

Claudette sighed. "He spent a lot of time with Marty in prayer for Brida, and more after we lost her. Powell found him that job with Chip Jenkins so he could stay near his kids. Then that nasty sawmill accident... Al and I spoke to Powell by radio the night of Marty's funeral. He said if we thought you could handle the kids he'd adopt 'em both."

"*Recuerdo.* He about made friends with Marty at choir practice, but now... he writes as if he's gone through as many changes as I have, though," Alyse said. "Maybe you can look at his letter, Claudette. I don't want to bother Dr. Green."

Claudette Green made a sympathetic noise. "Does Powell really not understand how hard you've been working, all these years?"

"I don't know," Alyse said. "What I do know is, I really, really don't want to start over from scratch someplace else, now. The house is paid for. I made a bit of money out of all those Croat raiders' horses, and Luis is as much help as I could want with the kids and the house. If I had steady money coming in, maybe Powell would reconsider."

"It's hard, but you know the Bible says a man must

be head of his household, Alyse," the pastor's wife reminded her.

"Says he's supposed to cherish his wife the way Christ cherishes the church, too," the tired Texan answered with asperity. "Powell's not reading those verses. *No entiendo nada. ¿Pero este? ¡Este no está ninguno bueno en absoluto—este no ayuda a nadie, este no hace nada que vale la pena!*"

The spate of Spanish left Mrs. Green behind as readily as it always had Powell. "Alyse!"

"I'm sorry, Claudette. I'm tired. I'm aggravated. I fall back on Spanish when I get upset." She sighed. "I don't understand Powell's thinking. What he's demanding isn't going to help anybody. It's not going to be worth the trouble."

"That's an understandable reaction," the pastor's wife said.

Silence stretched.

"Well, anyway, you called me about some horses and a wagon. I could probably have a team at the church before midnight, maybe scare up a freight sledge from Sundremda. But if you really need a wagon..."

"I really need a wagon," Claudette agreed. "I'll call up Huddy...no, I won't, at a quarter after ten with no real emergency. All the family members are safe at the church for tonight. I'll arrange a wagon through the Housing Office in the morning. Do you mind taking a team to pick it up?"

"I may bring Taylor with me. Luis can watch the babies while he does his homework," Alyse said. "I've got to finish up the tamales tonight to pack for Greta—remember Birdie's partner's wife?"

"That strawberry blonde who drives just like Hans Richter?" Claudette chuckled.

"It does make a person pack careful," Alyse agreed, chuckling herself. "I'll talk to you *mañana*, then?"

"I'll call you soon as I know what we need," Mrs. Green agreed. "Thanks, Alyse."

"*De nada*," Alyse answered. She hung up the phone and went back to her tamales, spooning out spicy shredded-meat filling into masa spread across corn husks laden with a dough made of cornmeal and acorn flour. Three tablespoons of masa, then two tablespoons of filling; tuck, roll and tie each husk, stack them in the steamer's racks. Not for the first time, she blessed her grandmother's taste in wedding gifts.

Abuela Adalia's last care package to Alyse's West Virginia address hadn't actually reached her until the Tuesday after the Ring of Fire fell; she'd gotten the package notice on Monday. So many years had passed since she'd opened that box to find another pristine but secondhand South Texas Junior League cookbook swaddled in a silk bandanna tucked among nearly a hundred packets of hand-labeled seeds; many manila envelopes also contained *Abuela*'s hand-ground spice blends, with her slightly listing copperplate handwriting explaining how to recreate them on the faces.

"*Dios bendice a la abuela*," Alyse murmured. She unfolded the onion paper air-weight pages of her grandmother's chatty letter again, wishing with all her heart that her husband's correspondence echoed the comfort and strength in her grandmother's letters. She read the account of the *tamalada* her great-grandmother had helped cook for during the big Viva Kennedy-Viva

Johnson gathering another time, though she knew the words by heart long since; Adelia's voice seemed to fill the room, reminding her that *las problemas de la vida* only seem impossible until people work together solving them.

For the tenth time since she'd gotten it in the morning mail, she smoothed Powell's latest missive from his office over the knee of her faded jeans. The clock ticked softly as she tried to read.

"I know," he wrote, "you think you're doing the best you can, but..." For the eleventh time tears filled her eyes before she could finish reading the thing, and she crumpled it in her fist. She sat in the old wooden kitchen rocker, still, head bowed, until she heard a patter of footsteps cross the front porch.

"Luis?"

"*Señora*," the boy replied. "Yes, I'm home. Is everything okay?"

She nodded. "I'm almost done with tomorrow's tamales. Want something to eat?"

The teen shook his head. "I had the last of the beans and cornbread before I left for class. I needed to go in early this evening. I had to buy that special eraser and shield for the drafting test."

She clucked her tongue. "I'm glad. I need your help first thing tomorrow. I'm taking a team to help at the church, but I don't know where the wagon's coming from yet."

"Okay," Luis said. "Will Greta be picking up the tamales again?"

"I'll pack them tonight," she answered. "Can you keep an eye on the younger kids while you're studying tomorrow?"

He leaned his head sideways. "Can we have tamales for breakfast?"

"There should be enough. I made twenty dozen this time. Birdie turned out to be right about the corn crop getting better."

"*Mucho gusto*," the boy said with a grin.

Late April 1635

"I'm told you're a horse whisperer." Slim, dusty, the stranger propped a trail-worn boot on the bottom rail of Alyse Ballantine Glazer's pasture fence. "*¿Verdadero, Señora* Glazer?"

"I'm Alyse Glazer. But I'm no horse whisperer; I just come from Texas," the sturdily built woman astride the trim bay mare replied. "My family are *Kiñenos* and *Kenedeños*. We've worked for the King and Kennedy ranches more than a hundred years."

"*La mujer mirando*," he sounded relieved. "*Ella quién trabaja milagros con caballos.*"

"Why are you looking for a woman who works miracles with horses?" Alyse reined around to face her visitor. She hadn't heard so much Spanish since her wedding day; the musical syllables spirited her, for a moment, back to a brushy pasture under South Texas' far warmer sun. She could almost taste hibiscus and the not-so-distant Gulf of Mexico on the Thuringian breeze.

"Señor Chad Jenkins"—ticking off names, her visitor folded in fingers—"Farmer Birdie Newhouse of Sundremda, and a Marine *llamen* Sergeant O'Keefe whom I met in *Ciudad* Magdeburg."

Chad and Birdie she'd worked with; the sergeant

she remembered as one of the few Marines not a danger to themselves around trained warhorses. "I know them. Who are you?"

A flashing grin lit his honey-colored eyes. "Pedro Sebastian Rafael de Treviño, *a sus ordenes.*"

"What puts Pedro Sebastian Rafael de Treviño at my service?" Alyse unsaddled, her morning's work irreparably interrupted. She swapped the mare a half moon of dried apple for the bridle-bit. "Fair warning. All that fancy business-school know-how Grantville's just soppin' with—that passed me by entirely."

Rafael shrugged. "I'm not looking for a woman of business. I'm looking for one to train horses·so they behave as if by magic."

"At your service," Alyse said, grinning in turn. "Working the *brasada*, our horses had to neck-rein and ground-tie; that's how I train mine."

"*Muy bien*," he said. "You are the woman whose help I need."

Alyse put her tack up on the railing as the mare ambled out to pasture. "If the Ring of Fire'd hit twenty-one yards yonder way, I couldn't help you for all the tamales in the world."

"What do . . . *tamales* . . . have to do with horses?"

"Tamales pay my rent."

By the look on his face, he still didn't understand. Sixty-three feet west, the Ring's fall would've included the MacCraes' house, professors Dale, Norma, and all. Much as she'd liked her neighbors, Alyse knew they'd fare better up-time. "Ring cut off the up-time owners' house. West Virginia County leases me this land, same price they paid in yearly taxes. Comes to sixteen dozen tamales every week at the Farmer's Market."

He still sounded puzzled. "Surely, whatever those may be, you don't need so much pasture for so few animals."

"They come with the lease."

"*¿Ellos qué?*" He gave his head a shake.

Now Alyse smiled outright. "'Til Powell joined the army, we looked after what stock the Ring brought through. Fifteen Rambouillets, a dozen mohair goats, a nice little Welsh mare, a few geese, ducks and chickens and those BLM burros Dale's grandkids adopted. Flo Richards bought Norma's Rambouillets, but I kept the rest. Didn't need the whole pasture 'til after the Croat raid."

"*He oído,*" Rafael said. "Richelieu paid a cavalry force to destroy your town and school, I have been told. Is that so?"

Alyse nodded. "Come nigh takin' out the school. Not the town."

"You were here"—Rafael sounded shocked—"the day of the raid?"

"Not right here," she said. "Evacuated downtown, like everybody but Irene Flannery. *Vieja pobrecita*— rest in peace. Made a sure 'nough bloody mess, from Dan Frost's *plaza matanza* clean out to the high school campus. Folks building nations don't have time for cleanin' up after battles, I reckon. 'Specially not carnage like Gretchen Higgins' busload of wannabe-gunfighters spread all over creation."

By then his eyes had stopped being saucer-sized. "*¿Qué hizo?*"

"What any sensible person would've done. Croats didn't need the horses anymore," Alyse said. "Swedes didn't want 'em all. Nobody else seemed interested in 'em either, so I commenced to gatherin' up strays."

Rafael's expression showed sharp interest. "War-horses? How many?"

Alyse felt her face harden. "Gretchen Higgins and her trigger-happy idiots shot 'em all to pieces. Must've been four hundred head to start with. I saved about a third of that *remuda*."

"Cavalry chargers?"

"Not many. Looked like the Croat *pendejos* stole remounts on the way. Even Grantville PD couldn't trace 'em back to their rightful owners," Alyse shook her head. "I did ask."

"And you have these horses still?"

"Not anymore," Alyse answered. "Along come Chad Jenkins needing draft teams to haul logs, so I fixed him up the gentlest ones. He paid half in peeled poles, or I wouldn't have pens or sheds. Duke Hudson bought a bunch for his Marines, 'n' paid me extra to teach his greenhorns not to let their own mounts kill 'em."

"That must have been quite a schooling," Rafael murmured. "A charger is as dangerous as any man, correctly trained. More so than many."

She raised her shoulders in a shrug. "Owin' to how they're handled. Cap'n Lennox bought my last few real trained cavalry horses for his embassy remount. I got a letter back—some cat named Ruy took a shine to a big liver chestnut Friesian I sold Lennox. Rattlesnake-mean, looked almost Andalusian. Lennox wants another'n just like it. That's liable to take a while. But I've got four of his foals in the pasture so far."

Rafael took his foot off the fence rail. "You raise horses here?"

"I will, if it'll make a little money. This sorta-livery business isn't very steady income, but I'd rather be here than emptyin' bedpans or scrubbin' floors in town. It beats starvin'. Speakin' of starvin', *tengo hambre*. Come on into the house. There's coffee." A moment later the heels of her boots rang across the wooden porch and the rock house's front screen door groaned gently under her hand. She watched the stranger watch her toe off her buckaroo work boots to leave on the rag rug just inside. "I'll pour, if you'll give me a couple minutes."

She peeked into the far bedroom on her way, where a black-haired teen sat, head bent over a lapful of homework as a scatter of toddlers and a cradled infant slept nearby. "Okay, Luis?"

"*Alles en* okay," the youth replied. Alyse ran a mother's gaze over the room anyhow. Neat as a pin, just like the children he watched while Alyse worked outside. "Greta says she'll stop back with your money after the market closes."

"*Bueno*," Alyse said. Ablutions tended, she headed to her kitchen. In the living room, she noticed as she passed, Rafael stood looking around, flat-crowned *lefferto*-style hat slung down his back by its storm thong. He had gray-streaked bronze-dark hair, and a light-olive complexion over high cheekbones and weather-creased wide-set eyes. "Quite a home you have, *señora*."

"Call me Alyse." She assembled coffee on a handmade mesquite tray: heavy mugs shaped like barrels, a silver pitcher and a hollow oval of dark amber with a grater, then a wicker basket lined with a clean kitchen towel, pastries nestled in its folds. "*Gracias*. Our mortgage with the university's credit union stayed up-time; I just pay for what upkeep I can't do myself and taxes."

She poured, handing off caramel-colored liquid.

Rafael sipped; his eyes went huge and round. "*¿Qué es esto?*"

"What that is, is *cafe con leche*—coffee and milk with Mexican *piloncillo*," Alyse said, offering the basket. He picked up a pastry the size of an emu egg. "Goes good with pumpkin empanadas."

"Mmm...if you were to sell these in the market..." He licked, little-kid-fashion, crumbs from his fingertips and mustache, making Alyse want to laugh aloud. She managed to avoid doing so by answering, "I do, when I can. Learned to make 'em out of one of *Abuela*'s wedding presents."

"Your grandmother must have been a formidable woman," he said.

"Not the only one—after World War Two and the Korean War, in South Texas the American G.I. Forum Women's Auxiliary raised money with tamaladas. *Abuela* bought me copies of about every Junior League cookbook from Corpus Christi to El Paso, then hand-wrote recipes in the blank pages at the back for me. When we got cheap cornmeal back, I could really go to town."

"Cornmeal?"

"*Harina de maiz*," she explained. "For the dough that makes tortillas and tamales. Birdie said this year's crop'd be better than the last one, and I'm glad. I've been stretching out the masa with acorn meal so long, I'm not sure I'd recognize real tortillas." She reached to refill his cup, and ran the amber oval down the grater, shaving coarse brown sugar into the coffee. "It'll be good to have enchiladas and burritos again, too. I put in a garden where Powell's lawn used to be."

"*¿El césped*—this grass with no flowers, no fruit,

nothing for the table? *¡Qué basura*—such waste of water, and work!" Rafael, finishing his third cup with alacrity, looked scandalized. His expression made Alyse shake her head.

"Some folks like it. For me, the garden's better. Ron Stone's apprentice crew cleans out my goats' and chickens' pens every week; they built me some nice raised planters last winter. Ron's stepmother wrote that contract; I furnish high-ammonia manure for Lothlorien's chemical work. They pick it up, pay two thirds in cash, and furnish me incidental labor for the rest. Birdie's co-op does the same with my horses' stalls. It's not just my sweat equity accumulated here—it's a balance between home and family and neighbors we all need, to keep us going."

Rafael leaned forward over the coffee table. "*¿Ayuda alguien?*"

"I do have some help—the contract work, and Powell when he's home," she affirmed. "Mostly Luis. Young'un's a quick study, and a good hand with little kids. Boards here for his evening classes at the Technical College. We can just about afford one another."

Now Rafael looked somber. "*Señora*, I wanted to make you an offer to move to Augsburg, come to work for our company there. I wanted to pay you well to train our horses and teach our riders to care for them. I can't make you that offer now."

"I couldn't say yes if you did, right now," Alyse replied. She didn't add how building her sweat equity for the past four years had helped her not to worry about Powell, let alone how long before his next leave. Instead she stretched into standing, gathering up the tray and taking the dishes to the sink for later washing.

"*Permitame otra oferta*. Could we send horses and their riders here, to learn to work together?"

"Owin' to what you want 'em trained for," she said judiciously, "maybe. But I have to tell you I'm not in any shape to house or feed your company's hands."

"*Los mesanjeros especiales*," Rafael said, sounding proud. "We will have a service of the couriers, the hub-and-spoke system, the special messengers, the special horses; we will have the stations and the relays. *Si*, radio takes important news to everyone. Thurn and Taxis handle mail very well, yes—where they are. We want to build a service like that, *un Correos*, too. But for things fragile or perishable, or that must be taken quickly, there will be our business. Our investor, H.A. Burston, tells us in the world he came from this is called FedEx."

Alyse wondered how Powell would feel about that.

The Marshal Comes to Suhl

Mike Watson

Grantville
Early March 1634

Judge Riddle sat behind his office desk. Harley Thomas, Dieter Issler, and Max Huffman were present, seated in well-padded side chairs. Archie Mitchell, however, was late.

Harley, Max, and Archie had been discharged from the Army just three hours previously. An hour before, with their families watching, Judge Riddle had sworn Max, Harley and Archie in as new SoTF marshals and Dieter as a SoTF deputy marshal.

The day was bright with a light southern breeze that brought a warming hint of spring. The warmth was a welcome break to the cold of winter and had melted the season's last snow. Vina Thomas and Greta Issler had decided to hold the ceremony on the Thomases' front lawn followed by a small reception. They prepared a selection of light pastries accompanied by a punch made from apple cider and ice cream. Frank Jackson had provided some unknown punch ingredient of approximately 100 proof. The new officers had been sworn in using the Issler family Bible, an enormous book that appeared to be old enough to have been printed by Gutenberg.

The marshals and deputy were now in Judge Riddle's office. Everyone was present except Archie Mitchell. Judge Riddle was about to ask Harley if he knew where Archie was when he heard footsteps in the hallway—footsteps that included the tinkle of jinglebob spurs. The door opened and Archie Mitchell stepped into the office.

"Good God Almighty!" the judge exclaimed. "What the hell is that?"

Archie walked into the room and said, "Sorry I'm late." He wore Tony Lama boots with spurs, dark brown canvas pants, and a white shirt with an accompanying black string tie. Over the shirt was a five-button leather vest; on his head was a light gray Stetson hat. Around his waist was a wide leather belt and holster on the right containing a Colt single-action .45 caliber revolver and a second pistol, in a cross-draw configuration, on his left-front side. The pistol belt contained a number of large, fat cartridges in leather loops. He carried an oilskin coat called a duster over one arm. The other hand held a cane.

Judge Riddle glanced at Max and Harley. Max's face was turning red and his shoulders were shaking. Harley was not as constrained and was openly laughing—loudly.

Archie stepped up to the desk. "Since you've made me a marshal, I thought I'd wear my marshal's uniform."

Max spoke up. "That's Archie's SASS costume. He

was a member of the Single Action Shooting Society up-time. They dressed up like that."

Riddle looked at Archie, his face turning red in anger. "Be very glad I'm not in court. If I were, you'd be looking at five days for contempt." He was not sure if he was being mocked or not. He needed this character, so he decided to overlook this affront to his dignity.

Archie's look of surprise and hurt finally convinced Judge Riddle that Archie's intent was innocent. Well, maybe not innocent, but at least not contemptible.

"Sit down, Archie, and don't try my patience."

Archie sat.

After a moment to collect his thoughts, Judge Riddle said, "I have your badges here. I asked Morris Roth to design and make them. My initial thought was to make them from some silver dollars I had collected, but Morris convinced me that would only attract thieves. Morris got together with Ollie Reardon and made these. Ollie had some stainless steel and brass stock left over from some job. Morris designed these badges. I had in mind something like the Texas Ranger badge, a five-pointed star inside a circle. Morris had other ideas. He likes six-pointed stars." He gave a slight grin.

"Dieter, come here," said the judge. "This is your badge. As a deputy, your badge is entirely stainless steel. Morris stamped your name, today's date, and the serial number on the back. Your badge is number four." Dieter stepped up, and Judge Riddle pinned the badge on Dieter's shirt.

"Max, Harley, and you, Archie, stand up," he said again. "The marshal's badge, like Dieter's, is made of stainless steel. The difference is that the points are brass-plated, leaving the center as polished stainless steel. You are all equals as marshals so we decided to assign the serial numbers in alphabetical order. Max, you have serial number one. Archie, you're number two, and Harley is number three. Wear them in good health."

He pinned the badges to the three new marshals and motioned them to sit down. "After much discussion with the other judges, Mike and Rebecca, Ed, and Frank, we decided to initially assign each of you marshals to some specific tasks as we build the larger service. Max, Doc Nichols doesn't want you to do much fieldwork for a while. Since you were a first sergeant in the US Army, we believe you would be ideal as the executive officer of the marshal's service. Harley, we thought the best area for you would be the marshal in charge of training since you did most of the tactical training for the old Marion County Sheriff...among other duties yet to be assigned. You'll be in the field, too. Since you hurt your knee again you're on leave until Doc Adams clears you for full duty."

Judge Riddle paused for a moment, looking at Archie and shaking his head slightly. "Archie, we had thought that you would be the best for the marshal in charge of field operations. I'm having some second thoughts after seeing you in that outfit, but the decision has been made. Don't disappoint me."

"Uhhh, yes...I mean no, Judge, I won't." *Perhaps*, Archie thought, *dressing up wasn't such a good idea*.

"By the way, how's the leg?"

"Well, for the most part, it's healed. Doc Nichols is being cautious, I think, but he said it will get better if I continue with the PT." Archie had been wounded in the leg the previous spring, and the wound had gotten infected, laying him up for months. The infection had caused some permanent muscle damage to his thigh and hip, hence the cane. He no longer needed it but he had become attached to the cane. It was made of hickory with molded alloy ball on one end and a steel cap on the other. It could be handy at times, he had decided—a knobknocker his grandfather would have called it.

Nodding to Archie, Riddle agreed, "That's what Doc Nichols told me; you've been released for duty."

Judge Riddle continued, "Max, for the time being, I want you to set up an office down the hall. The first task is to build a table of organization and equipment. All of us will be involved in that. One of the first tasks will be recruitment."

Turning to Harley and Archie, he said, "Harley... don't go hurting that knee again! I know he deserved it but next time, get someone else to kick the SOB in the ass."

Judge Riddle paused and looked at Dieter. "You are the only deputy marshal available, at the moment, to take cases. Fortunately for us, everything's quiet at the moment."

Riddle looked at the quartet again before he continued. "Archie, I would like you and Dieter to go to Suhl and find a suitable place for a court. Suhl has been a thorn in our sides since last year so we think one of the first courts should be there—establishing a presence of law and order, so to speak.

"The district court system is still being designed—how many courts, how many judges, their area of responsibility, all that. The current plan is each court will have a presiding judge who's in charge and two or three associate judges to help and take cases. You'll need to keep that in mind when you look for a courthouse. We're planning to place a troop of Mounted Constabulary there as well but that's not your concern once they're in place. They'll use the old Swedish garrison barracks. It's been turned over to us. Check it out when you get there; hire some people to clean it up and make any needed repairs. See if there is a site nearby for the court."

"How many constables will be in the troop?"

"Here is a copy of the proposed table of organization. It's still subject to change. Officially, it will be the 1st Mounted Constabulary Troop when it's all said and done."

Archie read the document. A captain, a sergeant, and ten constables, plus a saddler, farrier, blacksmith, medic, radio operator, and file clerk.

"Some of the headquarters folks, like the blacksmith, farrier, and saddler may be local people hired to fill just those functions," Riddle continued. "I would like you to spend some time with my son, Martin. He will go over everything in detail to answer any questions you may have. Do you think you could leave Monday for Suhl? That will give you nearly a week to get ready for the trip. We'll hire a bailiff to take over the admin for the court in May."

"Yes, sir," Archie replied. "Monday will be fine. Dieter?"

"That is fine with me, too."

"Well, that's it, everyone. Any questions? If not, then the meeting's over."

Grantville
Late April 1634

The sky was slightly overcast as Dieter rode up to Archie's home trailing a packhorse. In front of the house was a light wagon with a horse already hitched and another horse tied to the rear. In the back of the wagon were a saddle, worn and cracked, saddlebags, and two of Archie's old footlockers. Marjorie Mitchell was standing on their porch giving Archie a kiss and hug. They had been married over forty years and weren't used to being apart.

It was time to leave. "Bye, Marj. See you in a month?"

"'Bout that, I think. Be careful, Arch."

Archie nodded and carefully stepped down his front steps using his cane to support his weakened leg and carried his lever-action Winchester rifle in his other hand.

"Where did you get this wagon, Archie? I've not seen one like this before."

"I had it built in Saalfeld last year. It's called a buckboard. The wainwright built it from some pictures I had. A hundred years ago, Grantville time, these wagons were as common as automobiles were in the twentieth century."

"It doesn't appear too sturdy."

"It's not designed to carry heavy freight, just people and stuff, like a small pickup truck. Plus, I can haul more stuff than using a packhorse. Doc Nichols suggested that I not ride a horse yet."

"What are you doing with that old saddle?"

"That was my grandfather's. He used to be a cowboy

in Oklahoma before he married my grandmother. I've heard about a saddle maker in Suhl. I'm going to have him make me a new one based on this design. I did some horse swapping last week and got a couple of good, sturdy riding horses. This is mine," Archie said pointing to the horse tied to the back of the wagon. "Marjorie's old saddle fits her roan, but mine, the pinto here, needs a new saddle. My old saddle doesn't fit."

Dieter wasn't too familiar with horses or saddles. He just rode whatever was available. The new horse was a mottled white and brown.

He knew Archie had owned several horses before the Ring of Fire. He'd not thought about it much. Now that he had seen the wagon, he could see how useful it could be. Maybe he should talk to Greta about a wagon and some horses . . . He was well paid as a deputy marshal. Perhaps they should invest some of that money.

"Dieter, why don't you put your gear in the back of the buckboard and tie your packhorse to it. It's forty-five miles or so, a two-day trip to Suhl. That'll free your hands if it becomes necessary."

Dieter did so. The packhorse was to be his spare. Both of the horses had been assigned to him with his transfer to Suhl. Everything he and Archie needed for the trip, until their wives arrived, was now carried in the wagon. He frankly stared at the footlockers and bags that Archie had loaded in the wagon.

Archie, seeing Dieter's expression, said, "One of those footlockers is full of ammo, .45 Long Colt for my Winchester '73 and my revolvers, and .45 ACP for my two Colt Commanders."

"I brought .45 ACP and 12-gauge double-aught, too."

"Good, I've some 12-gauge, too, a mixture of

double-aught and slugs. Ammo weighs a lot. That's why I decided to take the buckboard—and I can haul enough fodder for all our horses. Grazing won't be all that good yet this time of year. Help me get this tarp over the bed and we'll be off."

Archie made sure the tarp covered the wagon bed in such a way that it would drain rainwater before he climbed into the wagon. A thick pad covered the seat to provide more comfort than would just hard wood. The steel leaf springs under the seat creaked. The pad helped soften the ride but Archie wasn't going to complain. Marjorie had made it using an old foam rubber camp mattress.

Once seated, he inserted the rifle against the front mudguard into a clip designed for that purpose next to his Winchester Model 1897 pump shotgun.

"Let's get going." He released the brake and snapped the reins. The wagon started off down the street. Dieter kicked his heels, caught up with the wagon and rode alongside.

Marjorie watched the wagon and rider depart down the street toward Highway 250 and the road that would eventually take them to Suhl. She stood on the porch, watching, until the two turned the corner down the block and passed out of sight.

She gave a sigh. She and Greta had work to do to move two households to Suhl. Time to get busy.

Suhl
Late April 1634

Archie and Dieter arrived in Suhl midafternoon. The sky had gotten darker. They had been rained upon a few times during the trip. Both wore their oilskin dusters to help shed the light rain. The string of wagons they had joined continued on toward Franconia leaving them at the gate.

After passing through the east gate, Dieter and Archie separated. Dieter proceeded to the inn where they would stay while Archie drove the wagon toward the saddler's shop.

He guided the buckboard through the streets toward the shop of the saddlemaker, Johann Zeitts. Archie would leave the pinto with Zeitts to allow him to make sure the saddle would fit. The new saddle would cost about the equivalent of forty dollars and the old cowboy saddle, he guessed. *We'll haggle some.* Archie suspected that Johann would get the better side of the deal with a template for a new-style saddle. *I wonder if I could get a new saddle for Marjorie if I traded that old McClellan cavalry saddle?*

Johann Zeitts' shop was located in the southern edge of town. He had started life as a cobbler. In fact, his son, Hans, still worked as a cobbler in a corner of the shop. Johann had become a saddlemaker by accident. One of the leading members of the Suhl council wanted a new saddle, and Johann had made a bid for the job.

He made saddles using techniques learned as a cobbler. His technique, using small brass nails and hand stitching, was new. Several competitors in the area were copying his methods, but Zeitts was more skilled. His business had grown and he was able to acquire a combination shop and home for his wife, married elder son Hans and younger son Christian.

Hans Zeitts saw the wagon pull up in front of the shop and walked out to welcome Archie. His father wasn't present, he said. Hans led Archie with the wagon and horses through the gate into the fenced-in area behind the shop where a small stable was located. The stable had room for several horses, with three already present. Hans helped Archie stable and groom his pinto.

"Your wagon and horse will be safe here while you meet with my father. My younger brother Christian normally takes care of the horses and the stable, but he's shoeing some horses at the moment. He's a farrier and journeyman blacksmith," Hans explained.

Johann arrived just as they finished with the horses. The elder Zeitts entered the front of the shop at the same moment Archie entered from the back, followed by Hans carrying the old saddle.

"*Wie Gehts, mein Herr! Guten Tag.* I'm Marshal Archie Mitchell from Grantville."

"Welcome, welcome, Herr Marshal Mitchell. I see you have arrived safely."

Why would I have not arrived safely? There's been no outlaws anywhere near here, Archie thought. The comment surprised him. He was under the impression that Suhl was mostly quiet and peaceful after the late unpleasantness with the gunsmiths and the CoC the previous year.

He dismissed the comment and followed Zeitts into the main workroom where Hans placed the old saddle on a wooden trestle that could be adjusted to meet the size of different horses. Johann lifted the stirrups, examined the leather fenders, skirt, cantle, and seat.

"Hmmm," he muttered. He flipped the saddle upside down on a nearby table to see the saddle's wooden tree visible through holes in the rotten leather. Hans rubbed his chin and hummed again.

"*Ja!* Now I see the differences. It is similar to some Spanish designs."

"True," Archie agreed. "The design evolved from saddles used by Mexican *vaqueros* up-time and they had Spanish ancestors. It is a working design to allow a horseman to ride comfortably all day."

"Do you want any embellishments? Any silver?"

"No!" Archie chuckled, "I'm not rich. I just want a good-working saddle . . . well, maybe a bit of leather tooling and embossing if it isn't too expensive."

"Very well." Johann seemed a bit disappointed. "When could you give me an estimate for cost and delivery?"

"Oh, yes, uhhh, tomorrow? Noon?"

"Noon, it is. I'll be here. I've other business in Suhl, but I'll make a point of being here at noon or as close to it as I can."

"Would you be available for dinner tonight, Herr Mitchell? Our quarters are above the shop, and I would like you to meet my wife and family."

"Thank you! I would be grateful, Herr Zeitts, but I'm not alone. Deputy Marshal Issler is with me."

"Bring him, too. We would like to have both of you. Besides, it does me honor to host the new marshal and his deputy."

Archie drove his buckboard back into town to the Boar's Head Inn where Dieter waited. The State of Thuringia-Franconia had a contract with the innkeeper to house them and their horses and gear until permanent quarters could be found. The innkeeper was being exceedingly helpful. He wanted them to remain at the inn as long as he could keep them. The SoTF was paying half again his current rate. More coins in his pocket.

Whoever had made the arrangements had requested a ground-floor room in light of Archie's injury. When Archie arrived, the innkeeper led him and Dieter to an area in the back of the inn where three rooms had been reserved for them.

It's a suite! Archie thought when he entered. The front room contained a desk, chairs, a table that could be used for conferences, a sideboard that appeared to be well stocked, and waist-high cabinets. A strong-room had been built out of a small windowless closet-like room off the main room for storage of their guns and ammo. It would also keep secure the funds that had been given to him for the purchase of the new courthouse and incidentals. Off the central room were two others made up as individual bedrooms. A door on one side of the central room led to the inn's bath, jakes, laundry, and an exit to the inn's stables in the rear. Someone had made an excellent choice in choosing this inn. He was surprised the innkeeper was so accommodating.

The innkeeper appeared and asked for permission to take Archie's buckboard and horse to the rear stable. "My stableboy will feed and groom your horse, Herr Marshal Mitchell. It will be in the stall next to Herr Deputy Marshal Issler's horse."

"*Danke, mein Herr.* I appreciate your courtesy."

The innkeeper left.

"Nice place, Dieter," Archie said.

"Ja. He bowed to me when I arrived. I almost thought he was going to add a *von und zu* to my name. I think he's glad to see us."

"I got the same impression from Johann Zeitts. It makes me curious. Everyone is happy to see us. It makes me wonder why."

"Perhaps I should wander around and listen to gossip? No one would think twice about me . . . at least for the next day or so, until I become known."

"Start tomorrow . . . and dress like you live here." Dieter was dressed much like Archie: oilskin duster, Western-style boots, pants, shirt, leather vest, and a copy of Archie's Stetson hat—Archie's unofficial idea of a marshal's uniform. "Tonight, we have dinner invitations with Johann Zeitts and his family."

It was dusk when Archie and Dieter arrived at the Zeittses' shop and home. Darkness came early this time of year. Johann welcomed them and introduced his wife Elizabeth, his son Hans and Hans' wife Lena and Johann's younger son Christian. Hans and Lena's two children were already in bed.

Johann and Elizabeth's ages were betrayed by their white hair but both appeared to be quite fit. Hans and Lena were in their late twenties. Christian was several years younger and had the shoulders and grip of a blacksmith. Hans was slighter than his brother although his hand was as calloused as that of the elder and younger Zeitts.

"Welcome to our home," said Elizabeth. "We are very happy that you accepted our invitation. Follow us, please."

She led them upstairs to the family area. It was much larger than it appeared from outside. Johann and Elizabeth had a separate room for themselves. Christian had his room, as did Hans and Lena. The rest of the upper floor was for common use by the entire family.

Dinner went well. Elizabeth and Lena had prepared a leg of mutton, roasted to a crisp, and a form of bread pudding for dessert. They had finished the dinner when, from the stables outside, they heard a scream from a horse. Everyone hurried downstairs, led by Hans and Christian who grabbed a lantern before leaving the shop. Hans saw two men in the stables with one of the horses. One had a knife in his hand.

Christian outran his older brother and yelled at the two intruders. One ran out of the stable and into the darkness. The other, the one with the knife, was slower. Christian threw the lantern at him and it hit with an audible *clonk!* The man stumbled, and fell to his knees.

Dieter arrived next and rolled the man over. A bloody dent in the man's temple from the heavy brass lantern was clearly visible.

Christian ignored the other man who had disappeared in the darkness. He ran into the stable checking the horses.

"He was trying to hamstring the horses!" he called, pointing to a slash on the leg of one of the Zeittses' horses. He soothed the shivering horse and examined the wound closely. "It's deep, but I don't think he cut the tendons."

Dieter checked the other horses. "The rest appear to be all right. I don't see any wounds."

Archie and Johann were the last to arrive. Hans picked up the lantern and relit it. He held the lantern closely to the face of the body. He, like Christian, was shocked. Christian clearly had not intended to kill the intruder, just stop him from hurting the horses.

"You know him?" Archie asked.

"No," replied Johann.

"Nor I," added Hans.

Christian walked over and looked closely. "He's one of Achen's men. I've seen him around."

"Who is Achen?" Dieter asked.

"He's . . . well . . . I . . ." Christian was hesitant to say more.

"Friedrich Achen is . . . uh . . . a . . . he calls himself a businessman. He has, what he calls 'a private security firm.' You pay him a fee and he guards your home and business," Johann said.

"If you don't, things happen," Christian added.

"His men came around wanting me to sign up for their protection. I refused. That is what the watch is supposed to do," Johann said.

"Except the watch is seldom seen after dark," said Hans.

"It isn't seen much during the day, either," Christian added.

Archie nodded. It was the old protection racket. He hadn't expected to see it here, in this time, but there was no reason why it shouldn't have occurred to someone.

"Did you report it?" Dieter asked.

"No. Why? It isn't illegal," Johann replied.

"It is if it includes intimidation and extortion."

"What do we do with the body until the watch comes?" Archie asked.

"Leave him there," Christian said. "The watch will show up eventually."

"Okay. Be sure it's reported in the morning if they don't come tonight."

☆   ☆   ☆

Dieter Issler rose early the next morning. The sky was still gray. He dressed as a down-timer, hiding his pistol inside his knee-length coat. His wide-brimmed hat would not draw attention. His boots were of up-time design but were unlikely to draw attention.

He left the inn and headed toward the riverside gate. That gate was not the one they had passed through yesterday. He was curious if it was manned at this time of the morning. Some cities in the SoTF had become complacent and failed to keep their gates well-guarded. As he walked, he kept an eye out for anyone about to dump their night soil. He didn't want to get splashed.

Archie, having finished an early breakfast, had one of his Colt Commander pistols disassembled on a large cloth on the table when the innkeeper announced a visitor. "Herr Marshal, *Bürgermeister* Feld would like to see you."

"Send him in," Archie said, rising to greet the *bürgermeister.*

"*Guten Tag*, Herr Marshal."

"And to you, too. I'm glad to see you. I had planned to see you later this morning but now will do. Please sit and please excuse the mess. I like to clean my weapons after they've gotten wet. It rained often on the way here."

Feld glanced at the pieces of the pistol, a collection of small, finely engineered pieces of a Model 1911 pistol, one of Archie's Colt Commanders, laid out neatly on the thick cloth. "Ruben Blumroder would like to get his hands on that."

"Ruben Blumroder?"

"He is the...not the guild master, because there is no guild as such here. He's the leader of the Suhl gunsmiths. He's also our representative to the new legislature. He's quite influential."

"I wouldn't object if he wanted to examine it. The pistol is easy to copy, the springs aside. It's the ammunition that is difficult. How did you know I was here?"

"Word gets around. The militia guard on the east gate sent word that you had arrived. A message from Grantville said you were coming. We didn't know when."

"Well, it isn't any secret. My deputy and I are here to secure a site for the new SoTF district court."

"Court?"

"Yes. It will provide justice and legal services for the district—administer SoTF law. The judges will report directly to Judge Riddle, the chief justice of the SoTF Supreme Court." Archie removed an envelope, wax-sealed with Riddle's official court seal, from his saddle bag on the floor. "I have a letter for you and for the city council."

Feld took the envelope. It was addressed to him and to the Suhl council. He weighed it in his hand. It was impressive. The envelope was heavy paper. Up-time, perhaps. He looked up to see Archie watching him.

"Should I open it now?" he asked hesitantly.

"If you wish...as soon as you sign this receipt," Archie replied, extending a form letter and pen to Feld.

Feld looked at the receipt form as if it were a serpent. After a silent moment, he reached for the form and signed it with Archie's pen.

"Thank you, *Herr Bürgermeister*. I've already given you a quick review of its contents," Archie said, nodding toward the envelope in Feld's hand.

"I suppose our ... difficulty last year is why the court is being established here."

"I wouldn't know. There are difficulties in Franconia and I assume the Mounted Constabulary will be sending many patrols there."

"They won't stay here?" Feld said with some alarm.

"There will always be some here at headquarters, but most of the troopers will be patrolling the main roads and areas away from the larger cities."

"We don't have many watchmen. The militia mans the gates and the city wall."

"That reminds me. I noticed the militia on my arrival. Who is the *wachtmeister*? There was an incident last night. A man tried to hamstring some horses and was killed during the commission of the crime."

"Crime! Uh, we don't really have much crime. Herr Heinrich Buch, one of our council members, oversees the watch and represents them, among others, in the council."

"How many watchmen do you have?"

"I'm not sure of the actual number. Herr Buch is the de facto *wachtmeister*. I think they're thirty-five or forty."

"That's all?"

"Well, the militia protects the city; the gunsmiths take care of their part of Suhl. The rest of Suhl is quiet. There haven't been any complaints and the cost *is* expensive."

"Suhl looks to be prosperous. You shouldn't have any difficulty raising the funds to add more."

"There are ... concerns."

Archie watched the *bürgermeister* sitting across from him. The situation wasn't new. Cities always seem to shortchange their safety whether external or internal, especially when no danger was on the horizon. "Neither the SoTF Court, the Marshal's Service nor the Constabulary is responsible for running Suhl. You are. It's up to you and the council."

"Yes, yes, we know. When we heard the rumor that the Mounted Constabulary was coming we thought . . ."

Archie said nothing. He was beginning to understand why he and Dieter were being welcomed so enthusiastically. "My deputy and I work for the court and answer to them. Suhl is your responsibility. I would suggest you and the city council review your needs. I believe you have some. That said, to whom should I report the incident?"

"Oh, well, Herr Buch, I suppose. We rarely have anything untoward reported."

"Very well, I'll pay him a visit. By the way, would you suggest someone I could see about what is available for a courthouse? The constabulary will use the former Swedish barracks."

Feld seemed startled at that piece of information. "I'll check with the council. One of them should know. I'll ask them to see you."

"Good, good. I appreciate your assistance."

Feld glanced at Archie, looked down to the envelope still in his hand and nodded. Rising, he said, "I'll present this to the council. *Guten Tag*, Herr Marshal."

"*Guten Tag, Herr Bürgermeister.*"

Dieter found the riverside gate manned by a very young militiaman, an apprentice to a local gunsmith he discovered. The youngster had a blue cloth tied to his sleeve and he was watching a farmer pass through the gate in an ox-drawn cart. The gate guard was unarmed as far as Dieter could see. He was just standing at the side of the gate watching people go and come. After a brief conversation, Dieter discovered the name of the inn favored by the journeymen and master gunsmiths. It was helpful. He decided to check the barracks next. He expected them to need minor repairs, being unused over the winter.

After Feld departed, Archie had some time before his appointment with Johann Zeitts. The hard wooden chair made his hip ache, and he felt tired. He hadn't slept well. The bed here was a simple pallet on a wooden frame. He would be sixty this year and he seemed to feel every one of those years. *God, I miss the twentieth century.* Marjorie was bringing some of their furniture when she and Greta came to Suhl. He hoped she would be able to bring his recliner. Hard beds made him restless and cost him sleep. Sleeping on the ground these last couple of days didn't help, either. It seemed the only time he could sleep well was in his recliner.

The innkeeper's wife cleaned up the remains of breakfast and swept the floor and the hallway to the stable. Archie made a mental note to tip her for her efforts.

He reassembled the Colt Commander, inserted a loaded magazine, chambered a round, and slipped it into his shoulder holster. The other Colt Commander was already on his belt. Rising from the table, he picked up his hat and walked through the inn's common room and out the front door. Johann Zeitts would be waiting for him at his shop. Archie hadn't taken but a few steps before he saw a familiar face.

"Hi, Archie. How are ya?" Anse Hatfield said. "I heard you were in town so I came over to visit."

"Anse! Good to see you. It's been, what, a year or more since we last met?"

"Yeah, 'bout that. It's good to see a familiar up-time face."

"I was just going out. I have an appointment."

"That's okay, I'll come along if that's all right? We can talk along the way."

Dieter approached the barracks and was surprised to see a number of workers on the site. They appeared to be tearing down the palisade walls. He walked up to the one who seemed to be in charge and asked what was going on.

"None of your business," Dieter was told.

"I'm Deputy Marshal Issler." Dieter showed them his badge. "That is SoTF property and the barracks of the Mounted Constabulary troop that should be arriving shortly. That makes it my business."

"Don't know anything about that. I was told to tear down the walls and that's what I'm going to do."

"Who's your boss?"

"That's none of your business, either. Now go or we'll make you go."

Dieter saw that he was outnumbered by six to one. He'd better pass this to Archie. "I'll be back. I strongly suggest you have your boss here when I return."

"... I managed some leave to talk over some business with Pat Johnson, on condition I bring back more guns, so I'll be leaving in a few days to rejoin the army. There won't be many up-timers here after that, just Pat, the Reardons, Gary and Gaylynn, and maybe one or two others," Anse Hatfield said.

"Marjorie is coming in a few weeks along with Dieter's wife, Greta. I don't think there will be any more up-timers here after she arrives." After a pause, Archie said, "You just didn't come to see me because we're old friends. What's on your mind?"

"There's a problem here, a gang. I was starting to get a handle on it but now I'm leaving. I wanted to fill you in and ask if you'd look into it."

"A gang that's running a protection and extortion racket?"

"Yeah, among other things."

"I've heard. I met one of them last night who was trying to cripple a horse. I understand he's one of Achen's men. Who is this Achen?"

"I don't know too much. I've heard that he's the new son-in-law of one of the city councilmen. They don't try much in my part of town but they work the rest of Suhl and outside the gates. The watch never seems to be around when something happens. When they finally show up, they don't do much. No one is caught and things just seem to get worse. It's getting so that it's not safe on the streets after dark."

"I thought the Jaegers were helping to take care of things?"

"Only in our part of town, and most of them are gone."

"That's twice you've said, 'my part of town.' What do you mean?"

"Where the gunsmiths are, their shops and homes. After the, ahhh, incident last year, they've kept the peace in their area. The city council is supposed to handle the rest of town. They don't. They think the militia is enough . . . you can't keep the peace by manning the walls and gates with unarmed boys."

"And the watch?"

"They seem more interested in patrolling the 'better' parts of town. The homes and businesses of the council members and others."

"I met with Feld, the *bürgermeister*, this morning. He said they only have thirty-five to forty watchmen for the whole town."

"I know. It's one of the problems here in Suhl. Saves them money, don'cha know. I'm surprised the council hasn't called for help. I've heard rumors that the council is deadlocked on that."

"They need about seventy-five to a hundred men if they are to have good day and night patrols," Anse continued. "They think the militia will fill in for their lack of watchmen. The militia has to provide their own weapons, and most militia members work for the gunsmiths and their families."

"Where have I heard this before?"

"Yeah. Almost like old times."

"Dieter Issler is my deputy—do you know him?"

"No...don't think I do."

"He's out scouting the town. I'd appreciate it if you'd have a talk with Pat and Gary and ask them to keep their ears open and give us a holler if they hear anything we should know."

"I can do that. I'm glad Pat and Gary aren't in the army. I don't really want to go but I haven't a choice."

"They kicked me, Max Huffman, and Harley Thomas out of the army and made us marshals. Frankly, I'm glad I'm not in anymore."

"I better get back. I'll drop by one more time before I leave."

"Thanks, Anse, I appreciate it."

Ruben Blumroder looked up from his workbench when Anse walked through the door. "Did you meet him?"

"Yep. I think ol' Arch will do. He asked me about Achen before I had a chance. He's already got some feelers out gathering information."

"Tell me about him."

"He's hard to describe. He's a SoTF marshal now. He was a deputy sheriff up-time, an army vet, up-time, not just here. He's a combat vet, too."

"What's he like?"

"Well, like many up-timers, Archie has some... eccentricities. He has always been a cowboy fan. Have you heard about Westerns?"

"Ja, but I don't think I understand."

"Westerns are stories about the American West in the nineteenth century—the American Frontier. Archie lives it. Up-time he was a member of a group that had action shooting matches using old-style weapons—revolvers, rifles, usually lever-action, double-barreled shotguns, weapons that were common in the nineteenth century. Sometimes they even shoot from horseback, and they dressed up in costumes like those from the West. Archie, too. Like I said, he lives it."

"Is he crazy?"

"No. Absolutely not. But, when we up-timers arrived here in the middle of the Thirty Years' War, it was a shock. People reacted differently. Some did well, some didn't. Everyone was affected in some form or another. Living as a real Old West marshal is Archie's way of coping—but don't doubt his competency. That would be a mistake. His, uh, eccentricity aside, he's a tough lawman."

"Good! We need someone like that."

"I think Archie will do."

"I have a meeting tonight with some of the other craft masters. I'll tell them about our new marshal."

"Guten Tag, Herr Zeitts," Archie said as he entered Zeitts' workshop.

"Guten Tag, Herr Marshal."

"Well, what do you think." Archie pointed to the disassembled saddle on Zeitts' workbench.

"I can do it," Zeitts affirmed.

When the haggling was over, Zeitts and Archie had an agreement. Zeitts would finish the saddle in two weeks unless there was an unforeseen circumstance to delay delivery.

Archie and Johann Zeitts were shaking hands on the deal when Christian entered the workshop with the aid of his brother. Christian had been badly beaten, one eye almost closed.

"What happened?" Johann asked, rushing to Christian's side.

"Achen's men caught him outside. They were looking for their man who didn't come home last night. It was their two on Christian until I arrived."

"Where are they?" Archie asked, referring to Achen's men. "Are they still around?"

"They ran up the street. I don't know where. Don't go after them," Hans said. "They outnumber you."

"I think I can handle them," Archie said as he left the shop. Outside he surveyed the scene. Zeitts' shop was next to the city's wall. A ring road ran parallel to the wall with homes and shops lining the cobblestoned street. A number of people were out walking the street but none appeared to be watching Zeitts' shop.

"They ran that way," Hans said, pointing to the left. The street ended where it met another that led to the eastern gate.

"*Danke.* Tell your father I'll look into this." With that, he stepped into the street and proceeded in search of Christian's assailants.

The buildings on the left side of the street abutted but did not actually touch the city wall. This gap provided space for wall maintenance and access in time of need. The right side of the street was like the left with narrow alleys appearing from time to time between buildings giving access to another alley to the rear.

I need a map, Archie thought. *This place is a maze. You could hide an army in these alleys and no one would know.*

Archie reached the intersection without seeing anyone or anything suspicious. He had stopped a few passersby, asking if they had seen two men running down the street, and no one had . . . or at least would not admit that they had. That was the problem with a gang. People were intimidated. Individually, they were at the gang's mercy. If they united, the gang would be ineffective and would soon be removed or would leave for easier pickings.

Archie headed back to the inn. He'd not had any lunch, and he was getting hungry. After he had eaten, he thought he would visit Ruben Blumroder. He seemed to be the real leader of Suhl. Maybe Blumroder would have more information.

Achen's two men watched the marshal walk past the alley where they had hidden themselves. Achen would not be pleased with their failure to extract information from the younger Zeitts.

Friedrich Achen was sitting in a corner of the taproom of Der Bulle und Bär, his favorite inn, when his two men entered. They walked over to Achen's table and sat.

"What did you find?" he asked.

"Nothing. We were interrupted. Zeitts' brother and some neighbors came before we had the younger one softened up. The new marshal was there, too, so we left."

"Conrad's dead. One of the Zeitts, maybe the marshal, killed him."

"How did you know?"

"Feld told my father-in-law who told me. Also, the other marshal, the deputy, was nosing around the barracks. He told the men to stop working. They refused but the deputy will be back, probably with the marshal to stop them."

"Shall we be there, too? Together we would have enough to take both of them."

"Do so. Keep watch. When the workers refuse, join them and overwhelm the marshals. Don't let them get away."

"You want them dead?"

"No, not yet. I need to know why they're here."

"Your father-in-law doesn't know?"

"He says not. I'm not sure I believe him."

"We'll find out. The marshal doesn't look all that strong. He uses a cane."

"Go. Wait for them as long as it takes."

After following the directions from several people, Archie arrived at Ruben Blumroder's shop located on the same street as Pat Johnson's US WaffenFabrik. He heard a shot from the rear of the building. Instead of entering the front, Archie walked down the adjacent alley to the rear where Blumroder and a couple of men were testing long arms. He stood watching them load the long guns with patched balls. Rifles, he assumed. The target was a wooden board attached to a large square wooden post that was at least a foot on each side. There were numerous holes in the board.

Bam! One of the men fired the rifle which produced a cloud of white smoke. Archie noticed the rifle produced significant recoil.

"Guten Tag!" Archie called as another shooter stepped forward to the line.

Ruben Blumroder, at least that is whom Archie assumed the older man was, appeared startled when Archie called. He turned his head swiftly and gave Archie a quick inspection. He stepped away from the other two, who ignored Archie's interruption once the elder man started walking toward the visitor.

"Herr Marshal Mitchell, I presume?"

"The same. I assume you are Herr Ruben Blumroder?"

"The same," he said with a grin. "I was going to visit you when I had some time. Herr Hatfield told me you arrived yesterday. And here you are. What is the occasion for your visit?"

"I don't want to interrupt your work but I would like to talk with you about Suhl. I understand you will be the city's representative to the SoTF legislature."

"Ja, that's so. The craft masters and their people elected me. We outvoted our opponents."

"The craft masters were able to control fifty percent of the votes?"

"Not alone . . . but with some other allies, we did."

"Politics?"

"Politics," he confirmed. "Come, let us go inside. I have some cider that I've been thinking about all day."

Archie chuckled and followed Blumroder into the rear of his shop. Inside the door, Archie stopped to let his eyes become accustomed to the unlit room. The few light sources were the open door and two windows facing the alley that Archie had used to reach the rear of the shop. To one side were three rifling machines next to a small forge that appeared to be used to make small metal pieces that would eventually become parts for the rifle's lock.

Blumroder walked down the aisle to a table where rifles and long arms were assembled. He picked up a rifle and handed it to Archie. "This is a copy, as best we can determine, of your Kentucky rifle. It's .50 caliber. Pat Johnson had a . . . magazine? . . . catalog? . . . that had an exploded view of this rifle. We created our molds from that and refined the final product to be this rifle."

To Archie, it appeared to be very much like a flintlock Kentucky rifle he had once fired. The smooth honey-colored wooden stock, forearm, and ramrod were expertly finished and varnished with fine checkering at the grip behind the trigger and at two points along the sides of the forearm. The brass side plates and patch box were polished to a mirror sheen that brought out the detail of the light engraving depicting a hunting scene. He hefted the rifle and found it to be perfectly balanced. "A fine piece of work," he told Blumroder.

"*Danke.* It is intended as a gift for the Landgrave of Hesse-Kassel. A working rifle, not some pretty piece that will never be fired. I can't say who ordered it but the commission was very welcome."

"I repeat, a very fine piece of work."

"A man who knows his weapons, I see."

"Of necessity. A reliable, accurate firearm can mean the difference between life or death. A man can be known by his weapon. I'm used to mine."

"If I may ask . . ."

Archie chuckled. "I've nothing fancy." He pulled his duster aside from one side to reveal a Colt Commander in a side holster, then pulled the other side of the duster aside to reveal a second Colt Commander in a shoulder holster.

"Ah, yes, the Colt model 1911A1. Anse Hatfield carries one."

"Almost, these are the Commander model," he said, pointing to his two pistols in turn. "The 1911 has a five-inch barrel, the Commander a four-and-one-half-inch barrel. It's not much shorter but it can make a difference if you have to draw quickly."

Blumroder walked into the shop where he had an office—a side room from a larger space where his apprentices and journeymen worked small pieces of metal to ensure they fit exactly into molds. This was the current method of standardizing parts. It worked well enough and helped keep parts interchangeable, more or less—a new concept introduced by up-timers. Using molds wasn't as precise as using a milling machine but would do until those tools became available.

After they were seated, Blumroder asked, "What can I do for you, Marshal?"

"I came, mainly, to introduce myself. Anse Hatfield, whom I've known for years, paid me a visit this morning. He mentioned that you were one of the city leaders. I've found it's best to know the PTBs."

"Excuse me, Herr Marshal, 'PTBs'?"

"Powers That Be. Folks like Herr Feld—and you. I keep forgetting few here know all our language foibles."

Blumroder chuckled. "I'm not in the same category as Herr Feld. I'm just a local craft master."

"Who effectively controls at least a third of the city."

"Um, uh, well, yes."

"And is the recently elected member to the SoTF legislature."

"True, as well."

"I think that qualifies you as being one of the PTBs, don't you Herr Blumroder?"

"Anse said you were different, Herr Marshal."

"Just call me Archie, if you would."

"Very well...Archie, and please call me Ruben."

"Thank you, Ruben."

"Now, what can I do for you, Archie?"

"Information, really. Anse alluded to some troubles here in Suhl—different from last year. A gang, he said."

"Yes, Friedrich Achen. He arrived a year or so ago. Married the daughter of Heinrich Buch, one of the city council members. No one seems to know from where he came. He has, as Anse had said, no visible means of support. He hangs out at Der Bulle und Bär, one of our more disreputable inns. He has a gang that extorts money from the shopkeepers, selling 'protection.' The watch, really the city council, hasn't done much to curtail Achen's activities. It's not our—the militia's—responsibility, either. Achen knows better than to bother us."

"Your militia?"

"The city's militia. However, we—the gunsmiths and the remaining Jaegers—are the largest contingent of the militia. The Jaegers answer to us...me...for the moment. Patrolling is not a responsibility I—we—want. It's been thrust upon us. We ensure our people are safe. That's all we can do."

"I see. It's not my responsibility, either. But, like you said, sometimes it is thrust upon us."

"Have you met the council, yet?"

"I met with Herr Feld this morning. He arrived on my doorstep bright and early. I had some documents for him and the council and gave them to him. The SoTF will be establishing a district court here in Suhl. I'm here to find a suitable building for the court. And a troop of the SoTF Mounted Constabulary will be stationed here in the barracks."

"I suspect the documents may disappear if he doesn't like their contents."

"I don't think so. He signed a receipt...and I have copies."

"I see Herr Feld's reputation has gone before him."

"Don't know about that. It's just a standard precaution."

"I wouldn't wait, Archie, to meet the council. I've been told there are workmen dismantling the barracks. If you don't lay claim, there may be no barracks, shortly."

Archie sat silent for a moment. "*Danke*, Ruben. I'll get on that."

"I have a meeting tonight with other gunsmiths and craft masters. If you don't mind, I'll tell them about the new court and the Mounted Constabulary."

"Feel free. It's no secret."

"Thank you for coming, Archie, but if you don't mind, I have some apprentices to oversee. Some need to be constantly supervised."

Archie chuckled. "I understand, Ruben. That is true even up-time. *Guten Tag.*"

"*Guten Tag*, Archie."

Dieter arrived at the Boar's Head Inn in time to see Archie enter before him. "Archie!" he called. "There's a problem."

Archie turned at the entrance to their rooms and asked, "The barracks?"

"Ja. It's being torn down."

"I know. Ruben Blumroder told me. He's the head of Suhl's gunsmiths. He'd be the master of the gunsmith guild if there was one."

"I told them to stop but they refused and there were six of them to my one."

"Get your gear. Let's pay them a visit."

Dieter disappeared into his room to shortly reappear dressed much like Archie—boots, canvas pants, white shirt and badge, leather vest, gun belt, shotgun on a sling and covering all, his duster. "I'm ready. Let's go."

They arrived at the barracks a few minutes later. "There they are. That one," Dieter said, pointing to a man in a leather coat watching the others, "is the leader." To one side were two other men leaning against a partially dismantled palisade wall.

Archie walked up to the man in the leather coat. "Are you the boss of these men?"

"I'm their overseer. So what?"

"Then I'm ordering you to stop work and leave—immediately."

"I don't take orders from you."

"You do now. That's SoTF property, and it's my responsibility. I have my authority here," he said, exposing his badge.

The man turned and shouted to the workers, "Get them!" and drew a large knife from under his coat.

Archie stepped back, shifted his grip on his cane and swung, knocking the knife from the overseer's hand. He slid his hand down to the other end of the cane, and on the backstroke hit the overseer's forearm with the alloy head, breaking both bones. The overseer shrieked at the sudden surge of pain.

Archie heard a click behind him. Dieter had switched off the safety of his shotgun that had been unseen under his duster. He had it leveled at the rest of the workmen. From the corner of his vision, Archie saw the two leaners running toward him. He turned and punched one in the stomach with the steel foot of his cane. That one bent double from the punch, blocking the path of the other before falling to the ground in a huddle. By the time the other attacker had stepped around the first, the cane's alloy head was swinging toward the attacker's jaw. It hit with a crunch and both attackers were out of action and on the ground.

The fight was over. Two men on the ground. One standing clutching a broken arm and five others with hands up, eyes on the muzzle of Dieter's shotgun. Archie was panting and wheezing.

I'm outta shape.

"Do you happen to know if Suhl has a jail, Dieter?" he asked between pants.

"No."

"I don't, either. Let's tie their hands and march

'em to Ruben Blumroder's place. I think he'll have a place to put them or tell us where's the jail."

Archie only had one pair of steel handcuffs. He and Dieter carried rawhide thongs instead of cuffs. Between the two of them, they had enough for the six men still standing.

"Archie, I think this one is dead," Dieter said, examining the one huddled on the ground.

"Well, crap."

Archie checked the two on the ground. The first one, the one he'd punched with the steel foot of his cane, was clearly dead. He opened the man's shirt to reveal a purple blotch covering most of his stomach. His cane punch must have ruptured some internal organ and the man had hemorrhaged to death. He checked the second man. He was dead, too. The alloy head of the cane had impacted the hinge of his jaw. His skull had caved in. *Hit him too hard. I need to practice with this cane more often.*

"Dieter, take the boss man's coat and cover these two. We'll send someone for 'em later."

Anse Hatfield was standing in the doorway of Ruben Blumroder's shop when he saw Archie and Dieter approach with their prisoners. *"Ruben!"* he yelled.

Blumroder, hearing the urgency in Hatfield's voice, strode quickly to join him.

"Archie's been busy," Anse said. "Told you so."

"Ruben, do you have somewhere to stash these folks?" Archie asked when they reached the doorway.

"I could find a place, a storeroom I suppose."

"Neither Dieter nor I know if Suhl has a jail. I assume there is one?"

"Yes, below the council chambers in the *rathaus*. I don't think it's been used much, not since last year."

"I don't think that jail would be the best place just now. Can you keep these people out of sight for a while, until the Mounted Constabulary arrives?"

"I can do that."

"Good. Dieter, go with them and get our cuffs back. I think we're going to need them."

Blumroder spoke briefly with one of his journeymen. He and a couple of apprentices armed themselves with pistols and marched the six down the street.

Archie sighed. "There are two dead men at the barracks, Ruben. Could you send someone to get them?"

"What happened?"

"They were waiting for us. The one with the broken arm was the boss of the crew tearing down the barracks. He refused to stop work and drew a knife on me. I have a sneaking suspicion the two deaders may have been a couple of Achen's men. While Dieter and I were taking care of the workmen, those two joined the fight. They rushed me and I got careless. I hit them too hard—with my cane."

Ruben eyebrows rose. "You killed them with a cane?"

"Unintentionally. I hit one too hard in the head with this"—he raised the cane to show the molded alloy knob—"and punched the other too hard with this." He pointed to the steel-capped foot of the cane. "They got too close to me. I had to use what I had. I was rushed."

Ruben nodded. "I understand."

"Does Suhl really have a watch? I've been here two days and I haven't seen one yet."

"They do. I don't know their patrol schedules. They

don't come here because we take care of ourselves. The council has not asked the full militia for help. Truthfully, I haven't really paid much attention."

"I'm thinking the watch should be rebuilt from scratch with a professional *wachtmeister* who can properly train, organize, and lead the watchmen. The only ones I've seen on watch are your militiamen at the gates."

"There are some on the walls, too."

"Guess I didn't look hard enough. While I'm thinking of it, I need someone to help me survey the barracks and see how much damage has been done. I'll need to hire some workmen to fix it up, repair any damages, and ready the place for the constabulary troop."

"I'll speak with some of the other craft masters. It's about time for our weekly meeting. I'll ask them to send you a man or two—tomorrow?"

"Good. Tell them we're staying at the Boar's Head Inn. If I'm not there, Dieter Issler, my deputy, will be. Feld is arraigning a meeting for me with the council sometime tomorrow."

A messenger from the *bürgermeister* arrived early the next morning. The council would meet with Archie later that morning. Archie sent a messenger to Anse Hatfield asking Anse to join him at the meeting. Anse knew, at least by reputation, many of the council members. Archie would have preferred to have Ruben Blumroder there, too. But that would appear to be political favoritism, Ruben being an SoTF official. If he needed a local representative, they would not be surprised to see Anse standing next to Archie. These folk understood family ties. They'd view the two up-timers as kith, if not kin.

Ruben had been good to his word. A master carpenter arrived early. He and Archie discussed the issue with the barracks. "Herr Heinrich Buch owns the barracks property," the carpenter said. "I heard he bought it from the council. He said he planned to build a warehouse on the site. It is prime property."

"I'm going to find out about that. It wasn't the council's property to sell. It belongs to the SoTF."

"I only know what I've been told."

"Is that going to be a problem with you? Herr Buch claiming it?"

"*Nein*. You said you would pay for the survey. It's guilders in my pocket either way."

"How long will you need for the survey? A day? Less?"

"Not a day. A couple of hours at least."

"Would this afternoon be good?"

"*Ja.*"

"Have you met my deputy, Dieter Issler?"

"*Ja*, when I arrived."

"Come back this afternoon. I have a meeting later this morning. If I'm not here, Dieter will go with you. He'll keep anyone off your back in case someone objects."

"I'll be here."

The carpenter departed. Archie glanced at his watch. It was time to meet Anse at the *rathaus*.

Archie was limping slightly when he arrived at the *rathaus*. He had been more active than usual. He had not been in a fight since he was wounded the previous year. He realized age was creeping up on him.

Anse Hatfield was waiting when Archie arrived. "Hurtin', Archie?"

"Some."

"Feelin' mean and ornery?"

"Yeah, why?"

"You'll need that with these folks."

The *rathaus* was a three-story building, the only one in Suhl as far as he knew, Anse said. The ground floor was an open space used for large meetings, weddings, and festivals. The city council met in a room on the second floor. The top floor contained offices of city officials and departments.

Archie's leg hurt more after climbing the stairs. If he needed to be feeling mean and ornery, he was ready. He and Anse walked into the council room. Herr Feld sat at the head of the table. Six other councilmen sat along both sides leaving Archie and Anse to sit at the end, opposite to Feld.

"Welcome, Marshal, and you, too, Herr Hatfield," he said. Without giving Archie the opportunity to respond, Feld introduced the other six members of the council. Heinrich Buch sat to Feld's right, Archie noticed. Each councilman nodded in turn as he was introduced.

"We are here at your request, Herr Marshal," Feld said.

"I appreciate you acting so swiftly," Archie began. "I am SoTF Marshal Archie Mitchell," he said, speaking to the entire council. "I assume you have read the documents I gave you, Herr Feld. Has the entire council read them?"

"No, I've not had time to make copies. A couple of the councilmen have read them, but not all."

"By chance, I have a copy with me. I'll read it to the council." Which he proceeded to do.

Several councilmen interrupted as he read, asking for clarification of one point or another. When Archie came to the part about renovating the barracks, Councilman Heinrich Buch interrupted. "That's my property!"

"No it isn't. It is owned by the government of the State of Thuringia and Franconia."

"Noelle Murphy transferred ownership to the city council. I bought it from the council!"

"Noelle Murphy didn't have that authority," Anse replied. "She was very aware of the limits of her authority. No one knew it had been transferred to the SoTF until Marshal Mitchell arrived."

"I have the document here. Right here! It's proof that she did, whether she had the authority or not. You can't take back what she has done."

"May I see that document?" Archie asked.

"No! It is my only proof."

"It is a transfer of ownership to Suhl, not you, Heinrich," Feld said. "Give it to him."

Grudgingly, Buch gave the document to the councilman sitting next to him. It was passed, councilman to councilman, until it reached Anse Hatfield.

Anse glanced at the document and looked up. "It's a forgery."

"What!" exclaimed Heinrich Buch, jumping to his feet.

"Look at it, Archie," Anse said. "Look at the signature."

"What about it?" Archie asked.

"Look at it. Is it written by someone who is right-handed or left-handed?"

Archie looked down at the document again. "Right-handed. Why?"

"Noelle Murphy is left-handed. I carried messages for her whenever I went back to Grantville. Whoever wrote this was right-handed."

"You're a liar!" Buch shouted.

"If I am, it can be refuted in a few days. I can send a radio message for samples of Noelle Murphy's signature. They can get here by courier in a couple of days."

"They'll be fakes! You just want to steal my property."

"Now why would we want to do that when no one outside Suhl even knew you claimed the barracks?"

Buch stood white-faced, trembling. Abruptly, he sat. He muttered something to Feld who in turn said, "We await your proof, Herr Hatfield."

"In the meantime," Archie said, "I'm having the barracks surveyed to determine what is needed for its full restoration. No work will be done until the council has proof the transfer of the barracks to Suhl was fraudulent. I also warn you now that the Court of the State of Thuringia-Franconia will be very interested how this all happened."

". . . that was the end of the meeting," Archie told Dieter. "I'm very glad Anse was there. Otherwise, we'd be in a mess, a big lawsuit probably. Just the thing to kick off the new court here in Suhl. So how was your afternoon with the carpenter?"

"Interesting. A stonemason joined us at the barracks. Apparently, the Swedes had built a stone armory for their munitions and a stone outbuilding that could easily be converted to be a jail, guardhouse, whatever you call it. Strong fitted stone walls and floors, and thick iron-studded doors. A little dark, no windows, but the stonemason said those could be added if we wanted."

"I think we'll have to do that. If we make that the holding prison for the court, the prisoners will need access to light and air."

"He's coming by here tomorrow. I can tell him then. He and the master carpenter will draw up some estimates for us, cost and time to do all the renovation."

"Good. Now, we have to find a courthouse."

"I think I found one."

"Oh? Where?"

"Right next to the barracks. You remember that building right next to the place where the wall had been torn down?"

"Vaguely."

"It's part of the barracks. It was quarters for the officers and their headquarters. They didn't like the spaces in the barracks proper so they included that building when they appropriated the property for the barracks. I was told Buch had owned it before it was seized by the Swedes."

"That explains much."

"Yes, it does."

"I didn't go in today but I think we should give it a look over as soon as we can."

"I agree. Tomorrow?"

"Let's see, the carpenter and stonemason are coming in the morning. We could go with them. I don't remember any other appointments, do you?"

Their conversation was interrupted by a knock on their door. The innkeeper entered. "Herr Marshal, this message just arrived for you."

"*Danke*. I appreciate your promptness."

The innkeeper left to return to the taproom in the front of the inn. Archie tried to read the message but it was handwritten, and poorly at that. "Can you read this, Dieter?"

"Well. Uh, it's from Heinrich Buch. I think he is offering an apology and would like to meet you tonight at"—he glanced at his watch, a gift from Greta—"at around 9:00 P.M., if I'm reading this right. His handwriting is terrible!"

"Huh! I wonder what he wants? After the meeting today, I wouldn't think he wants to meet for hugs and kisses."

"What?" It was another of Archie's witticisms that always surprised Dieter.

"Never mind. Ask the innkeeper to send a messenger to Buch and tell him I'll be there. Remind me that we need to budget for messenger service."

"I'll do that. Is it alright if I don't go with you? One of my horses has cast a shoe. I'd like to take it to Christian Zeitts and get it shod."

"Go ahead. I don't think Buch is going to try anything, not now that all has been exposed."

Archie entered Buch's shop. The smell of burned powder still lingering on his duster and clothes.

Heinrich Buch approached from the rear of the cabinetry shop. "Herr Marshal."

"Herr Buch. I think you have a mess out front. There are four dead bodies."

"I heard." He sighed. "I need to confess."

"Luring me here to be killed?"

"No! No, I . . . I didn't know what was planned. My son-in-law told me to invite you here. He . . . uh . . . he forced me."

"How?"

"My daughter. She's six months with child. Achen beats her. I'm afraid he'll kill her."

"Isn't that frowned upon?"

"Yes, no, the church won't interfere. It's not against the law if it's just a beating. There's no one."

"I know how that can be. I've seen it often enough. Back up-time, if something like this occurred, a man gathered his friends and family and fixed the problem, put the son of a bitch in the hospital. No one talks, nothing can be proved."

"I don't have anyone that I could trust to not talk. This whole scheme with the barracks is his idea. He told me to build a warehouse and storefront at the barracks. When finished, it and the building next to it could be sold for three times what it cost me."

"And what did it cost you to buy the barracks?"

The price Buch gave was astonishingly low. "Who pushed this through the council? You?"

"Feld. He gets a percentage of the profit when the buildings are sold."

"Somehow, I'm not surprised."

"Now, where can I find your son-in-law?"

"He's usually at Der Bulle und Bär this time of night. He lives, sometimes, here with my daughter. They have rooms upstairs. But most of the time he's there."

"Will he be there tomorrow?"

"He should be."

"Don't warn him I'm coming."

"No—no, I won't."

"I think Suhl needs a new councilman and *bürgermeister*, don't you?"

Buch didn't speak but just nodded and hung his

head. He'd be lucky to get off with some jail time and a heavy fine. He and Feld both. The SoTF was hard on public corruption.

Archie wished he hadn't given Dieter time off to get his horse shod. He wasn't up to bracing Achen in his own territory. He didn't know how many men Achen had. Seven of them were now pushing up daisies. He could easily have more. Tomorrow would do. He and Dieter would scout Der Bulle und Bär. If Achen was there, he and Dieter would arrest him . . . one way or another.

He headed back to the Boar's Head. He felt fine. The adrenaline hit made his aches and pains slip away.

He walked through the Boar's Head doorway and made his way over to a table in the corner. He didn't drink much but, once in a while, he liked a beer. *"Ein bier, mein Herr,"* he called to the innkeeper. The beer arrived in a large mug, still foaming. The innkeeper brewed it himself. It wasn't what he liked, but in the time since the Ring of Fire, he had become accustomed to the down-time brew. It would do.

Archie slept late the next morning. He had left Dieter a note on his bedroom door to postpone the follow-up with the carpenter and stonemason for a day. He and Dieter had law business to attend to today.

A visit to the jakes, a bath, and he was ready. He retrieved his Model 1897 shotgun from their makeshift armory and dumped a handful of double-aught shells in his side coat pocket. He loaded the shotgun with five more shells of double-aught buck. The shotgun was once known as a trench gun. It had a twenty-inch barrel, and, at one time, a bayonet lug. Archie had never owned a bayonet for the shotgun. He was well off without it. All a bayonet did, in close quarters, was get in the way.

Dieter stood waiting. He, too, had his double-barreled shotgun ready and his Colt 1911 on his belt. The two walked out through the front of the Boar's Head Inn, Archie in front with Dieter following. The innkeeper did a double take as they passed. They were armed and appeared ready for business.

Der Bulle und Bär was in a part of Suhl that Archie had not yet visited. It was nestled in the shade of the city wall. Archie and Dieter walked up to the entrance. Dieter opened the door and stepped aside to let Archie enter first.

Archie walked in and stepped to one side. Dieter followed and stepped to the other side. Neither were silhouetted against the open doorway.

Schlick-schlock! The strange sound caused Achen to look up, interrupting his conversation with his last two men.

"Friedrich Achen," Archie said. "You are under arrest for fraud, extortion, assault on an SoTF marshal, and murder. Place your hands on your head and stand up!"

Achen looked into three shotgun barrels, the double-barrel in Dieter's hands and the one in Archie's. Both marshals stood covering the inn's common room, their six-pointed badges clearly visible in the dimness of the inn.

No one moved. Then, Achen slowly raised his hands, put them on his head and slowly rose. The other two sitting at his table didn't move, neither scarcely breathed.

"Step forward and turn around."

Achen did so.

"I'm using my good steel handcuffs on you, Achen.

The rest of you—don't interfere. Stay where you are and don't move until we're gone. Don't follow us either. We can take you all out if necessary."

The room remained silent. None doubted his word. Archie and Dieter pulled Achen with them and backed out of the room. Dieter kept watch as they headed for Ruben Blumroder's shop.

"We *really* need a jail, Dieter," Archie said as they neared the gun shop. "This is just getting repetitious."

Suhl
Mid-May 1634

A Mounted Constabulary trooper dismounted outside the entrance of the Boar's Head Inn. The inn's stable-boy took the horse's reins and led it to the stables in back for watering while the trooper went inside the inn. "Where may I find Marshal Mitchell?" he asked.

"He's in back. Wait. I'll get him," the innkeeper replied and disappeared into the rear of the inn to reappear a few minutes later with the marshal.

"I'm Marshal Mitchell," he told the trooper.

"Sir, the 1st Mounted Constabulary Troop with Frau Mitchell and Frau Issler should arrive in two hours. Captain Gruber sent me ahead to tell you."

"That's very good news, trooper." Archie walked back to the rear doorway and shouted, "Dieter! They're here. Want to ride out to greet them?"

"Yes!" Dieter replied from the rear of the inn.

Archie returned to the trooper and said, "Have a beer on me while we saddle our horses. We'll ride back with you."

"*Danke*, Herr Marshal." The trooper never refused

a free beer. He took his time to finish it and then walked out the front entrance in time to see Archie and Dieter appear on horseback with the stableboy leading the trooper's horse.

"Lead off," Archie instructed after the trooper had mounted, and the three departed.

They rode down the road that ran along the river until they found the troop and several accompanying wagons coming toward them. Archie saw Marjorie sitting on one wagon. Greta was seated on another. Both wagons, covered by waterproof tarps, were heavily loaded and driven by MC troopers.

"I think Marjorie and Greta brought everything but the kitchen sink," Archie said to Dieter as they approached the troop. Archie greeted the officer in the lead and then rode down the column until he reached Marjorie's wagon. Dieter rode on to the next wagon and Greta.

"Hi, Marj, I've missed you," Archie said, pulling up next to the wagon.

"Arch, I missed you, too . . . I'm glad to be here. You're looking good."

"Feel good, too. I was really whupped when I first got here. Dieter and I had some troubles but that's all cleared up."

"I see you got a new saddle."

"Yeah, I made a good deal. Where're your horses?"

"My mare and the gelding are in the string back behind the wagons with the MC's spare horses. I rode most of the time, but too much made my rear hurt. I'm not up for long rides on horseback anymore."

"I hear ya. Dieter and I found a nice house in town. It's two stories and big enough for all of us with room to spare. It's not far from some new friends of mine, Johann Zeitts and his family. I think you'll like them."

"I brought your recliner and our bed. I had to disassemble them to get everything in the wagon but I knew you'd want them."

"Thank you. I really miss that recliner. The beds here are okay, but my leg starts hurting in the middle of the night."

Captain Gruber rode up next to Archie and introduced himself. "Is the barracks ready, Marshal?"

"Almost. The workmen should finish up today—just minor stuff. The trooper barracks and the stables were finished first. I left two tall trees standing for the radio antenna according to the instructions I received."

"Good. I brought a permanent radio station with me and two radio operators. They'll work for the court. Did you find a blacksmith, farrier, and saddler?"

"Yes, I did. Johann Zeitts and his son, Christian. I have them under contract to give you twenty hours each, each week. Johann Zeitts is a saddler. He made the saddle I'm sitting on. His son, Christian, is a journeyman blacksmith and farrier. I don't think you'd need them more than twenty hours a week."

"No, that should be sufficient. The horses were all shod before we left."

"Before I forget, I did make one commitment for you."

"Oh?"

"There's been a shakeup in the Suhl city council. The city watch has been pretty much ineffectual. They've not been competently led. The militia has been manning the gates and the walls but that's all. The new city council has asked for some suitable *wachtmeister* candidates. I told the council that you would provide troopers to help train the watch and help patrol the city until a new *wachtmeister* takes over or for two months, whichever occurs first."

"Hmmm. I think I can do that. Some of them can do double duty for a while."

"I'm glad you agree. I was put into a spot, and I hate to make commitments for other people. My deputy and I have been helping to improve the watch's overall capability and with some on-the-job training on a few promising watchmen. We've been making random patrols through the city with them but we're just two, and when the court is established, we'll have our own work to do."

"I must start sending out patrols as soon as I can, but we'll need some time to get everything set up and to rest the horses and men before we start. I think we can work something out."

"Thank you, Captain."

"You are very welcome, Herr Marshal." Gruber kicked his heels and rode up to the head of the column. Archie stayed with the wagon and Marjorie.

They rode silently for some time, he on horseback and she on the wagon seat next to the driver. Archie broke the silence. "I really missed you, Marj. I don't like living alone."

"What? No dancing girls in that inn?"

Archie laughed. "No, no dancing girls. I hope you like the place Dieter and I found for us. It was a bakery at one time. I had some walls added to divide it into two apartments, one for us and the other for Dieter and Greta."

"It sounds good, Arch...Arch, I'm ready to go home."

"Me too, Marj, me too."

The Tower of Babel

Iver P. Cooper

Grantville
1635

Federico Ballarino took an appreciative sip of the Thuringian Gardens lager. It had been a long day; his train from Magdeburg to Grantville had suffered a breakdown, costing him two hours. When he finally arrived, he dropped his gear off at "Cair Paravel"—the name Princess Kristina had insisted on giving to her official Grantville lodgings. Being her dancing master did carry some perks. And then he made a beeline for the Gardens.

Having arrived later than usual, he hadn't been able to get his regular seat. But it could have been worse. At least he had found an empty table—the last one, in fact. He pulled out some of his translation work. No rest for the wicked, he mused.

A well-dressed stranger walked up to his table and addressed him. "May I sit down?"

Federico made a welcoming hand gesture. It was de rigueur at the Gardens to fill up the tables, even if that meant seating strangers with each other. Anyway, Federico was a bit curious; the stranger's English had a slight French accent.

"My name is Claude Hardy," the stranger said. "I am a counselor to the Court of Justice in Paris. Are you the Federico Ballarino that acts as a translator for Words International, perchance?"

"Why, I am," Federico said, and smiled at what he took to be a prospective customer. "Do you have something that needs translating from French? I can translate French, or for that matter English, into German, Ital—"

"No, no. Earlier today I asked an acquaintance where I might find you, as I suddenly realized that you would be just the sort of person to appreciate my invention." He raised his chin slightly. "I have developed a universal language. Conceptually, at least."

Federico wistfully eyed the nearest exit. "I see."

"The languages you mention, they are all illogically constructed. What is needed is a language based on philosophical principles."

"Uh-huh," said Federico, trying to strike the right balance between politeness and discouragement. By now there were people standing, drinks in hand, between the tables. The crowd was thick enough that only the experienced barmaids dared plow through, like icebreakers in polar waters.

"As a mathematician of some note—you perhaps have read my commentary on Euclid?—it initially occurred to me that mathematics is itself, in a sense, a universal language and thus we could express all thought as a series of numbers."

"Really?" asked Federico, as he contemplated whether, being a dancer, he could make a quick escape by leaping from table to table in the direction of the exit. "How would you obtain the numbers?"

"Why, if we could assign prime numbers to basic characteristics, then any concept could be expressed by the product of the numbers assigned to the basic characteristics that define that concept. And then all we need for a universal language is to agree on the pronunciation of those numbers."

"So if being human were denoted by 2, and being crazy were denoted by 3, a crazy human would be a 6," prompted Federico. He had decided that if he could not escape, he could at least amuse himself.

"*Exactement!*" cried Claude.

"But what if a concept were a composite of a dozen concepts? Then the number to express would be the product of a dozen prime numbers. Would you just teach the product by rote, or would you expect everyone, to be literate, to do the arithmetic in their heads?"

"I see your point." Claude shrugged. "Anyway, I decided that it was not possible for the word for a thing to convey all characteristics of the thing. Rather, I needed to devise a hierarchy of concepts, with enough levels and branches that all things could be assigned their proper place. But I kept changing my mind as to which characteristics to give primacy to. For example, should animals first be subdivided by reference to whether they are carnivores or herbivores, or by whether they walk, swim, or fly?

"I was in a state of despair, until I happened upon a wonderful book in your Grantville library."

"Which book was that?" asked Federico, who was in a state of despair himself by that point.

"*Roget's International Thesaurus,*" Claude declared. "The fifth edition, to be precise. It arranges English words, not in alphabetical order as in a dictionary, but according to the ideas that they express."

"But isn't it just a writer's aid, to make sure that one has chosen the word that best matches the thought?"

"I suppose, but it is also a useful guide for constructing a useful language. For example, class one encompasses words pertaining to the body and the senses. Suppose we were to specify that all such words were to begin with the syllable *ba*. Then each of the categories within the class is identified by the second and if need be the third syllables. One combination for the category 'birth,' another for 'the body,' yet another for 'hair,' and so on. And the final syllables would identify the particular word within the category. Thus, we have a unique word for everything on this earth. Ingenious, no?"

"Have you ever played Twenty Questions?" asked Federico abruptly.

"Excuse me?"

"It's an American word game. One person thinks of something—an animal perhaps—and the other person may ask up to twenty questions in an attempt to guess the animal. The problem-setter must answer truthfully, to the limit of his or her knowledge. You can't ask 'What animal is it?', but you can ask about its characteristics—where it lives, how it moves, what it eats, and so on, and also classification questions, such as, 'Is it a kind of whale?' Finally, you ask whether it is a specific animal, say, a blue whale."

"Interesting."

"It can be amusing, but only if the poser knows

enough about the mystery animal. If the answer to too many of the questions is 'I don't know,' the game becomes frustrating. And that's the problem with your proposed universal language. To name a thing, you must know a great deal about it."

Hardy sighed. "That is pretty much what Descartes wrote to Mersenne, and Mersenne passed on to me. If the primitive words are chosen to reflect the natural order, they may be easily learned, but finding that natural order would require perfect understanding of the things the words represent, and that true philosophy is achievable only in terrestrial paradise.

"But your Grantville's presence in this world is the result of a miracle, none can honestly doubt that, and I hoped that here I might uncover the secret of universal language. If the answer lies not with *Roget's International Thesaurus*, then surely it is somewhere else in Grantville. Could a merciful God intend us to be divided by language until Judgment Day? Is there any doubt that if men understood each other better, that war might become a thing of the past?"

Federico took a long look at Claude Hardy and felt a little ashamed of treating him as a fool. Founding a universal language on philosophical principles was surely a will-o'-the-wisp, but the greater objective was a noble one.

"As far as I know," said Federico, "no 'universal language' in which the words were based on some sort of encoding of the properties of the things was ever devised that could be spoken fluently by someone other than its inventor—if that. But there have been artificial languages that made use of a vocabulary drawn from a variety of languages—French, German, and so on—so that all Europeans would suffer equally in learning it.

"The most successful of them was Esperanto. It had something like a hundred thousand speakers in old timeline 2000, but remember, that's out of ten billion people."

"And where can I find out how to speak Esperanto?"

"Unfortunately, there isn't much in the public libraries. You can find a few paragraphs in the encyclopedias about the grammar and how the words are constructed, that's about it. It is possible that there's an enthusiast here in Grantville, but I wouldn't count on it. After all, the adult population of Grantville at the time of the Ring of Fire was only about twenty-six hundred. The odds are against you. . . .

"You could of course construct your own version of Esperanto. But if you must invent and promote a universal language, I would suggest an alternative. My colleague Nicole told me that around the end of the nineteenth century, some mathematician created a language called *Latino sine flexione*. That is, a Latin with a simplified grammar and minimal inflection of words. As I understand it, it had only the ablative case for nouns, no gender, one kind of plural, one plural form, one adjectival form, one definite article, and verbs aren't inflected for person or number, only for tense."

Claude pondered this. "That would certainly make it easier to learn."

Federico added, "And Latin is already the closest that Europe has to a language that is universal in a practical sense, that is, widely known." He paused. "I take it that you know Descartes and Mersenne because you have communicated with them on mathematical questions?"

"Yes," said Claude, "but not just as a fellow mathematician. I understand Arabic, and I have translated selected passages from several of the great Arabic treatises for them."

"Really? Can you also understand Turkish then? Or Persian?"

"Both, but believe me, it is not because I know Arabic. There are a few words in common, but the sound and the grammar are very different."

"That's very interesting," said Federico. "Sooner or later the eastern empires are going to sit up and take notice of what's happening in Grantville, or vice versa, and there will be demand for translation between English and those languages. Perhaps, if you are still in town then, you might help us out at Words International.

"In fact, if you have the time, let me show you around Words International now. I don't know whether my colleagues will be there, but it's possible—they teach at the school during the day and translate at night."

Claude agreed, and they called the waitress for the check. In due course they were out in the street.

They had only traveled a block when Federico held up his hand. "Do you hear that?"

"Some sort of commotion," agreed Claude.

They reached the intersection, where a narrow side street crossed the road they were on and beheld two wagon drivers screaming at each other. The street in question wasn't wide enough for them to both pass simultaneously, and neither seemed inclined to yield.

"'Here lies the body of Solomon Grey, who died defending his right-of-way,'" Federico recited.

"Pardon?" said Claude.

"I am sorry, I was quoting an American limerick I thought apropos."

As they came closer, it became apparent why they had failed to negotiate a resolution so far; one was speaking in German and the other in French.

"They appear to be at an impasse," said Claude, "and soon it may come to blows. Shall we mediate?"

Federico nodded. "Yes, we should suggest that one with the shorter distance to backtrack should do so," and Claude agreed. A moment later, Claude approached the French-speaking driver and Federico the German-speaking one.

After a brief exchange, Claude walked back to Federico to report. "He says that while he has the shorter distance to backtrack, he turned onto the street first."

Federico returned to the German and passed this on. A moment later, he cursed and told Claude, "And this one insists that his load is the harder one to back up safely and so the Frenchman should yield.

"Should we let these two idiots remain where they are until Judgment Day?"

"How about a coin flip?" suggested Claude.

The two drivers grudgingly agreed, the Frenchman won the toss, and the German backed up. The Frenchman drove past and fortunately refrained from giving the German the finger as he did so.

"You see, the world needs a common language!" declared Claude triumphantly. "If they had that, they could have settled their differences without our help."

Federico sighed. "I think what the world needs is more common sense."

☆　　　☆　　　☆

Author's Note: This story was inspired by reading Arika Okrent's *In the Land of Invented Languages*. Federico Ballarino, a created down-timer, appears previously in my stories "Federico and Ginger" and "Lost in Translation." The French mathematician, linguist and lawyer Claude Hardy (1604–OTL 1678) did propose a universal language to Mersenne (for review by Descartes) in 1629, but the letter is lost and his system is unknown. What is known is that Descartes didn't think much of the practicality of any universal language based on philosophical principles. A math-based language in which the word for each thing was the equivalent of a mathematical product of the numbers representing the properties of the thing was proposed by Thomas Urquhart in 1652 and by Francis Lodwick in 1647. A hierarchical classification approach to a philosophical language was proposed by John Wilkins in 1668. Wilkins' classification in turn inspired Roget's Thesaurus. While Roget composed a "catalogue of words" in 1805, he didn't publish his classification system until 1852. Note that the arrangement in the 5th edition (1992) is very different from that of earlier editions, although it, too, is hierarchical.

Dr. Phil Rules the Waves

Kerryn Offord and Rick Boatright

Prague, Bohemia
September 1636

Dr. Phillip Theophrastus Gribbleflotz, president for life of the Royal Academy of Science, knew what was coming the moment Samuel Hartlib, the secretary of the Royal Academy, stepped into his personal laboratory at the top of the Mihulka Tower—there could be no other reason for him making the climb. "What am I being dragged off to this time?" he protested as he put away his pen and got to his feet.

Samuel had the cheek to smile. "Radio Prague is almost ready to begin transmissions."

"And?" Phillip asked as he replaced his white lab coat with a jacket in a beautiful shade of orange.

"Someone from the Royal Academy has to be there when it is declared operational."

"Why me?" he asked. "You're the secretary. Why don't you go?"

"Because, Herr Dr. Gribbleflotz, sometimes only the president will do."

Phillip sighed. "And I suppose you're going to tell me that this is one of those times?"

Samuel nodded. "This is one of those times, Herr Dr. Gribbleflotz."

Phillip glared ineffectively at Samuel, whom he was sure was laughing at him. "There seem to be a lot of these 'one of these times' events," he protested as he gave his laboratory one last check to make sure he hadn't left anything on. Unfortunately, it seemed there was nothing more to delay the inevitable. "I'm ready. Let's go."

The room was full of the usual band of hangers-on for whom being seen in the right place, and more importantly, being seen talking to the right people, was important. Phillip managed to pretend most of them didn't exist—and thus he didn't have to greet them—as Samuel hustled him to a place of honor.

Phillip found himself seated alongside Vernon Fritz, the up-timer with overall responsibility for getting Radio Prague built.

"Hello, Dr. Gribbleflotz," Vernon said as he held out his hand.

Phillip knew enough to accept the offered hand. "Herr Fritz," he said as they shook hands.

"Sorry to drag you away from whatever you were working on, Doctor."

Phillip waved the apology away. "No need to apologize." He shot a glance in Samuel's direction. Yes, he was watching. Phillip redoubled his efforts to keep a smile on his face. "So Radio Prague is ready to go on the air?"

"That's why we're here," Vernon said. "Have you got your speech prepared?"

"Speech?" Phillip just managed not to shout it out, instead keeping it to a loud hiss, mostly directed at Samuel.

Samuel passed Phillip some papers. "Frau Kastenmayerin and I prepared something for you."

Phillip scanned the pages, shooting Samuel repeated glares as he did so. Samuel and his own wife were taking advantage of his disinterest in anything to do with the running of the Royal Academy to advance their own agenda. With a final glare that was intended to show Samuel that he knew what they were up to, Phillip put the prepared speech to one side and turned his back on Samuel.

Vernon had a grin on his face. "You weren't aware that you would be giving a speech?"

"Of course I knew I would be giving a speech," Phillip said, lying through his teeth. "It's just that I was so caught up in my research that I didn't get around to preparing anything."

"It's fortunate that you have such good support in Herr Hartlib and your wife."

Phillip shot another glare in the general direction of Samuel Hartlib. "Yes, it is," he muttered. "So, Herr Fritz, what do you do now Radio Prague is ready to go live?"

"I'm contracted to hang around for another six months to deal with any teething problems."

Phillip understood about teething problems—he had a son and daughter who'd been born on the 29th of February. Fortunately the nursery maid his wife's stepmother had located for them had known what to do. "We'll miss Frau Rutilius and Herr Bockelmann when they leave."

"Oh, they won't be leaving when I go. They're on two-year contracts."

"They are?" Phillip hadn't known that. It opened a whole new world of opportunities. "Would there be a problem with them wiring my apartment so that I have electric light?"

Vernon shook his head. "There shouldn't be a problem with that. Both Mags and Dietrich are qualified electricians. They'll just have to do the work on their own time."

"Naturally," Phillip said, even as he wondered how he could get them to do the work in their normal working hours. Nothing leapt to mind, but maybe Samuel could help. Sorting out that kind of problem was what he did best.

Samuel slid up beside Phillip. "Herr Doctor, it's time."

Phillip gave Vernon a smile before picking up the prepared speech. "I'll catch up with you later," he said before following Samuel to the podium.

Phillip nodded his head as a token bow to acknowledge the applause his speech was being accorded. After a few minutes he held up a hand to silence the applause. "Thank you, thank you. Now, it is my proud honor to pass the baton onto"—he paused to glance at Samuel, who, like the good secretary he was, was indicating the next person—"Herr Vernon Fritz, the man responsible for bringing us Radio Prague." He stepped back to allow Vernon up to the podium.

Phillip tuned out while Vernon spoke to the crowd. At some point, he was sure, someone was going to flip a switch. Obviously it wasn't him, because Samuel would have told him so. He edged away from the podium so he could whisper into Samuel's ear. "How much longer?" he asked.

"The formalities will end soon, Phillip, but you'll be expected to hang around and talk to people," Samuel said.

Phillip sighed, probably a bit too loudly judging by the way Samuel's brows lifted. "I have experiments I have to get back to," he protested.

"Have to?" Samuel asked. "What could be more important than keeping the Royal Academy in the public eye?"

Phillip knew that to Samuel keeping the Royal Academy in the public eye had priority over everything else. He also knew that if it weren't for Samuel acting as a gatekeeper, he'd constantly be pestered by people wanting the Royal Academy to fund their pet projects. In the interests of keeping Samuel sweet, he kept his mouth shut, settled back in his seat, and waited for the evening to end.

A few days later

Vernon Fritz was walking down the street listening to Radio Prague on a portable crystal set he'd knocked up out of some bits and pieces he happened to have lying around. Reception on his portable set was good, which, considering how close he was to the transmitter, was as it should be.

In addition to checking reception, Vernon wanted to check on the local reaction to the new radio service. Obviously he wasn't going to find many people wandering the streets listening to the radio, and he could hardly go knocking door to door to ask if people were listening to the radio in their homes, so that left just one option. He was going to have to visit inns and taverns to check. It was a tough job, but someone had to do it.

He couldn't hear a radio playing at the first tavern he stopped at. He discovered why when he stepped into the main room. There were people listening to the radio alright, but they were taking turns listening to a single crystal set. That wasn't what he'd expected from a tavern. He approached the barkeep.

"Hello, I'm with Radio Prague, and I was just wondering what you think of the new radio station."

The barkeep snorted loudly and shot a glare at the single crystal set in the room. "It's useless. I thought I was being smart buying a crystal set, but while everyone wants to listen, they are too busy trying to hear to buy drinks. At least with the newspapers they buy drinks."

Vernon was nodding as he listened to the man's tale of woe. "What you need is a proper radio, not a crystal set."

"I most certainly do," the barkeep agreed, "but do you have any idea how much one of those things costs?" Before Vernon could utter a word the man continued on. "And then there's the cost of batteries. The crooks that run the recharging service charge a fortune." He stared at Vernon. "You're an up-timer, aren't you?"

Vernon nodded.

"Well, why aren't you doing something about it. What I need is a radio that can be heard anywhere in my tavern, that doesn't need electricity to work."

Vernon backed away, promising to see what he could do. It would have served no purpose to tell the man that a radio for his tavern that didn't need electricity was an impossibility—radio needed power in order to function.

The man shot a final couple of sentences after Vernon. "Maybe that Dr. Gribbleflotz can do something. I understand he's the world's greatest scientist."

Vernon sniggered as he walked away. Dr. Gribbleflotz was not the world's greatest scientist. If he was the greatest anything, he was the world's greatest and luckiest fake, and there was absolutely no way he was going to invent anything that could solve the man's problem. He headed for the next tavern, and this time he intended buying a drink before trying to talk to anyone.

Meanwhile, at the HDG Laboratories facility at the Mihulka Tower

Thump! Clatter! Thump!

Magdalena "Mags" Rutilius looked up from the new instrumental circuit she was struggling to assemble and saw a red-faced Georg Hoffman scrambling to pick up his crystal radio's earpiece. "Stop!" she said. "Now, jump on it."

Georg looked at her in horror. "But that would break it," he protested.

"Really?" she asked. "I thought that's what you were trying to do." She looked over her four assistants. This wasn't the first time an earpiece had been dropped since Radio Prague went on the air, but on top of a fast approaching deadline to deliver the theremins they were making, Mags' left arm was itching like crazy under its cast—she'd broken the arm saving Dr. Gribbleflotz's lucky crystal from would-be thieves—and as a result, her temper was not its usually sunny self.

"Look," she said, trying to keep her temper in check. "This just isn't working. You're spending half your time fiddling with your earpieces instead of working." She gestured to the incomplete theremins lined up against the back wall. "We need to get these theremins completed by the end of the week," she told them, "so, I'm afraid I'm going to have to ask you to listen to the radio only during your breaks."

"But, Frau Rutilius," Fritz Schmieles protested.

"Put them away now!"

No one was expecting the command voice from the small woman. All four laborants scrambled to remove their earpieces and stow their crystal sets. As they did so, Mags caught sight of their faces and suppressed a groan. The expressions on their twelve-year-old faces put her friend and mathematics tutor Daniel Pastorius' best poor beaten puppy expression to shame, but Mags dare not show any apology for roaring at them however she felt.

The four boys quietly turned back to their respective tasks, but their air of abject misery permeated the room.

"It's no good trying to make me feel guilty," Mags informed the boys, schooling her face to sternness. She had no intention of telling them that they were succeeding.

"Why can't we have a radio like they have in the kitchen?" Georg asked.

Mags laid down her tools and reached out to cover

Georg's hand with her own. "I'm sorry, but radios are expensive, and they need a source of electricity, which we don't have, even if I could afford an electric radio."

"But the Gribbleflotz Magneto-Etheric Theremins don't need electricity," Fritz said, gesturing to one of the said machines sitting against a wall in the room awaiting the installation of the components Mags was working on.

Mags' initial reaction was to smile at how Fritz insisted on giving the theremins their full name, with a lot of emphasis on *Gribbleflotz*. Clean clothes, three meals a day, and a warm bed to sleep in bought a lot of loyalty. She was just about to launch into an explanation about how the theremins converted the power generated by pumping the treadle into electrical power to drive the oscillator and amplifier when she realized what she was about to say and froze.

"Is there something the matter, Frau Rutilius?" Michael Thurn asked.

"Noooo," Mags managed to say. "Hans, Fritz, bring that theremin over here." She pointed to the space on her right.

"Lift it, don't drag it," she added when she heard the scrape of the theremin's wooden legs on the floor.

"What are you going to do?" Hans Grünhut asked as he and Fritz carried the nearly completed Gribbleflotz Magneto-Etheric Theremin over to Mags.

"Give me a moment," she said. Mags studied the amplifier unit she'd been working on. If she replaced the oscillator inputs to the coil with the crystal set outputs . . . A smile spread across her face. She might have a solution to the earpiece problem. She disconnected the oscillator and turned her attention to the nearest crystal radio. Unfortunately, it was on the other side of the room, close to where the boys had been sitting.

"Okay, let's get everything over beside that crystal radio," she said, pointing to one of them.

The boys leapt into action and carried, not dragged, the theremin to the crystal radio Mags had pointed to. It took just a couple of minutes for Mags to solder the wires to connect everything.

"Do you want this?" Georg asked.

Mags glanced round to see Georg was offering her fuel for the flame triodes. She shook her head. "Thank you, but we don't need the flame triodes for this," she said before she started to pump the foot treadle that spun the Alexanderson alternator's rotor. Soon she could hear Radio Prague through the speaker.

A *few days later*

Vernon walked into the radio station expecting to see everyone busy. They weren't. They were gathered around a door watching something happening in the machine room. That didn't bode well for the rest of the day.

Ernst Goetz, the locally employed manager of the radio station, looked up. "Herr Fritz. We have been looking everywhere for you. Hans here has a problem."

"What's the problem?" he asked as he walked over. The sight that greeted him wasn't pleasing. Hans had an access hatch of the main power cabinet open. He could hear that the Alexanderson alternator was operating, which was comforting. It wouldn't look good for the station to be off the air so soon after going live.

Hans Rohfritsch lifted his hands in a show of

frustration as he pulled his head out from inside the cabinet. "Someone managed to break a coolant pump. That meant the coolant in the first bank of liquid rheostats started to boil, which resulted in a surge going through the main power supply. Fortunately, the backup system kicked in as it was supposed to."

Vernon's whistle wasn't particularly pleased. "How the . . ." He managed to bite down on the expletive before it escaped. "The system is supposed to shut down before the coolant starts to boil."

Hans shrugged apologetically before turning accusing eyes onto Ernst. "Someone pulled the override."

Vernon turned his gaze onto the current villain of the piece. The override was only supposed to be used during maintenance operations and there were supposed to be safeguards in place to stop it being accidentally pulled during normal operations.

Ernst immediately started to stutter out excuses. "It was an accident," he said.

Vernon raised his brows. It must have been some accident, he told himself. "You're a front room guy, Ernst. What the heck were you doing in the machine room?" That got more mumbled excuses from Ernst. Vernon raised his hand to silence him. "Let's forget about how it happened for now and just worry about getting it fixed." He turned to Hans. "Can you fix it?"

Hans backed away from the cabinet he'd been working at and shrugged. "I'm pulling the boards to check on them. Meanwhile, it would be good if someone could unbolt the covers from the liquid rheostats." He paused. "Maybe Frau Rutilius?"

"She's still on the sick list," Vernon said.

"But it's her left arm that is broken, Herr Fritz,

and she's right-handed," Hans said. "If Frau Rutilius can get at the mounting bolts..." He gestured to one of the enormous liquid rheostats to complete the sentence before going on. "Otherwise..." He left that sentence hanging, because Vernon would know exactly what the otherwise option was.

Vernon looked at the rheostats and realized that there was a design problem and winced. The bolts holding the heavy liquid tank covers in place were virtually inaccessible from above, blocked by another cabinet mounted above them. The space between them was far too small for Hans. He could unbolt the front of the covers from below, but there was no way for him to reach the bolts at the back.

He checked the rest of the watching team. Some of them were smaller than Hans, but they were all giants compared with the pint-sized Mags. If she could get into the gap between the rheostats and undo the bolts holding the covers in place, then they wouldn't have to disconnect complete rheostats, unbolt them from the floor, and lift the heavy units up just to remove the tops. It would save them days of backbreaking work. He made a note. The next time the station was down, they would have to move the upper cabinet. Meanwhile Mags was the answer. "I'll drop by and see how she's doing."

"Dietrich has said that Frau Rutilius is suffering 'cabin fever,'" one of the other technicians said.

That statement amused Vernon. Dietrich was actually Dietrich Bockelmann, an electrical trades graduate from Grantville who had graduated in the same class as Mags. The rest of the team at Radio Prague happily called or referred to him by his Christian name. Meanwhile,

Mags was still Frau Rutilius to everyone but himself and Dietrich. As for the cabin fever, he could easily believe that, and he was pretty sure Mags would leap at the chance to get back to work. It was going to be his job to stop her from making her injuries worse. "If I don't think she's fit to come back to work, she won't be coming. So, Hans, I want you to look at ways to get at those rheostat covers while I'm gone. Meanwhile, the rest of you can get back to work."

Mihulka Tower, HDG Laboratories (Prague)

Vernon made his way into the workroom where Mags was muttering to herself as she fiddled with one of her retail crystal sets. He watched quietly for a while, listening to the sound of Radio Prague coming from one of the other work rooms. The reception was good, as was the sound quality. Eventually Mags looked up and saw him.

"Herr Fritz!" she said as she scrambled to get to her feet.

Vernon waved a hand. "Stay seated. I just dropped by to see how you were getting on."

Mags glared at her arm in its plaster cast. "I can do most things, but the cast gets in the way when I need to hold something."

Vernon nodded. He'd observed the difficulties Mags was experiencing as she worked on the crystal set. But he'd also noticed that she had ways to work around the problems. "How would you like to get back to work?"

Mags' eyes lit up momentarily, then she frowned. "But I can't work with a cast on my arm," she muttered.

"Not in your normal area of expertise, but they've

managed to boil the coolant in a couple of the rheostats, and..."

"Boil a rheostat? How did they manage to do that?"

Vernon shrugged. He wasn't ready to apportion blame until he had the full story. "That's not important. What is, is that Hans Rohfritsch can't get at the bolts securing the rheostat covers, and we're faced with the prospect of lifting up each unit just so we can get at the bolts so we can remove the tops... So, are you interested in helping?"

"Yes," Mags said as she carefully put the equipment she'd been working with down and started collecting her tools. "I'll need to get changed," she said as she got to her feet.

"No problem. Five minutes here or there won't make much difference."

While Mags dashed off to change, Vernon examined the crystal set she'd been working on. He'd been impressed enough with the earlier versions he'd seen back in Grantville to hire her over graduates from the electrical trades course with better grades. He could see that she was working on a new version, this time using a flame diode as the detector, replacing the finicky cat's whisker and galena crystal method of demodulating the AM radio signal. He wondered how well it would work, but seeing that she'd even thought to try it reassured him that he'd made the right decision. Even if she'd managed to get herself on the sick list for the last few weeks by breaking her arm.

"I'm ready," Mags called from behind him. "We just need to tell Frau Mittelhausen where I'm going."

Vernon nodded and let Mags lead the way.

There was another radio in the kitchen. Or at least Vernon imagined it was the kitchen, judging by the sounds and smells coming from beyond the door. He shrugged. Obviously Dr. Gribbleflotz, or more likely, Frau Mittelhausen, believed that it was worthwhile investing in radios to keep his staff happy. It wasn't as if he couldn't afford to buy several—and the batteries to keep them going.

Mags shoved her knuckles into her mouth and sucked on them. The taste of lubrication oil was offset by the taste of her own blood. Next time she saw her boyfriend's father—Jason Cheng Sr. of Kitt and Cheng Engineering and the head of the engineering department at the state technical college in Grantville—she intended to have words with him about doing more to get engineers designing things for ease of maintenance rather than just concentrating on designing for ease of manufacture.

She pulled her knuckles out of her mouth to survey the damage. She now had a complete set of skinned knuckles on her right hand. The only reason the left hand wasn't similarly decorated was the plaster cast that made it difficult to use the hand also protected her knuckles. She made a mental note: work gloves.

"How's it going?" Vernon Fritz called from behind her.

"Just the last bolt to loosen, and we can lift it free."

"So?" Vernon asked.

Mags took the hint and got back to work. A couple of minutes later she removed the last nut and washer. "Okay, you can lift it now," she called out as she stepped as far back from the liquid rheostat as she could.

Using a block and tackle, the other workers quickly hauled the top of the rheostat free and swung it onto a cart, leaving Mags still in the cramped space she'd been working in. "Could someone help me out, please?"

Two-hundred-forty-pound Dietrich stepped as close as he could before putting a hand under each of Mags' arms. "Alley-oop," he said as he easily lifted her less than eighty-pound body out from between the rheostats.

"Thanks, Dietrich," Mags said when he set her back on her feet. She turned to Vernon. "What do you want me to do now?"

"You can help try and breathe new life back into those rheostats."

Mags sighed. It wasn't what she'd hoped to hear, but the likely alternative was being sent back home.

Kitt and Cheng Engineering, Grantville

Jason Cheng sent the radio-controlled model of Hans Richter's Belle into a tight turn as he tried to get it into the six of the model airplane being flown by his friend and fellow apprentice mechanical engineer, David Kitt. However, with two almost identical models, gaining an advantage in a close-in dogfight was next to impossible. He broke off and sent his model in search of altitude.

The bell of the timer rang out, calling an end to the flight. Jason circled while David landed his model of Colonel Woods' Belle before landing his own model.

They were shutting down their respective models when Barry Thompson, their current immediate supervisor, walked up. "That last flight can't have lasted more than ten minutes. Are you two slacking?"

Jason ran a hand over his aching neck. Keeping an eye on a model airplane meant you were constantly looking skyward. "We were dogfighting, Barry. Ten minutes is pushing the limits for that kind of intense flying."

"Yeah," David said, rubbing his own neck. "You can't afford to lose your concentration when you're flying planes that aggressively that close together. Otherwise you'll collide and *bang* go two models."

Barry nodded. "Okay then, ten minutes is the limit for close flying. I'll pass that on to the movie guys." He paused a moment. "Should I tell them the models are ready, or have you two not finished playing around with them yet?"

Jason glanced over to David. He got a shrug in reply, which meant, if David was thinking the same as him, that he didn't think they could put off handing over their handiwork any longer. "Go ahead, Barry."

He would have said more, but just then Rosina Trempling, the office manager, appeared. "Jason. Your father just rang. You were supposed to be home half an hour ago."

Jason shot a glance at his watch. "It can't be that late," he protested. He looked around at all the gear that had to be put away before he could head home. He was going to be in soooo much trouble.

"Just leave it and go, Jason," Barry said. "David and I can put everything away."

"But you'll owe me," David said, making move-along gestures with his hands.

"Thanks," Jason said before grabbing his personal gear and making a run for it.

Meanwhile

Jason's older sister, Diana had her nose buried in a book. It was no ordinary book. It was an offset-printed photographic reproduction of Dr. Shipley's copy of *Gray's Anatomy*, and the very expensive book's presence in her personal library was a good reason to be glad of her family's relative wealth.

She was reaching out to turn the page when there was a knock on her bedroom door. She sat up. "Yes?" she called to the still-closed door.

"Dinner will be ready in ten minutes," her mother called.

Diana groaned and muttered about yet another interruption to her studies. "Coming," she called. She placed a bookmark in her book before closing it and got to her feet.

Some time later

Jason made his apologies as he pulled out his chair and flopped down. "Sorry. But David and I were test flying the Belles and lost track of the time."

"How are they going?" his mother, Jennie Lee, asked.

With that question, coming from his mother, Jason knew he wasn't in any trouble. "They're working perfectly. The engines are firing without a hitch." That last was important, because he'd built the engines himself, copying one of the engines his father had made. Sometimes it helped to have a father who was a mechanical engineer who had been heavily into radio-controlled aircraft before the Ring of Fire.

"So you're ready to hand them over to Gino?" Jason Sr. asked.

Jason nodded. Gino Bianchi was the director and producer of the proposed Hans Richter movie, and the person who had commissioned the two radio-controlled scale model Belles. "Barry's going to give the studio a call and let them know they're ready." He looked inquiringly at his father. "So, what are you going to have David and I work on next?"

"Funny you should ask that," Jason Sr. said, "because we've been asked to send someone to Prague to help with a problem the radio station has experienced."

"Prague!" Jason said, all excited. "Can I go?" Mags, his girlfriend of more than four years, was currently working there, and he hadn't seen her since June—not even to check up on her after she'd been injured in an encounter with a couple of housebreakers.

His father nodded. "You'll be going, as will the rest of us." He looked pointedly at Diana.

"What?" Diana protested. "But I can't go to Prague. I've got an anatomy test to prepare for, and I've got assignments to write, so I need access to the library."

Jennie Lee turned to Diana. "You, young lady, need to cut back on your studies and relax a little."

Jason stared at his mother in disbelief. "Who are you and what have you done with my real mother?" he asked.

"What he said," an equally incredulous Diana said. "The only reason you haven't grounded him for life for graduating only second in his class is because he was beaten by Daniel."

"Who happens to be a certified genius," Jason said, "with an IQ off the scale."

Jason Sr. and Jennie Lee smiled at each other before turning to face Jason and Diana. "That is beside the point," Jennie Lee said.

"Teacher's pet," Jason muttered, referring to the fact his mother was one of Daniel Pastorius' mathematics tutors, and that they shared a true love of mathematics.

His mother glared at him. "I was speaking to your sister," she said before turning her attention back to Diana. "You're getting too far ahead of the rest of your intake, and the teaching staff are running out of material to give you before the class is scheduled to start working on the wards."

Jason Sr. smiled at Diana. "We're proud of you. You're going to complete the BSN curriculum six months ahead of the previous best by any student, and your mother and I think you deserve a short break."

"But what will I do in Prague?" Diana protested. She gestured toward Jason. "It's all right for him. He gets to visit his girlfriend. But what will I do while we're in Prague?"

"You could visit the hospital," Jason suggested, "to see what's happening with Dr. Gribbleflotz's vibrating bed experiment."

Diana snorted. "That's a load of crock," she said. "There's no way vibrating beds can help patients heal faster."

"And how do you know that, young lady?" her father asked. "At least Dr. Gribbleflotz is willing to test the theory before reaching a conclusion."

"And," Jason said, eager to add his two cents' worth, "your friends on the veterinary program did say that cats' purrs help speed up healing in animals."

He got a glare from his sister in response to that. "If it was a viable treatment someone would have been doing it up-time," she said.

"Just because you've never heard of anyone researching the field doesn't mean it won't work. Keep an open mind!" Jason said. "You never know; it might turn out to be a revolutionary cure."

"You mean your girlfriend's hero might finally manage to invigorate the *Quinta Essentia* of the human humors," Diana said.

"Children!"

Jason and Diana froze. Their mother very rarely raised her voice. There was a mutual exchange of glares as they fell silent.

"Thank you," Jennie Lee said. "We are all going to Prague. That's final. Now, let's start planning the trip."

A couple of days later, Grantville

Jason Cheng Sr. slipped into the drawing room as quietly as he could. His son and his fellow apprentice mechanical engineer were attempting to produce accurate engineering drawings of two completely different bearing housings. When their drawings were complete they'd be checked for errors and corrected before being turned over to Ollie Reardon, who would then hand them on to some of his machine shop apprentices, asking them to make the bearings.

He edged up beside Barry Thompson, the company's head, and only, qualified machinist. "How are they doing?" he quietly asked.

Barry whispered back, "They had a few teething problems finding things in the engineering drawings standards manual, but they seem to have worked out what they're supposed to be doing."

Jason Sr. nodded. The drawing standards manual laid down the conventions to be adhered to by engineering and drafting personnel in the preparation, revision, and completion of engineering drawings. If his son or David Kitt deviated from the standards, it was likely Ollie's apprentices wouldn't be able to follow the drawings. It was, naturally, a test—testing Jason and David's ability to produce proper engineering drawings, and, after they'd been corrected, the ability of Ollie's apprentice machinists to follow said drawings.

Before too long Barry called out that time was almost up. That resulted in a brief flurry of activity as the two youths gave their drawings a final check, making subtle alterations here and there.

"Time's up," Barry announced a few minutes later.

Both Jason and David laid down their pencils, pushed their chairs back, and stood. "Why do we have a time limit?" David asked as he rubbed his neck.

Barry glanced to Jason Sr., inviting him to answer.

"If you had all the time in the world," Jason Sr. said, "you'd never make a mistake, but we're running a business, and we can't afford to have you spending hours we can't charge preparing drawings, so you have to learn to work to a time limit."

Jason and David exchanged looks. They'd learned about chargeable and non-chargeable hours when they first started their apprenticeships. Chargeable hours were included in the quote and produced income, while non-chargeable ones cost the company. David's mother had told them in no uncertain terms not to accrue non-chargeable hours.

"Barry, if you don't mind, I'd like a few words with Jason and David."

Barry glanced around, raising a brow in Jason Sr. "Hey, no problem. I'll just collect the drawings and start checking them."

"Thanks." Jason Sr. turned to the two boys. "I've just been on the phone to Gino..."

"Is there something wrong with the Belles?" Jason asked his father.

"No, but it is about the Belles." Jason Sr. grinned. "How would the pair of you like to show off your flying skills to the good people of Prague?"

"Hey, cool," David said.

"Why does Mr. Bianchi want us to fly the Belles around Prague?" Jason asked.

"He wants to use them to raise interest in his movie."

"But he hasn't made the movie yet," David protested.

"Is he trying to get investor interest, Dad?"

Jason Sr. shrugged. "Maybe, but that's not our concern."

"Mum'll be very concerned if we aren't going to get paid," David said.

"Yes, your mother would be concerned," Jason Sr. agreed. "However, we have been paid for our work to date."

"Including the Belles?" David asked. "We only just turned them over."

"The check is in the mail," Jason Sr. said. Then he grinned. "Actually, your mother has already deposited the check."

"So if we're taking the film company's Belles to Prague, what happens if anyone asks to have a go?" Jason asked.

"You tell them no," his father replied. "We can't risk the Belles in the hands of people who don't know what they're doing."

"Even the king?" Jason asked.

Jason Sr. winced. The king was probably a special case. "We'll have to make sure the king doesn't want to try flying one of the Belles. Gino can't afford to lose either of them before he finishes shooting the movie."

"There's an easy solution," David said. "Just take some round-the-pole or simple control-line models."

"That's a good idea, David." He stood up straight and smiled at the two boys. "I'll leave you two to sort out what you need in the way of models and spare parts."

A *few days later, Prague*

Jason Cheng was enthralled with what he was seeing and hearing as he observed his father investigating what was wrong with the Radio Prague installation. He glanced quickly at his fellow apprentice mechanical engineer and smiled. It looked like David was also enjoying the opportunity to see an expert at work. Of course, Jason was still a teenager, having only recently graduated from high school, so although his brain was one hundred percent attentive to what was happening, another part of his body had other considerations. It had been more than four hours since his stomach had received sustenance, and it didn't approve. It voiced this disapproval with embarrassing audibility.

Jason Sr. turned at the first audible rumblings from Jason. "Are you feeling hungry?" he asked.

"I'm good," Jason said, waving his hand, but his stomach disagreed, releasing another loud rumble.

"We can stop now," Vernon Fritz, the up-time installation manager for the Radio Prague project, said with a grin.

Jason Sr. glanced over at David. "How about you? Are you 'good' like Jason too?"

David grinned. "Actually, I am feeling a little hungry," he said.

"Well," Vernon said, "rather than let your apprentices starve, how about we find somewhere we can talk while we eat?"

Jason Sr. cast an expert eye over the machine room and nodded. "Let's."

Jason stepped into the inn just behind his father and Mr. Fritz. The first thing he noticed was how quiet it was. He managed to hold onto his curiosity until they were seated and their orders taken. But once the waiter walked away he lost no time asking. "Why's it so quiet? I would have expected them to have a radio going."

Vernon glanced around the inn. "There are radios in here." He pointed to several small groups at the wall end of their tables. "Those people are listening to crystal sets."

"Crystal sets?" David muttered. "I would've expected an inn to have proper radios."

"Shush!" Vernon said. He glanced around quickly before turning back to David. "It's a bit of a sore point with a lot of the public houses. They want proper powered radios, but even those that can afford them are being held ransom by the battery suppliers."

"Can't they just use some other source of power?" David asked.

"What?" Vernon asked. "I'm sure that if someone could come up with a viable alternative to the crystal sets the innkeepers will beat a path to their doors."

Jason stared at Mr. Fritz as the workings of his mind tried to process what he'd said. The only reason he and Mags hadn't seriously pursued the idea of getting married was the inability to afford to establish and maintain their own household. If he could come up with a way of powering radios... But then reality reared its ugly head. There were two insurmountable problems preventing the inns from using radio. Firstly, there was the lack of affordable amplifiers—the only ones available were up-time ones, and then there was the fact radio needed electricity. A crystal set might be able to feed an earphone using just the faintest bit of broadcast energy, but an amplifier needed real electricity, from either a main supply or batteries. He sighed. It had been a nice dream while it lasted.

That evening, the castle

Dietrich Bockelmann stopped and pointed to a window set high up in the exterior wall of the Mihulka Tower. "That's the window Liova came flying out of."

Jason looked up and whistled. The window in question was just below the tower's conical roof, about five floors up. Mags' cat must have fallen at least fifty feet. "How the heck did he survive falling that far?" he wondered aloud.

Dietrich shrugged. "I'm just glad he did. Can you imagine how Mags would have felt if..."

There was a lot of body English in Jason's wince as he hunched his shoulders protectively at the potential repercussions of Liova dying. Mags loved her cat almost as much as she loved him, or at least he hoped it was in that order. "She would have been inconsolable."

"Yeah, well, fortunately, he didn't die, and the only person hurt was Mags."

There was something in Dietrich's tone that drew Jason's attention. A quick glance at his face told Jason that Dietrich was still feeling guilty for not being there to protect Mags. "You were at work when those guys broke into Dr. Gribbleflotz's lab, Dietrich," Jason said. "I don't blame you for what happened to Mags, and I'm sure she doesn't either."

"I blame me," Dietrich said.

There wasn't anything Jason could say in reply to that, so he changed the topic. "Shall we go in?" he asked.

"Sure," Dietrich said before leading the way in.

They were confronted by a woman the moment they stepped into the building. She looked Jason up and down before turning to Dietrich. "Would this be Mags' young man?" Ursula Mittelhausen asked.

"Yes, Frau Mittelhausen. Allow me to introduce Jason Cheng." Dietrich nudged Jason toward Frau Mittelhausen. "And this is Frau Mittelhausen, without whom nothing would get done around here."

Ursula held out a hand, and with a quick glance Dietrich's way for reassurance that it would be correct, Jason took the hand in his and shook it. "It's a pleasure to meet you, Frau Mittelhausen. Mags has spoken about you often." Which was true, Mags had, although not always in a complimentary manner.

Ursula's smile suggested she suspected as much. "I expect you'll want to see Mags. She's up in the workroom." She stared hard at Dietrich. "Dinner will be in half an hour."

Dietrich grabbed Jason and started to tow him away. "I'll see that they're both down in time," he said.

Jason cast a despairing look at the fresh bread on the kitchen bench. "What's the hurry?" he demanded.

"Mags has got something you need to see."

"What?"

"She's made something I think has real prospects." He set off toward the workrooms.

"What?" Jason repeated his demand as he chased after Dietrich. The last thing she'd made was her theremin, which had been adopted by the Prague chapter of the Society of Aural Investigators as the Gribbleflotz Magneto-Etheric Aural Detector. That was a nice little earner. He wasn't sure what the current market price for them was, but he did know the first one sold for thirty Venceslasthaler, or about three thousand dollars. "What's Mags made this time?"

Dietrich glanced over his shoulder. "Follow me and you'll find out."

He stared at Dietrich's departing back for a few seconds before hurrying after him, catching up with him just outside the main workroom in the Mihulka Tower.

There was sunlight shining through a window, illuminating Mags. Jason just stood there, taking in the vision before him. Meanwhile, Dietrich made their presence known, and Mags' head shot up. She saw Jason, burst out of her chair, flew across the room, and threw herself at him. Fortunately, Jason was able to catch her, even as she swung her arms around his neck.

"Ouch!" Jason protested when Mags' plaster cast hit his head.

"Sorry," Mags said before hauling herself up off the ground to kiss him.

"Hey, Georg, who told you to stop pumping?" Michael Thurn called out.

To Jason's disappointment the shout by one of the laborants caused Mags to break off the kiss and lower herself to the ground, but not out of his arms. He looked over to where a laborant was starting to pump the treadle of a theremin box. He glanced down toward Mags and was just about to ask what was going on when he heard the theremin's high-pitched note turn into music. Hearing it, he realized there had been music playing when he first entered the workroom, and if the music was restarting as Georg pumped the theremin . . .

"Is that a radio?" he asked, pointing at the machine emitting the music.

Mags shook her head, but Dietrich contradicted her. "Yes," he said.

"But it's not," Mags protested, turning her head toward Dietrich. "It's just a theremin I rewired so that the input is from a crystal set instead of the oscillator."

"Which makes it a radio." Dietrich looked toward Jason. "I only discovered what Mags had done a couple of days ago, after we heard you were coming to Prague, otherwise I'd have told Herr Fritz."

"But why would you want to tell Herr Fritz that I'd wired a crystal set to a theremin?" Mags demanded.

Jason pulled Mags until her back was against his chest, and hugged her. "Because there is a demand out there for radios," he said.

"Especially ones that don't need electricity," Dietrich said.

"But it uses electricity," Mags protested.

"Dietrich is talking about mains or battery power, Mags. And your new radio doesn't need either."

"Yeah," Dietrich agreed. He turned to Jason. "How do you think it'd work in a bar?"

Jason thought about it for a few seconds before deciding he didn't have enough information. "I think we need to find out," he said. He turned to Mags. "Do you have one we could take to a local inn or tavern?"

"No, I don't," Mags said. "I have orders for modified theremins for the Society of Aural Investigators to fill."

"We only need one," Dietrich said.

"And just for one night," Jason added.

Mags glared at Jason.

"Please."

Mags released her breath in a noisy sigh. "All right. But only for one night, and I go along with you to make sure it comes back."

"Well of course you'll come along with us," Dietrich said. "We need someone who knows how to set it up."

"But not until after dinner," Jason hastened to add. He'd already been embarrassed once by his stomach today, and he didn't want a repeat.

"Sure, after dinner suits me, too," Dietrich said.

"Men," Mags muttered.

Later that evening

"It's just down here," Dietrich said over his shoulder as he led the way along the Loretánská, the main street heading west from the castle.

"Where are we going?" Jason asked. He was carrying the legs and treadle unit while Dietrich carried the theremin. Mags, of course, with two strong males to do all the heavy lifting, didn't have to carry anything more than the three hand tools she'd need to put everything together.

Dietrich pointed. "Over there. The Black Ox."

Jason looked at the sign hanging above the entrance. If he squinted, he thought the animal could be called an ox, and as for the color, given the light, he was willing to call it black. "How do we handle this?" he asked.

"I go in and ask Pavel if he wouldn't mind letting us test a prototype human-powered radio in his tavern."

Jason noticed the use of the man's Christian name. "Just how well do you know this guy?" he asked.

"Dietrich moonlights at The Black Ox as a bouncer," Mags said.

"Ahh!" Jason had no difficulty accepting Dietrich was moonlighting as a bouncer. He lacked the solid, neckless look of the stereotypical up-time bouncer, but at over six feet and two hundred forty pounds he had a more than adequate physical presence. Add brains to that, and he was probably every bar owner's dream bouncer—able to enforce the rules, but smart enough to know he didn't have to actually hit people to do so. "So you don't think there'll be any problem?" he asked.

Dietrich shook his head. "Nope. Not unless it works so well Pavel wants to keep it."

"What?" Mags demanded. "I thought this was just going to be a test."

"It is," Dietrich said, "but Pavel is running a business,

and if he can have a proper radio going, he'll get more people buying drinks."

"We'll cross the bridge when we come to it," Jason said. "Meanwhile, how about getting this show on the road?"

"Sure thing," Dietrich said, before leading the way into the tavern.

"Dietrich!" a swarthy man in a filthy apron called as they entered. "And you have brought friends. Please, introduce me."

"Pavel Dusek, the proprietor of this establishment," Dietrich said. "And these good people are Jason Cheng and his betrothed, Magdalena Rutilius."

"A pleasure to meet you," Pavel said. He turned back to Dietrich. "So what brings you around to my humble establishment at this hour?"

Dietrich grinned. "This," he said as he doffed the theremin radio he'd been carrying strapped to his back.

Pavel ran his eyes over the wooden box before turning back to Dietrich. His brows rose in question. "And why might I be interested in a Gribbleflotz Magneto-Etheric Aural Detector?"

"Ahh," Dietrich said, "but this isn't just a Gribbleflotz Magneto-Etheric Aural Detector. Magdalena here," he said, gesturing toward Mags, "has managed to combine the technology of the Gribbleflotz Magneto-Etheric Aural Detector with a crystal receiver to create a human-powered radio."

Pavel's eyes opened wide. "A what? A radio, you say?" He took another look at the device. "Does it work?"

"Of course it works," Jason protested. "That's why we brought it here."

"Actually," Dietrich said, inserting himself between Pavel and Jason, "although we know it works in the laboratory, we don't know how well it works in a proper working environment." He smiled at Pavel. "We're hoping you'll allow us to test it."

"And how much will this cost me?" Pavel demanded.

"Not a pfennig," Dietrich said. "After all, you are letting us test it in your bar."

"Although we would like your honest opinion of how good or bad it is," Jason said.

Pavel nodded, as if understanding and accepting the conditions. "Where would you like to set it up?" he asked.

"I'll need access to an aerial and earth," Mags said.

Pavel nodded again as he surveyed his bar. A few seconds later he pointed toward a table set up against a wall. "Can you set it up over there?" he asked.

Mags nodded. "Come on," she said to Dietrich and Jason. "Let's get it up and running."

It took only a few minutes to set up the theremin radio and connect it to the aerial and earth wires that had previously been servicing a crystal set. Then Mags started pumping the treadle. Soon the sound of Radio Prague could be heard coming from the speaker. Around them the bar quieted as customers stopped talking to listen to the radio.

"Can you make it louder?" Pavel asked.

Mags nodded and started pumping the treadle harder. The harder she pumped, the louder the radio grew.

"That's good." Pavel nodded approvingly. "Just keep it at that level."

Some three hours later

Mags was still feeling a little confused by events when they finally arrived back at Dr. Gribbleflotz's residence in the castle. They entered to be greeted by Frau Mittelhausen. She looked the three of them over, surely noticing the absence of the human-powered radio.

"Did Pavel like Frau Rutilius' human-powered radio?" she asked.

"He loved it," Dietrich said.

"He loved it so much he's paying Mags ten dollars a day to keep it," Jason added.

"Well, of course he is," Dietrich said. "He'll get more than ten times that in increased customers once word gets out that he has a radio you can hear without an earpiece."

"I thought that might happen," Ursula said. "And no doubt, within days, other bar owners will be beating on Dr. Gribbleflotz's door demanding he make one for them." She smiled. "It'll be just like the Society of Aural Investigators, except there are a lot more bars than there are investigators." She turned to Mags. "I think you need to resign from your position with Radio Prague and start making radios full time."

Mags stared at Frau Mittelhausen, terrified at what she'd just suggested. "But I can't do that. I can't afford to give up my job."

"You will have a job, Magdalena, making radios . . ." Ursula tilted her head as she looked at Mags. "You could call your business Mags Electrical."

"Mags Electronics would be better," Jason said.

Mags whirled round to face Jason. "What are you

talking about?" she demanded. "I can't just quit my job at Radio Prague."

"Sure you can." Jason reached out and dragged Mags closer so he could hug her. "You've been on light duties since you broke your arm, so they'll hardly miss you. And, Mags, you could become filthy rich. The Higgins Sewing Machine Company will have nothing on Mags Electronics. The demand for radios must outweigh the demand for sewing machines by a couple of orders of magnitude."

Mags blinked. That certainly appealed, but she could see a major problem Jason and Frau Mittelhausen were missing. "I don't have the money to start a business like that, and"—she turned to glare at Jason—"don't suggest that your parents can lend me the money."

"Mags," Dietrich said.

She swung round to look at her friend, who was casually leaning against the doorjamb. "What?" she asked.

He gestured toward Ursula. "I think Frau Mittelhausen might be about to suggest that Dr. Gribbleflotz lend you the money."

"Oh!" Mags swung her attention back to Frau Mittelhausen. "Dr. Gribbleflotz?" she asked.

Ursula smiled. "Dietrich is right. Not that it'll be the doctor himself putting up the money—he has little interest in anything outside his personal lines of research—but rather the holding company that owns HDG Laboratories. And I'm not thinking of lending you the money. I think we should form a company together. You contribute the know-how, while we provide the money for facilities, materials, labor, and of course, distribution and marketing."

"And just how much of this company would the holding company own?" Jason asked.

"Let's be generous and call it a measly eighty percent," Ursula said.

"EIGHTY PERCENT?" Jason roared.

Mags turned to her boyfriend. "Settle down. That's just an opening offer."

"Not only are we offering startup capital, but we are also providing access to the distribution channels we already have in place for the doctor's products," Ursula said.

Mags nodded. "Yes, but without my knowledge, there's no product to sell." She ran her tongue around her lips. "I might be prepared to go as high as fifty percent."

"Hold it!" Jason said. "How about I talk to Mom and Dad and see what they think before you sign your life away, Mags?"

"And you'll probably want to consult a lawyer, too," Dietrich said.

Mags glared at her two companions. They were ruining her fun with logic. She turned to Frau Mittelhausen. "I guess I'd better see what Jason's parents think."

"You do that," Ursula said, "but there is no way you're getting to keep fifty percent."

Jason drifted into the inn where he and his family were staying while they were in Prague, his mind more on the prospect of Mags leaving her job at Radio Prague and returning to Grantville than on what time it was. That attitude came to a screaming halt when he stepped into the room and was confronted by his parents, his sister, and David Kitt sitting around the table playing a board game in the light of an oil lamp.

"Did you have a good time?" his father asked in a very conversational manner.

"Yes," Jason said uneasily as he removed and hung up his coat before changing his outdoor footwear for a pair of indoor slippers. "Dietrich took us to a bar he knows."

"I would have thought you and Mags had better things to do with your time than hang out in a public bar," David said.

Jason grinned. "Yeah, well, normally you'd be right," he said. "But when I got to her lodgings I discovered she'd built herself a human-powered radio. Me and Dietrich thought there might be a good market for such a thing, so we all went to a bar Dietrich knows to see how well it works in situ."

"A human-powered radio?" Jason Sr. asked. "From what Vernon had to say, I'm sure there would be an eager market for such a thing. How does it work?"

"She's feeding the output from a crystal radio through a theremin," Jason said.

"Using the theremin as an amplifier." His father shook his head ruefully. "I can't imagine why I didn't think of it earlier."

"Same here," Jason admitted. "It's one of those things that's so obvious once someone else has already thought of it."

"So how well did it work in situ?"

"Really well," Jason said. "We could hear it from the other side of the room, even with the usual noise you'd expect from a bar at night."

"So you spent all night at a bar?" Jennie Lee asked.

Jason shook his head. "No. We had dinner first..."

"Why am I not surprised," Diana muttered.

Jason ignored his sister's sotto voce comment and

continued as if she hadn't spoken. "... before going to The Black Ox. We were only there for a few hours, but Frau Mittelhausen was waiting for us when we returned." He grinned. "She wanted to know how well it worked, too. Anyway, Frau Mittelhausen thinks Mags should quit Radio Prague and go into business making them full-time. The demand is going to be astronomical. Every public house that can receive a radio signal will want one."

"I'm sure Frau Mittelhausen is right, but there's no way we can help Mags start such a business," Jennie Lee said. "Kitt and Cheng Engineering has to be our first concern."

"That's okay, Mom," Jason said. "Frau Mittelhausen suggested Mags go into business with Dr. Gribbleflotz's parent company. Mags will be responsible for making the radios and aural detectors while she sees to everything else. She said she wanted eighty percent of the new company for the parent." He turned to his father. "That's a bit much, isn't it?"

Jason Sr. nodded. "Eighty percent is more in line with what a *vulture capitalist* rather than a venture capitalist might demand. I wouldn't have thought Frau Mittelhausen would demand that much."

"I don't think it was a demand," Jason said. "I think it was more an opening gambit in a negotiation. Certainly that's how Mags treated it. She came back with a counteroffer of fifty percent, but I don't think Frau Mittelhausen will go that low."

"Mags shouldn't make any agreement without consulting a lawyer," Jennie Lee said.

"That's what Dietrich said," Jason said. He turned back to his father. "I told Mags I'd ask what you thought might be a reasonable distribution of owner-ship of the company."

"That's a tough one," Jason Sr. said. "Let's see"—he prepared to count points off on his fingers—"Mags is contributing the intellectual property, while Frau Mittelhausen, for Dr. Gribbleflotz, is offering capital and marketing." He held up three fingers. "There are three parts to the deal, and Frau Mittelhausen is offering two of them. Maybe Mags should be prepared to let them have up to two thirds of the company."

"But she shouldn't make any commitment without seeing a lawyer," Jennie Lee repeated.

"No, she shouldn't," Jason Sr. agreed. He turned to Jason. "When can we talk to Mags and Frau Mittelhausen?" he asked.

"I'm supposed to meet Mags after she finishes work tomorrow to go over the details." He looked at his parents. "Can you come too?"

"I wouldn't miss it for the world," Diana said.

"I wasn't talking to you," Jason said.

"Children!" Jennie Lee said. "We will all be there."

"Does that include me?" David asked.

"Sure," Jason said. "You're welcome to tag along."

Next day, the Mihulka Tower

Mags was waiting with Frau Mittelhausen and Lips Kastenmayer, a younger brother of Dr. Gribbleflotz's wife, when the Cheng party arrived. Mags made the introductions before leading everyone into a workroom where she had set up a theremin radio.

"That the radio?" Diana asked.

Mags smiled at Jason's sister. "I know, it just looks

like a theremin, but it works." She looked at Jason. "Would you mind?"

"No problem," Jason said. He walked over to the theremin and started pumping the treadle.

The sound of Radio Prague started to emerge from the speaker and everyone stood quietly and listened for a few minutes.

"That's enough, Jason," Jason Sr. said. He waited for the radio to fall silent before speaking again.

"So, Mags, we hear you're planning on quitting your job with Radio Prague to start your own business?"

Mags sighed and looked appealingly at Jason. "I want to, but Frau Mittelhausen can't see any role for Jason."

"Don't you worry about me, Mags. Mom and Dad are planning a major expansion at Kitt and Cheng Engineering, and I'll be part of that."

"Really?" Mags asked, darting glances to Jason's parents.

"Really," Jennie Lee said.

"Yes," Jason Sr. said. "You might think you've invented a radio, but what you've really done is created the basis of a new sound reproduction industry, and Kitt and Cheng Engineering intends being in on the ground floor supplying you with all the components you're going to need."

"One moment," Ursula Mittelhausen said. "What do you mean by a sound reproduction industry?"

"Mags' radio just connects a radio signal to an amplifier in the theremin," Jason said. "Well, there are plenty of things that can use that same amplifier. We did a bit of brainstorming earlier, and came up with a few things Mags could add to her production line."

"In addition to the aural detectors and radios, there

are also record players and public announcement systems," Jason Sr. said.

"Also sound systems for performers," David said. He mimed playing an electric guitar and smiled at Mags. "That was my idea."

Mags winced at that. She'd heard David playing his electric guitar before, and she didn't think the world was ready for that noise. "Fortunately, you'll have to be your own power source, limiting you to twenty or so watts."

David clasped his hands to his heart. "You wound me. My music is brilliant, and the louder the better. Which is why your boyfriend and I want to borrow one of your spare thercmins so we can experiment with installing a glow plug engine to spin the Alexander alternator."

"I don't have any spare theremins." She gestured to the one across the room that she'd used to demonstrate her radio. "That one belongs to a member of the Society of Aural Investigators."

"That's okay," Jason said. "Dad's happy for David and I helping you build some more."

"We're going to need to take a couple back to Grantville with us for development work," Jason Sr. said.

"Is your company going to be competing against Mags' company?" Lips asked.

"No." It was a resounding declaration from all four of the Chengs and David Kitt. For a moment they smiled at each other before Jason Sr. took charge. "We're happy just helping design peripherals and making components for Mags' company. We're even happier to leave her company to put them together and worry about marketing."

Prague
October 1636

Vernon Fritz was once again conducting an unofficial survey of radio reception and listener satisfaction around Prague. He was walking down the same street he'd been walking down on his first monthly survey thirty days previously when he noticed a crowd gathering around the entrance to one of the many public houses that lined the street. Curious to see what had them gathering around the bar, he approached.

As he got closer he was sure he could hear the current broadcast from Radio Prague emanating from the open door. He checked the portable crystal set he was wearing and confirmed that the sound was from Radio Prague. He increased his pace and quickly arrived at the door, where he forced his way in.

The room was crowded with men sitting at tables chatting quietly while they drank or ate. In the background was the sound of Radio Prague. He had questions to find answers to and glanced around the barroom, seeking the barkeep.

The bar owner met Vernon's eyes and hurried toward him. "The man from Radio Prague," he said as he reached out a hand to Vernon. "You have come to admire my new radio. It is one of the new Gribbleflotz Ethereal Plenitude Auricular Amplificators." The man smiled at Vernon. "I told you Dr. Gribbleflotz would find a solution."

What Price for a Miracle?

Terry Howard

Augsburg, an Imperial City in the USE
December 1634

"Horatio Alger Burston! Why is this piece of junk cluttering up our *eingang*?!" This gale force greeting assaulted H.A. Burston's ears as he walked through the front door of his home at five minutes before noon, and he smiled. He knew, without looking, that the suit of armor he had recently purchased had arrived. Yes, there it was, standing in the entry hall to the right of the stairs, just as he had instructed. His pregnant and visibly annoyed wife was standing on the stairs next to it and staring at him when she wasn't scowling at *it*. H.A.'s smile widened significantly.

Catharina had a fine set of lungs. When she filled them completely, as she usually did when she had a strong, negative opinion, he often found himself distracted by the side effects. This was an additional reason he enjoyed teasing her.

A friend once compared the way he teased to a picador pricking a bull and said he was cruel to do it because he did not have even a picador's excuse. H.A. disagreed. He was just teasing, as had his father and his grandfather before him, and he was sure it was harmless. When he was told that he was wrong, it was tormenting and it was not harmless, he answered, "Well, I'll concede that I might be wrong. But I am not the least bit uncertain. And until I see something wrong with it, I will keep right on doing it."

"Because," he quietly responded to his wife's question, "if I put it in our bedroom then how would anyone know we have it except us?"

Catharina said firmly, "Get rid of it!"

"I don't think so."

"I am serious, Mr. Burston! Store your junk elsewhere until you are ready to send it to the scrap dealer."

"Mrs. Burston, you know that I would do almost anything for you. But not that. The armor stays."

"I will not have it. Get rid of it or I will have the servants throw it into the street!"

He continued smiling. Then in the mild, polite, reasonable voice he knew drove her absolutely mad when she was already angry, he said again, "I don't think so."

"Well, I do!" she screamed. "What do you want with it anyway? No one wears armor like that anymore! It's old and it's ugly. And no one else has anything like it."

"Well, Kate, up-time, when I was growing up, a rich man always had a suit of armor somewhere in the house. So if I am rich I am going to have a suit of armor. You married me because I was rich," he reminded her.

She freely admitted it, and saw no reason not to. After all it was right and normal, wasn't it?

"Well, of course I married you because you were rich. What better reason for a well brought up lass to marry, or for a widow to remarry? I want this piece of junk out of here!" Her demand filled the whole house.

"Kate, did you say well brought up or well bought up?" It sounded like an accusation, and it was one of his favorite lines when this topic came up. Catharina did not understand why he found it amusing. And her husband either would not or perhaps could not explain why he found it funny.

Her temper cranked up another notch—as he'd expected when he'd called her Kate. He was surprised he had to do it twice before she responded.

"My name is Catharina, thank you very much, and calling me any other name is disrespectful. If you were a polite gentleman you would use only my full first name and even both my full first and last name occasionally. If you must abide by your strange up-time customs, you could address me as Mrs. Burston! But I do not work below the stairs. I am not a Kate!" Their ongoing clash of cultures frequently had "proper address" as its keystone. H.A. watched, smiling expectantly.

His very exasperated wife said, "Horatio Alger Burston, I do not know how many times I have asked myself how you can be so good at business when your head is so full of foolishness. You did not have a suit of armor when you were in Grantville!"

"When I lived in Grantville I wasn't rich."

"I did not see a single suit of armor when we were there!"

"Grantville's not full of rich people," he said. "The rich are moving out of town."

"I did not see and have not heard of any suit of armor in any other up-timer's home!"

"Have you looked in their bedrooms? Would you prefer to have this set moved to ours? Besides, a lot of them still don't consider themselves to be rich. The ones who do are often trying to fit in. I'm not. I'm rich and I am going to live like a rich man, and a rich man, *when* I come from, has a suit of armor in the entryway."

Smiling, H.A. passed by his lovely, young, pregnant, sputtering wife. He headed for his hot lunch. It would be on the table at twelve noon sharp, or his French chef would be out of a job. He knew Catharina would calm down and join him because there was nothing else she could do. Over a midday meal of cream of tomato soup (H.A. had nagged the chef until, at last, he could make something H.A. couldn't tell from the real thing) and a grilled cheese sandwich (which took even longer for the cook to get right), Horatio asked, "How is your search for a painter coming?"

She wanted a family portrait painted. Respectable families had them done, she said, and H.A. agreed. But he insisted on a Dutch painter, or at least an Italian.

"We could be sitting right now if you were willing to be reasonable about this! There is a perfectly good German painter in town currently."

"Nope," he said. "All the best painters are Dutch. We can afford the best. If you want a portrait get a Dutch painter. Though I will settle for an Italian if we can't go Dutch."

"Horatio Alger Burston, you are a most infuriating man."

H.A. laughed. "I can afford to be."

"Another glass display case arrived this morning," she said. "I do not understand what you want with that, either."

Actually only the front was glass. The hardwood case had a leather gasket on the door to seal out damp, and an aerated box in the bottom to hold chalk or dried wheat to absorb any moisture inside the case. When it became available, Horatio planned to add a nitrogen atmosphere system to preserve the books and artifacts.

"Are you spending more money on another old Latin Bible when you can't even read Latin?"

"Nope," he said, and smiled as he helped himself to a second sandwich. "Six Gutenberg first edition Bibles are enough, unless a really good one or a really cheap one comes along."

"What is this case for? Surely you have enough of those English Bibles. You don't read any of them either," Catharina said, genuinely curious. Some of the things H.A. wanted, like the foot-long bronze chariot which he said was over a thousand years old, needed no explanation. It was simply beautiful.

"No, I don't read them. If I were going to read a Bible it wouldn't be a 1611 Authorized Version, that's for sure. Six first edition King James Authorized Bibles are enough. I didn't buy them to be read."

"Then why did you buy them?"

"Catharina, when I was a boy, I collected stamps because I could afford to. I wanted to collect old and rare books but I did not have the money. So I studied to be ready and dreamed of the day when I could afford to buy them. Well, I have the money and right now they're dirt cheap. Any one of those Bibles when I was a lad would have been worth a fortune. There are millions of dollars setting on those shelves, if not now, then in time, and if not in time, then in my mind. Having them makes me feel rich. Just like the suit of armor. I like feeling rich."

"What is this case for?" she asked again.

H.A. smiled. "It's a surprise."

"Well, what is it?"

"Can you keep a secret?" he asked.

She huffed at him. The first time he asked that she had replied, "Yes, of course I can." And he had answered, "So can I." She hadn't fallen for it since.

"Well, since you are rich, a rich man should have some relics on display!" Catharina repeated a much promoted idea. "For the sake of piety, we should have some relics."

Patiently, watching her bosom, he said, "We've been over this before. Most of them are fakes. I could buy you a piece of the True Cross, but why? When Henry the Eighth threw the Catholics out of England there were enough pieces of the True Cross in England alone to make two and a half crosses. Would you like the skull of John the Baptist? Would you like two of them? Three? I believe there are three for sale on the market and at least six on display in various places. Should I buy you some of the clay that was left over from making Adam?"

"You could find something that has made miracles."

"My love, you are married to a man who was born in 1953. Surely that is miracle enough."

H.A. could tell she still was not impressed by this argument. The truth was that nearly two years ago when she had first brought it up, shortly after they married, he had set a chain of events into motion so she could be the owner of some genuine artifacts. The display case that had just arrived would exhibit the fruits of that labor.

A few weeks later H.A. came home for lunch early, to check in on the sick children at home. He'd talked to the doctor the first day he came and the doctor had been back every day since. Catharina had insisted even though the physician had repeatedly assured her there was nothing he could do. The doctor said it was measles. "Keep them warm, and dry, fed and most importantly hydrated." Catharina was sure they were dying and was upset. She was equally upset with her husband's apparent lack of concern.

"Catharina," H.A. told his wife, "it's just the measles. I had them when I was a kid. It's no big deal."

"People die from the measles."

"Yes, something can go wrong, but it is very rarely serious." H.A. dredged up what he knew about it from a conversation with his mother years ago when he was a kid and the measles were going around. She told him, amongst other things, that he had already had them so he could not get them again.

But his wife had a different experience with measles than her husband had. "Here and now, measles are always serious. I'm worried. You should be, too."

When he started upstairs to check on the kids, Catharina met him on the staircase. She was smiling for the first time in days. It was a tired smile on an exhausted face.

"The fevers have broken. They are going to be all right," she said.

"That's good," H.A. replied.

"It is an answer to prayers, which would have been more effective if we had a relic in the house."

H.A. realized that a relic was more to his wife than just keeping up a pious appearance. If she actually thought her prayers would be worth more for having a trinket in the house, then who was he to deny her?

So H.A. made some inquiries as to what was available on the market and made a purchase.

"It's beautiful," Catharina said as her husband closed the door of a display case. "What is it?"

"It is beautiful, isn't it? A poet once said, 'A thing of beauty is a joy forever.' Something that beautiful needs no other reason to exist than the fact that it is. It was in England up until Henry the Eighth; then it floated around through France and Germany until now. You will be pleased to know that inside that beautiful work of art there is what is claimed to be a hair off of the donkey Christ rode into Jerusalem. Whether it is indeed what it claims to be and not just a recent fraud, it still has any number of attested miracles to its credit."

"But," Catharina said, "you've always said you would not buy any relic that was not verifiable."

"I didn't buy the hair for me. I bought the hair for you," H.A. replied. "What I bought for me is the case it is in. It claims to be over two hundred years old. Whether it is or it isn't, really does not matter. It is just plain beautiful. Beauty needs no other justification to exist. Which is why I married you.

"How is the search for a painter coming?" H.A. asked.

"Horatio, we could be sitting now if you were not being so difficult." But the passion which usually went into her protest was lacking.

Two weeks later Eliyahu, from the local Abrabanel office, was waiting for H.A. when he arrived home from work along with another man.

"H.A., this is Abram. He is from Jerusalem and he is the man who went to the Sinai for you. He's on his way to Grantville. Since he arrived in Venice with the first item he was insistent that he wanted to bring it to you in person. So he could meet you."

"That's flattering," H.A. said.

Eliyahu smiled. "Not really." What he said next reflected the bond that had grown between the two men, which far and away exceeded their working relationship as men of finance and business. "He said he had to meet the craziest man in the world."

Abram blushed. Of his four languages German was the weakest. He had only started learning it when he decided to move to Grantville. But it was still plenty good enough to understand what his associate had just said.

H.A. laughed. "Can you stay to dinner? I'm sure the chef can come up with something suitable." The kitchen wasn't kosher, but if asked the chef could put together a dairy kosher dinner in short order, and the staff would enjoy the whole of whatever meat had been destined for the dinner table instead of just a portion of it.

"We would be delighted," Eliyahu answered. Abram and Eliyahu were part of the extended Abrabanel family. They were Sephardic Jews, and they considered themselves to be cosmopolitan, men of the world, understanding fellows willing to be less strictly observant than some of their more conservative co-religionists.

"Let's install what you've brought. I've got a display case waiting for it. And then you can tell me why you think I am crazy, over dinner."

When his wife came to the table H.A. said, "Catharina, you know Eliyahu. He brought Abram from Jerusalem, and Abram brought a relic from St. Katherine's Monastery in the Sinai. I just put it in the new display case. We are now the owners of an absolutely genuine piece of history. Abram here was about to tell me why he thinks I'm crazy."

"That is not surprising in the least," Catharina said. "I have had the same thought myself at least once a week since we married. And now I have it every time I look at that hideous suit of armor."

"That is not quite correct, Herr Burston," Eliyahu said. He had been translating to Abram and now he was translating from Abram. "The monks at St. Katherine's are greatly puzzled, and they are sure you are quite strange, but they were very pleased with what you were willing to pay for copies of manuscripts. The money you sent was very generous. But with the advent of printed copies of the New Testament they were puzzled by why you wanted handmade copies."

When the soup was served, Catherina excused herself from the table. She was having morning sickness, for the usual reason, and morning sickness can happen anytime of the day, after all. Something about the pleasant smell of the soup course sent the poor lass off to find a bucket in a hurry.

Abram continued in her absence, "That you sent three Bibles all the way from Germany along with a substantial gift in hard currency, just to loan them to the monastery's library was a bit odd. Though they were completely puzzled by why you sent a Latin Bible and two English Bibles when they use the Greek texts. That you asked them to place the smaller of the English Bibles in storage in the *genizah* with the worn-out manuscript rolls and codices, when it was clear that all it needed was some minor repair to the binding was cause for almost as much discussion as the book itself.

"I was repeatedly asked, was it really printed in 1988, and where was Indianapolis, USA. It will be a while before it ends up in the *genizah*. They are insisting that it be copied first. Also they have sent letters to all the houses they correspond with asking for a visit by a monk or scholar with English proficiency willing to teach. The printing, the binding, and the paper were all very talked about, but the half of the book that is not biblical text has them poring over the book with great interest.

"While I was there they discussed what you meant by a permanent loan and concluded that you meant they should treat it as if it were staying permanently but that someday you might ask for it back.

"But then, when I mentioned that you asked to buy works already on their shelves and in the *genizah*, my warm welcome became very cold. When I said you were only interested in making such a purchase if they would agree to store the works on site in perpetuity for you, then they relaxed. But it was then that they decided you were completely odd if not truly mad.

They understand that because of the dry climate, books last longer there than anywhere else. They also decided that even if it proved to be that you were not mad, you were unquestionably quite mean. You really should send them a dictionary. The monks are combing the English Bibles looking for words and then trying to figure out what they mean by reading the Greek textual equivalent. It really is driving them crazy because there is clearly not a word-for-word correlation."

H.A. chuckled. "Yes, I guess a dictionary or two would be in order. I really never thought that they might be interested in reading them. I guess it was silly of me not to think of it. I sent them there to be warehoused and preserved. I wonder if maybe one of the pastors in Grantville might have a 'Teach Yourself Greek' book or a Greek–English lexicon he would part with." H.A. looked at the senior Abrabanel. "Do you think they will find a teacher who will be willing to go?"

"Not likely. It is a long way, and traveling is expensive."

"Find me a Greek scholar with English or an English scholar with Greek. I'll pay his expenses. Have him stay no less than two years. Tell him to write a book about the trip and I will have it published. Considering the kind of men who would seek a life like that, having books you can't read would be torture."

Eliyahu did not ask if Herr Burston was serious. He had gotten enough odd requests from the man asking him to handle strange and unique undertakings to know better. He sent the three Bibles to an oasis in a desert mountain range. And he had arranged for his colleagues in Jerusalem to negotiate with the Orthodox Christian Patriarch to establish a new Christian monastery at Masada near the Dead Sea. It turned out that this was rather a matter of restaffing a long-closed institution. This fact went a long way toward getting government permission. And it helped that they had the backing of the Romans and Armenians. They had actually offered to share the old Anchorite site. He did start thinking of whom to write to, to find a man willing to make the journey to the Sinai and what to charge, and just how much the commission and charges would add up to five years down the road when the man was back and the book he would write was finally printed. H.A. Burston handled commercial accounts for several interests in Grantville and elsewhere. But there were odd and one-off items he farmed out rather than handle himself. And Eliyahu was happy to oblige him. The smile on Eliyahu's face did not change even if it did become a bit more sincere.

Eliyahu prompted the man from Jerusalem to continue. "When I told them you were interested in the oldest texts they had, eyebrows went up. When I told them you were especially interested in the second-oldest known copy of the Gospels in Syriac but that it was a palimpsest under a work dealing with female martyrs, they tried not to laugh out loud. But when I insisted they did go looking for it and when they got over the embarrassment of having something they did not know about, they were quite excited. As I said already, when I said you were willing to buy them, the atmosphere became a bit tense and suspicious. When I told them you would only be willing to buy them if they agreed to store them for you and your heirs in perpetuity, and that while the works could be viewed there with due care, they were never to leave the monastery under any condition, that was when they first asked what sort of man you were and if you were as completely insane as you seemed. Of course I couldn't answer them because I did not know. But they warmed back up. That you were willing to pay to have copies sent to you, while they kept the originals after selling them to you—well, it was the first time anyone had ever asked such a thing. While they agreed, they again asked me—why? I promised to ask if I ever got the opportunity and to send them a letter with an explanation.

"So I am asking? Why? Specifically, why buy something and then have the seller keep it for you? Why send three Bibles they cannot read?"

H.A. felt Abram's gaze lock on to his face. The man not only wanted to hear the answer, he wanted to gauge the truth of it. H.A. smiled a slight smile. "St. Katherine's is in the middle of a very dry desert. It is hard to get to and there is nothing there that an army would be at all interested in. Books last next to forever there. That is why I sent one of my copies of the first edition King James and a first printing Gutenberg on loan to them for safe keeping. If I should have a fire here I would still own a copy of the two most important books ever printed. The study Bible I sent is falling apart. The owner who wore it out knew it was cheaper to replace it than have it rebound. He gave it away and it was important to the person he gave it to. When I ended up being responsible for it, throwing it in the garbage just didn't feel right, so I sent it to where it could be stored with other worn-out Bibles.

"In the future, more and more people will be increasingly interested in the oldest texts available. In our history back up-time a German scholar working for the czar of Russia absconded with the particular Bible I was most interested in. He gave it to the czar as a gift. It was later sold off by a new government that did not care about such things. Most of it would have ended up in the British Museum in London. Now they can't sell it, or loan it beyond their walls, because it is no longer theirs. So it should be safe where it is until the scholars are ready to deal with it.

"My wife"—H.A. beamed a broad smile at the empty chair where the love of his life was recently sitting—"for piety's sake wants some relics. Now she owns the oldest complete Bible in the world. It is being stored where it will be best preserved. When it is ready we will have a copy to display."

The next morning on his way out the door, H.A. observed his wife peering at the book that was opened for viewing in the newest of the display cases. He approached her quietly, put his arms around her and looked over her shoulder at the codex. "How are you this morning?" he asked. While she was pregnant she chose to sleep in a separate room from her husband. In the early stage of an uncomfortable pregnancy with a lot of nausea she did not want to disturb his sleep. In the later stage when she was large she did not want him to disturb hers. So some mornings he did not see her until he came home for lunch.

"So this is a copy of the oldest Bible in the world?" she asked a bit skeptically.

"No, it will be nearly a year before that arrives. It will take that long for a scribe to copy it out. This is a copy of the Gospels in Greek. The cover letter says it's a copy from an eleventh-century codex. It's associated with a name I don't know anything about. The other copy of the Gospels I want, the Sinaitic Syriac, will be just as long in coming as the full Bible even though it's shorter. It's a palimpsest, which means it was reused for something else so someone has to figure out what is underneath what is written over it. But a copy of the oldest Bible in the world, which we now own by the way, is being copied out for us. It happens that someone had just made this new copy and sent it to us while they make a second copy for their library and the original gets put away in a cool, dark room cut into the stone of the mountain, where it will be safely out of sight, and scholars three and four hundred years from now can see the original and take photographs when someone gets around to making low-light film so the harsh light doesn't hurt the old texts."

"But, husband, if the books are that valuable, when word get outs about how much you paid for them, won't thieves flock there to steal them? Can the monks keep them safe?"

H.A. nuzzled the back of his young wife's neck. "Actually, I didn't pay hardly anything for the originals. They sold them very cheaply. After all they are still in their possession. An emperor of Rome once created a tribe of Romanian Bedouins, well, Macedonians anyway, the Gebeleya, to guard the monastery.

They're still there. Perhaps I should send them some modern firearms."

"Horatio Alger, a recent copy of the Gospels, no matter how old, is not a relic." The quiet but very sincere young woman added, "And rich man really should have relics for piety's sake."

"My lady wife, you notice that the top shelf holds the codex. The second shelf will hold the Syriac copy when it arrives. There is a shelf for the copy of the whole oldest Bible. The bottom half has no shelves. Something is coming from a place called Masada on the Dead Sea which is south of Jerusalem. It is an absolutely genuine, over sixteen-hundred-years-old item which absolutely without doubt or question once belonged to Herod the Great while he lived."

"Herod? The one who condemned Christ?"

"No. The father. The one who tried to have the Christ Child killed."

"And you have procured something that belonged to him?"

"Yes. When it arrives we will have an absolutely genuine relic complete with letters of authenticity establishing its provenance, proving that it is what it claims to be." He kissed the back of his wife's head, patted her gently on her bottom and left for work.

Some weeks later H.A. installed the artifact in the display case.

"What is it? It looks like a piece of broken pottery. It ought to be thrown out!"

"It is a piece of broken pottery. But beyond any doubt it was once the property of Herod."

"Does something which belonged to King Herod qualify as a relic?" Catharina asked.

"It is one of the few things I can think of that claims to be more than sixteen hundred years old, which is indisputably what it claims to be."

"Has it produced any miracles?"

"No."

"Then it is not a relic," Catharina pontificated.

H.A. sighed. His wife wanted a miracle. Then a thought popped into his head. There was a blind Irish harper, an acquaintance of one of the resident staff, visiting below the stairs. A shit-eating grin spread across his face as a scheme was hatched. If Catharina wanted a miracle then he would give her a miracle. It would cost almost nothing and that was almost a crying shame because having a happy wife was one of the few things in this life that truly was worth spending a fortune on.

Fredrick Hertfelder, H.A.'s valet, went to see his distant cousin Bernhard Hertfelder, the abbot of the Benedictine abbey that now inhabited only half of the Church of St. Ulrich and St. Afra near the end of *Maximilianstrasse* behind the Hercules fountain. The other half of the complex had been claimed by the Lutherans. It was sometimes a bit tense, and sometimes it worked out rather well. Not that they wouldn't like it all back and, in time, when the writ of restitution was enforced it would all be theirs again.

"What do you want, Fredrick?" The abbot demanded.

"Is that any tone to take with a close kinsman?"

"Kinsman, I'll grant you. Close, I will not. And you want something. You always do. If you need money, I am sorry I can't help you. Under the current circumstances the abbey is struggling."

"Then we can help each other."

The abbot just looked at him.

"I mean it. If you had the right to display a genuine miracle-working relic with a line of people out the door just to touch it, and each and every one of them would pass the poor box donation stand as they came in and another as they went out, that would go a long way to helping out your empty purse."

"And of course you want me to buy this relic."

Fredrick smiled a lying smile and waited to get his cousin's goat. When he had confirmed his cousin's opinion with his silence he gave that lie up. "No."

"Then you want a portion of the proceeds."

"No."

"What do you want?"

"My boss—"

"Your what?"

"My boss—it's an up-timer's word—my employer, Mr. Burston—has a miracle-working relic. It once belonged to King Herod, the one who tried to kill the Christ Child. He wants to place it on public display."

"Why, and why here? He is not Catholic."

"In truth, he's not anything. He eats with Jews and the way they get along I suspect he is secretly one of them. But that does not matter. You see, he wants to display a miracle-working relic. He asked me to arrange it and I thought of you."

The abbot looked extremely doubtful. After all, this was Fredrick he was dealing with. "Why does he want to display it and again why here?"

Fredrick smiled. "In part because this is a shared site. So he has the favor of both the faiths. And to answer your first question, he wants to make his wife happy by making his piety publicly known.

"He will send it in a display case. He will provide an armed guard for as long as it is accessible to the public. He will leave it for as long as you like but for at least a week."

"I never heard of any miracle-working relic associated with any Herod."

"It has just come from the Holy Land. He has papers documenting that it once belonged to the Herod who tried to kill Christ. And if it fails to produce at least one miracle he will donate one thousand dollars to the joint maintenance fund."

"There is no joint fund. We are each responsible for our half."

Fredrick smiled. "There won't be, either. Because there will be no donation. There will be miracles or at least *a* miracle. The offer is Herr Burston's way of, as he says, putting his money where his mouth is. This is a miracle-working relic."

"Still, who ever heard of a Herod miracle?"

"He sought to kill the Christ Child and failed. Wasn't that a miracle?

"Look, it won't cost you anything to let him display. It will generate interest and donations. Isn't that enough of a miracle?"

"I guess. What sort of miracle are you expecting?"

"The usual. The blind made to see, the mute to talk. The relic has a special affinity to saving children and making them well. Herod failed to kill the Christ Child. His possessions continue in the failure of seeing children suffer and die."

"Fredrick, why am I sure I am going to regret this?"

"Why my dear cousin Bernhard, why ever would you say something like that?" Honey could have learned something about sweetness from his voice. "When have I ever led you astray?"

"Lucinda and her sister in the hay loft?" Bernhard answered.

"That wasn't my fault. I was just as much a victim as you were. Those two wayward girls were—"

Bernhard cut him off. "When? Fredrick?"

"The boss is having a display case made and arranging some promotional materials. Give it a week or two. I'll let you know."

The town was plastered with broadsides, with when and where and what. The inns and taverns were full of tales. A favorite was the story of how a donkey would walk the five miles from the mount that held the monastery built on the ruins of Herod's mountaintop stronghold to the garden by the sea because the monks asked it to. Some said the very donkey blessed by having carried the Christ Child lives on to this day. When it arrived it would knock on the door of the gardener's shack with its nose and he would load it up and tell it to go home. But it only listened to the monks.

And the stories of the blind seeing, the deaf hearing, the mute talking, the lame walking were all overshadowed by the tales of the desperately sick children facing certain death who lived after they touched the relic or were touched by a bit of cloth that touched it.

The stories overshadowed the people who asked why no one had ever heard of it before. Some people asked why something belonging to the arch-villain Herod would now work miracles. The idea that Herod's failures lingered on in his possessions after his death satisfied some but not all. So there was a great deal of skepticism.

It was a fair day, overcast but warm, when the abbey was first scheduled to show the Herod pot. Some people were claiming it was Herod's chamber pot. They said that if you touched it you should touch the outside only. A line formed early. Near the front of the line a blind Irish harper played and sang. A skinny little girl with red hair and big blue eyes stood beside him and with a hand on his hip moved him forward. When he didn't need to move she would work the crowd around her with a begging bowl. There were always a few small coins in it. There was never less than half enough for a good meal for one and never more either, at least not for very long. But you would have to watch closely to see the child make the extra disappear. For the last week he had been making the rounds of the inns and taverns. Playing, singing, and telling tales. Most of the stories of Herod's chamber pot could be traced back to him.

But the main story though was his dream. In the dream he was told by the Virgin herself to come to Augsburg and he would receive his sight, being spared from a life of blindness through Herod's failure to kill the Christ Child. It had been a well-received story, for it was well told. The journey had been fraught with peril and full of close escapes. But the real genius was the child. What man's heart would not melt at those big blue pleading eyes. "Please, if we don't get enough to feed us both he won't eat, and I am worried for his health."

The day was warm, his music was pleasant, the

doors opened, and he moved forward at a touch on his rump. At the door he quit playing. The church was not the place for a con man's music. "Shaun," the little girl said, "we're almost there. There is a fine wooden cabinet with four legs standing on feet of balls in the clawed hand of birds. The pot is broken. There is naught but the base.

"Now, give me your hand." And with those words she placed his hand onto what was left of the storage jar.

Shaun stopped and stood absolutely still. "What is that?" he called out in a loud voice. "What is that? It's warm but it isn't. Is that light? Lass, take the harp lest I drop it." He handed off the harp and ripped the rag off of his eyes. When he did he yelped as if in pain and closed his eyes. "I can see! Lass, do you understand? I can see! It is as the virgin told me in my dream. Herod has failed, the Christ Child lives. I can see!"

Calls came from outside.

"What is happening?"

"What's going on?"

And people called back, "It's the blind harper. He can see."

And the news was spread down the line. Those who had passed through and were on their way out rushed off to share the news or take the bits of cloth home to sick children. The harper's tale spread like wildfire.

The musician took a seat on the steps of the church and played a hymn to Mary. Mostly he kept his eyes closed and would from time to time open them a crack to squint out. The little girl stood beside him, bowl in hand. And no matter that everyone passing by was dropping a coin the bowl seemed always empty. The harper smiled. It had been a good turn of luck when he had stopped to visit an old friend. It had been better luck her employer had asked her point-blank if he was truly blind and she had told the honest truth. "Of course not. He's Irish, and we Irish are all terrible liars now, aren't we?"

He was paid well to linger in town and play the miracle. But that was nothing compared to what he was pulling in on the steps of the church. Before noon, the word of the first healing from a rag carried home to a sick babe was in the streets. At noon someone afflicted with gout left their canes on the floor between the legs of the cabinet and walked out without pain for the first time in years. In the square he shouted the news. The harper's mouth fell open in surprise or shock or maybe awe. But his pondering of whether the relic was genuine or not did not stop him from playing a jig. When the man now free of gout heard the music he danced.

By evening there was another story of a healed child being told in the streets. By the next day there were two more.

H.A. arrived home that first day to find the maid by the door. She rushed into the dining room where his wife was entertaining a number of women friends who suddenly found her company desirable. "Mistress, the master is home."

Catharina rushed to his arms. "Tio," she said, giving in to his wish that she address him informally, "Thank you. You were right. It is a relic." She smiled. "We will have something that no one else has. I have never heard of anybody having anything that once belonged to a Herod."

"Well, we will be the only one for only a while. I have one hundred pieces of Herodian plunder. We will be swapping out the first one tonight to establish that all of Herod's pots are touched with the gift of healing. Shortly Herodian relics will start turning up in curio cabinets of the very rich across Europe." H.A. did not mention that the price he had been planning to ask for Herodian relics had just shifted a decimal point and he had not planned to sell them cheaply to begin with.

"But? Why? You should give them to churches. You do not need the money."

"Others will give them to churches. And while we do not need the money, the monks on the shores of the Dead Sea do. It is a hard place to make a living. I do not want to pay to keep them there forever out of my own pocket."

"They were doing okay before, weren't they?"

"No. This is a newly reestablished monastery. And they need to be there. There are special things on that mountain top that will be stripped and lost if they are not guarded."

"But they are selling them, are they not?"

H.A. Burston smiled. "I have an agreement with the Patriarch of Jerusalem. As long as I buy enough to keep the monastery going and a bit more for him of course, then they will sell only to me. So the monks need to sell an occasional broken pot, of which there are tens of thousands of pieces, to protect the rest of the site. And in time they will charge tourists to see the special areas. So the world slowly gets miracle-working relics and the mountain fortress is guarded for posterity. That is why we will not be giving the pot shards away for free."

Fredrick stopped by nightly and if there had been a reported miracle that day he would swap out the artifact. The miracles kept happening. The area between the legs was filling up with crutches and canes. The poor box was filling up with offerings. The tales of the healing from the little white rags being sold by the monastery and carried by pilgrims were coming back from ever farther away.

Fredrick told H.A., "Boss, when I told my cousin that we wanted one hundred letters attesting to the miracles of Herod's pots Bernhard told me we only needed ninety-nine. He says they are keeping one of them. I reminded him that it was just on loan. He said you have ninety-nine more, and you agreed to display it for as long as they wanted. He said you can afford to make them a long-term loan of one of them for the good of your soul."

H.A. chuckled. "My wife wanted relics for piety's sake. Leaving the last one there will please her. Tell your cousin ninety-nine letters attesting to the miracles will suffice."

The Three Stooges

Brad Banner

Late Spring, 1632

Dr. Les Blocker snorted moonshine out of both nostrils. Gagging and coughing, he spat the liquor out on the floor of his screened porch. *"Dammit all, even the batches of shine taste different since the Ring of Fire and this batch tastes like burnt billy goat assholes. The sun comes up in the wrong place. Much of my family was left up-time. I've volunteered to be one-half of the face of up-time veterinary medicine. Like two people are going to educate new vets, preserve centuries of progress in treating animals, treat hurt and sick animals of multiple species, and keep animal and human disease epidemics out of Grantville and the area. Well I can either keep dragging my dobber in the dirt about it or get on with it as best I can."*

Les was startled out of his reverie by his wife, Ruth Ann, calling him. "Les, you gone deaf; dinner is on the table." She and his grown daughter Leslie were already seated at the kitchen table. The two women could be twins—a generation apart. Both were tall, thin, and lean-faced. Unlike Les, who was short, round-faced, and tending toward fat. They always tried to share as many meals together as they could. Leslie began the banter that the family had shared for years. "How's my favorite Daddy?"

"The only one you have," Les replied. "Unless your Momma has a secret."

Ruth Ann winked at Leslie. "Well that garbage man was one fine-looking man."

"Hung like a Missouri mule, too," added Les. Sometimes it was the garbage man, or the meter reader, or the milkman (even though they never had a milkman). Though Les was a good Christian man, he had never been a prude. His colorful language and "for mature audiences only" stories were something of a legend in Grantville. Ruth Ann and various Baptist ministers and deacons quit trying to reform that part of him years ago.

Today's early supper was poke salat, squash casserole, plus ham and redeye gravy. Washed down with milk from their Jersey cow.

As they ate Les noticed that Leslie was quieter than normal. "Everything okay with Jeff? Do I need to show him the burdizzos?"

Leslie laughed and shook her head. "No, Dad, remember, I told you—no burdizzos, especially with fiancés. I remember when you showed it to Harry Lefferts when he worked for you in high school. He wasn't worried until you told him it was for castrating cattle without breaking the skin. I thought he was going to pass out."

"Oh lord," Les said. "What was I thinking of when I let Harry, Cory Joe, and Darryl work here together.

It's a wonder that the clinic is still standing. Just the fist fights among them... Those three could fu...errr mess up a rock fight. Looks like those three stooges turned out okay though, just a little wild."

"I believe that every wild child in Grantville worked at the clinic some time or other," Ruth Ann said. "You never seemed to hire any good kids."

"Pass the poke salat please, Ruth Ann. Those good kids didn't need the money or direction. And I know what it's like to be a wild child." Les handed the bowl to Leslie. "Want some greens? Your momma assured me she boiled them three times and isn't trying to poison us. So if it isn't Snider, why so glum?"

"Dad, you know I don't like poke salat. It's Dr. Adams. His wife and kids being left up-time is bothering him more than he lets on. Plus, all the extra jobs he's been doing since the RoF. Can you talk to him? You're the best grief guru I know. Ever since Emma was killed in the car wreck up-time, you've been so good with people that've lost family. I don't think Momma and me could have stood it without you or stood losing Hoss, Dan, Mary Jo, Jean and the kids when they were left up-time."

Les got up from the table and put his dirty dishes in the sink then headed to the bedroom. "I'll see what I can do. I've got to work on me first."

Ruth Ann motioned a puzzled Leslie into the living room. "I'm getting really worried about your daddy. He sits on the porch and stares into the distance, sipping his tea. Sipping shine too when he thinks I've gone to bed. He won't say boo about it, since he thinks he has to be strong for everyone else. You didn't know about it, but when your sister was killed by the drunk driver, he nearly went crazy. Drank and drank and drank. Had bad dreams again from his time in Vietnam as a USAID veterinarian. One really bad night, I found him getting his SKS out of the closet, the one the Green Beret sergeant gave him. He said, 'That sorry MF burnt my baby up.' I had to get down on my knees and beg him to think of us if he went to prison. The truth was I wanted that SOB dead too, but we had to think of you kids."

"Whatever happened to that boy that ran into Emma?" Leslie asked. "Did he ever get out of prison?"

"He never went to prison," Ruth Ann replied. "He got out of jail on bail and just up and disappeared, left the country I reckon, his people never did hear from him again. I hope he fell down a mine shaft.

"Anyway, soon after the gun deal, Les put down the bottle and the dreams mostly went away. He began helping other folks who had lost a loved one. It was his ministry. He hasn't been doing any counseling since the Ring of Fire. The dreams have started again and he calls out to the kids in his sleep."

Their conversation was interrupted by a knock on their front door. When he opened the door, Les saw an obviously agitated cavalryman. It was one of the three young military farriers that were recently accepted as veterinary students. "Mr. Oliver, what can I do for you."

The tall, broad-shouldered, dark-skinned Ulster Scots trooper replied, "Dr. Alexander sent me to fetch you; we all think we have some remount horses with glanders in the quarantine pen."

"Let me tell my wife where I'm going." Les rushed down the hall into the living room. "Well, it's started,

Ben has found glanders in some cavalry remounts. I wondered how long it would take for it to show up."

Leslie looked puzzled. "What's glanders? I've never heard of it."

"It is a very deadly and contagious bacterial disease of horses and people," Les explained. "It was eliminated from the US is why you never heard of it. I better get going, the sooner we can get rid of the infected horses the better."

On his arrival at the quarantine pens, Les saw his colleague, Dr. Bentley Alexander, in mask and gloves, royally chewing out the other two military farriers. Ben looked like the Marlboro Man. Tall, wiry build, high cheekbones—in his usual attire of jeans, khaki shirt, and Resistol cowboy hat. Sergeant Robert MacGregor, the horseshoeing instructor, also properly attired, was vigorously adding his two bits. Robert was the red-haired Scottish version of Ben. Since the troopers were not wearing masks and gloves, Les had a pretty good idea what the butt-chewing was about.

"Howdy, Les," his fellow veterinarian said, "you know what these three were doing? They were examining the glandered horses without using their gear before Sergeant MacGregor and I got here. Well, Mr. Oliver was using gloves, which is why he got to go get you."

"Bloody idjits," added MacGregor.

Les motioned to the three abashed troopers. "I'll talk to you shit-for-brains in a minute." He turned to Dr. Alexander. "You think the horses have glanders, Ben?"

"Yeah, I do," Ben answered. "The boys think so; so does Sergeant MacGregor."

Les once again faced the three young farriers.

"What part of 'you will wear protective gear around glandered horses' did you three stooges not understand? Three stooges fits you three. Mr. Ross Oliver, your name is now Mo. Mr. Daniel Banner, your name is now Curly. Mr. Lawrence McDonald, your name is now, uhm, Shemp."

Hearing the chuckles from the other masked and gloved veterinary students, who were sitting on the corral fence watching the show, Dr. Blocker turned on them in full fury. "All y'all pissants get your asses over here right damn now." Dust flew as the students sprinted over to him. He asked, "Ms. Clinter, did you recognize the glanders in the horses"?

"No sir, I didn't," she answered.

"These boys did," he said as he pointed to the troopers. "Mr. Harr, can people get infected with glanders?"

"Yes sir, they can," the student replied.

"What happens to people with glanders of the respiratory system, Mr. Schmidt?"

"They die, Herr Doctor."

Les nodded his head. "Right, they die, yet none of you made sure that your classmates were properly protected before handling the horses. Look folks, Dr. Alexander, Sergeant MacGregor and I've told you over and over that you're all in this together. You each have your strengths so you have to help and teach each other. We aren't going to wash one of you out of the program. One flunks, you all flunk and this program shuts down for good. Okay, let's look at the horses."

Les put on a mask and gloves then led the group over to a small herd of horses. He saw that some of the animals were very, very ill. Most had ropey nasal discharge and lumps on various parts of their body. Some showed no signs of infection. "Dr. Alexander, would you lead us through medical rounds about these horses?"

"Glad to, Doctor." Ben pointed to the horses. "Mr. Oliver, please show us the lesions that we usually see in glanders."

"See these large ulcers in the nose. Those are typical for glanders," the student explained. "When combined with the thick pus coming from the nose, you know it is glanders. See the thick swellings on the head and neck of the next horse over. They look like ropes under the skin. That's the skin form of glanders."

"Good," the doctor said. "Mr. Banner, what are some other common names for glanders and how is it transmitted?"

"We Germans call it *Rotz* and the skin swelling is sometimes called 'farcy' by English speakers," the young man said. "The bacteria that causes the disease is spread by droplets in the air from the horse sneezing and coughing. It can also be spread by direct contact of the pus from the nose and the skin swellings to the skin of an animal or person. The bacteria can live in the environment on a feed bucket or fence post for some time."

Ben was pacing back and forth, his brow furrowed. "Very good, Mr. Banner. Mr. McDonald, how do you tell the difference between glanders and more common diseases like horse strangles?"

The young man, who was built like a pro linebacker, said in his thick Scottish brogue, "The usual strangles only has knots under the jaw and never has the sores in the nose. Sometimes it's very hard to tell bastard strangles from the farcy. If they have knots all over it could be either. In that case you have to wait till the ropes form from one knot to another. Then you know it is farcy. And the pus is more cheesy and thick with strangles usually."

Ben nodded. "Good summary, Mr. McDonald. Ms. Clinter, tell us the dangers of glanders to people."

"If people get the respiratory or systemic forms of the disease they will probably die. Even up-time antibiotics don't work well against glanders in any form. The cutaneous form is often disfiguring and requires the abscesses be drained multiple times over several months."

Ben wrote a note on the clipboard he usually carried while teaching. "You did a good job of hitting the high points, Ms. Clinter. I may have told y'all this before, but in the first up-time veterinary school—in France in the 1700s—there were multiple fatalities among students and faculty studying glanders. Everyone get a good look at all the horses. Let's get some good photos of the horses and of the lesions."

As the students moved toward the horses, the doctor turned to his colleagues. "Sergeant MacGregor, could you tell your glanders horror stories again?"

"Be glad to, Doctor," said the sergeant.

"Scare the piss out of them, Robert. I don't want one of our students dying because they don't take the disease serious enough."

The sergeant grinned. "Oh, I always try to make my lads and lassies wet themselves at least once a day."

Ben watched as Les walked over to the fence and stared into the distance between the fence rails. It wasn't like Les to stay upset about anything for very long. When Ben worked for Les as an undergraduate, Les had chewed him out plenty of times, but five minutes later the older vet would be laughing and cutting up. Les' sense of humor seemed to have been mostly left behind after the Ring of Fire. Ben ambled over to the fence and put his hand on Les' shoulder. "Students pull stupid stunts," he said. "That's a given. Remember the dumb stuff I used to do?"

"I can't stand to lose anybody else," Les said. "I've tried, but I just can't get past leaving my sons and grandkids behind. It's bringing back things that I would rather forget, Emma, for one. Damn it, I know all the right things to say to folks that lose someone, but they aren't helping me the least little bit. Makes me wonder if I've been talking nonsense to them all these years. I know it's irrational, but I can't shake the gloom, if that makes any sense. The thought of losing one of these kids, to anything, is too much to bear."

Seeing his friend and mentor in pain disturbed Ben. All he could think of to say were clichés, but he felt compelled to try. "The students aren't kids. They're young adults that are responsible for their own actions. We can't hold their hands or they'll never learn to think. And that's one of our goals—to make them think critically. I'm sorry about Hoss and the others left behind after the Ring of Fire. There are just no words that are adequate. I miss Hoss, even though the silly rascal spent all his time getting me in trouble." Ben hugged Les close, whispering, "We need you, boss man. Hang in there; we'll get it all figured out. Just like the students, we're in this together. You hurt, I hurt."

With all the conflicting emotions, Les could barely

speak. "Thanks," he said. "I didn't mean to lay all that on you. I'll either get over it or not. Just need some time, I guess." Les doubted that time would heal his wounds this time, but didn't want his friend to worry.

Les watched the five horse traders who owned the glandered horses striding stiffly toward the students and Sergeant MacGregor. "Looks like trouble," he said to Ben. "You armed?"

"Yep," said Ben. "So is Robert, and have you ever seen the farriers without the new play pretties we gave them? You?"

Les grinned and patted his revolver. "Never leave home without it."

Les heard the demanding voice of the roughest-looking trader, an Englishman, well before he and Ben walked up to the group. He looked more like a hardened mercenary than a horse trader. The man addressed the sergeant. "If you won't buy the horses, give them back and we'll find other buyers that are interested."

"Nay, not in Grantville you won't and the poor animals that are near dead won't be going anywhere again," Sergeant MacGregor said. "I saw you read the signs about diseased animals by the gate. You had your chance to turn about, but didn't take it." The Englishman made a show of opening his coat to reveal a couple of horse pistols. Sergeant MacGregor winked at Mr. McDonald standing beside him. Banner and Oliver had made their way behind the men. The rest of the students were making a semicircle around the small band of traders.

"I'm glad to see that the sergeant has been teaching

y'all more than just horseshoeing," Les said to the students. To the traders he said, "The very sick horses will be humanely shot and burned. All the other horses, including the ones you are riding, will be branded on the left jaw with the letter G, for glanders. No one from Grantville will buy the branded horses. And we hope that soon nobody anywhere will buy disease-branded animals. If you try to resist the order, it will be done anyway and you will be permanently barred from Grantville."

The Englishman said, "I've never heard of such nonsense." Les was about to reply when Sergeant MacGregor pointed to the man and said, "Don't give me that shite; I've seen you trading horses to King Gustav's army. You're lucky Colonel Stock isn't here yet, he would simply hang you from the nearest tree. These Americans are a wee bit more tolerant of the likes of you than the colonel is."

The head trader began gasping for breath and there were loud murmurs from the other traders. "Rittmeister Stock is coming here? When?"

"Aye, soon," the sergeant replied. "And it's Colonel Stock now. He's a horse marshal in King Gustav's army. He's eager to exchange ideas with the doctors."

The horse traders' attitude changed from arrogant to cringing in seconds. "We will be glad to cooperate with whatever you gentlemen decide," said the head trader. "Colonel Stock doesn't have to hear of this, does he?"

Les was pleased that there was no shooting. He said, "We'll discuss it among ourselves, but I think we can handle it without involving the colonel this time. Don't ever bring diseased animals to Grantville again.

Understood? I recommend shooting all the animals with glanders; they will infect your own mounts if you keep them long enough."

The horse trader looked puzzled. "Infect?" he asked. "What do you mean?"

Les always looked for chances to educate people about the science of diseases, so he took his time explaining glanders and infectious diseases in general to the traders. When he was done with his lecture he said, "Do you have any questions? I know you may have a hard time believing that invisible organisms are responsible for such things as glanders, but it is absolutely true. We know beyond doubt that it's true."

The horse traders were still somewhat bewildered after the doctor's lecture, but the leader was quick to say, "We believe you, Doctor. Please, you will tell Colonel Stock that we believe you?"

Les was puzzled and annoyed but saw that it was very important to the man. He said, "I'll see to it personally."

The traders were all very loud and enthusiastic in thanking Les. Les glanced over at Sergeant MacGregor. The sergeant was at attention and grinning broadly. Les knew that when MacGregor looked like that, he was suppressing either a laughing or screaming fit. He heard a humming sound coming from deep in the sergeant's throat. Humming meant laughter, strangled growling noises meant screaming. So Robert was amused. Les would have to ask him about that later.

Ben, seeing Les' bemusement and MacGregor's amusement, took charge of the situation. He said, "Dr. Blocker, I'll get the students and these gentlemen to lead the diseased horses over to the burn pit."

Ben led the group to a remote area screened by trees and well away from running water. This was the first time that all of the students were involved in mass euthanasia, so Ben hoped that everything would go smoothly. He turned to the three farriers. "Since y'all have done this before you'll help me with the first horses." To everyone he said, "The way we do this is draw a line from the base of one ear to the inside corner of the opposite eye. Then we do the same from the base of the other ear. Where those lines cross is our target. Hold the gun as perpendicular to the target as possible. Done correctly, the horse will be dead before it hits the ground. Respect the animal and respect the procedure. Euthanasia is the last good thing that we can do for God's creatures who have served us and have often been our friends. It's never to be taken casually or lightly. Harden your mind to what must be done. But don't harden your heart. Let's get on with it."

Shooting the horses went as well as any very unpleasant procedure can go. Several students had tears in their eyes well before all the horses were shot, but all did their parts. Ben was pleased at how gentle and respectful the students were in handling the animals. The bodies were pushed into the pit, covered with tree limbs and burned.

The horses that the traders kept, which showed no signs of disease, were hot-branded on the jaw. Ben watched as the students handled the horses. Sergeant MacGregor supervised the branding. Les had the traders laughing in another part of the corral as he told ribald stories and jokes. Ben walked over to the sergeant and students. "Someday, we'll have enough dry ice or liquid nitrogen to do cold branding instead of hot branding. It doesn't hurt as bad and doesn't scar horses' thin skins as much." He called to Les, "I'm going to send the students who aren't on duty on home. It's beer-thirty." Les nodded and waved as he continued to talk with the traders.

Ben had a special assignment in mind for the students. "I want y'all to break up into at least three teams. Make sure that there are up-timers and down-timers in each group. I want a paper from each group about all aspects of glanders, tuberculosis, brucellosis, and rinderpest from both up-time and down-time perspectives. Those are the diseases we must keep out of the Grantville area at all costs. The paper is due in two weeks." There were half-serious groans from the students. Ben grinned his best grin at them. "What? You think you already have enough to do? Poor babies. Get on home or wherever." The students left the corral chattering and carrying on like a flock of crows. No doubt they were headed to the nearest watering hole to imbibe some liquid refreshment. Vet students never passed up liquid rounds where the day's cases were discussed with the aid of beer and whisky.

Les watched the horse traders riding and leading their remaining animals away from Grantville as the sun went down behind the hills. "Nothing like a good dirty joke to calm down an irritated horse trader. Same as back in West Virginia. That Englishman leading them worries me, though; one minute he was acting like he wanted to kiss my ass and the next kick it." He smiled and shook his head. "Ben, would you make a report about today's activities to Willie Ray and the agricultural committee? I'll brief Dr. Adams and the medical committee. Robert, if you don't have anything better to do, could you make sure the students heading to the beer joint behave themselves? It's been almost a month since the three stooges cleared out a bar. Those boys like to scrap. I don't want to bail them out of jail again."

Robert laughed and shook his head. "I never mind sitting in a pub, but when those lads get the bit between their teeth, it is hard to whoa them. I could beat them bloody and work them half to death, but that only lasts a wee bit. After the last ruckus, I had a little talk with them. I told them if they continued in their foolish ways, I had no choice but to tell Colonel Stock about it. They've behaved better since."

"That reminds me," said Les. "Is he a nine-foot-tall ogre that eats babies for breakfast? I know he's your commanding officer and is one of King Gustav's horse marshals. Should I regret sending him a letter asking him to visit Grantville?"

"Nay, he's no ogre, though he doesn't mind if dishonest sutlers and horse traders think so. He hanged a horse trader that sold glandered horses to the Swedish army. But that was more because several of his men got sick and a couple of them died. I was one of the ones that got sick. My cousin died. We were careless in handling the horses even though he had taught us better. He is the best officer I've ever served under. He cares about his men enough that he won't tolerate having them hurt because of their foolishness or lack of training. So he can be a very tough taskmaster and will take the hide off your back if he has to. But the worst is the look of disappointment in his blue-gray eyes. He has remarkable eyes. Rarely raises his voice.

His men love him and will do anything for him. I never want to see the look of disappointment in his eyes again or get another quiet, icy reprimand from him. Those hurt worse than the lashes that lesser officers think is the only way to discipline."

"That sounds like what Mr. McDonald told me," said Ben. "Didn't his family have a riding school that was destroyed in the wars?"

"It was a *ritterakademie*, which teaches much more than riding. It's a 'knight academy' in English. It is much like a combination of your up-time military academy, riding school, and martial arts school. Anyway, I had best run along if I'm going to catch up with our youngsters."

Robert was having a pleasant conversation in the Gardens with two Grantville locals close to his own age. One said he was a retired U.S. Marine and the other laughed and said he was a retired biker. Whatever a biker was, Robert could tell that he and the Marine were hard men. Robert liked to converse with mature, hard men who had no reason to prove their manhood by being troublesome. The three young military farriers and the other students were talking with a Grantville local that taught martial arts—as they called it here. The farriers were friends of his and often practiced their skills at his gym. There was no hint of trouble until three twenty-something up-time soldiers joined the students at their long table. They had the look of hard men still learning their craft.

The bearded biker glanced over at the table. "So much for a quiet evening." The Marine chuckled and said, "Boys will be boys." But there was no trouble for a long while. Of course the farriers and the three locals were circling each other like wary gamecocks. But the conversation seemed pleasant enough.

Then one of the Grantville lads said, "...and then we'll go to Ireland and kick all the English and Scottish invaders out." Robert MacGregor of Clan MacGregor was mildly irritated but he knew that Lawrence McDonald, whose family had served as gallowglass mercenaries to Irish kings for centuries, would be offended. Robert watched as McDonald slowly rose to his feet and growled something in Gaelic. The offending party also stood. "What did you say?" he asked. The tall, dark Ross Oliver was also on his feet. "He said, quite lyrically I thought, my arsehole is more Irish than you are, arsehole."

The three farriers and the three up-timer soldiers were facing each other across the table. One of the other up-timers removed his coat, which revealed a large bowie knife sheathed at his belt. Grinning, he slid the knife out of its sheath and laid it on the table. "Friendly fight, I figure."

Oliver had an equally predatory grin that his companions knew too well. His knife had appeared in his hand seemingly from nowhere, and he too laid it on the table. "I'm told dueling is forbidden in Grantville, and I'm a law-abiding fellow. Getting a beating, though, seems legal enough."

As Robert pushed his chair back he said to his tablemates, "I may need your assistance to stop this from getting out of hand. McDonald is the strongest man I know; Banner is an excellent pugilist and grappler, but I may have to shoot Oliver to keep him from slicing your man to ribbons." The biker pointed to one of the young Americans. "We may have to shoot them both—he's a pretty good hand with that bowie of his."

Shooting anyone proved unnecessary. Robert heard an icy quiet voice that he knew so well say in German-accented English: "Corporal Oliver, please put your knife away." The knife disappeared as quickly as it appeared. The pale-faced Oliver stood at rigid attention, as did his two companions. Everyone at the two tables was standing very still if not at attention. Robert was amused. An angry Colonel Carl Stock seemed to make everyone want to stand at attention, whether they had a military background or not. The colonel was an impressive figure. Tall, broad-shouldered, dressed in a dark, floor-length, padded leather riding coat that some Americans called a duster. Deadly sword, long knife and horse pistols on his belt. But Robert knew it was the ice in the blue-gray eyes—killer eyes—and in the quiet voice that froze people in place. And the concern in the voice and eyes at the same time. The colonel commanded respect from all who met him; he did not demand it; something in him made you want to not disappoint him.

Colonel Stock seemed to glide across the room to the table of the combatants. Several other hard men followed him. Behind them were a dignified middle-aged woman and a young woman barely out of her teens. Robert watched as the colonel said to the farriers, "You three see to our horses and the wagons. We have come a long way today and the animals need food, water and shelter. I assume you can carry out those duties without causing a riot?" The farriers replied as one, "Yes, sir," and all but ran out the door. The three young Americans also started toward the door.

Colonel Stock gestured broadly. "Gentlemen, please, we all have too many common enemies to have our young men fighting among themselves." The Marine growled at the three Americans, "I agree with the colonel; y'all sit and drink your beer. And try not to make anyone else want to carve you up tonight if you can help it." Still scowling, the three sat.

Robert introduced his tablemates to the colonel and those accompanying him.

Colonel Stock gave each man a slight bow and gestured to the other table. "And these young people?"

Robert introduced each veterinary student in turn. "They are some of the other students that I wrote you about that are being trained in veterinary medicine. The others are on duty at the veterinary hospital." The three up-time soldiers then rose, saluted and formally introduced themselves.

Colonel Stock nodded, "I am Carl Stock, horse marshal for his Imperial Majesty Gustav of Sweden. May I present my wife Barbara, who cares for our library, and my daughter Katerina, who hopes to become one of your veterinary students. My officers are Captains Giovanni Caldarola, Aert VanZandt, Emile Billiot, Otfried von Meusebach, Ragnar Ljungberg, Bill Wallace, and Esteve Fages y Callis. All are experts in their homeland's schools of swordsmanship and are master horsemen. These young men are Frantz Kuhler and Jorgen Jönsson, apprentice military farriers and two of my family's traveling *ritterakademie*'s students. May we join you and the students at your table?"

Sergeant MacGregor sat down at his adjoining table after the newcomers were seated and said, "Mr. Harr, please go ask Doctors Blocker and Alexander to join us after their meetings if it is convenient. I reckon both committee meetings are at the elementary school."

After everyone ordered food and drink, there was lively discussion in a mixture of German and English, all of Colonel Stock's party being fluent in German and speaking and understanding some English. The food orders arrived a few minutes before the veterinarians came in the door.

MacGregor got up out of his chair when he saw them. "Colonel Stock, Drs. Alexander and Blocker are here." Colonel Stock rose and bade the others to keep their seats. He walked with the sergeant to greet the pair. MacGregor made the introductions and they all walked to the long table where more introductions were made.

After everyone was seated, Les turned to Colonel Stock. "Colonel, we are very happy you decided to visit Grantville. Sergeants MacGregor and Lennox and Captain Mackay think very highly of you as a man, officer, and horse doctor. They all say you are the best horse doctor in Europe. Dr. Alexander and I hope to learn everything you can teach us about your treatment methods and medicines."

"There are some equally good horse doctors in Europe," The colonel replied. "Some, like me, studied human medicine at universities in order to better understand the science of treating animals. Others taught themselves science and medicine in order to understand animal disease. I had to leave university prematurely to help with my family's *ritterakademie.* You say you wish to learn from me. I came here hoping to learn from you. The Scots say you two doctors are miracle workers."

Ben joined the conversation. "No, we're definitely not miracle workers. We're country veterinarians who stand on the shoulders of those who have come before us. Veterinary education in the time we come from is more rigorous than human medical education in some ways. We are trained to treat more than one species. Robert showed us your writings on diseases after we asked about current treatments. He had to translate them for us. They are scholastic gems. We use them as textbooks."

"Grantville appointed Dr. Alexander and me as the veterinary medical examining board," Les said in a solemn and official-sounding voice. "The board is authorized to grant veterinary licenses to practitioners that we think are qualified. As the veterinary school, we have the authority to award Doctors of Veterinary Medicine to qualified individuals. Sergeant Robert MacGregor has Grantville veterinary license number three. He won't accept a DVM yet. We've discussed it and we'd like to offer you license number four and a DVM degree. Please believe us, we offer them to you because we think you are very qualified. We hope you will accept and join us as an equal colleague at the veterinary school and on the examining board."

Colonel Stock sat in silence for a few moments tapping the steepled fingers of both hands against his chin. He folded his hands as he began to speak. "Dr. Blocker, Dr. Alexander, you honor me. I came here expecting nothing. These wars have made us all lose hope in humanity at times. My only thought was to find a place that is safer for the dependents of the *ritterakademie*. And to learn what you would teach me. I will accept upon several conditions. My first duty is to King Gustav, the second is to the staff and the families of the *ritterakademie*. I'm afraid that the veterinary school must come third for some time."

Les was smiling as he stood and extended his hand. "Welcome to Grantville, Colonel. We welcome your staff, students, and families as well. We have room for you and your family and several others at my house and we'll find places for everyone to stay. Robert has told us your first duty is to King Gustav. We understand that. Please understand you'll be our full partner. True colleagues never stop learning from each other."

Colonel Stock smiled as he shook Les' hand. "Then I accept. I understand some horse traders tried to sell horses with *Rotz* and you turned them away. And that Captain MacGregor's charges drew your ire. Yes, Robert, I said Captain MacGregor. I won't allow you to turn down the commission this time. One thing I don't understand is why you called them the three stooges. They are quite intelligent when they aren't breaking things or causing trouble."

Les laughed. "Exactly, Colonel. Exactly. The Three Stooges were comic actors that were always breaking things and creating a ruckus."

Les spotted the three young American soldiers sitting at the table. "Colonel, have you met these three? They worked for me when they were teenagers. They were my original three stooges. Y'all tell the Colonel some of the things you did when you worked for me. You've been behaving yourself tonight, I assume?" Everyone within earshot roared.

A waitress interrupted the conversation at the table. "Les, Daniel Banner is on the phone. He wants to speak to you and a Colonel Stock. He asked for Sergeant MacGregor, but I told him you and Ben were also here. He says it's an emergency."

Everyone wondered what kind of emergency would require talking to Les and the colonel. The two men were passing the phone back and forth. They all soon had their answer. "This is an all-hands-and-the-cook situation," said Les. "Two things are going on. First, there is a very sick boy in the horse traders' camp a couple of miles outside of Grantville. He probably has glanders. The farriers are going to the camp to scout and fetch him to the hospital if there are no problems at the camp. The boy's name is Adolf Dudensing. His father Axel is in camp with him, along with several other horse traders. As soon as we got off the phone I had them alert the hospital. The second problem is the reason they are approaching the camp cautiously. There's a large gang of bandits about two days' ride from Grantville. They are ex-mercenary cavalrymen led by an Englishman named Charlton. They're holding the families of the horse traders hostage. They made the traders try to sell glandered horses here today. The Englishman that led them is on his way back to Charlton's main camp. Colonel Stock knows more about these bandits."

"Yes, Bannister Charlton deserves his evil reputation," said the colonel. "He has about forty to fifty men with him. Ross Oliver captured a boy who was scouting the veterinary hospital. The boy had been sent by the Englishman to find a hidden route into town. The bandits plan a raid to steal stock and whatever else they can carry off. The boy's real motive in coming to the hospital was to find help for his sick friend. Sergeant, I mean Captain MacGregor, I need to talk with Mackay and to someone in the Grantville military. We need to hit Charlton before he can raid Grantville."

"I'll go to the cavalry command post," said Mac-Gregor. "There's usually an officer or two there."

The young American with the bowie knife stood. "Colonel, I'll alert Mike and Frank. What do you need from us?"

The colonel thought for a moment. "We need men that can ride and fight. We must attack them before they break camp. If we do not, they will scatter and gather again someplace else. And they may kill their hostages. I will be at the hospital. Anyone you two find can meet me there."

A party on horseback, which included the sick boy's father, arrived at the hospital. They were met by both veterinarians, and Dr. Adams, Colonel Stock, nurses, and several Scottish cavalrymen—all wearing surgical masks. Lawrence McDonald carefully handed Adolf down to the men, who placed him on a gurney. Dr. Adams did a quick exam of the boy. "Take him to the isolation area we prepared. We don't need everyone to come in with us, just the one or two who know the most about him and his condition. Drs. Blocker and Alexander, please join us. You probably know more about glanders than me or any of the physicians."

"Colonel Stock should come with us," said Dr. Blocker. "He's seen cases of glanders before and may know down-time treatments that will help."

Dr. Blocker was carrying several thick books. "I brought all the books that have anything about glanders in them. Between us and the books we'll figure something out."

The nurses quickly started an IV on Adolf, taking his vital signs and drawing blood for lab tests. Axel watched the procedures on his son with concern. "You're not going to bleed him, are you? I've never seen that help. We've given him some willow bark to decrease his fever."

Dr. Adams looked up from his examination of the patient. "No sir, we don't use bleeding. We're taking samples of his blood for testing."

Colonel Stock approached the worried father. "Herr Dudensing, how long has your son been ill? You have seen glanders in people before?"

"Adolf fell ill three days ago. At first I wasn't worried. I thought it might be a cold or something. But then he started getting knots on his neck, a bad fever started, and he started coughing. I've seen glanders before. This looks just like it."

The colonel turned to Dr. Adams. "The boy has been sick three days. Herr Dudensing has seen glanders before and so have I. We are both positive that the boy has glanders. I do not know of any cures. I use willow bark to reduce fever and the father has already done that."

"Thank you, Colonel," said Dr. Adams. "Dr. Blocker, what are y'all finding in the books?"

The two veterinarians were thumbing through several thick volumes that were scattered on a table. "Nothing very helpful or very hopeful," said Dr. Blocker. "Neither the medical or veterinary texts recommend a specific antibiotic. They list several that have been tried with varying results. Success in treating systemic glanders with anything is fifty-fifty at best. I think hitting him with every antibiotic we have left is the best course. I had one of the students bring the injectable antibiotics from the veterinary hospital. I recommend ceftiofur to start with, unless you have a similar fast-acting cephalosporin with a human label. It can be used intravenously, but giving it intramuscularly works nearly as fast. We also have florfenicol, enrofloxacin, and trimethoprim-sulfadiazine. We've already given you most of our injectable tetracycline. I recommend using it also unless you have doxycycline you can use. Doxy is one of the recommended antibiotics. The good thing is that all of the antibiotics should be safe. They're all used in multiple species of animals."

Dr. Adams frowned. "Doesn't look like we have much choice. You vets had more injectable antibiotics than all the physicians and even the pharmacy had at the RoF. Let's start with the ceftiofur, then give the others one at a time. That way we can tell if he has a bad reaction to one of the drugs. We'll monitor him closely, and then it's just a waiting game."

Dr. Blocker explained the treatment regimen to Colonel Stock, who translated for the father. "The doctors are using the machines to watch Adolf's condition. They are giving him medicines to try to cure the glanders. But there is a problem: Even in the future, treating glanders is very difficult. The horse doctors seem to know more about it than the physicians and are advising them. They are even using some animal medicines. It is in the hands of God now."

Axel smiled for a few seconds. "Good, I've always trusted good horse doctors more than human doctors. Yes, may God guide these good people that my son may live. Colonel, I hope you know that we are honest horse traders. We would never buy or sell glandered horses. The bandits are holding our families hostage. Please, can you free our families?"

The colonel's eyes seemed to ice over. "I assure you that we will free your families. I am going outside to talk to the military authorities now."

An hour later a nurse reported that Adolf's temperature was dropping and he was breathing easier. Les and Ben left the care of the patient in Dr. Adams' care and joined the discussion on freeing the horse traders' families. Colonel Stock came back inside when the council outside concluded.

"Herr Dudensing, stay with your son. The other traders will lead us to the bandit camp. We will free your family."

"My son is getting better, praise God," said Axel. "Thank you, Colonel. Go with God."

Axel sat at his son's bedside as the door to the isolation room opened. His wife and children flooded into the room—all wearing surgical masks. His mask didn't hide the joy in his eyes. Two days later, a large abscess in Adolf's lung burst, causing a massive hemorrhage. He was sixteen years old when he died.

After Adolf Dudensing's funeral, Colonel Stock, Ben, Les, and Robert rode back to the veterinary hospital together. It was an overcast, dreary day, which matched their moods. Les was the first to speak. "I'm stooge number one to think we could save that boy or even keep glanders out of Grantville."

"I'm stooge number two," said Ben. "I didn't even think to ask the horse traders if any of them were sick."

"I am the third stooge then," said the colonel. "I knew Charlton was out there raiding and stealing, but I did not make it a priority to stop him."

"Does putting a DVM behind your name make a man daft?" said Robert. "Les, you and Ben kept that boy alive long enough to say goodbye to his family. Without you he had no hope. Colonel, you united and led men of several countries to save the families and to put paid to the Charlton band. If you're stooges, it's because you think you can fix this present world. Only Jesus can do that. If you're stooges, then you're stooges of hope."

The men rode on in silence for a while. "Colonel, my three American stooges and your three did good in the raid on the Charltons," said Les. "I guess we'll have to quit calling them stooges."

"Please call me Carl. They made some mistakes that enthusiastic young men always make, but overall they did well. I think they should keep the name a while longer. To keep them humble.

"Robert, how are your studies going? We need a fourth old stooge to help keep the six young stooges out of trouble."

Robert laughed for the first time in days. "I don't think all of Grantville and the Germanies can keep those six in line for very long."

Stolen Reputations

Anne Keener

Leiden
June 1634

Bonaventure Elzevir was a happy man as he bustled toward the bookshop nestled in the grounds of Leiden University which he owned with his nephew Abraham. The high sun shone down on Bonaventure's stylish black breeches and doublet, white shirt and wide lace collar, plump frame, and his warm and genial face, a tool which helped when befriending the best scholars in Europe in order to find promising manuscripts and convincing merchants and nobles to buy the resulting books.

His shop, a small building sporting a couple of large windows covered with thin vellum, smelling heavily of rag paper, ink, and leather, had been built fifty years before by his father after the Spanish had forced his family first from Antwerp and then from Wesel and Douai. One entrance, usually used by scholars or customers, led straight to the office, and the other, which Bonaventure preferred to use so he could examine his domain, straight through the workshop. Unlike most publishers who had to send their books out to printers, increasing the cost of their books and slowing their ability to produce more, he had six presses, purchased from his nephew Isaac ten years ago. They were housed in a slightly larger nearby building that sported similar large vellum-covered windows, always smelled of ink, and seemed to constantly quake from the action of the presses.

Thinking about Isaac still brought a twinge of pain. Isaac had sold the presses and building to buy a commission in the Dutch navy and had been murdered the year before by the loathsome Spanish and the traitorous French and English. It was at that larger building, purchased from his late younger brother, that Abraham spent most of his time, overseeing the printing to his meticulous standards and producing sheets that were works of art, while Bonaventure made sure the books were exquisitely bound and found homes on the best and most lucrative shelves in Europe.

While he was trying to place some of his wares on those shelves, his family's world had been altered forever. Bonaventure had traveled to the 1633 Frankfurt-am-Main fair with a new treasure to sell, the New Testament in Greek, compiled from some of the oldest versions of the Bible available. He had expected to receive a large number of orders for the exquisite book, but the fair had been a disappointment. The book had sold some copies and made a small profit, but not nearly what his house had hoped for, and most galling of all, the most exquisite and desired books at the fair were the ones claiming to come from a place called Grantville, and a future that would not be.

There were a great many rumors swirling around Grantville, some claiming they were sent by the devil, others claiming they were sent by the Almighty, and all claimed there were wonders beyond belief to be found there, including a multitude of books that were higher quality than any his family could produce. Other tales, including the story of the so-named up-timers burning Spanish troops with unquenchable fire in a castle, had brought a grin to Bonaventure's face, while the sight of the books from Grantville had quelled it and left him feeling sickly and ashamed. After the fair, he had chosen to travel home with a side journey to Grantville, trying to sell his wares along the way to lessen the blow of the disappointing fair and to see what wonders he could find that he could use to the glory of his house.

The rumors had been an understatement. He had been taken aback by the sheer number of books in Grantville. He produced maybe a handful of copies of thirty to fifty books a year, with maybe a few dozen of a new work, but Grantville had thousands upon thousands of them. There were books even left carelessly in taverns or in places of business for customers to read. Not mere cheap pamphlets—though there were plenty of those which the up-timers called magazines, journals, and newspapers—but books. Many were bound in a matter that was only a small step up from a pamphlet, but there were a handful of books so finely bound that it had made him weep from despair. He had seen earlier at the fair that the quality of the books made the offerings of his house look like the work of apprentices. The multitude of books had driven home the danger that his house was in if he did not obtain any books to publish in Grantville.

He had expected to search all over town to find interesting books to copy and inquired at the inn he chose to stay at, The Maddened Queen, so chosen because he had been told it was preferred by scholars at the fair who had been to Grantville, as well as its connection to the Crucibellus letters. He was informed that, fortunately, the up-timers kept the texts that would most appeal to the faculty and students of Leiden University at the National Library, so after settling into his room, he traveled directly there. Oddly, a few people at the inn seemed to recognize his name, but he was too overwhelmed by the wonders of Grantville and worries about his house's future to inquire why.

But while thumbing through a promising-looking book of anatomy at the National Library, an unusual etching on the frontispiece had caught his eye. It was an unmistakable picture of an elm tree wrapped by a grape vine, with a figure standing next to the tree and the words NON SOLUS appearing on the opposite side of the tree. He had nearly dropped the book in surprise. It was *le Solitaire*, the device his family put on many items printed by Abraham and Isaac before him, and the name Elsevier was above it. The book, *Gray's Anatomy*, wasn't the only one in the library to bear the publishing mark of his house. It seemed like half of the journal section and a number of the books bore *le Solitaire* and the name of his house. Now he knew why people at the inn had recognized his name.

He had been trembling when he approached the research desk, asking to know more about the history of the publisher of the book and his family. The librarian had appeared about to faint when he revealed his name, and had guided Bonaventure to several Elsevier texts which had sold well at the spring Frankfurt fair.

After returning home, Bonaventure had closely followed the news from Grantville and the rest of the Dutch Republic. The year had been a heavy one but familiar to his family, with one nephew killed by treachery in battle and the other forced to flee from the siege of Amsterdam with the clothes on his back. But there was good news. The up-timers had kept the Spanish from destroying the Dutch Republic entirely, and they had devastated the treacherous French, orchestrators of Isaac's death, in battle on both land and sea.

Other news of the up-timers had brought a smile to his face. Bonaventure had been secretly gloating when the up-timers had persuaded the United States of Europe to adopt their laws on copyright. While some claimed you could not own items produced by yourself in the future that was not to be, clearly a portion of the rights on all of those valuable publications belonged to him and Abraham. In fact, his family should have first claim on the right to print them, not those shops in Grantville. It was clear to him that his and Abraham's exacting standards had paid off, for his house was a giant in publishing in that future that would not be. The solicitor had drafted the lawsuits already. All that was needed was the proof that Elsevier was founded by his family.

He had barely entered the building when shouting erupted from the office he shared with his nephew Abraham when his nephew wasn't overseeing the printshop to his exacting standards. Several of the handful of journeymen and apprentices working at large tables in the bright, airy shop flinched and buried themselves deeper into their proofreading or bookbinding, while others looked around to find the source of the shouting. Just then a heavyset man wearing disheveled ink-smudged clothes burst out of the office. "Those bastards! Those backstabbing, thieving bastards!" Abraham shouted over and over again as he waved a packet of documents in his hand.

Bonaventure quickly walked over, seeking to calm him down, a frequent task with his mercurial, exacting nephew. "What is wrong, Abraham? Did someone steal the university contract from us? Did someone copy our recent edition of the New Testament?"

"We received a response from Grantville about the history of our family and the print house Elsevier," Abraham replied as he slammed the offending documents down on a worktable. "The documents state that you and I were the peak of our family's success. We were most renowned for our editions of the New Testament in the original Greek and a book printed four years from now written by Galileo after the Papists forbade him from writing. Several of our sons and nephews carried on our business, but were not as successful and by 1712 our family left the printing and bookselling trades."

"If our family stopped printing in 1712, why do the up-timers have hosts of books printed under our name using our device? Who printed them?" asked Bonaventure in a confused and worried tone. He swept his hand out toward the shop. "Did someone trained by our house borrow the name and device?" He could see all of the publications he thought his family had claim to disappearing in his head, along with the fortune that came with them. Dark thoughts flashed in his mind toward the group of journeymen and apprentices. Did one of them steal the name and device, or did they carry it on with the family's blessing?

"A group of thieves in Amsterdam started publishing in 1880 using our name, mark, and reputation!" Abraham spat out. He slapped his hand on the papers. "We were famed for publishing works in Greek and Latin, as well as books of natural philosophy. They took that reputation and started publishing scholarly works in a variety of fields. Those bastards built an empire on our good name. I know the up-timers claim 'imitation is the sincerest form of flattery,' but we were robbed."

Bonaventure walked over to his agitated nephew and draped an arm across his shoulder, and with the other grabbed the documents in question. Although he was still reeling from the news, as the older member of the partnership, he was expected to be the rock to his nephew, although only ten years separated them. He also wanted to review the documents himself. He then steered Abraham into the office, closing the door behind them, and started pouring a measure of genever for each of them to soften the blow of the terrible news.

After a bottle or two, a thought struck Bonaventure. "That other firm built a reputation for publishing scholarly works. While we have no claim to what they published, we may be able to use their reputation just as they stole ours. The up-timers know Elsevier as the place to send scholarly articles and report new discoveries in natural philosophy." His arm swept out to the case of exquisitely bound books. "They will want us to print and sell their books."

"Start publishing academic articles? Solicit them from different universities? Would we have to produce masses of mere pamphlets?" Abraham slurred drunkenly as he reached for the bottle again. His arm brushed some of the documents and letters on the table in the office. "Would that weaken our contract with Leiden University and our reputation as booksellers?"

"Not if we use it as a way to raise Leiden's prestige and access to knowledge. The university is less than fifty years old, although it is well-funded and has attracted some prestigious scholars. We can become the avenue to circulate discoveries and hold academic debates with distant scholars. We will not sell mere pamphlets—we will produce high-quality journals with fine illustrations. The up-timers used those to quickly circulate new knowledge. The fact that we are associated with a university will just enhance our access to scholars and scholarly reports." Bonaventure leafed through some of the papers on the table. "Several groups in Grantville, including the *Bibelgesellschaft*, the high school, and the Grange have sent works to be published. We can even suggest that we become the place to reprint scholarly reports in order to circulate them among the scholars of Europe."

Abraham cupped his chin in his hand. "We'll need to figure out some way to produce those fine illustrations. Those up-time reports have a lot of complicated illustrations, as do the new ones written in Grantville. They will be difficult to engrave."

"We may not have to engrave. The up-timers have a whole host of ways to print. Little Louis is a journeyman and will soon be ready to run his own shop. The historians claimed he would do so in four years' time. Your son Jean is twelve. It is time to begin an apprenticeship. I know you planned to send him to France, but perhaps it would be better to have him train in Grantville or perhaps Jena if no one in Grantville will take him. We can ask Little Louis to escort Jean to Grantville so they can both learn new techniques and bring them back here. If Louis does so, we will happily vouch for him so he can become a master sooner than expected when he brings back new techniques. If he sets up his own shop, whether in Grantville, Jena, or Amsterdam, hopefully it will be closely affiliated with our shop."

The two men exchanged bemused glances. While they knew Louis would welcome the chance to truly journey again, he would not enjoy traveling with his temperamental and imaginative young cousin.

Abraham grinned and brushed the papers from Grantville with his hand. "Maybe those thieves did us a favor after all. They stole our reputation and we can in turn steal theirs." Abraham raised his glass as did Bonaventure. "May our kinsmen be more successful than in the future the up-timers came from."

The Invisible Dogs of Grantville

Jackie Britton Lopatin

Magdeburg Railway Platform
September 1634

"Who said anything about there being invisible dogs in Grantville?" Allan Dailey, coordinator of the Imperial College's Military Engineering program, demanded of the hapless young soldier.

The private flinched and stammered out, "Um, uh, nobody in particular, Lieutenant, you know, just rumors."

With a sideways wink to his companion, fellow faculty member Thomas Holcomb, Allan stared fiercely at the young man. "Well, if there *were* invisible dogs in Grantville, Private, they'd be a highly classified military secret, and anyone spreading rumors about their existence would be subject to military discipline." With a self-satisfied smile, Allan rocked back on his heels and tugged at the hem of his uniform's jacket.

"Military discipline?" the young man squeaked. "But my cousin Georg sent my mother a sign to place in her window, announcing to all that her home is guarded by an invisible dog."

517

"What?!" Allan loomed over him.

"Y-yes," he cringed. "It's written in both English and German. Georg also told me stories that he said he heard directly from the up-timer, Billy Bob, about the invisible poodles and Chihuahuas."

"Oh, well, if your source is Billy Bob Robinson," Holcomb interjected, "you can discount everything you heard. Billy Bob tells a great story, but he's one of the biggest liars in Grantville."

"B-but, my cousin said he *saw* an invisible dog being walked down the street. And—and, look!" he pointed at a woman walking along the platform. Allan and Thomas followed the line of his finger and saw that the tote bag she was carrying featured the outline of a poodle in red with a caption underneath that read: "Beware the Invisible Dogs of Grantville!"

"Yeah, well, my cousin, Laramie, found an invisible dog leash in our grandmother's attic and found a way to make money off it without actually selling it." Bledsoe Kline was clearly enjoying being the center of attention of the gathering sprawled around Allan's classroom that evening. In his early thirties and a high school dropout, he wasn't one of the typical students here in the Imperial College of Science, Engineering, and Technology, but rather had been assigned here by the USE Army as an assistant to Jere Haygood, one of the few honest-to-goodness civil engineers who had come through the Ring of Fire.

Allan looked around and noted with approval that most of the up-timers here at Imperial Tech were present. Only about eighteen of them, but even at that, this particular year probably represented the largest group of up-timer students it would ever have. This class included any older Americans with the desire— and the money—to learn engineering, as well as a few recruits from the latest high school graduating class. Hereafter the college would likely get only a few up-timers each year as they graduated from high school and showed a desire for engineering studies.

"He had notices printed up and is selling them through the bookstore and gift shops in Grantville," Bledsoe continued.

"Then some other clever entrepreneur with a good source of canvas and burlap decided that tote bags are the new T-shirts for displaying clever slogans and pictures and came up with an entire line of invisible-dog tote bags."

"Really?" Henry Swisher, one of the youngest students, leaned forward to ask. "What kind of slogans?"

"Lessee." Bledsoe paused and thought a minute. "Some of the bags just say simple stuff like 'Beware the Invisible Dogs of Grantville!' or 'I ♥ My Invisible Dog.' But more elaborate tote bags have been printed promoting various different breeds, with a high-end line of signed and numbered bags being sold exclusively through the Higgins Hotel." He paused to chortle sharply. "Wearable artwork with the virtue of being useful!"

As the guys sitting around chuckled, Bledsoe continued. "Some people have been spinning yarns about these invisible dogs and speculating about the nature of the various breeds. Poodles are said to be both smart and vicious, while nobody wants to mess with the invisible Rottweilers, either. Everyone's quite glad that none of the invisible Doberman pinschers came back through the Ring of Fire, and some rather wish a breeding pair of invisible Chihuahuas *hadn't* come back with us.'"

"Grr-rh-ha-rh-ha-rha!" Vincent Kubiak, another recent high school graduate, snarled at the chuckling room in a high-pitched Chihuahua fashion.

"Apparently a bunch of good ole boys are upset that none of the best tracking hounds have come through, but they're going to try to breed some up," he said, winking. "But some of the visiting artists have been commissioned to make portraits of the various breeds."

Allan's eyes started rolling as he tried to visualize portraits of invisible dogs.

"Did you find out *how* the artists are able to paint the invisible dogs to their patrons' satisfaction?" Armand Glazer finally asked, a quizzical expression on his face.

"Apparently the customer specifies a breed and a pose, the artist paints their picture, and then blurs the background in the appropriate shape; kinda like in the *Predator* movies when the cloaked predator moves. They've become quite a status symbol and cost accordingly."

Armand nodded and sat back in his chair, a thoughtful look on his face. As the oldest up-timer present and a fine commercial artist, he was one of the few there who had probably seen someone walking their "pet" during the height of the original invisible dog craze, and Allan suspected the stories were giving him some ideas.

"On the cheaper end, you can get hand-painted tote bags that say something like, 'My Invisible Dog can beat up your Invisible Dog!', or a picture of the invisible breed, or sometimes both."

"I can understand how you can print different sayings on tote bags," Armand spoke up, looking puzzled. "But since we don't have the supplies to make our up-time silkscreens anymore, how the heck do you put an invisible dog on a tote bag? Carving or etching even one blank for printing a picture would be incredibly expensive."

Bledsoe started laughing. "It's so stupid it's simple," he said. "It's kinda the same as silk screening, but not as slick. You take a piece of paper shaped like the outline of a dog—sitting, standing, whatever—and use it as a stencil to block out the ink that gets sprayed or dabbed over the rest of the bag; and there you have it, one picture of an invisible dog. The poodles have proven to be quite popular."

"Poodles?"

"Yeah, apparently they've been given a reputation for being quite vicious. 'Beware the Invisible Poodle Dogs of Grantville!'" he declaimed grandly, throwing out his hands dramatically as they all laughed.

This is good for us, Allan thought, leaning back and looking around the cramped classroom. A temporary arrangement, the Imperial College was currently sharing quarters with a Latin school in the *Altstadt*. A new roof to replace the one damaged in the sack of the city had convinced the *schule* that it could make do with the crowded conditions until the college's first building was finished outside the city walls. For this meeting he'd pushed most of the furniture back against the wall and pulled the chairs into what proved to be an inadequate circle, resulting in some sitting in chairs, some perching on tables outside the circle, and some lounging around in the middle of the floor.

They were all happily munching on snacks he'd had a servant bring in and pass around. *We should get together on a regular basis, even when the new college gets finished. It's too easy for us to get isolated from each other. We need a comfortable place to kick back, decompress and have a chance to talk with others who understand our background, language, and the culture clashes which are inevitable.*

When he noticed the servant leaving the room, he couldn't help wondering what he had thought about the whole invisible dog shtick. Shrugging, he turned back to the discussion as the jokes started flying even faster.

Three days later he found out just how seriously the servant had taken the concept when he was summoned to the office of Wilhelm von Calcheim genannt Lohausen, the Imperial College's civilian administrator and representative of Emperor Gustavus Adolphus II.

Without preamble, von Calcheim demanded to know how the invisible poodles were being deployed and berated him for keeping this kind of secret from their allies.

"*Why* did you not tell us about these dogs?" he demanded.

Allan rolled his eyes and took a deep breath. "Because we don't actually have invisible dogs?"

"Of course you don't," von Calcheim replied, one corner of his mouth turning up. "The idea is ridiculous. But the idea of missing such a window of opportunity is even more ridiculous."

"Sir?"

"I have heard the stories your Vietnam vets tell of Captain Pierre Kirk and his joking order over the radio which had the Viet Cong believing that the fiction of phasers was real. I have read the book *The War Magician*, and the second thing I thought of when I first heard about the invisible dogs from Grantville—after my first thought of disbelief—was that this was a wonderful way of 'bamboozling' our enemies. Any strange sound or disappearance? Blame it on our well-trained *hunde*.

"It will take very little effort on our parts to have our enemies looking over their shoulders, never knowing where to look. Are they about to be bitten by invisible dogs as our soldiers march toward them?" He paused and smiled. "Imagine the solitary sentry at his post, trembling in fear of the attack which he cannot see. A brilliant subterfuge; all it takes is instilling that little bit of doubt in the enemy.

"We have engineering students now, and if they cannot think of pranks to play and devices to use on our enemies based on the notion of invisible dogs, then they don't deserve to graduate. War is as much a game as a fight, and any mind games which save lives are good."

"*Herr Rektor*, we can't do that," Allan protested. "The spirit of Grantville consists of a couple of thousand Americans living side by side with people who don't necessarily share our exact ideals. While I can agree that anything which gives our enemies pause before attacking us is a good thing, we have to protect our reputation for integrity first. Being known for having a civilian population with a warped sense of humor is one thing; being known as outright liars—if not worse—is something else again."

"*Ja*, I can see that," von Calcheim agreed sadly. "I can respect and understand your reasoning, too. As a joke it might work once, but yes, it is not a good long-term strategy."

October 1634

"Hey, Allan, take a look at this!" Jack Bartholow thrust a squarish box at him in the empty hallway outside his classroom in the late afternoon.

"What's this?" Allan looked down at the box. Jack, a tall, rangy man just beginning to go a little gray around the edges, grinned at him.

"That's the winner of the first annual Fake Invisible Dog Competition which my kids insisted we hold."

"Huh?"

Jack nodded. "That's pretty much what my reaction was when it was proposed to me last week. I had told my class about one competition I'd heard about up-time—using elbow drinking straws and Q-tips to build different devices—and then one of my kids suggested a much more practical down-time competition . . . tricks and snares designed to fool the unwary into thinking invisible dogs are real."

"Uh, you *did* explain to them that the army isn't promoting the whole fake invisible dog strategy?"

"Oh yeah, but *you* try talking kids out of a good gag. It can't be done."

Shaking his head, Allan lifted the lid off the box and slid it underneath. Inside was the reel off a fishing pole with the clear fishing line attached to an old yellow tennis ball.

"Hey, where's the fishing pole to go with this reel?" he demanded, lifting it out. "It'd be a lot more fun to cast this ball at a long distance."

"Yeah, but the whole rationale behind leaving off the pole is that it's much easier to hide the reel under a coat. Think how much fun it'd be to throw out the ball and playact it back to yourself as if an invisible doggie were really bringing it back to you." Grabbing up the ball, he threw it down the length of the hallway.

"Get it boy, get it!" he called. Taking the reel out of Allan's hand and hooking it onto his belt, he began reeling it in with a bouncy motion with one hand while making little kissy sounds and patting his leg with the other. When the ball came within grabbing distance, he reached out as if trying to wrest it from a reluctant dog's mouth. "Come on, boy, good boy, let it go, come on, drop it, there's a good boy."

Allan swallowed a snicker. "Oh, that's really awful."

"That's pretty much what I said when I first saw it," Jack nodded, "but they're all having such a good time one-upping each other in tall tales and gizmos to keep the myth going that there's no stopping them. This engineering program is not only capturing our students' imaginations and developing their competitiveness, it's helping them push our technological envelope as far and as fast as possible.

"They've even got Jerry discussing potential strategies for using invisible dogs in war situations."

"You're kidding!"

"I wish I were." Jack shrugged. "So he's put together a packet using dogs and fishing line and various other snares, trip wires, and gizmos as the basis of mathematical problem-solving. 'If you have two dogs, each holding onto a ball attached to a reel of fishing line, circling around a squad of enemy soldiers from different directions"—he made circling motions with his hands—"how long of a line would each dog be having to pull to be able to circle around the squad twice and trip them up?'"

"That's ridiculous!"

"Yeah, but it's a lot of fun and it's making them think. And ultimately, thinking outside the box is what this engineering program is about. It's making them laugh, and funny is easier to remember when it comes to math and science."

"Sheesh, what's next?" Allan asked, taking the ball out of Jack's hand. "Catapults for pet rocks?"

He had just heaved the tennis ball down the hall and was tugging it back when he spotted the servant out of the corner of his eye. *Oh no*, he thought. *Just what we don't need ... more rumors about invisible dogs and pet rocks!*

A couple of weeks later Jerry Calafano came into his classroom and held up several strips of paper. "Hey, Allan, look what Armand got for us ... freebies for the Billy Bob show this weekend at the Higgins Hotel!"

Allan groaned. "Not more of that invisible dog nonsense! I can't believe that gag is hanging on the way it is."

"Aw, come on, it's gonna be fun. A bunch of us are all going up to Grantville tomorrow, anyway, so why not take a break and catch the show?"

"Hey, Dalton!" Allan called out across the crowded lobby of the Higgins Hotel. "How ya doing?"

Dalton Higgins grinned as he worked his way over to where Allan was standing with his fellow up-time teachers, reminding him of the young kid he'd been when they were both in school in the seventies. Dalton had dropped out of high school to put his muscles to work in a U-Haul business, but Allan had gone on to college and earned a degree in chemistry, ending up at the water treatment plant where he'd worked until the Ring of Fire changed everything. Now Dalton was mechanical support for the various branches of the military, and Allan was an officer in the army and a professor at the Imperial College. "Professor," Allan chuckled wryly to himself. *Back home I wouldn't have been qualified to teach chemistry in high school, let alone college. But times change and all of a sudden I'm one of our best-educated men and Dalton's an expert on all things mechanical and salvageable. When something breaks down, people come to him to see if it can be repaired, replaced, or repurposed. Life. It do get strange.*

"Lookit you!" Dalton exclaimed, thrusting out his hand in welcome. "All uniformed up and everything. I thought you were teaching these days!"

"I'm wearing a ridiculous number of hats these days, Dalton." He grinned back ruefully as they shook hands. "I've been assigned to the Imperial Tech school in Magdeburg, mostly teaching practical chemistry, but I've been coming up here about once a month to help develop a series of advanced chemistry lectures for the high school and tech college, while still helping out where I can with military research. But these yahoos here"—he jerked his thumb over his shoulder—"talked me into taking some time off tonight and coming to see Billy Bob's show while we're in town. You know Jerry Calafano, Christine Gaddis, Armand Glazer, and Jack Bartholow, don't you?"

"Sure do," he said, shaking hands with each in turn. "Don't hardly see you guys any more, now you're mostly down in Magdeburg."

"So, you're here to catch Billy Bob's lyin' act?"

"Yeah, Armand here got us some free tickets."

"Free? That's the least Mom could do for someone who's made her as much money as Armand helped her make with those booklets she sells in the gift shop."

All heads swiveled to stare at Armand as he grinned sheepishly.

"How could I resist?" he said, shrugging. "It's just too much fun. After putting in a day's work drawing illustrations for military training manuals, I found myself kicking back and designing training manuals for invisible dogs. 'The Care and Feeding of Your Invisible Dog,' 'The Many Breeds of Invisible Dogs,' 'How to Avoid Being Bitten by Invisible Dogs.'"

"My personal favorite is 'The Dangers of Allowing Invisible Dogs to Form Packs,'" Dalton interjected with a grin. "I took out a big ole ad on the inside back cover for my salvage business."

"Uh, you *do* understand we're trying really hard not to mislead people, don't you?" Allan asked.

"Oh, nobody's taking it seriously," Dalton said with a shrug, "But it's getting a lot of people laughing, buying souvenirs, and showing up for Billy Bob's show.

"Speaking of which, I highly recommend sitting near the back and watching the audience as much as Billy Bob. It's a hoot seeing who laughs at what. We know it's lies, but some of the down-timers don't know whether to believe or not. Y'know, it's one of those things you're afraid to believe because you'd look silly, but afraid to *not* believe, just in case it's true."

Once they were seated, Allan noticed that he, Christine, and Jack in their uniforms were getting quite a few looks from the down-timers filing past their row, but everyone in up-timer garb—whether blue jeans and T-shirts or dress pants and shirt—seemed to be coming in for their share of looks, too. *Great, it looks like we're part of the show.*

"Apprentices are trouble." Billy Bob, dressed in well-worn blue jeans and checked western shirt, had begun speaking into a handheld microphone from his perch atop a tall stool at the front of the room. "Every master knows that. A bored apprentice is even more trouble. And a bored apprentice in Grantville, this small town from the future which somehow landed smack in the middle of the Thirty Years' Wars, is a dangerous thing.

"Fortunately, this American apprentice had him a sense o' humor. Low humor, to be sure, but at least nuthin' malicious.

"This apprentice shoulda been in school, but he had talked his mother into the notion of homeschooling him and his sister early in the mornings so they could start learning a trade during the rest of the day. He'd had dollar signs in his eye, a-course; they always do. Two years into his apprenticeship with Gruenwald Brassworks here in town and he started scroungin' around for something else he could do to make some money on the side. After all, this was Grantville! Up-time Americans and down-time Germans alike are makin' money hand over fist. Whatever an American's interested in doing, they kin find others interested in payin' good money to teach 'em about it, simply because they were usually the best in their field. At the very least, they knew that if sumpin' was popular at some point in American history, that down-timers would like it, too.

"So it started when that scroungin' apprentice found an old gag in his grandmother's attic and started a rumor goin' around."

Billy Bob dropped his voice dramatically. "'Americans been keepin' secrets from us. They ain't been tellin' us about their invisible dogs.'"

Reverting to his normal voice, Billy Bob continued. "Then the rumors grew as rumors often do. 'Beware o' them invisible poodle dogs—they's vicious.'"

Allan chuckled and looked around. Some of the Germans—who far outnumbered the Americans—looked puzzled by the laughter around them. *They've just never experienced pet poodles in quite the same way as us Americans. Yappy little things with ridiculous haircuts.*

"Them rumors mighta died down or been disproven as setch rumors often are, 'cept that one of the first people asked about them invisible poodle dogs was a concierge right here at the Higgins Hotel; he was asked right out why Americans had been a-keepin' them invisible poodles a secret."

Billy Bob leaned toward his audience. "Oh, he was a prideful man, he was. He drew hisself up in all his well-dressed glory, stared down his nose at that tourist and demanded right back: 'Why do you think?'"

Shifting his stance and pitching his voice to indicate different speakers, Billy Bob continued.

"'Oh, of course,' that tourist said. 'Now it makes sense. The church would have taken them as evidence of witchcraft and consorting with demons.'"

While some of the audience gasped in terror, Allan and the other Americans in the room couldn't help laughing out loud.

Billy Bob waited, nodding and grinning, until the laughter died down. Which took a while.

"Heh," he was finally able to say. "Back when our computers was hooked up to what we called the 'internet,' the computer geeks had all kinds of abbreviations that meant this and that. If someone found sumthin' funny, they'd type the letters el-oh-el, for 'laughing out loud.' My friends' reactions over there? That woulda been typed out are-oh-tee-ef-el, for 'Rolling on the Floor Laughing.' Much more, and it woulda qualified as 'Rolling on the Floor Laughing Ma Ass Off.'

"'Cause ya see, that's one answer we never woulda thought of. We ain't never hadta worry about the church accusing nobody o' witchcraft or nuthin' like that . . . not fer hundreds o' years. 'N thas a *good* thing and one of the many reasons why our American forefathers insisted on separation of church and state. We don't believe in magic or burnin' people at the stake. Our guv'ment pertected us from all that nonsense.

"Anyways," he continued, "back to the concierge and that there tourist. The concierge didn't laugh in the tourist's face, but he did swell up some in indig-*nay*-shun.

"'Certainly not!' he snapped. 'That's ree-dick-a-lus!'

"'Then Grantville really doesn't have invisible dogs?'

"'I can neither confirm nor deny the existence of any such invisible dogs,' the concierge said all stiff-like. 'If they exist, *I* certainly have never seen them.'"

With a dramatic pause, Billy Bob looked around and grinned before continuing.

"Looking relieved, the tourist went on into the hotel."

Billy Bob paused, leaned over to pick up a glass of water from the base of the stool, and took a sip.

"'Invisible dogs, indeed,' the concierge repeated to himself. 'Someone's been a-tellin' some tall tales. Or resurrectin' old gags. What's next, someone a-takin' their 'invisible dog' for a walk down Main Street?'"

Billy Bob paused again, to nod in satisfaction at the audience.

"Now, havin' a rather low sense of humor hisself, the concierge couldn't help announcin' to the kitchen staff that he'd had a question that day about the Americans' invisible dogs. He loved the way Brunhilde's eyes got *real* big as she envisioned invisible dogs. She'd come to Grantville from a small mountain village where hunting hounds was the only dogs for miles around and she were still rather ... unnerved ... by the way many Americans kept dogs and cats as inside pets. Several of the Higginses' long-term guests keep setch pets and one of 'em—a Chihuahua—takes exception to anyone entering his territory. He terrorizes the maids and is one of the reasons Brunhilde prefers to work in the kitchen.

"'I understand the invisible poodles are quite vicious and should be avoided at all costs,' that concierge said with a straight face.

"Now it so happened that I was a-workin' down there on that very day, sharin' the secrets of my down-home barbecue sauce with the head chef, and I couldn't resist.

"'Shoot,' I said—with an even straighter face—'them invisible poodles ain't nothin' compared to them invisible Rottweilers.'"

Allan put one hand up over his face as some in

the audience responded with a sharp intake of breath. *Say what you may about Billy Bob Robinson*, he thought, shaking his head in admiration, *he's a damn fine storyteller. He's got this audience right in the palm of his hand.*

"Now this caused all the kitchen staff to pale at the thought, even the concierge who knew better. One of the police officers in town owns a Rottweiler-Chow mix and he scares the bejeezus out of anyone walkin' by his lot. Fortunately, he's been fixed, to everyone's great relief. No little Rottweiler puppies coming along unless someone takes the time and effort to breed 'em up.

"Three days later, though, that scallywag of an apprentice was seen a-walkin' his 'invisible' dog outside the Higgins Hotel, making a big production outa havin' the dog sniff around the fire hydrant. The concierge thought the little plastic pooper-scooper was a particularly nice touch," he added, with a grin. "He was unsurprised to see the apprentice being 'led' up the steps into the hotel and equally unsurprised to have him ask to talk with the person responsible for buyin' stuff for resale in the hotel's gift shop. After the kid went down the hall, the concierge started t' laugh but turned it into a cough when he saw several visitors a-starin' after him with their jaws hangin' down in disbelief.

"'And so the legend grows,' the concierge thought to hisself. 'I wonder what that kid's gonna try to sell . . . bumper stickers, maybe, that say "I brake for invisible dogs?" Or more silly gag leashes? With all the things we *do* need made, we certainly don't need to be a-wastin' resources on gags.'

"The next day that concierge found himself a-shakin' his head at the small signs he found for sale in the hotel's gift shop proclaiming 'Beware! This house is guarded by an invisible dog!' in either English or German. Or both on the same sign.

"He weren't the only person who wanted to cash in on this sudden recurrence of an old gag, neither.

"It seems as if everyone in Grantville who ain't figgered out some way a-makin' money on their up-timer knowledge was able to thinka some kinda invisible dog slogan they could slap onna sign or a tote bag. 'I Visited Grantville and Have the Invisible Dog Bites to Prove It!' 'I Love My Invisible Dog!' 'I Heart My Invisible Dog!' or 'Don't step on my invisible poodle dog—she bites!'" With each slogan mentioned, Billy Bob dramatically waved his hands as if slapping a huge bumper sticker up in the air.

"I, of course, have appointed myself the teller of the 'Tales of the Invisible Dogs of Grantville.' Back up-time I couldn't hardly get anyone to listen to my yarns . . . now I git invited to tell 'em to great audiences like you."

As the audience enthusiastically applauded, Billy Bob got up off his stool and strutted back and forth with his microphone, expanding on the marvels of Grantville's invisible dogs.

Allan couldn't believe just how much truth Billy Bob managed to work into his tales, but in a way that made it hard to believe. People are very, very polite and law-abiding in Grantville, because they never know when acting up may get the dogs sicced on them. Invisible dogs are trained by whistles that can't be heard by human ears. The concept made *him* snort in disbelief and he *knew* dog whistles are real.

He had about cracked up when Billy Bob put in a plug for "gettin' you a picture o' your family painted here in Grantville, with the invisible dog of your choice." *How is someone going to paint a picture of an invisible dog?* he wondered. Maybe the same way some artist plagiarized the "Dogs Playing Poker" concept on black velvet, only with one of the dogs represented with a hand of cards suspended in midair about where a dog would be holding it.

He had thought that suggesting people get themselves a pet rock so they could shy it at any invisible dog that was bothering them was pushing the limits until Billy Bob suggested that people "put them a buckeye for luck in one pocket and a pet rock in the other to cover all the bases. Luck should keep the invisible dogs away, but the pet rock would be there . . . jist in case."

"And as for that there apprentice," Billy Bob concluded, returning his microphone to its stand, "he's happy having a little extra pocket money . . . money he wouldn't've earned if he hadn't gotten bored one day and decided to have some fun.

"Now, it's good to share the fun, but when someone's telling you what sounds like a tall tale, remember that if there were near the number of invisible dogs in this town as people make out there are, we'd all be up to our knees in invisible doggy doo-doo."

As the Imperial Tech group was exiting the room afterwards, Allan noticed down-timers staring at their uniforms and whispering to themselves. *Maybe coming to this show wasn't such a good idea after all,* he thought. *The last thing we need is for people to get it into their heads that we actually have invisible dogs and are using them for military purposes.*

*Imperial College of Science, Engineering, and Technology
March 1635*

"Professor Dailey?"

Allan looked up to see one of their brightest students, USE Army soldier Friedrich Schumacher, standing in the doorway of his classroom.

"Yes, Friedrich," he said, gesturing him inside, "what can I help you with?"

"Professor, you know how you keep saying Grantville has no invisible dogs?"

Allan sighed. *Can I ever get shook of this whole stupid gag?* he wondered.

"Friedrich, have you *ever* heard anyone in the military claim that we have invisible dogs?"

"*Nein.*"

"Have you ever read anything in any of the up-time books about invisible dogs?"

"*Nein.*"

"Do you understand that the souvenirs and gags that talk about invisible dogs are just jokes and tricks?"

"*Ja.*"

"So, all that being said, what would you like to say about invisible dogs?"

"It's just...sir, *mein Onkel*—my uncle—raises the *Pudelhunde,* the swimming dogs that look like the little American poodles, only bigger. I told him about up-time training techniques and he's very interested. Do you think the Army would be interested in his dogs if he can train them like we've been talking about in our military strategy sessions?"

Allan sat back, his eyebrows raised in surprise.

"A well-trained K-9 corps could be very useful for a lot of different jobs—military, police, and fire and rescue teams—but what does that have to do with invisible dogs?"

"My uncle was interested at first in breeding his *Pudelhunde* to your invisible poodles, but when I explained about how it was just a big joke, that Americans have never had invisible dogs, he suggested that his dogs would be almost as good as invisible dogs."

"But, Friedrich, most of the suggested uses in war, the discussions in class about how dogs could be effectively used in battle, presupposes dogs that can't be seen and shot at a distance."

"*Ja.*" He grinned and nodded down at Allan. "But it occurred to us that if the fur of his *Pudelhunde* is bleached and dyed in an up-time camouflage pattern before they go into battle, they would blend into their background like the Predator beast and be very hard to see before they were right on the enemy."

Allan looked up at Friedrich and began to laugh. "You could even put leaves and twigs in their fur like a little doggy ghillie suit!" Sobering a bit, he continued, "This whole thing may have started as a gag, but I can see all kinds of uses for well-trained dogs, invisible or not. So sure, get your uncle as much information on up-time dog training as you can find up in Grantville. In fact," he said, pulling out a sheet of paper and starting to scribble on it, "I'm giving you an assignment in Grantville. Take the train, spend a week, find what you can in the libraries, and talk to some of the veterinarians. They should be able to give you some good pointers."

A Season of Change

Kerryn Offord

Grantville
July 1633

Stephan Greiner was but a poorly paid and barely
acknowledged cog in the machine that was the
Schmucker & Schwentzel print shop. He wasn't a
printer. He was a sales rep, and his job was to sell
printing services and books. He was paid a basic
retainer plus a commission on anything he sold.
Unfortunately, printing was a very competitive business, especially in Grantville, where the guilds didn't
hold sway, which explained why he was poorly paid.
He wasn't married, but given his financial position
that wasn't unusual. However, he did have a young
woman with whom he had hopes, however faint, of
marrying. Anna Margaretha Gall was five years his
junior, and she was an employee at Grantville Canvas
and Outdoor—one of Stephan's best customers.

He walked out of yet another store in Grantville
with only a few orders for books. Where would he be
without the *Grantville Genealogy Club's Who's Who*

of Grantville Up-Timers? It was the print shop's most successful publication, already into its second-print run, with a third being planned. The commission on his latest orders would more than double his week's income. He screwed up his nose at the thought. The shops were placing orders for the new releases, and it would be a month before the next set of new releases. What was needed was something to catch the imagination of the buying public. Something that would have them going to the book shops in droves to buy books in numbers that would pay him enough to marry. Of course, part of the problem was the price of books. The *Who's Who* sold for five hundred and seventy-five dollars, unbound, and the cheapest books they were printing, reprints of up-time novels, retailed for twenty dollars. The stumbling block was the price of paper, and it wasn't getting any cheaper.

Stephan wandered over to the outdoor tables of the café and slumped into a chair. A quick perusal of the menu confirmed that prices had gone up again. Not that he'd ever really been able to afford to drink coffee, even without sugar.

"Can I help you, sir?"

"Herbal tea and a roll please," he told the waitress.

With his order placed, Stephan started to bring his order book up to date. It didn't take long, nor did it make for particularly good reading.

"The new paper isn't as good as rag, but at the price they're asking, the boss doesn't care."

Stephan had been contemplating the low probability of a life with Anna when he overheard that comment. He hadn't meant to listen, but he'd been aware of the group since they ordered coffee with their rolls. Now he was all ears as he struggled to hear the conversation going on behind his back. Then he caught the price the man's boss was paying, and he couldn't control his curiosity any longer. He turned around to look at the people sitting behind him. He didn't recognize either of them, but they looked like down-timers.

"Excuse me, but I couldn't help overhearing you. Are you really are able to buy paper suitable for printing that cheaply?"

The man who'd had his back to Stephan turned to face him. "Who wants to know?" Daniel Krausold asked.

With a practiced flick of his hand Stephan presented the man with his business card. "Stephan Greiner, Schmucker and Schwentzel Print Shop."

Daniel looked up from the business card. "I'm Daniel Krausold, the *Grantville Times*; my friend is Christoph Heinz."

"The Spirits of Hartshorn Facility," Christoph said, naming the Gribbleflotz Laboratories ammonia production facility in WVCo.

Even before he knew what he was doing Stephan sniffed the air, raising a wry grin from Christoph. "I'm with packing and dispatch."

Stephan smiled an apology, even if he was sure he was catching a whiff of Spirit of Hartshorn, before turning his attention back to Daniel. "Where are you getting paper that cheaply? Or is that a trade secret?"

Daniel shook his head. "No. A couple of days ago Gottfried Spengler had an open day for all the newspapers where he demonstrated his new mill and handed out samples. The boss went and was really impressed. He was even more impressed when he found it took print at least as well as rag newsprint."

This was all very interesting, but Stephan hadn't got to the ripe age of thirty without being aware that there was always a catch. He asked for the catch to the cheap paper.

"It'll age badly, but as the boss said, who cares if their newspaper changes color after six weeks?"

"Do people keep newspapers that long?" Stephan asked.

"Of course not. That's why the boss has already placed orders for the new paper."

Stephan thanked his new friends for the information, and turned back to finish his tea and roll. What a difference a few minutes could make. He suddenly felt a lot better and fully intended stopping in to see Anna, just as soon as he had spoken to someone at the *Grantville Times*.

A few days later Stephan walked into the lioness's den with some trepidation. He could have gone to see Johann Schmucker or Friedrich Schwentzel, the two journeymen printers who'd started the print shop that bore their names, but at some stage he would still have had to present his idea to Frau Fröbel, the real driving force behind the success of the business. This way he only had to persuade one person of his idea and not three.

"Frau Fröbel, I have an idea I'd like to discuss with you," he said from the doorway.

"Well, don't just stand there, come in and tell about me this idea you have," Ursula Fröbel said.

Stephan entered and sat on the chair she pointed him to.

"Well?" Ursula prompted.

Stephan emptied the contents of his briefcase onto her desk before sliding a copy of the *Grantville Times* across to her.

Ursula picked it up, glanced at it, and then turned her eyes onto Stephan. "What am I supposed to be looking at?"

"That copy of the *Grantville Times* was printed on new paper that is much cheaper than the cost of the old newsprint." Stephan stopped there because he could see he'd plainly lost his audience. Not that he was worried. He had confidence in Ursula Fröbel's intelligence, and given the way she was gently fingering the paper the newspaper was printed on, he was sure she was seeing what he'd seen.

"Why haven't I heard about this new paper?" Ursula demanded.

Stephan shrugged. "I don't know. I'm in sales, not purchasing. But, it might be because Herr Spengler didn't think we'd be interested in his new newsprint."

"Spengler? Do you mean Gottfried Spengler, the man who used to run Heinrich Merkel's mill?"

"That's the name I was given, but I was also given to believe he was running his own mill."

Ursula nodded. "That's right. He's got that new mill on the road to Saalfeld. So, he's producing cheap newsprint? I wouldn't have expected that of him. He was always proud of the quality of the paper he made. So, if it's that much cheaper, what's the catch?"

"The paper is made from wood fibers and it turns a dirty yellow-brown color after six weeks or so."

Again Ursula nodded. "I think I understand why Gottfried might not have thought of us. Nobody is interested in news that is six weeks old. Of course, we do print broadsheets, and they could benefit from the cheaper paper. I shall have to have words with that young man."

Stephan had completely forgotten about broadsheets, and even about advertising flyers. Neither of which would provide him with much in the way of commission. No, what he'd been thinking of was books. His commission on them was much bigger. "I was thinking that maybe we could offer a line of very cheap books."

"Pulp fiction?" Ursula suggested. "Yes. I'm sure we could try some of our less popular titles in that format."

Pulp fiction was an up-time term used for a certain kind of cheap novel. They were easy reading, cheap, and had sold in enormous numbers up-time. "I was thinking we might also offer such publications as the *Who's Who* in the cheaper format."

They both paused for a few seconds to silently honor the *Grantville Genealogy Club's Who's Who of Grantville Up-Timers* before Ursula voiced an objection. "We'd be cannibalizing our own market," Ursula said.

Stephan shook his head. "I don't think so. The fine edition printed on high quality rag paper is a prestige item that will always have a market, but its high price limits the *size* of the market. If we were to offer a cheaper edition, like the up-timers did with their hardcover and paperback editions, we'd be covering both markets." He looked at Ursula expectantly.

She had gone from shaking her head to chewing her lip. That was always a good sign. It meant that she might progress to nodding her head. "We might lose some sales of the quality edition, but it is possible that a lot of people who wouldn't otherwise be able to afford the *Who's Who* might buy it."

Stephan decided to hit her with his greatest fear.
"And, Frau Fröbel, if we don't make an edition available in a cheaper format, someone else might."

Stephan pretended he didn't hear the expletives
Ursula muttered. Book piracy was a problem the
up-timers still hadn't managed to stop. There were
some copyright laws, but they always stopped at the
border, and you couldn't stop someone across the
border selling his pirated copies of your book to your
customers via one of the multitude of mail-order
catalogs that were springing up.

"Do you have any more good news?" she asked.

"This." He offered her a small sample of cardboard
that had been sent round just that morning.

Ursula prodded and bent the cardboard before
dropping it onto her desk. "And why is the person
who is in sales, not purchasing, showing me a piece
of corrugated cardboard?"

"I called in to see Herr Blume about a new design
for his invoices and he showed me the new cardboard
he was planning on making. He asked if I thought
Schmucker and Schwentzel might be interested."

"And what did you tell him?"

"I promised to show it to you if he sent some
samples." Stephan didn't have to say that if Schmucker
and Schwentzel decided to buy the new cardboard
that he would receive a present from Herr Blume.
Such an arrangement was expected.

"And why should we buy it?"

"We are currently using cardboard products made
from recycled rag paper. That"—he pointed to the
sample—"is made from the new newsprint. Herr
Blume plans to start commercial production using

recycled newsprint when it becomes available in sufficient volumes." The smile that blossomed on Frau Fröbel's face was encouraging. "Naturally, it will be a lot cheaper than the rag-based cardboard."

"As much of a difference as the pulp paper?" Ursula asked.

"I'm sorry, but not quite that cheap."

"Wolfgang is not going to be pleased if we stop buying from his supplier."

Stephan returned Frau Fröbel's smile. Wolfgang Diller was the print shop's purchasing officer, and no doubt he was receiving a present for every purchase from the current cardboard supplier. "But Herr Blume's cardboard will be significantly cheaper," he replied innocently.

"You're a bad boy, Stephan. Get back to work while I think about this new paper and cardboard."

September

When Stephan first started working for Schmucker & Schwentzel two years ago, Grantville Canvas and Outdoor had operated out of the basement of Tracy Kubiak's house on Mahan's Run. Recently, much to the benefit of his poor legs, they had set up a new manufacturing facility in the industrial zone just outside the Ring Wall. He wasn't sure why they moved, but he certainly approved, as the new facility was on the regular tram route and he no longer had to make the three-mile hike along the road, or the shorter, but more strenuous route over the hills to get to the workshop.

He walked in to find Frau Kubiak's adopted downtime daughter bashing a pair of shoes against her desk. He stood watching silently as he tried to work out what she was doing.

An extra dozen or so blows later Richelle Kubiak finally realized Stephan was watching. "Pointe shoes. I'm conditioning them," she explained as she tried flexing the dainty little shoes.

Stephan actually knew what she was talking about. Schmucker & Schwentzel printed the programs for the Grantville Ballet Company's regular public performances in the middle school's theater, and as a token of appreciation for the low price the shop charged for the work, they were provided with free tickets to performances, which, as Anna liked to see the ballet, Stephan didn't pass on to anybody else. "Is Frau Kubiak about?"

"Mom's in the workshop. The heavy-duty overlocker has been acting up."

Stephan had fond memories of the heavy-duty overlocker. It was the machine Anna had been operating when they first met. "I'm sure Frau Kubiak will soon beat it into submission."

Richelle giggled at his joke. "You know the way. Just remember to grab a coat and ear protectors."

"Thank you." The coat was a simple blue hemp jacket that covered his clothes. He wasn't sure if he had to wear it to protect his clothes from the fluff and threads floating around the workshop, or to protect the fabrics being worked on from contamination from the outside world. The ear protectors were, he knew, almost essential, as some of the newer machines in the workroom were quite loud.

He could have found Frau Kubiak sooner, but he stopped to say hello to Anna first and make arrangements to meet later. When he arrived at the industrial standard overlocker, Frau Kubiak was in the final stages of reassembling it. She was smiling, which suggested the problem had been fixed. That was always good, because a client in a good mood was always easier to deal with.

"Hi, Stephan. Do you want to follow me into the office?" she said as she wiped her hands clean on some paper offcuts. She gave instructions to the operator of the overlocker before leading Stephan to her office.

Tracy placed several pages on her desk and pushed them across to Stephan. "Those are what we want to show in the next catalog."

Stephan looked at the line pictures. "Do you want them produced exactly like that, or can Fabian put them on bodies?"

"How much more is that likely to cost?"

"The new technique he's been working on is actually cheaper than the old method, Frau Kubiak. And it encourages free drawing."

"Cheaper? Then it must be one of the few things getting cheaper in Grantville. Okay, you can let Fabian loose."

Fabian Schlitte was Schmucker & Schwentzel's seventeen-year-old engraver. The biggest thing about him was his ego, but even Frau Fröbel was willing to forgive him that because he was, if anything, even better than he thought he was. Not that anybody at Schmucker & Schwentzel would publicly admit that. Frau Kubiak had met Fabian when he was sketching dancers for a ballet program, and admired some of his work.

"I won't put it to him quite like that, Frau Kubiak.

Now, this is what I think we should do for your new invoices..." The conversation turned to Tracy's printing requirements, and Stephan was able to join Anna for lunch with another order to his credit.

Stephan and Anna had been exchanging sweet nothings and silently staring into each other's eyes for most of the lunch hour when Richelle Kubiak walked past hand in hand with her and Tracy Kubiak's daughters. Anna waved to Leyna and Terrie, and both girls waved back. "Aren't they adorable?" she asked Stephan.

The two girls were about two years old, and as Anna had suggested, quite adorable. He thought about the chances of having children with Anna and sighed. "Yes."

"Richelle showed us the most beautiful photograph of her with Leyna the other day."

Stephan knew what was expected of him, and nodded. "I'll be sure to ask her to show it to me next..." Suddenly what Anna had said penetrated. For Richelle to suddenly have a photograph of her and her daughter, it had to have been taken recently. Stephan leapt to his feet. "Where is this photograph?" he demanded as he dragged Anna by the hand after Richelle and the children.

"I don't know," Anna said as she was dragged along. When they reached the entrance to Grantville Canvas and Outdoor she grabbed Stephan's hand and hauled back on it. "Stephan! What's got into you?"

He turned to look down into Anna's eyes. He ducked down his head and kissed her. "Photography. Someone is still taking photographs."

"And?"

Stephan hugged her. "I'll explain after I've spoken to Richelle."

The moment Stephan stepped out of Richelle's office Anna grabbed him and dragged him outside. "Well?"

Stephan sat down on the bench seat set up with a view of the river and pulled Anna down beside him. There was still too much space between them, so he put his arm around her and dragged her closer. "The photograph was taken by a family friend, a Frau Lettie Sebastian. Not only does she still have some up-time photographic supplies, she is also working on reintroducing photography."

"And?" Anna asked.

The confused expression on Anna's face was so appealing that Stephan leaned closer and kissed her. "Fabian claims that he knows how to make printing plates from photographic negatives."

"Oh!"

Stephan nodded. "If he can really make it work, it means we can make printing plates from up-time books without having to set the type, and we can reproduce images without Fabian having to spend hours delicately engraving the plates."

A few days later

Any protest Fabian Schlitte might have made about being dragged away from his work had been easily silenced with one word—photography. He'd begged for more information, which Stephan had refused to give, other than to say that he'd made an appointment to talk to a woman who might be able to help them.

The bus had dropped them off half a mile from the house they wanted, and they completed the walk in companionable silence. They were met at the door by an elderly up-timer.

"You'll be the boys from Schmucker and Schwentzel? I'm Lettie Sebastian."

"Frau Sebastian . . ." Fabian started to say.

"Please, just call me Lettie. Frau Sebastian makes me feel old."

"Lettie," Fabian said. "You can take photographs?"

Stephan was all ready to reprimand Fabian for his lack of manners, but Frau Sebastian didn't seem to mind. In fact, she'd already launched into a conversation with Fabian that went right over Stephan's head. He decided to let things take their natural path and settled down to listen and wait for any questions Frau Sebastian might have that Fabian couldn't answer. It was a long wait.

Fabian was bright and cheerful as they walked back down Gray's Run toward the nearest bus stop on Route 250.

"She and her husband were really into photography up-time," Fabian said. "Not only did they collect cameras and other photographic paraphernalia, they also had their own darkroom. That's why she has the stuff I need for my research."

Stephan thought about correcting him and saying "we," but decided that would be petty. "So you will be able to make printing plates from photographs?"

"It's a simple step from the process I've been using to create illustrations for customers. Of course I'll need some new chemicals, and a carbon arc light."

"And then you'll be able to make printing plates of some of the up-time books?"

Fabian shook his head.

"No? But you said all you needed was access to photography," Stephan protested.

"And a supply of film. Lettie's supply of up-time film is limited, but she is working on making new film. Fortunately, her late husband was a reenactor."

Stephan stared at him blankly. He knew what a reenactor was. The military training he'd been forced to undergo as a member of the militia had been run in part by up-timers who'd been reenactors, but what did soldiers have to do with photography?

Fabian explained. "Herr Sebastian used to reenact as a Civil War photographer. He had all the equipment to do wet-plate photography."

"What's wet plate?" Stephan asked before he could put a brake on his tongue. Naturally Fabian filled him in, in excruciating detail.

Eventually Fabian ran out of words. "And you can use this technique to make color plates?" Stephan asked, not without some trepidation, lest Fabian cut loose with yet another outpouring of information Stephan didn't really need.

"Only as long as I have access to Lettie's up-time supplies," Fabian said before entering into a particularly detailed explanation of the science of color sensitivity of emulsions. The gist of it was that any new photographic emulsions would need special dyes, which Lettie's friend, Celeste Frost, an up-time-trained chemist, was currently working on, to make any new film anything like equally sensitive to most of the colors of the spectrum.

"Of course I'll be limited to still life, because you can't keep people absolutely still while you change the filters."

"Filters?" Stephan knew he was going to regret the question even as he uttered it. He was right. Fabian entered into a long and detailed description of how important filters were.

"How difficult is it going to be?" Johann asked when a couple of days later Fabian and Stephan presented their report of the meeting with Lettie Sebastian to Johann Schmucker and Ursula Fröbel.

"Well," Fabian started. "I'm going to need a carbon arc light source, a vacuum cleaner, some sheets of glass as flat as possible onto which I will have to draw half-tone grates, and a selection of chemicals."

"Nothing too expensive then," Johann muttered sarcastically.

"You're going to need electricity, and that means you'll have to set up in Grantville somewhere," Ursula said.

"Which adds more expense," Johann muttered.

Fabian nodded. "Stephan suggested we should try and work a deal with Herr Kindred of the *Grantville Times*."

"And why would Stephan make such a suggestion?" Ursula asked Stephan.

"Because if we can make printing plates from photographs, then the *Grantville Times* will want to use them too," Stephan said. "I'm sure Herr Kindred would be happy to share the research and development costs in order to be able to print photographs in his newspaper."

"I'll talk to him," Ursula said.

October

The photographic research laboratory of Schmucker & Schwentzel was set up in Lyle Kindred's garage, which had the necessary power for the carbon arc light.

Stephan, by virtue of being pushy and insisting that the technique offered new opportunities he could sell to clients, had a front row seat as Fabian presented his first printing plate made with the new technique. He was joined by Lyle Kindred and his senior pressman, Dice Clifford. They crowded around when Fabian placed the finished copper plate on the worktable.

"It's a bit rough," Dice noted, "but for a first effort, it looks pretty good."

"Can we see how it prints?" Lyle asked.

Fabian carried his copper sheet to the small proofing press they had installed in the laboratory, and while Dice inked it, he prepared a sheet of paper. A short time later the pair of them gently peeled off the completed print and laid it on the worktable.

"It's not bad for a first attempt," Lyle said.

Stephan reached out a hand and patted Fabian on the shoulder in sympathy. They'd had such high hopes.

"There's not enough white," Dice said. "You need to leave it in the acid bath a little longer."

"You think that's all that's wrong?" Fabian asked.

Dice grinned. "It's a start. As soon as you get that right we'll find something else that's wrong."

"So we try it again." Fabian sighed and set up another treated plate to be exposed to the carbon arc light.

A *few days later*

Stephan stood at the door to the compositing room at Schmucker & Schwentzel and watched as the operators pounded away at their Treiber TypeSetters. The machines were a long way from being up-time Linotype machines, but they allowed the crew of a young female copy typist and three boys to set as much type in an hour as it would take eight experienced printers. Naturally, they were paid based on their skill levels, which were generally low, and not according to their productivity. The new machines were making it possible to produce more books and monographs at lower prices. Unfortunately, Schmucker & Schwentzel weren't the only print shop to have the new machines.

Stephan turned away from the door and headed for his tiny cubicle. There he sat down and checked the new offerings. They had secured the rights to Lettie Sebastian's catalog, and had a number of negatives they could use to produce covers for their paperback books. It gave the Schmucker & Schwentzel paperback imprint a point of difference, even if the image selected didn't always bear any relationship to what the book was about. The new covers were boosting sales and Stephan was laughing all the way to the bank. His hopes of being able to afford to marry Anna were rising every day. All they required was a supply of the special chemicals needed to actually produce photographs so they could do color and they'd be off.

He slowly worked his way through his in-basket until he came across the message asking him to contact Lady Beth Haygood at the I.C. White Technical School about the Grantville Ballet Company's scheduled performance of *Nutcracker*. Stephan didn't know the Americans used titles like that, and just like any down-timer wanting information about an up-timer, he decided to look her up in the library's copy of the *Who's Who*.

Of course that wasn't the Rudolstadt library, which did have its own copy, but rather Schmucker & Schwentzel's own library, which in addition to a selection of other books had at least one copy of everything they'd printed. He looked up Lady Beth Haygood and smiled when he saw that it was a name, not a title. How like the Americans to say how they didn't want a nobility, and then adopt their titles as names. He shut the *Who's Who* and returned it to its place. It was all very well knowing who Frau Haygood was, but why was she writing to him on behalf of the Grantville Ballet Company, Frau Matowski's baby? He shrugged. There was one sure way to find out. He headed for the post office to phone Frau Haygood and make an appointment to see her.

It was a walk of only a few miles from the print shop at the Rudolstadt end of the industrial zone to the high school just inside the Ring of Fire. It was commonly called the Grantville High School, but Stephan, who'd managed to sell them stationery, knew the official name, as stated on all of the stationery, was Calvert High School, just like the I.C. White Technical School where Frau Haygood worked, was typically referred to as either the Vo-Tech or Tech School.

"Hi, Herr Greiner. Lady Beth is expecting you," the

young girl manning the reception desk said when he entered. She jumped to her feet. "Follow me."

Stephan was sure he knew the girl from somewhere, but it wasn't until he had observed the graceful way she glided down the hallway that he realized she was one of Frau Matowski's dancers. She'd obviously recognized him from when he'd attended performances, and by the time they reached Frau Haygood's office he'd managed to put a name to the shapely pair of jean-clad legs. "Thank you, Frau Haggerty," he said with a gentle bow.

"Herr Greiner to see you, Miz Haygood," Glenna Sue Haggerty announced before guiding Stephan into the office.

"Thank you, Glenna Sue. Herr Greiner, please take a seat."

The door shut behind Glenna Sue, leaving Stephan in the room alone with Lady Beth. He broke the silence by turning immediately to business. "You asked to see me about printing a program for the Grantville Ballet Company?" he asked.

"That's right. For the New Year's Weekend season of *Nutcracker*."

"Season?" Stephan asked. "I thought it was just going to be a single performance."

"That was before Mary Simpson got involved," Lady Beth answered. "It is now going to be a season of three evenings and a Sunday matinee over New Year's weekend. And she's bringing a number of her friends to the premiere."

Stephan's whistle was spontaneous and unconscious. "People from Magdeburg are coming to Grantville to watch Frau Matowski's *Nutcracker*?" His mind was already rushing beyond printing a program and progressed to thinking about how many books could be sold to the visitors.

"That's what I said," Lady Beth confirmed. "And we'd like to present them with the best possible program, so that they go off with a very good opinion of ballet." She pulled a number of glossy booklets out of a drawer. "Bitty said you could borrow these."

It took a few seconds for Stephan to see beyond the quality of the paper and the printing and identify the booklets as up-time ballet programs. He flicked through them, admiring the quality of the printing and how well the photographs of the actors and scenes from the ballet had been reproduced. He carefully placed them back on Lady Beth's desk and reached for the satchel of samples he'd brought with him. "We can't do anything that good, but here is what we can do," he said as he laid down some of the best images Fabian had produced.

Stephan dawdled on the way back to the print shop. He'd been told to mock-up a program as best he could based on the programs he'd been lent. He knew they could do the head-and-shoulder portraits of the cast, and Lady Beth had told him that they had commissioned Prudentia Gentileschi to paint a scene from the ballet, which he knew Fabian could reproduce using his new camera and fancy filters. The problem was doing scenes from the ballet.

Stephan had a light-bulb moment and quickly dug out the programs he'd been lent. They were all for performances of *Nutcracker*. If Fabian could reproduce a painting, surely he could reproduce some of those photographs. Then an even better idea struck him. Why stop at using them in the program? Surely the up-timers had to have some ballet-themed books that could be prepared for publication in time for the season of *Nutcracker*. They would have to push their translators hard, but if Fabian was already making printing plates of ballet scenes, surely they could use those same plates to print the cover illustrations?

Stephan continued the walk back to the print shop in a bit of a daze as he considered what he was proposing. Frau Fröbel was surely going to jump at the opportunity.

Friday, December 30, 1633

The tickets to the premiere of *Nutcracker* were horrendously expensive, and Stephan had failed in his attempts to get hold of a couple of free tickets. He'd had to settle for tickets to the matinee, but that didn't mean he couldn't turn up to see the rich and powerful file into the auditorium, with their copies of the full-color program grasped in their hands.

They were nothing like as good as the up-time programs, but they were the best they could do with the materials they had. They were also new and unusual, and Schmucker & Schwentzel was the only print shop currently able to do such work. After tonight Stephan expected to be flooded with inquiries.

January 1634

Stephan started his post-ballet-season tour of the bookstores with a degree of trepidation. There had been massive orders for books, especially the new titles with the ballet-themed cover art in the lead-in to the season of *Nutcracker*. Now he was going to find out how good the sell-through had been. He was paid his commission on orders, and a good sell-through would mean more orders, whereas poor sales would result in returns, and even worse for Stephan, a reduction in new orders.

His first stop was the DiOn Book Shoppe. It was a small store run almost as a hobby by two up-time women, Cassie Difabri and Mary Rose Onofrio. He started there because Frau Onofrio was actually a Kubiak by birth, and thus related to Richelle Kubiak, which had made them a prime target for the new ballet titles.

He stepped into the little shop and was immediately confronted by the shop's ballet-themed display. Several copies of the posters that had been produced to advertise the season of *Nutcracker* surrounded a sadly depleted book display. In pride of place in the middle of the display was a full-color reproduction of the painting by Prudentia Gentileschi that had been on the cover of the program. That had been the best of the posters, and had earned Stephan a nice commission. He quickly checked his order book to see how many books they'd ordered, and whistled. If their shelves were that bare...

"Hello, Mr. Greiner. Didn't they do well?"

Stephan reached out for Frau Difabri's hand and lowered his head to drop a kiss on it. If it had been Frau Onofrio saying that, she might have meant Richelle and the other dancers, but coming from Frau Difabri he knew she meant the titles. "You appear to be almost sold out."

Cassie smiled. "Yes. Of course, without the ballet to

bring attention to the ballet-themed books, we won't be placing such a big order for them this time, but we'd like a few more of them. Oh, and can we get a bundle of the posters of Carl and Staci as Cavalier and Sugar Plum Fairy? We had a few people wanting to buy our display copies."

Stephan stared at the poster Frau Difabri was pointing to. It was the full-color reproduction of the Prudentia Gentileschi painting, and Stephan immediately realized they'd missed a trick. Of course they would have to negotiate a fee with Frau Gentileschi, but it looked like they might have a new line. "I will see what I can do. Would you like copies with or without the advertising?" he asked.

Cassie stared at the poster for a while. "Without, I think. How much will they cost?"

Stephan still had a smile on his face when he presented his sales report to Frau Fröbel later that day.

"You're looking bright and cheerful today. Was the sell-through good?" Ursula asked.

"Sell-through for the ballet titles was over ninety percent," he announced. This was almost unheard of for a book not sold by subscription, especially in such a short time frame, and Stephan was justifiably proud of his initiative.

Ursula smiled. "That's very good."

"And a number of outlets would like to order copies of the Prudentia Gentileschi poster, without the advertising."

Ursula's brows shot up. "Posters of the painting?" She paused for a few seconds. "I'll have to talk to her agent."

Stephan nodded. "That's what I told everyone, but there seems to be a lot of interest." He paused to collect himself. "What other paintings could Fabian turn into posters?"

"I shall look into it," Ursula said. "I'm sure there must be something that will appeal to the market."

Ursula made some notes and then looked up and stared Stephan in the eye. "Schmucker & Schwentzel has done extremely well this financial year. Sales and profits are up, and we have a good list. We have decided that you need an assistant. As of today you will no longer be on retainer, but on salary as befits your new position as sales manager." She passed a letter across to him.

"Salary?" He looked at the letter. It was a formal offer of employment, laying down his new and quite livable salary, with profit sharing. It was a dream come true. With his new salary he could afford to marry Anna.

"You've earned it. Now why don't you take some time off to tell your young lady your good news?"

Stephan stumbled out of Frau Fröbel's office and out onto the street. The day seemed especially bright right now. He checked he still had the letter from Schmucker & Schwentzel, and confirmed that he had read the salary and conditions correctly. With a smile that put the sun to shame, he set course for the Grantville Canvas and Outdoor facility down the road.

The Seven Dwarves and the Generals Jackson

Bjorn Hasseler

Northwest of Magdeburg
April 1634

The Red Lion Regiment was in the field for a few days instead of snug in their barracks, which were only a couple hours away. Four of the dwarves were sitting around the fire. Ever since Drill Sergeant Sloan had demoted them from recruits to dwarves after that snipe hunt, everyone called them that—even though they were officially privates now. Some things never changed.

Schliemann, Tüntzel, and Tüntzel's wife—the nondwarf members of the squad—were at the Committees of Correspondence meeting tonight. So were Snow White and Angry—officially known as Corporal Barbara Danker and Private Johann Metzler. Sarge—Andreas Strauss—was at sergeants' school, and Boller—Dopey dwarf—had already gone to bed. Some things never changed. So the other four had nothing to do but share stories they had heard about the various commanders—and invite a couple of recent volunteers to join them.

"Give me that," Gunter told Hans Tauler. He took the stick Tauler was poking the fire with. "You are Clumsy. *I* am Torch. Tell them about our commanders."

The new guys, Martin and Bertrand, looked interested, so Tauler started at the top. "There is General Torstensson, of course, and then there is Jackson. I do not know much about him, but I heard he is a lot older than the prince. Do you think he is too old for the campaign?"

"*Nein.* He is an expert soldier. He has fought in three wars before," Johann Mohr declared.

"Three?" his buddy Karl Sauer asked.

"The Viet Nam . . ." Mohr pronounced it carefully with a short *a.* "The up-timers' Civil War . . . and . . . I know there is one more."

Martin frowned. "I thought their Civil War was long before they came back to our time?"

"I am telling you, General Jackson was in their Civil War." Mohr was emphatic.

"*Nein!*" Sauer remembered something. "Jackson fought the English in some French city."

Tauler came up with it. "Orleans, *ja?*"

"*Nein, nein,*" Gunter insisted. "Jackson is the one who made his men march very far, very fast. As we ourselves have found out."

"All of you are correct," Mohr insisted. "The Viet Nam, their Civil War, and the French and English War."

"Drill Sergeant Sloan did say that in their Civil War the up-timers named their armies after rivers. And he talked about a river in the Viet Nam. . . ." Sauer remembered half of what the drill sergeant had said. That was typical for him.

Tauler came through again. "The May Kong."

"That is it!"

"So the English and the French have fought him before?" Bertrand asked.

"*Absolut*. That is why they allied together in the League of Ostend."

Martin and Bertrand paid very careful attention to everything the dwarves said. They learned almost all the details. Alas, they never learned that Sauer and Mohr were dwarves Moron and Nutty. If they had, they might have questioned their intelligence windfall.

Once the dwarves started to settle down for the night, Martin and Bertrand made a beeline for a certain sutler.

"I told you not to come here! You are supposed to be with your company!"

"It is an emergency!" Martin hissed. "We have been tricked!"

"What do you mean?"

"Jackson was not really demoted," Bertrand explained. "It is all a ruse! The Swedes are trying to conceal that he is a very famous up-time general!"

Sergeant Matt Lowry was lying behind some crates in the back of Sutlers' Row. It was his turn at surveillance again tonight. Matt remembered a time when he'd naively dismissed the idea of assassins and spies. Not anymore. Maybe someone would finally say enough that he could have the MPs throw this sutler out. Perhaps even arrest him.

Martin and Bertrand laid out what they had learned.

Lowry spent the next ten minutes with the leather strap of his cartridge box in his mouth, to keep from laughing.

Matt knocked on the captain's door early the next morning.

"Sergeant Lowry?"

"Sir, it seems we have some French spies in the camp."

The captain snorted. "It seems we have some fleas in the barracks, too. Tell me something I did not already know."

"Well, a couple of the new men got talking to the Seven Dwarves last night." Lowry smirked. "They may have come away with a slightly inflated view of Colonel Jackson, sir."

"Go on."

"It seems that *General* Jackson marched his Union Army of the Mekong thirty miles a day while leading them to victory over the English at Orleans, France— where they fired at them from behind the Stone Wall. And then he outflanked the Confederates."

The down-time captain broke up laughing.

"And then those two men went straight to our favorite sutler."

The captain stopped laughing. "Did they now?" He fiddled with his mustaches. "Matt, go tell the men to stop talking about military secrets. Just make sure you are not too successful at it."

Lowry had a very evil grin on his face. "I understand, sir. I will go take care of that right now."

Quelles Misérables

David Carrico

Paris
March 1634

Armand-Jean du Plessis, priest, bishop, Cardinal-Duke
of Richelieu and of Fronsac, and chief minister to His
Most Christian Majesty, King Louis of France, thir-
teenth of that name, stood at the window and gazed
at the gardeners at their work in the early afternoon.
He watched as they plied their craft with spades and
trowels and snips. He admired their skill and focus,
and from time to time he was even a bit jealous.
There were days where the thought of having honest
dirt on his hands and the smell of honest manure in
his nostrils appealed to him more than the spiritual
reek of the court. But then, there was no one who
could do his work as well as him, so if he didn't do
it, things would become even worse. Although he was
beginning to have hopes of young Mazarini.

"Your Eminence."

Richelieu looked back over his shoulder to where
Servien stood inside the door. He raised his eyebrows.

"There . . . is a visitor, Eminence."

Richelieu considered his intendant. If he didn't know better, he'd have thought that Servien was . . . uncertain. And that was a condition he had seldom seen in his intendant in all their years together.

"Has this visitor a name, Servien?"

"He is one Abbé Jehan Mercier, Eminence."

A low-ranking cleric. Perhaps he was wanting to speak to the cardinal rather than the chief minister. That might be refreshing.

"Is he one of our informers?"

"No."

Richelieu frowned. "Who did he bribe to get this far?"

"He, ah, carries an introduction from your niece."

"From Marie-Madeleine?"

"Yes, Eminence."

Well, that put a different light on things. If the Marquise de Combalet sent a lower-ranked cleric to see her uncle, it behooved him to meet the man. And it explained why Servien was handling the matter instead of a porter or guard.

"Then you had best admit him, Servien. We would not want the marquise unhappy with us."

"Indeed, Eminence."

Servien withdrew, then moments later ushered a short, round figure into the room. Abbé Mercier was dressed in what was apparently his best priestly garments, but they were somewhat on the fusty and shabby side. Richelieu was almost prepared to dismiss the man as a waste of his time, but for two things: the marquise was not a fool, and the abbé's eyes were both bright and focused.

Richelieu held out his ring. The abbé bent with a certain aplomb to kiss it, then straightened with a slight smile on his face. Richelieu was a bit intrigued and waved a hand at the chair placed before his desk.

"Please, Abbé Jehan, be seated. Servien, see to refreshment, please." Servien beckoned to a servant. As Richelieu rounded the desk, he heard the servant offering coffee, tea, mocha, and wine. Richelieu settled into his chair as Servien took a stance against a side wall, close enough to be available to Richelieu if needed, yet far enough away to not be part of the conversation.

"Perhaps a little wine," the abbé said in a high-pitched breathy tenor as he took his seat. Moments later, he was holding a Venetian glass of a red to rival the claret contained within it. Richelieu picked up the cup of mocha that had appeared at his elbow and took a sip. Perfect mocha in the American style. He took a larger sip, then set the cup down.

"How do you know the Marquise de Combalet, Abbé Jehan?"

A large smile appeared on the priest's face, transforming the roundness of it to almost beam like the sun. "I minister at and through a hospice located outside Paris, mostly for poor folk who are dying, usually of consumption. The marquise learned of the work and has become one of our largest supporters. She has, upon occasion, invited me to her salons."

"Ah."

Richelieu gave a slight nod. His niece was given to works of charity, and it would be just like her to invite someone like this priest and set him in the middle of her usual salon set. On the other hand, that was another indication that there was more to Abbé Jehan than one might assume. She would not expose some-one she valued to the eyes, ears, and tongues of the salons unless she was certain he could hold his own.

"So do you seek the face of the cardinal or the chief minister, Abbé Jehan?"

An expression of almost sadness crossed the priest's face. "Perhaps both, Your Eminence."

Richelieu made a "continue" gesture with one hand as he picked up his cup again with the other. Abbé Jehan drained the wine from his glass, then held it in both hands and leaned forward slightly.

"Your Eminence, I am concerned about the spiritual welfare of Paris, and indeed, all of France."

That took Richelieu a bit aback. That was not what he would have expected from a man cultivated by his niece.

"In what manner?"

Mercier took a deep breath, and began, "For some time, Eminence, I have been aware of—not a flood—a current, shall we say—of works of literature that have been making their way into France from Grantville. Some of them are translations of works written mostly in English, but more than a few are works written originally in French. Or what passes for French in the up-time. And these have begun to attract attention, even notoriety."

"Dumas," Richelieu murmured.

The priest made a moue, then continued with, "Yes, yes, everyone is reading Dumas. And it's not *his* work I'm most concerned with. Despite his licentiousness, the man supports—supported—whatever the correct phraseology should be—the proper order of things. The divinely ordained order, if you will.

"And of course, there are the adventures of Asterix the Gaul, copied from the up-time books and sent this way." Mercier shrugged. "They are, of course, overtly pagan, but I deem them no threat. As lampoons, they have their uses, and I confess that something that sticks a thumb in the eye of the Romans as often as these stories do warms my heart a bit. They will provide no more harm than Plato or Aristotle."

The priest held up a hand with the index finger standing alone.

"But, there is another, one whose work is becoming more widely available, whose work concerns me: Monsieur Victor Hugo."

Richelieu raised his eyebrows and settled back in his chair, holding his cup in both hands. The abbé leaned forward a little more.

"This man apparently lived at much the same time as Dumas, yet his works were very different. His most well-known work, *Les Misérables*, has been discovered by some enterprising soul mining the archives of Grantville, and an effort has begun to replicate the work today and disseminate it among the people of France, in particular the people of Paris, from what I can determine. It focuses on the lives of downtrodden poor and folk who were unfortunates in a time of rebellion and strife, when the very warp and weft of Paris and France were in danger of being pulled asunder.

"If Hugo were another Dumas, or even a fabulist such as Jules Verne, I would have little concern over him or the effect of his work. But the man was no such thing. From his writings, he appears to have been at the very least a subversive republican, if not an outright anarchist. Yet he was such a writer that he can reach into the minds and hearts of men and set them aflame. Even now, every couple of weeks or so a new signature of the reproduction of *Les Misérables* appears, and with each appearance the circle of readers widens and deepens. Even amongst my little flock, I hear rumblings of discontent being stirred by the ladle of those pages, and I fear that they are but the merest hint of what is simmering on the fires of the times." Mercier's voice had grown louder and more impassioned as he spoke. He made an obvious effort to sit back and take a deep breath.

Richelieu judged that the man was seriously concerned about the matter. This was not just something he was using as an entrée to the higher levels of the court. In another man, that would have been a very likely consideration, but the abbé, despite his apparent sharpness of wit, didn't seem to be maneuvering that direction.

The cardinal took a sip of his cooling mocha, then cradled the cup in his hands. "So, again, do you come to me as cardinal or as chief minister? What recommendations do you bring?"

"I come to you in whatever manner you stand as guardian of the spirituality of the people of France," the priest responded with some passion. "I urge you to do what must be done to protect the souls of France from the pernicious influence of the writing of Victor Hugo. I urge you to suppress his work, to declare it unworthy of France. At the very least, I ask that you be aware of it, and have your eyes and ears follow it, lest it become a source of active unrest in the corpus of France."

Richelieu stared over the rim of his cup at the

abbé as he finished his mocha. He set the empty cup down on his desk, clasped his hands before his midriff, and focused a long gaze on the priest, who was staring back at him earnestly, apparently having spent his passion.

"As it happens," Richelieu said at length, "we are aware of the matter you have raised. It is a matter of some concern, this wholesale importation of unauthorized works that bids to upset the normal channels of our *ancien régime*. So, you may take some comfort from that."

The expression of relief that spread over Mercier's face gave an almost palpable air within the room. The smile that appeared seemed to take a few years off of his appearance, leaving Richelieu to wonder if he had overestimated the man's age.

"Thank you, Your Eminence," the abbé said, his tone reflecting a certain amount of both humility and gratitude. "I had hoped that my concerns were not new to you, but it is good to know that you are well informed and already have the matter in hand."

"Indeed," Richelieu said. "Those who are printing these scurrilous publications cannot make a move that we are not aware of. We are simply watching to see who has become entangled in their nets."

"Ah," Mercier said, with a bit of a knowing nod. "Well, since that is the case, I will apologize for having bothered you with my petty concerns and take my leave. God's blessing on you, Your Eminence." He rose as he spoke, and Servien materialized to take the wine glass from him.

"It is of no matter, Abbé Jehan," Richelieu responded. "And do, if you see or hear anything that bears on the matter, give us word of it. Or as much as you can without breaking the seal of the confessional, of course."

"As you direct, Your Eminence," the abbé responded. He gave a final bow, and allowed Servien to usher him from the room.

Richelieu chuckled when Servien slipped back into the room. "Ah, if he only knew, eh, Servien?"

"Indeed, Eminence," the intendant responded with a small smile.

"Wait until he encounters Voltaire and Camus," the cardinal said. Another chuckle followed. "Make note of him, Servien. He might prove to be useful."

Servien placed a folder on the desk. "The latest report at last, Eminence."

"Ah?" Richelieu placed a possessive hand on top of the folder. "And why was this late, Servien?"

"The local distributor said that it was delayed by some officious guard at one of the city gates."

"Make a note of that as well, Servien."

"Yes, Eminence."

And with that, Servien slipped out of the room while Richelieu opened the folder. "Now, let's see what Jean Valjean and Monsieur Thénardier have to say this week." He bent over the folder and began to read.

You've Got to Be Kidding

Tim Sayeau

As Colonel Nils Ekstrom worked his way through the various reports sent to Lübeck from Torstensson's adjutants, he spotted an oddity.

Thorsten Engler, that sergeant the princess wanted made a count, had captured *both* the French cavalry commander and the French army commander!

"Oh, splendid! That's one problem solved at least! Bring me a map," he commanded his nearest aide, one Major Dag Rödvinge. "Nutschel. That's about where the capture was made."

"What's this about, Nils?" asked Frank Jackson, having just come in.

Ekstrom explained about Thorsten Engler, Caroline Platzer, and how Princess Kristina had come to name Engler the Count of Narnia. Ekstrom concluded with, "We'll just inform the villagers that the emperor—their emperor now—has decided to rename their village to honor the great victory."

"Rename it what?" asked Frank Jackson.

"Narnia, of course. That gives us a fallback

position—that is the American term, yes?—in the not unlikely event the emperor capitulates to his daughter."

"You've got to be kidding."

The fish-eyed look Ekstrom sent Jackson's way would have done credit to the holds of a fleet of Baltic fishing vessels returning to port. "You *have* met Princess Kristina, I believe."

"Good point. Yeah, I have met her. Narnia, huh? Well...as long as they don't spell it in Fraktur."

As Ekstrom and Jackson conversed, Major Dag Rödvinge considered the odds.

I'm not the only one here, he thought. *Not counting the colonel and Frank Jackson, there's Viggo, Loke, Svante, and Tor. They're all close by, and they heard the conversation just as well as I did, so there's absolutely no reason to—*

"Rödvinge!" called Colonel Ekstrom.

—*run!* finished Dag, his eyes closing in dismay.

Rapidly disciplining his face to show only utmost readiness, Major Rödvinge turned to his doom.

"Yes, Colonel?"

"You heard Jackson and me talking, so I don't need to repeat myself. Write up a proclamation for the emperor to announce and, once the Navy has defeated the Danes, take charge of this Nutschel business and get it settled to everybody's satisfaction."

"Yes Colonel, I'll work it out right away," said Rödvinge, making a quick note on a nearby sheet of paper.

And I'll also arrange the Second Coming of Christ, thought Rödvinge as he scribbled. *To everybody's satisfaction, of course!*

☆   ☆   ☆

Thirty minutes later Dag Rödvinge was in deep conversation with Lübeck Mayor Dieterich Matthesen in the latter's council office.

Seated within a deep leather chair, Mayor Matthesen stared at Rödvinge across an ornate desk.

"You've got to be kidding!"

Rödvinge looked him straight in the eyes.

"No, I am not. The emperor wants Nutschel's name changed to Narnia, and he wants it done yesterday. That's not exaggeration, by the way!"

Matthesen leaned forward.

"This is ridiculous! This high-handed conduct is... it's... I could believe it of that Saxon twerp John George or that fool Charles in England, but Gustav Adolf? Has he gone mad? And besides, what is a Narnia anyway? And why should Nutschel change its name to that, anyway?"

"Mayor Matthesen—Dieterich—listen to me. Please. I beg you, let me explain. And this will go much faster if you don't ask questions until I'm finished. Yes, that's high-handed, but believe me, it's better that way, it really is. What is going on is this. There's a flying artillery sergeant called Thorsten Engler—"

"...and that's why Nutschel has to be changed to Narnia," finished Rödvinge.

Silence. Then, from Matthesen—

"Major—Dag—let me see if I understand this. Because Princess Kristina on a whim named a man the Count of Narnia, which is a fantasy land in a series of up-timer children's books, now the village of Nutschel *has* to be renamed Narnia? Do I have that right?"

"Essentially, yes."

Matthesen stared at Rödvinge for several long seconds.

"Do you have any idea how silly that is, Dag? That grown men, supposedly intelligent grown men, will indulge a willful seven-year-old girl's wish?"

"That willful seven-year-old girl is the daughter and heir of Emperor Gustav Adolf II of the USE and the king of Sweden, Dieterich. Your *emperor*, my *king*, Dieterich. He dotes upon his daughter as a father should, and besides, this Thorsten Engler did capture the highest-ranking members of the French army, so as silly as it may be, on this Princess Kristina gets her wish, and anyway—"

"And anyway it is rather sweet, I suppose," finished Matthesen. "How otherwise sane and supposedly mature men of high consequence and grave bearing make themselves into the willingly indulgent slaves of a headstrong little girl!"

Relieved at Matthesen's unexpected good humor, Rödvinge smiled. "It is a wonder to see. And not just Kristina, mind. Little girls do make grown men go soft in the head and the heart in the best way possible."

"That they do, Dag, that they do. Even when you know they're doing it to you. Which I suppose is how I shall try to make the CoC see this. And the village council. And the people of Nutschel. Because otherwise—this really is high-handed, you know. It's not even that it's so bad, but the way in which it is being done! This really is being done bass-ackwards, you know."

"Bass-ackwards? Amideutsch, right? And yes, I agree. The thing is, nobody knows anything. Which I deny ever saying, but it's the truth. The USE has just begun, after being first the NUS and the CPE; they're working it out as they go along. I'll see if there are any copies of those Narnia books in Lübeck, if not the Air Force can ship some in. Not just for you and me, but for the people of Narnia. That should help. Anyway, once the proclamation is made Nutschel becomes Narnia, the princess gets her wish, and that's the end of it."

Oh my friend, thought Matthesen, as they walked together out of his office. *I'd tell you, but enjoy this respite while you can.*

I hope you *get a countship out of this, you'll deserve it!*

Two days later the official proclamation went up on the Nutschel St. Jacob's Church door.

It would have been only a day later, but no copies of the Narnia books had been available in Lübeck, and Rödvinge had successfully argued introducing the books into Nutschel at the same time as the proclamation "would help settle matters; at least when people are busy reading the books they're not wondering what this Narnia is all about."

Ekstrom having agreed, a special delivery had been made from the bookshops of Magdeburg to Wismar to Lübeck by the Air Force. Colonel Jesse Wood did grumble about "not being a mobile library, damn it!" but supervised it personally—"if we have to do it let's get it done right."

(A few days after the flight somebody painted a winged horse and the name "Fledge" on the nose of the Gustav plane that flew the books in. Nobody ever admitted responsibility, but the nose art stayed.)

The proclamation, as expected of one on behalf of both the Lion of the North and Aslan the Lion of Narnia, was impressive.

In bold, large print it announced:

WHEREAS   In May 1634 the Joint Forces
               of the Kingdom of Sweden and
               the United States of Europe
               under the Commands of General
               Lennart Torstensson did Ably
               and Admirably Rout the French
               Invaders,

WHEREAS   Sergeant Thorsten Engler of
               Colonel Straley's Flying Artillery
               Did Capture at Great Personal
               Risk Count Jean Baptiste Budes
               Guébriant, Cavalry Commander of
               the French,

WHEREAS   Sergeant Thorsten Engler Did
               Again at Great Personal Risk
               Capture Charles de Valois, Duke
               of Angoulême, Commander-in-
               Chief of the French forces,

THEREFORE   In Recognition of his Bravery,
               Courage and Service Sergeant
               Thorsten Engler is Raised in Rank
               and Distinction to

Imperial Count of Narnia

FURTHERMORE   By Virtue of the Capture of
               Charles de Valois, Duke of
               Angoulême, having Occurred
               in the Vicinity of the Village of
               Nutschel, the Aforementioned
               Village is

HENCEFORTH   Recognized and Renamed as

The Village of Narnia

Proclaimed This Day by Order of

Gustavus II Adolphus

King of Sweden,
High King of the Union of Kalmar,
Emperor of the United States of Europe.

Along with the official proclamation on the church
door of St. Jacob's were smaller proclamations, handed
out to every passerby and churchgoer. The copies of
the *Chronicles of Narnia* flown in to Lübeck the day
before proved greatly popular among the Nutschels,
once it was realized these books were free.

Rödvinge's reason to delay the proclamation proved
perceptive; the villagers were interested in the books,
in the free books, in the free books from up-time,
in the free books from up-time that were among the
favorites of Princess Kristina Vasa herself!

What interested a princess greatly interested the
villagers. Conversations centered around the books.

"Narnia? What sort of a name is Narnia?"

"Aslan? The Lion? All right, with Gustav Adolf the
Lion of the North now Narnia makes sense."

"No, it doesn't! Why change Nutschel to Narnia when
it was at Ahrensbök that the real victory was won?"

"Children's stories? This is all because of children's stories?"

"They're not exactly children's stories, are they? The books themselves talk of Christian imagery."

"Witch? *Witch! Heresy!*"

"Shut up, you idiot. The witch doesn't live, read the book!"

"*Dawn Treader*? What a poetic name! Dear—"

"All right, but still, for a fishing punt?"

"Magician's Nephew? *Magician! Her—*"

"Shut up, you idiot!"

"Can you build me a wardrobe? One like in the books."

"All right, but you do know it won't actually take you to—"

"Of course not, I meant one that looks like the one. Although maybe a secret compartment or two? Don't tell me where they are, I want to find out on my own."

"Aslan is Christ? Christ as an *animal*? *Blasph—*"

"Do I have to say it?"

"Who do you like the most?"

"Well, don't tell anyone, but—Eustace."

"Him? He's scum!"

"I know he starts off that way, but he changes into a hero, and I like that."

"That's it, horse! You've rolled in the mud once too often, from now on your name is Puddleglum!"

"You can't name your kitten Aslan!"

"Why not?"

"Because I named my kitten Aslan first!"

☆   ☆   ☆

Those were the initial conversations about the books. The ones people had while they were still reading the free books, still distracted by the free up-time books Princess Kristina herself read.

Then came the *real* conversations. The ones Matthesen had known would come and hadn't yet wanted Rödvinge to worry about.

"You know, these stories are all very well and good, and I guess Narnia is a pretty good name, but—"

"Yeah, but now what? Who do I pay my rent to now?"

"Can I still run my tavern out of my house?"

"I have the leases on a farm west of here, at least I did, but now I don't know."

"What's this count of ours like anyway?"

"So who's in charge now? Is it this count or Lübeck?"

"I liked it before, I knew who did what and who to go see when I had a problem. Now—"

"Will this new count let me stay as the schoolteacher? And if he does, who pays my salary?"

"A new broom sweeps clean, I hear."

"Yeah, but this new broom isn't doing anything."

"Hasn't even come round to see us."

"At least before we knew what was what."

"I admit the French weren't here too long to do much damage, but they did do some. Who do we see about getting repairs done?"

"What about the woodlot there? It's common property, you know that!"

"I knew that, but now I don't know, I don't want to be in trouble for gathering firewood."

"This is just not right. Somebody needs to do something. Maybe write to Lübeck and ask what's going on."

"Yeah, I'm going to do that. I mean, I don't know if I should, I don't know what this Engler guy is like, but he can't leave us like this, he has obligations!"

"That's right he does!"

The letters came first. Then the people.

The people, like the letters, were mostly respectful. Stating facts tactfully and requesting information, advice and aid with modesty and grace.

Those who weren't either wrote letters anonymously or requested others make their case for them.

The anonymous letters found use in the Rathaus jakes.

Some of the requests made it to Lübeck. Others were forgotten on the way.

What Mayor Dieterich Matthesen and Senior Rathaus clerk Leo Anslinger could handle they did.

What they couldn't, they set aside for Rödvinge.

After all, he had been put in charge of Nutschel/Narnia.

Fortunately for Rödvinge, Matthesen and Anslinger waited to inform him of ongoing matters in Narnia only as long as it took for those matters to become a mild curiosity instead of an overwhelming necessity.

So it was only a small packet with an accompanying letter that landed on Major Dag Rödvinge's desk somewhere in Copenhagen instead of a mailbag.

The official letter from Matthesen stated the following:

Mayor's Office
Rathaus, Lübeck, USE

To: Major Dag Rödvinge
Army of Sweden
Copenhagen
Re: the Countship of Narnia

We of the Lübeck City Council write to you to express first our continued loyalty to and full support of the Emperor, and to request clarification of an increasingly difficult legal matter.

Simply put, who is in charge of Narnia? When the name was changed, what else if anything changed with it? Does the Count of Narnia own only the name of Narnia, or does he also legally own the village and surroundings of Narnia?

If the former, then everything is as it was before the name change and will proceed according to established custom, tradition and law.

If the latter, as we personally feel it must be, then for the past few weeks Lübeck has been assigning to itself the Count of Narnia's privileges and responsibilities, much as Grantville did those of the Saxe-Weimar brothers.

That was of course an exceptional, even miraculous situation, a True Act of God.

In Lübeck's case, should the status of Narnia not soon be officially determined, we in Lübeck increasingly fear we risk a charge of lèse majesté, possibly even High Treason against the Emperor.

As our lawyers have made clear, the action

of taking to ourselves the privileges of the Count of Narnia, ennobled by the Emperor himself, could be considered usurping the privileges of the Emperor himself.

We therefore request an immediate clarification of the legal situation concerning the village of Narnia.

We add that until such time as the legal and official status of Narnia be known, the Lübeck City Council cannot in good conscience and lawful obeisance to the Emperor continue its relations with Narnia.

Accordingly we must and will defer all such decisions to the lawful authority of the Emperor and his duly appointed representatives.

> *Signed this day by*
> *Dieterich Matthesen,*
> *Mayor of Lübeck,*
> *United States of*
> *Europe*

Inside the letter Matthesen included a handwritten note.

Dag—sorry to do this to you, but this is what happens when things are done bass-ackwards. We aren't really afraid of being arrested for treason, but the fact is, stranger things have happened.

Another fact is, what is Narnia? Is it only the village or is it a county? If so, whose? The count's, the emperor's? Who handles the rents, land sales and ownerships, leases? You said it yourself, "They're working it out as they go along."

This is something that needs to be worked out.
I swear, the Rathaus will do everything possible
to help, but we need to know what it is we're
helping to do!

                                    Sincerely, Dieterich

Major Dag Rödvinge of the Swedish Army, currently
in Copenhagen for the Congress of Copenhagen, finished reading both letters from Dieterich Matthesen.
He picked up and weighed the packet that had come
with the letters. Then he considered his options. *The
Republic of Essen, that's where I'll go. Close by, and
I speak the language.* Instead, he picked up the letters,
then went to speak with Colonel Ekstrom.

Four hours later Major Rödvinge was at the Copenhagen aerodrome, awaiting a USE flight to Lübeck.

As he sat in the "command headquarters" of the
airfield—really a rather large shed, incongruously
supplied with panes of stained glass and luxurious
chairs—and stared out one of the few clear windows
at the construction of King Christian's "flying cottage,"
he considered his verbal and written orders.

Colonel Ekstrom when presented with the developing situation had quickly presented Rödvinge with the
authority and funds to solve it.

"The emperor stated we'd borrow the Habsburg
model. The only Habsburg counts without land are
those who've gambled it away. So, Engler gets land.
Here's your authority to negotiate purchases of lands
and leases, plus a letter authorizing you to draw on
the Abrabanels. Speak with their Copenhagen branch
before you go—if they don't know who's the best lawyer

in Lübeck it'll be because there are no lawyers in
Lübeck and that's impossible, they're always underfoot.
Make sure the first thing you do in Lübeck is hire
whomever they say. You have two weeks."

Two weeks! Goodbye, sleep!

He checked again the leather saddlebag swung
over a shoulder.

Authority to negotiate and purchase, check.

Authority to disburse funds to purchase, check.

Authority to call upon the services of the local
USE forces, check.

Abrabanel recommendation of a lawyer, one Ludwig
Hautzmeyer, check.

First flight in an airplane, coming up soon.

As he repacked the letters and authorizations, in
walked an Air Force NCO.

"Major Rödvinge, sir? Your flight is ready. Weather
reports clear skies to Lübeck."

Oh good, thought Rödvinge. *I get to see everything!*

Ludwig Hautzmeyer proved to be everything the
Abrabanels said and more.

Apprised of the situation, Hautzmeyer had quickly
read the attached letters, the official—*Nicely done
there, Mayor*—and the unofficial—*Bass-ackwards?
Amazing, never heard it before yet fully understood*—
made notes on how to handle the complaints and
requests in the packet—*Hmmm now this can wait,
this fellow here must be doing it for the attention.
Yes, all right, God is your witness but His affidavit
would be more help*—and drew out the whole story
of Princess Kristina and Narnia from Rödvinge almost
without asking any questions.

At the end of the interview, as Hautzmeyer and Rödvinge prepared to leave Hautzmeyer's offices for the Rathaus, Rödvinge asked why Hautzmeyer hadn't once questioned or wondered about the sense of the whole thing.

"Don't you find it rather odd, all this for what is essentially a little girl's whim?"

Hautzmeyer drily replied, "Not at all, Major. Odd is changing one's will based on the phases of the moon, which I only talk about because that was one of my grandfather's clients, and it's been done with for years. Still haven't solved the murder... As for this matter of Narnia, it can be done in two weeks but I warn you, that will cost. Not only my services. Depending on what we find in the Rathaus files, there could be any number of issues: Access rights to the Trave, for instance. Road maintenance. This Thorsten Engler may find being a count less pleasurable than he expected."

Rödvinge considered what he knew of Engler. He'd formed a good opinion of the man, having met him at the Congress.

"I don't think he can find it any less pleasurable than he already does. Actually, that came out wrong. I've actually met Engler. At the Congress."

Warming to the topic, Rödvinge continued. "I made sure of that; I really wanted to meet the guy who got this whole Narnia thing going. Quite a good sort really; it's not that he hates the whole count business but I got the feeling he's only going along with it to humor Princess Kristina. Which is an odd way to view becoming a count, but that's the best way to put it. He's planning to become a psychologist after he gets out of the army. I think that'll reconcile him most to being a count—he'll be able to afford the time to study."

Hautzmeyer paused.

"A psychologist? What the—no, let me guess. *Psykhe*, from the Greek, spirit. Logi, logist, probably Greek again, so *logos*, logic, study. Logic, study of the spirit, is that it?"

"Actually, yes. As he explained it, it's all about studying the mind, figuring out why people act as they do, restoring sanity. Grantville apparently has all sorts of books on the subject, especially at their Leahy hospital."

"Huh," replied Hautzmeyer, resuming his preparations. "Well, if he's going to be studying in Grantville, he's going to need his countship. The income, especially. I hear all sorts of stories about the place, is it true that—"

They were warmly greeted at the Rathaus by Mayor Dieterich Matthesen and senior Rathaus clerk Leo Anslinger.

While Matthesen and Rödvinge talked, Anslinger and Hautzmeyer got down to business.

"We knew this would be coming before the major even left," confided Anslinger. "So I had all the files on Nutschel pulled and set aside. Then had my juniors going through a few of the files each day, checking for any misfiles. Didn't find anything on Nutschel so far, but sorted out a few things all the same. Really ought to do that much oftener—amazing what gets put where."

"Thank you, Leo. This makes my job much easier. The major's too."

"Our pleasure, Ludwig. The major's a good sort,

so helping him out is only right. Don't cheat him too much on the fees, that's what I'm saying."

"Leo, I'm a lawyer," said Hautzmeyer, reaching for a file. "We never cheat, we finesse. There's a difference. When the major is done with the mayor, show him in here, will you? I should have some idea of what's what by then and be able to give him the good news or not."

"Will do."

Some time later Rödvinge entered the room where Hautzmeyer was busy checking through files. "Sorry for the delay, Ludwig. Dieterich wanted to know all about what's going on in Copenhagen. He says it's for his wife, but I wonder."

"Hmm. Mine will want to know about Copenhagen, too. Something tells me I'll be working late at the office tonight. Well, I'll have to anyway, to get this worked out as fast as your colonel wants, but now I won't have to pretend. So far nothing I've come across is anything exceptional. Now, I have to finish going through these files, so you can either stay here and read through the files yourself, or . . . actually, I don't know what else. I usually have a law clerk to take notes, but I don't know if that's suitable . . ."

"It is. I even have legible writing."

"Oh, good. All right then, first thing I've found; the local miller . . ."

It took four days.

Working sixteen to eighteen hours a day, sending out for meals and arranging to sleep overnight in the Rathaus, Ludwig Hautzmeyer and Dag Rödvinge worked out everything connected to Narnia.

Not by themselves, not after the first day. After

the first day, Hautzmeyer called in one law clerk after another from first his office, then from a colleague's.

First one room in the Rathaus had been taken over, then another and another. Notes and files were passed around, clarifications requested, law books requested and studied, files and laws studied again, then again passed around and studied.

The horrible thing, as Rödvinge came to realize, was that Nutschel—*Narnia*—was not a particularly remarkable village.

It wasn't particularly small, nor particularly large.

Issues of land ownership, rights and leases were not particularly complicated nor particularly significant.

But until now, nobody had ever sat down and actually worked out every particular detail of a particular village.

Those had always been handled on an individual, case-by-case affair. A transfer of a land lease here, an issue of a cottager's access to the common lands there.

Individually no one issue was particularly noteworthy. But add them up all at once, and then!

Once an issue was determined, Hautzmeyer informed Dag Rödvinge, who then entered the detail into ledgers set aside for that purpose.

(Not that Rödvinge and Hautzmeyer and the clerks were ever to know it, nor would they have cared other than to snarl "How nice!", but decades later social historians would praise them for their work, citing it as an authoritative study of a north German farming village in the early years of the USE.)

The sixth day, refreshed after taking the injunction of Sunday as a day of rest and sleeping through it, Rödvinge and Hautzmeyer met at Hautzmeyer's office.

Hautzmeyer opened up the ledger reserved for his and Rödvinge's use.

"Most fine handwriting, Major. A pleasure to read. Now, as I hear the Americans say, come the hard parts. Buying Narnia. Running Narnia."

"Let's work on buying Narnia first. For the running part, perhaps you could do that"—Hautzmeyer glared at him—"...or recommend somebody," Rödvinge quickly added.

"We'll handle the buying part first. I've gone ahead and listed all the lands and leases for Narnia along with the likely purchase cost of each and all together."

Hautzmeyer handed Rödvinge several sheets of paper.

Rödvinge looked at the final page, dropped the pages, and sat down hard on the floor.

"It's not as bad as it looks," said Hautzmeyer dispassionately as Rödvinge tried to stand up, his legs failing him. "Not everybody is going to want to sell, and it's not as if it has to be all paid back at once. However, for this count to be viewed seriously, he has to be the majority land or lease owner."

Back on his feet, Rödvinge bent down and picked up the sheets. He sat on a nearby chair and studied the pages. Finished, he held them in his lap and looked at Hautzmeyer.

"This is going to take longer than a week."

Hautzmeyer, seated as well, leaned forward across his desk.

"Yes. It is. As your lawyer, and by extension the count's, I have several recommendations.

"First, arrange to have the funds to make purchases. There are three banks in Lübeck that can probably handle that much, one for sure.

"Second, we both go to Narnia. The people there are going to have questions and concerns, and we need to be there to answer them.

"Third, unless you want to be here for the next three to four months, appoint me as your representative. I know I glared at you before, but after those four days at the Rathaus..." Hautzmeyer paused in recollection, then shook himself and continued explaining matters to Rödvinge.

"As your representative I'll send in weekly reports, and by all means come in unannounced to check on me whenever you like. You won't find anything wrong, but best to get into the habit of doing so. Not everybody you meet and employ is going to put your interests ahead of their own, and even if they do that's no guarantee there won't be mistakes made along the way. Trust, but verify. If more people did that there wouldn't be a need for lawyers. Well, not as much need," amended Hautzmeyer.

Rödvinge nodded agreement at the points Hautzmeyer made. He thumbed through the pages, examining them in more detail. Finished, he turned to Hautzmeyer.

"Sounds good to me. After the bank, let's first see Matthesen. Lübeck owns and leases land in Narnia, and I'm sure they'll sell."

"Hmmm...it'll have to be decided in a special meeting of council, but you're right, I'm sure they will. For the bank, I advise setting the purchases up this way. While you are here, full disbursement. When you aren't, arrange it so that I can disburse the funds into escrow pending your approval. That way, the seller knows the money is there, you retain approval, and the possibility of embezzlement is lessened."

"Lessened?" Rödvinge asked, raising an eyebrow.

Hautzmeyer solemnly nodded. "Lessened. Believe me, that's the best that can be done. The creativity of people when it comes to money...I tell you, Jesus kicking the money changers out of the temple should rank as one of His miracles."

Rödvinge looked discomfited. "That arrangement would make it seem I don't trust you."

Hautzmeyer shook his head in refusal. "Major, you are planning to make some rather large outlays of funds. That attracts the envious, the desperate, and the greedy. The envious will find any way to make the most aboveboard and honest transaction seem criminal, the desperate will find any way to grab what they can, and the greedy will find any way to grab what they can."

Hautzmeyer stood up and walked around the desk to stand next to it. He looked straight into Rödvinge's eyes.

"Believe me when I say this Narnia business can go from a child's fancy to a tragedy within an eyeblink. Faced with that, the question of whether or not you seem to trust me isn't a concern. My concern as your lawyer is making sure everything goes well for you, for the count, and yes, for Narnia. As a lawyer, and hopefully as a good man, I've seen and heard enough tragedies to know I want no part of those." Hautzmeyer paused. "And that's quite enough of that talk for the morning. The week, even." He picked up a sheet from his desk and handed it to Rödvinge. "Here's a list of those banks I mentioned."

Rödvinge examined this new sheet.

"Let's see—Fugger Bank I know, who doesn't? But Berenberg Brothers and Sparkasse zu Lübeck?"

"The Berenberg Brothers are Hans and Paul,

although only Paul is around. Hans died a few years back. They started off in Antwerp and moved to Hamburg to escape the Duke of Alma. They're fairly new to Lübeck but are solid in Hamburg."

"And Sparkasse zu Lübeck?"

"Is the one wholly Lübeck bank on the list. Well, the name shows it, Savings Bank of Lübeck. Like the Berenbergs it's a family bank, the Dossenbachs. They started off as jewelers three centuries ago, then moved into the amber and timber trade with shipping investments and from there to banking. They're solid too, even though they did just change their name."

"They did? Why?"

"Like everybody else, including me, once they heard of Grantville they sent off to find out what history remembered of them. Didn't find anything, so they asked around for anything about Lübeck. Somebody had a postcard showing a Lübeck street scene, and there it was, *Sparkasse zu Lübeck*, so they took it for their own."

Rödvinge looked again at the sheet of paper listing the recommended banks.

"Which do you recommend?"

"Honestly, Berenberg and Sparkasse together. I said they're solid and they are, but I'm not sure either could handle Narnia alone."

"Why not the Fugger Bank, then? They loan to the pope and the Habsburgs. They could handle it all."

"I know the Fuggers could handle it all but they're too rich as it is. Besides, they're Catholic, they're in Bavaria, and as a Lutheran and Lübecker and I guess now a USE citizen, I'd rather have the business kept here."

Rödvinge drummed his fingers on his chair as he thought about his upcoming decision.

I'm a Swedish Army major, what do I know about banking? Ah, blast it, forget the Fuggers, Lübeck's one thing but who wants to go to Bavaria?

"All right, the Berenbergs and the Sparkasse together, but how does that work? Do I have to go see them one at a time or what?"

"They're bankers—they'll work it out. With your permission, I'll contact them now and ask to have representatives meet us on our way to Matthesen and the Rathaus."

"So fast? And without even seeing them first? Will they even come?"

"Major, they already know you're here and why. They contacted me yesterday. I made no promises save that if you agreed, I would send for them. Besides, for a chance to do business with the Abrabanels and Emperor Gustav only a Spanish banker would say no. Probably say no. But now, we're expected, I'm sure."

They were. As Rödvinge and Hautzmeyer discussed banking, the Lübeck City Council was in session. By that time every member of the council knew why Major Dag Rödvinge was in town. Matthesen, true to his word about doing everything to help, had made sure of that. Of course, not every member of council was all that interested in helping Matthesen keep his word.

"But it makes no sense!" cried one burgomaster.

"Neither does that name!" voiced another.

"Does it have to?" asked Matthesen. "Or do you really want to say no to Gustav Adolf, to the emperor who came to Lübeck under siege and stayed here? To the Lion of the North whose forces broke the League of Ostend at Ahrensbök?"

"No," admitted the first to speak up, one Josef Jacobs. "It still makes no sense, though I admit, better this than whatever King Christian would come up with. Did you hear the latest out of Copenhagen, about that up-timer lieutenant and Christian's daughter?"

"Yes. My wife told me all about it. She and her friends all think it romantic."

"So does mine," admitted Hans Rolfes, the second council member to speak up. "I blame it on the newspapers, serializing all those Austen writings. I admit she and that Heyer one wrote well, but the women take it too far! Plus, I heard from a friend in Bamberg about something called a Romance Readers' Book Club. I dread the day it comes here. I tell you, every woman in Lübeck will be signing up once they hear of that."

Council Member Alois Rodlauer chuckled. "Not *all*. Only the ones who can read. This is why I thank God I only have sons."

"Don't joke about it, Alois," retorted Rolfes. "You know darned well 'only the ones who can read' *is* all of them. Except the blind, and they're sure to find somebody to read the stories to them. I tell you, there isn't a man in Lübeck who won't curse the day that gets here."

"Don't remind me," mourned Jacobs, who after six daughters had glumly accepted his sorrowful lot. "The dowries! Thank God I got three of them married off before Grantville came. I thought I had suffered before, but now the other three and my wife are getting *ideas* from all those damnable serials. My house is filled with talk of *Directoire* and *Empire* dresses, *Regency* riding habits and *Spencer* jackets, *reticules* and *parasols*, and I don't want to know what else!"

"It could be worse," piped up fellow sufferer Georg Kenzian, with four daughters. "They could want a submarine!"

"True," laughed Matthesen. "Somehow I think that whim of Christian's is going to become very popular among the lords and ladies of Copenhagen. Not the fathers, though. Thank God it's there and not here."

"That said, we do have a monarch of our own to deal with. Opinions?"

Jacobs waved a hand. "Sell. Not like we could say no to him anyway, or have a good reason to refuse. And with the Abrabanels backing him, we'll actually get good money for it."

"And for a good price," added council treasurer Fritz Pütter. "I for one insist on that. Bad enough we have to lose the revenue from Nutschel—from *Narnia*—but let's at least get a good price for what we have there."

"All right. What would you call a good price?" asked Matthesen.

"Double or triple what we paid is what *I'd* call a good price. The emperor ended our independence and tossed us into the USE. He should pay for that as well. However"—Pütter raised his voice and a hand, forestalling objections—"a *fair* price overall would be what we paid plus nine percent. Taking into account what we have in Narnia, what we paid for it and when we paid for it, that really is fair. If Rödvinge wants to haggle or somebody above him does, seven. Even then we'd lose a bit on some of the lands and leases, but anything less and we'd lose on all."

"Do we really want to haggle with the emperor?" questioned Kenzian. "To play devil's advocate here, you said it yourself Dieterich: he came to Lübeck under siege and stayed here. All before the Danes were cleared out of the Baltic, I point out."

"I admit Gustav Vasa deserves his accolades," stated Pütter. "I even admit that if Lübeck had to lose its independence and neutrality, better to Gustav than anyone else. All the same, for all that I respect the man himself, we are in the USE now. I hear we have a constitution and a Bill of Rights before which even an emperor must bow. Well then, as we have those let's use those. Accommodating the emperor on this Narnia business is one thing. Spoiling him is another."

"Hear, hear," cried other burgomasters.

"Right then," said Matthesen. "All in favor of selling Lübeck's holdings in Narnia to Major Dag Rödvinge on behalf of the emperor of the USE for cost plus nine percent, seven if need be, raise your hands."

The motion passed with full support.

"Very well then. Fritz, I want you with me when Dag and Ludwig come here. Show them the figures, make it clear we really are cooperating as best we can."

Accompanied by Carl Menckhoff from the Berenbergs and Albert Dossenbach from the Sparkasse zu Lübeck, Rödvinge and Hautzmeyer met in the mayor's office with Matthesen and Pütter.

The offer of cost plus nine percent was accepted by Rödvinge. Even so, Hautzmeyer insisted there be some negotiation before the actual transfer of lands and funds.

"Best to start at fifteen, Fritz, so the major can

argue down to nine. Silly, I know, but if my client takes the offer right away somebody is going to go looking for evidence of bribes or kickbacks. When they find nothing they'll consider that evidence and lay charges."

Rödvinge stared at Hautzmeyer, eyes and mouth wide open.

"So...I have to argue with Dieterich and Pütter even though we're already in agreement?"

Hautzmeyer quietly replied, "Yes, Major, you do."

Rödvinge glanced at the others in the room, all of whom were nodding in agreement. Rödvinge closed his eyes. Opened those.

"God in Heaven, give me a battle any day! All right, if we *have* to do this—Pütter, fifteen percent? Dieterich, when you told me the council would do anything to help, you left off 'yourselves'! Fifteen percent? I wouldn't give my mother fifteen percent! Five, if she made me *lutefisk* beforehand!"

Matthesen shook his head, his face expressing appalled disbelief at Rödvinge's inability to grasp simple economics.

"Rödvinge, take a look at the numbers! Twelve is the best we can do!"

Rödvinge, face heating, answered back with, "Twelve? *Twelve?* I'll give you seven, for the seven deadly sins—that's more fitting!"

Matthesen, close to shouting, riposted with, "There are also seven blessed virtues, none of which I see in you! You'd only give your poor mother, who raised you, who fed you, loved you and cared for you, five? Even doubled at ten would be a serpent's tooth!"

Rödvinge snorted in contempt. "Ten? I'm surprised

you can count that high without checking your hands first! I'll make it easy for you, one hand and three of the other, that's eight!"

Then it got personal.

"Ten, you Swedish thief!"

"Eight, you Lübeck lout!"

"Ten, you—Major Dag Rödvinge, you!"

"Eight, Mayor Dieterich Matthesen!"

Who without changing his tone shot back, "I'd say we've taken this far enough. You?"

"Agreed!" shouted back Rödvinge. Then, in a more temperate tone, stated, "Let's sign the papers. I still have to get to Narnia and work that out to everybody's satisfaction, I'm told. How much of Narnia is being transferred now, anyway?"

Hautzmeyer examined his notes. "About . . . forty percent, more or less."

"Which already makes this Thorsten Engler the majority holder, you could leave it at that," opined Pütter in a diffident voice.

"I thank you for the suggestion and no. It would work for Thorsten and his betrothed Caroline, but the colonel would order me back. Even if he didn't, somehow I don't see it working for the princess. And . . . it's odd, I've never met her, but . . . I don't want to disappoint her," finished Rödvinge, his tone that of a man realizing an unsuspected truth about himself.

The room was silent for a moment after that.

Carl Menckhoff spoke first. "I presume you'll be wanting myself and Albert to accompany you and Hautzmeyer to Narnia then, Major? If so, we can arrange a coach to take us there by tonight. We can bed overnight in Narnia and begin at first light tomorrow."

"Is there enough room in the coach for myself and Fritz?" asked Matthesen. "I know that as of now Lübeck has nothing to do with Narnia, but we should speak and explain matters to the villagers."

"It has room for eight, so there's enough," said Dossenbach.

"Splendid! But does that work for you, Major?" asked Hautzmeyer.

"It does, and thank you both."

"Speak to Leo about sending for the coach," piped up Pütter. "And best tell our families we'll not be home tonight. Pity that, there's a new Heyer starting in the evening paper and I was looking forward to reading it."

"Oh? What's the title?" asked Dossenbach.

"*A Civil Contract*. I'm sure it's only a coincidence, though."

The trip to Narnia was uneventful. On the way they reviewed what was likely available in Narnia and discussed possibilities. Menckhoff and Dossenbach were brought up to speed on why and how Narnia had come into existence. Rödvinge noted to himself they hadn't needed much extra information. *Not that why I'm here is really a secret, but honestly, do even the fish in the harbor know?*

They arrived late in the evening at Narnia and put up at the local tavern. After assuring the owner that yes, he could continue to run his tavern out of his home, they obtained beds throughout the village. "Good thing," voiced Hautzmeyer. "By tomorrow morning everybody will know we're here. Some will even be right as to why."

☆ ☆ ☆

The morning showed Hautzmeyer's prediction right. Excluding those who had to work in the fields, after breakfast most of the village of Narnia was sitting in the tavern. The day being sunny, Dag asked for tables and benches to be set outside "to discuss and explain what's happening and answer as many questions as we can."

The *dorfschulze*, the village representative, one Otto Fruhner, took the lead from there. Rödvinge was pleased to see Fruhner didn't just order; he helped move the sturdy wood tables and benches.

Once set up, Rödvinge spoke. Drawing himself to his full height, Rödvinge used a modulated parade voice, one designed to carry to all assembled without shouting or berating.

"My name is Major Dag Rödvinge of the Swedish Army, here on detached duties on behalf of Emperor Gustav II Adolf of the USE. This gentleman seated to my right is Ludwig Hautzmeyer, lawyer. Next are Carl Menckhoff and Albert Dossenbach, bankers. To my left are Dieterich Matthesen, Mayor of Lübeck, and Fritz Pütter, Lübeck city treasurer."

Each man nodded or waved a hand at the villagers as they were introduced.

"We are here because of the change in Narnia's status, from being the village of Nutschel located within the lands of Lübeck to being the village of Narnia, with USE Sergeant Thorsten Engler proclaimed Imperial Count of Narnia at the Congress of Copenhagen for his bravery at the Battle of Ahrensbök.

"We are here because over the past few weeks we've realized almost everything connected to that has been done bass-ackwards."

A murmur ran through the assembled villagers at

that admission. Those seated next to Rödvinge glanced warily at him.

"We—*I*—am here to change that for the better. I'm here to resolve the status of Narnia and yes, to buy lands and leases. When and if people are willing to sell, and only then. There will be no forced buyouts. I've personally spoken with the count, and that is the last thing he wants and needs."

Must remember to tell him that; I'm sure he'll agree.

"That's already happened, as Mayor Dieterich Matthesen and Treasurer Fritz Pütter will confirm."

The two silently nodded in confirmation.

"That's also why Ludwig Hautzmeyer, Carl Menckhoff, and Albert Dossenbach are here. Hautzmeyer *and myself* to buy, Menckhoff and Dossenbach to guarantee payment. *Full, fair,* and *good* payment."

He paused a moment for effect.

"But not today."

That caused everybody to sit up and take notice. Everybody. The villagers were surprised, Menckhoff and Dossenbach stunned, Matthesen and Pütter stared at each other, and Hautzmeyer stared warningly at Rödvinge.

Ignoring them, staring straight at the villagers, Rödvinge explained.

"No, not today, because today not everybody is here. Because today is the first anybody here has heard of this. Because today we need to *talk*, to listen, and to learn. Because today, and tomorrow, and the day after, and in the days to come we need to figure out where we are going with this, with Narnia.

"That won't be done in a day, a week or a month. It will take time. What we can do today is *start*.

Start by asking questions and by providing answers. And here's the first question. For you, Herr Fruhner. What do you want? And here's the second question. What do you hope for?"

Please answer. Damn it, I should have set this up beforehand, help me out here!

Fortunately Otto Fruhner picked up on his unrehearsed cue.

"Well, I guess what I want to know is about that woodlot there. People keep asking me if it's still for the community, and I don't know what to tell them. Is it, and I hope it is, I've been saying use it."

Thank you, Fruhner. You too, God.

"As long as it's used properly, and I can see from here that it is, it remains and stays as it is: for the use of Narnians."

Encouraged by the friendly answer, another Narnian spoke up.

"This count we are told we have now—is he going to change all our names?"

"What?"

"Well, in Narnia there are names like Digory and Jill and Polly and Puddleglum and Cloudbirth, and we are in Narnia, so do we all have to have names like in the books?" explained the villager, face and stance genuinely serious and concerned.

How could anyone think . . . well, the village name was changed so it makes sense—no. Don't go there.

"No, not unless you want to. I would stick with the English names for now if you decide to change your names. Otherwise, keep your names, I assure you Count Thorsten Engler has no interest in changing your names."

But in you he'll have interest, once he completes his education!

"Does this mean we don't have to change our church name to Aslan or Emperor Beyond the Sea then?" asked another. Again in all seriousness.

Rödvinge, familiar with the Chronicles of Narnia and their mythology, was not fazed by this. Forcefully he stated, "No. St. Jacob's remains St. Jacob's."

The villager turned toward another. "See, Hans? Told you!" Hans scowled back. As did Otto Fruhner.

Sensing the mood, or else genuinely curious about the answer, another villager quickly asked another question.

"Major Rödvinge, what about the wasps?"

Flummoxed, Rödvinge asked back, "What wasps?"

Otto Fruhner explained. "Major Rödvinge, what it is is that wasps built a nest in Helga Fischer's garden. They swarmed and badly stung Kurt Gruber's dog. He wants compensation. Helga says she isn't responsible for what wasps do; Kurt says they came from her garden so she is responsible."

This is more like it. Not that I expected wasps, but finally a sensible question. That I haven't the slightest clue how to answer...

"Ah... tell me, how would such a dispute usually be handled?"

"Well, before we'd leave it for the judge for the area to decide, but now with this count, we don't know—does it still go to the judge or to the count?"

Another save, thank you! Fruhner, I swear if I have anything to say about it Engler will keep you on the job for life!

"To the judge. Believe me when I say that although there has been a change of name, the usual administrative, judicial, and village procedures remain. Treat matters as you normally would"—*Why do I think that won't solve much?*—"and carry on as before. I have met Thorsten Engler, I assure you he wants matters to remain as normal as possible. I don't say there won't be changes, our being in the village of Narnia instead of Nutschel is proof of that, but any other changes will not be as dramatic nor as noticeable. Keep on doing what you were doing before then. Yes, you fellow, with the hand up," finished Rödvinge, pointing to a rather runty-looking villager.

"What's he like?"

"Pardon?"

"This Thorsten Engler, what's he like? I mean, I know you say he wants matters to stay pretty much the same, but"—the villager asking had an apologetic look on his face—"we don't know him. He's never been by, after all."

Do you know, I think that's the . . . bravest . . . question I've heard. You look like mice could beat you up, yet . . .

"He won't be, not for a while. He's still in Colonel Straley's Flying Artillery, so it will be a while before he can come by. It isn't that he doesn't want to come here—he's as new to all this as you are—he really *can't* come by, he isn't free to do so."

"How long until he can, then?"

"Well . . . at least as long as it takes the emperor to conclude the wars . . . however long that is."

"That makes sense, but still . . ." The villager looked both apprehensive and determined now. "What's he like, Major? You've met him—what's he like?"

Smarter than me, he'd have answered your first question before now.

"He's . . . he's solid, I guess is what you would say.

Dependable. Reliable. Honest. He's from a farming village himself, you know. He's the sort who'd be the *dorfschulze* or even the *amtmann* for villages for years. He'd be in the job for so long children would grow up believing he'd always been there and always would be."

"I hear he knows Princess Kristina, is that true?" asked another villager, a woman this time.

"Yes, he does."

"Huh. How's a guy from a farming village meet the princess, then?" asked another.

"From what I heard—understand, I don't know all the details, just some gossip and little things he talked about—he met the princess at the settlement house where his betrothed works."

"What's a settlement house?" asked the female villager of a moment ago.

This really isn't what I planned, but we're talking, so—

"It's—I'm not too sure myself. From what I gathered, it's a charitable institution the rich ladies of Magdeburg run and work in as well. They run something called a *tag-pflege*, where parents leave their children to be cared for for the day while the parents work. Or at night, if that's when they work. They also do something called a 'soup kitchen,' that gives free meals to hungry people."

"A 'soup kitchen'? Sounds American," observed another villager, previously silent.

"So this betrothed, she's a rich lady of Magdeburg, then?" asked another. She sounded disappointed somehow.

"Caroline Platzer is her name, and yes, she is a lady. In the best sense of the word. But no, she isn't rich or even from Magdeburg. She's from Grantville."

There was a collective gasp from the assembled villagers.

"From *Grantville*? You mean she's an *up-timer*?" asked the woman who had spoken in disappointed tones before.

"Yes, she is an American, an up-timer."

"How did he meet *her*, then?" asked the villager, excitedly.

Let me guess, you are the village gossip. Which works out great! Probably.

"He met her at her workplace, at the"—Rödvinge stumbled over the unfamiliar phrase—

"De-part-ment-of-So-cial-Ser-vi-ces."

"What's that?" asked the gossip.

"It's like the settlement house, only the government runs it."

"Why was he there then? Does he have children he had to drop off?"

"Or looking for a meal?" asked another villager, a male this time.

What's with that disparaging tone, fellow? Feeling jealous, are we?

"No, he does not have children." *Yet.*

"And no, he was not 'looking for a meal.' Besides, after what he did at the coal gas explosion he could get a free meal in Magdeburg anywhere."

"The coal gas explosion?" gasped the village gossip. "We heard that here in Nut—Narnia! You mean he was *there*?"

"Yes. Back then he was a foreman at the coal gas plant."

"Oh, come on!" cried the sour one. "Next you'll be telling us he helped the Prince deal with the explosion!"

"Yes. He did." *And he should have gotten his*

countship for that, not capturing two Frenchmen too exhausted to do anything other than surrender.

The sour one looked as though he were going to object, then saw the look on Rödvinge's face. He shut up.

The other villagers also saw Rödvinge's look. They didn't shut up.

"You mean our count knows the *Prince of Germany Michael Stearns himself?*" cried the gossip.

Huh. It's true. It's not what you know or what you do, it's who you know.

"Yes. Helped the Prince prevent a worse explosion, put out the flames, then dealt with the dead and the maimed."

"Well!" said the gossip, her words expressing the reverential look on the faces of the other Narnians, even the sour one.

Although other questions were asked by the villagers after that, it was clear that from then on Thorsten Engler would have to work hard and long to lose respect among the Narnians.

(A century later the town history, *The Chronicle of Narnia: One Hundred Years of the Lion*, would claim the villagers of Narnia quickly accepted their new status. Although true enough, the fact was that it was *that* moment when the villagers first considered themselves Narnians and Thorsten Engler their count.)

Hautzmeyer that night congratulated Rödvinge on his tactics.

"I had no idea where you were going when you said we weren't going to buy anything today, but my God that was inspired! Thorsten Engler should *adopt* you for that! Dear God, *I* should!"

The other four added their congratulations. "The villagers will probably pay us to buy land from them now!" Albert Dossenbach joked, with Menckhoff agreeing.

Matthesen, with a wink to Rödvinge, congratulated Pütter. "To think you managed to get him up to nine percent! Even none would have been amazing, facing Dag!"

Pütter, also winking at Rödvinge, agreed. "My best day ever and his worst. Otherwise, I'd have sold Lübeck!"

Elsewhere in Narnia conversations mostly centered around *their* count.

"Faced death alongside the Prince, *astounding!*"

"*And* he knows the princess as well. I hear she's remarkable for her age. I was speaking with Heinrich the other day, and his cousin was in Magdeburg the day the princess spoke to everybody there. He says she was impressive."

"Engaged to an up-timer woman—he must really have something on the ball then. The stories you hear about up-timers—"

"Was a farmer himself, so he won't be stupid about things, not like most of 'em."

"We might even get to meet the princess ourselves one day, you know."

And other matters:

"What have you decided for the names?"

"I had been thinking Maria or Kurt, but now—I mean, we do live in Narnia, and Digory or Polly sound nice—"

(Pity the Prince, *The Chronicle of Narnia* would say. Only in Narnia is the name Michael uncommon in the USE. Instead Digory, Kirke, Peter, Edmund, Clarence, Eustace, Cole and Colin are near-obligatory for boys born here. As are Jill and Polly, Susan and Lucy, Letitia and Gwendolen for girls.)

"Joachim showed me that wardrobe you made for him. Really fine piece of work, and the secret compartments are a nice touch."

"It is, isn't it?"

"Could you make me one like that? Maybe with a lion head at the top."

"All right, but you'll have to wait, I have three orders in already, and they all want secret compartments. This keeps up, I'll have to get an apprentice."

(As *The Chronicle* would later explain, thus began the Narnian tradition of *Wardrobes*. With production limited to master carpenters living within the county, using only wood sourced from the county and with all fittings handmade, *Wardrobes*, with their secret compartments and carved depictions of scenes from the Chronicles, were by then recognized internationally as an art form of furniture, with the prices to match.)

Three days later when Rödvinge and the others left Narnia they could and did compliment themselves on a job well done.

There hadn't been much buying and selling done, but there had been a bit. Enough that Thorsten Engler now had the leases on two more farms and the right of first refusal on several more lands and leases.

Apart from that, there hadn't really been much call for Menckhoff and Dossenbach, but when Rödvinge apologized for bringing them in, they quickly corrected him.

"Big deals are all very well and good, but it's little and medium ones that are the backbone of any bank," explained Dossenbach.

"Besides, it's early days yet; this is just priming the pump," added Menckhoff.

Back in Lübeck, they all came to see Rödvinge fly off to Copenhagen.

"Amazing invention," said Matthesen admiringly.

"Yes, amazing," agreed Pütter, although the green tinge to his face as he looked at the Gustav made it plain that slipping the surly bonds of earth would never be his ambition.

"Now remember to check on me unexpectedly," insisted Hautzmeyer. "Otherwise I'll charge extra for noncompliance."

Once reinstalled in Copenhagen, Rödvinge quickly reported the results of the land-buying to Colonel Ekstrom and through him to the emperor and the princess.

Rödvinge pointed out that Thorsten Engler was now the majority land- and leaseholder in the farming village and surroundings of Narnia, with the prospect of the gradual acquisition of more lands and leases in the following weeks and months.

He emphasized the remarkable aid and assistance of the City Council of Lübeck, particularly that of Mayor Dieterich Matthesen, City Treasurer Fritz Pütter and senior Rathaus clerk Leo Anslinger.

Praise was handed out unstintingly to lawyer Ludwig Hautzmeyer, whose ongoing legal help, advice, and work was credited as chiefly responsible for the smooth transition of lands and leases.

Sparkasse zu Lübeck and Berenberg Brothers were strongly recommended to the Abrabanels, with particular thanks to their representatives Albert Dossenbach and Carl Menckhoff.

Lastly, Rödvinge thanked the villagers of Narnia, especially Otto Fruhner, for their quick acceptance of the 'new normal' and willingness to help their count in his endeavors both in Narnia and outside.

With that done, Major Dag Rödvinge returned to his usual duties as an aide to Colonel Nils Ekstrom.

Some weeks further on, Rödvinge was along with the other aides and everybody else in the Swedish and USE armies up to his ears in preparations for the next campaign.

While he was ensconced at his desk, his fellow aide Tor Svensson popped in his head and told him, "The colonel's asked you to come see him now."

Startled, Rödvinge looked up. "Did he say what it was about?"

"No, although he did say to tell you it wasn't anything bad. But, you do have to go see him now."

"Good thing, actually. I see one more request for dynamite, and, I swear, I'll explode myself. Try and explain the up-timers don't have much left if any, nobody's making much just now, and anyway it's not all that helpful to us, but nobody believes me. The worst are the Germans, who think since up-time it was a Swedish invention and I'm Swedish *of course* I can get them some. Then there are those who ask me for it knowing I have to refuse, so since I didn't get them that, could I see my way clear on this *other* thing they want..." He rolled his eyes to the ceiling in righteous exasperation.

Tor nodded in commiseration. "I've got this one quartermaster who somehow heard about hot or warm pockets, whatever those are, and keeps asking for pants with those. I'm tempted to send him some with matches in the pockets, except I know he'd light the pockets on fire and then wonder why the pants burned!"

"Anyway, duty calls, see you!"

Ekstrom was in his office waiting for Rödvinge. "Ah, Rödvinge. This came for you." He handed over an envelope—a thick, cream-colored envelope, clearly of the most expensive stock.

Rödvinge opened the red wax seal. Inside the envelope was a letter, itself on expensive high-end paper. It was a personal letter from the emperor, written in his own hand.

Greetings, Major Dag Rödvinge.

I join with Colonel Ekstrom in praise and thanks for your astounding accomplishment in Narnia.

The villagers of what was once Nutschel have by all accounts taken to their new status of Narnians with a good will that I could and do wish all in this world would have.

My daughter joins her thanks to mine and expresses her hopes to one day thank you in person for making Narnia real.

Sincerely,
Gustavus II
Adolphus Vasa

Rödvinge read it. Then read it again. Touched Gustav Vasa's signature with the fingers of his hand, as if to assure himself it was real. He looked up at Colonel Ekstrom, eyes wide.

"Congratulations, Major. You have earned it. A personal letter of thanks from His Majesty is a true honor. Cherish it."

Overcome with emotion, Major Rödvinge wiped his eyes clear with a sleeve. "I—I—I do, Colonel. Sorry, I can't seem to—I . . . I . . ."

Ekstrom was sympathetic. "Take your time, Dag. You've earned it."

"Th-thank you, Colonel. I—I'll be all right, I will. I—I am all right."

"Ah. Good. As it so happens, I received a letter from the emperor as well. Nothing so grand as yours, alas. A note, quickly written, scrawled really. All about future affairs."

"Very well, Colonel. With your permission, I'll return to my duties."

The colonel affected not to hear.

"As I said, all about future affairs, some of which concern you, Major."

"Concern me, sir? How?"

At this the colonel looked—sympathetic?

"Major—please sit down. Rather than explain, I think it best you read the note. And—I'm sorry."

"Sorry?"

"Read the note, Major," said Ekstrom, handing it over.

In writing far less measured and elegant than that of his letter to Rödvinge, indeed in the scrawl Ekstrom had termed it, were the emperor's words.

His chilling, horrific, terrifying words.

Nils—It occurs to me that when Thorsten Engler was made Imperial Count of Narnia we also made that scapegrace Eddie Cantrell Imperial Count of Wismar. Plus, Kristina insists her governess Caroline Platzer is Countess Oz.

Since Rödvinge has demonstrated remarkable talent in this area, put him to acquiring Wismar Bay for Cantrell. Since it's in Mecklenburg and I'm the duke, he has my full permission. Same with Miss Platzer, and as she's betrothed to the Count of Narnia, tell Rödvinge to get her land close to Narnia. If there's no good land there close by, then Lübeck again or Hamburg—actually, make it Hamburg, the Lübeckers have been generous enough.

Leave this until after Saxony and Brandenburg, but tell Rödvinge this now so he won't have to rush as much as he did for Narnia. He can get some preparation done in advance. Once we're finished with my oaf of a brother-in-law, this gets his full attention.

"You've got to be kidding!" escaped Rödvinge's lips. Then he looked up at Ekstrom, his eyes pleading, begging for succor.

"Sir, I resign my commission effective immediately!"

The colonel was amused. "Forget that, Major. As the Americans don't say, no good deed of land goes unpunished!"

Acknowledgements

Kevin H. Evans,
February 2, 1956 to December 23, 2020

Karen C. Evans,
June 27, 1955 to March 30, 2021

It was so long ago that I don't remember clearly when I first met Kevin and Karen Evans. Karen's memory was that it was at the 2007 WorldCon, but that was the one held in Yokohama, Japan, and I wasn't there. Besides, it had to have been earlier than that because the convention in Yokohama was held in the fall of that year and Kevin's first article in the *Grantville Gazette*, "Steam: Taming the Demon," was published in the February 2007 issue of the magazine—which means he must have written it in 2006. I think she was misremembering and we actually met at the WorldCon that year, which was held in Anaheim, California. That was the first WorldCon I ever attended.

Fifteen years ago, in other words, which seems about right. Kevin and Karen go back to the early years of the Ring of Fire series project, which began with the publication of my novel *1632* in February of 2000. Over the years, the two of them—sometimes working together, sometimes writing alone—produced many stories and articles for the magazine, as well as three volumes for Ring of Fire Press: *No Ship for Tranquebar, Fire on the Rio Grande* and *Tales from the Mermaid and Tiger*.

Aside from his writing, Kevin and his sometimes-partner-in-fiddling Rick Boatright would build equipment designed to prove to nay-sayers that, "baloney, people in the seventeenth century COULD have built that gadget." Kevin built two firearms, a slam fire shotgun of his own design and a rifle based on a design by Gorg Huff, both of which could have easily been constructed at the time. Gorg's rifle was the AK series that figures prominently in the Russia novels of the Ring of Fire series (of which there are two, so far: *1636: The Kremlin Games* and *1637: The Volga Rules*). The best known rifle of that series is the AK 4.7, named after the seventeenth-century designer (in the novels; he's not real) and gunsmith Andrei Korisov. After the first novel came out, Kevin built a working model of the AK 4.7, which figures prominently in two battles in the sequel, *1637: The Volga Rules*.

Yes, the gun works. So does Kevin's shotgun. We took them out and tested them on firing ranges.

Kevin's great love, though, was steam power. He and friends of his built a full-size working steam locomotive. He also built and tested a half-scale model of the steam engine that is used several times in the Ring of Fire series to power dirigibles. And it was he and Rick Boatright who explained to David Carrico and me just how devastating a steam explosion can be, which we used in a critical episode in our novel *1636: The Devil's Opera*.

Kevin was born in Rexburg, Idaho, on February 2, 1956. He joined the SCA (Society for Creative Anachronism) in 1970, at the age of 14, and was knighted ten years later. That same year, he joined the National Guard Green Berets.

He and Karen met in 1984 and got married in 1987 and moved to Pirmasens, Germany. In 1982, they transferred with their two children to Fort Reilly, Kansas. In 1996, Kevin left the army and they moved to Norman, Oklahoma.

Kevin got a job with the FAA in 1996 and moved to Texas two years later, when he was promoted to Airway Systems Specialist. He and Karen transferred to Rio Rancho, New Mexico, in 2001. That same year, they began attending science fiction conventions.

Karen was born in El Paso, Texas, on June 27th, 1955. She studied at Eastern Washington State College and continued her studies at Southern Utah University, where she graduated with a BA in English and Elementary Education. Karen joined the SCA in 1983 and became Kevin's Squire in 1984.

She traveled to Recife, Brazil, on her mission as a member of the Church of Jesus Christ of Latter Day Saints later that same year and returned in 1986. She and Kevin began dating when she returned. They married June 5, 1987.

Karen had a love of languages. She understood several ancient Celtic languages and could speak both Portuguese and German fluently. She and Kevin both were part of the chase crew for the Possmann Bembel balloon at the International Balloon Fiesta in New Mexico for many years.

Karen was the *chocolatier par excellence* for the

fans of the Ring of Fire series. She gave a memorable talk at one of our conventions on the history of chocolate, which included providing everyone with samples of cocoa and chocolate going back centuries to its Mesoamerican origins.

Kevin and Karen are sorely missed and will be for many years to come.

　　　　　　　　　　　　　　　　—Eric Flint
　　　　　　　　　　　　　　　　April 16, 2021

Story Acknowledgements

RING OF FIRE SERIES
(with Eric Flint)

1635: The Papal Stakes
PB: 978-1-4516-3920-9 • $7.99

Up to their necks in papal assassins, power politics, murder, and mayhem, the uptimers need help and they need it quickly.

1636: Commander Cantrell in the West Indies
PB: 978-1-4767-8060-3 • $8.99

Oil. The Americas have it. The United States of Europe needs it. Enter Lieutenant-Commander Eddie Cantrell.

1636: The Vatican Sanction
HC: 978-1-4814-8277-6 • $25.00
PB: 978-1-4814-8386-5 • $7.99

Pope Urban has fled the Vatican and the traitor Borja. But assassins have followed him to France—and not only assassins! The Pope and his allies have fled right into the clutches of the vile Pedro Dolor.

STARFIRE SERIES
(with Steve White)

Extremis
PB: 978-1-4516-3814-1 • $7.99

They have traveled for centuries, slower than light, and now they have arrived at the planet they intend to make their new home: Earth. The fact that humanity is already living there is only a minor inconvenience.

Imperative
PB: 978-1-4814-8243-1 • $7.99

A resurrected star navy hero attempts to keep a fragile interstellar alliance together while battling and implacable alien adversary.

Oblivion
PB: 978-1-4814-8325-4 • $16.00

It's time to take a stand! For Earth! For Humanity! For the Pan-Sentient Union!
